THE GREAT
GOLDBERGS

Also by Daniel Goodwin

FICTION
Sons and Fathers
The Art of Being Lewis

POETRY
Catullus's Soldiers

THE GREAT GOLDBERGS

A NOVEL BY

DANIEL GOODWIN

 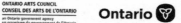

We acknowledge financial support for our publishing activities: the Government of Canada,
through the Canada Book Fund and The Canada Council for the Arts; the Government of
Ontario, through the Ontario Arts Council, Ontario Creates, and the Ontario Book Publishing
Tax Credit. We acknowledge additional funding provided by the Government of Ontario and
the Ontario Arts Council to address the adverse effects of the novel coronavirus pandemic.

LIBRARY AND ARCHIVES CANADA CATALOGUING IN PUBLICATION

Title: The great Goldbergs / a novel by Daniel Goodwin.
Names: Goodwin, Daniel, author.
Identifiers: Canadiana (print) 20230218202 | Canadiana (ebook) 20230218253 |
ISBN 9781770866591 (softcover) | ISBN 9781770866607 (HTML)
Classification: LCC PS8613.O6485 G74 2023 | DDC C813/.6—dc23

United States Library of Congress Control Number: 2023935154

Cover design: Angel Guerra / Archetype
Interior text design: Marijke Friesen
Manufactured by Friesens in Altona, Manitoba in June, 2023.

Printed using paper from a responsible and sustainable resource,
including a mix of virgin fibres and recycled materials.

Printed and bound in Canada.

CORMORANT BOOKS INC.
260 ISHPADINAA (SPADINA) AVENUE, SUITE 502,
TKARONTO (TORONTO), ON M5T 2E4

www.cormorantbooks.com

THE GOLDBERG FAMILY TREE

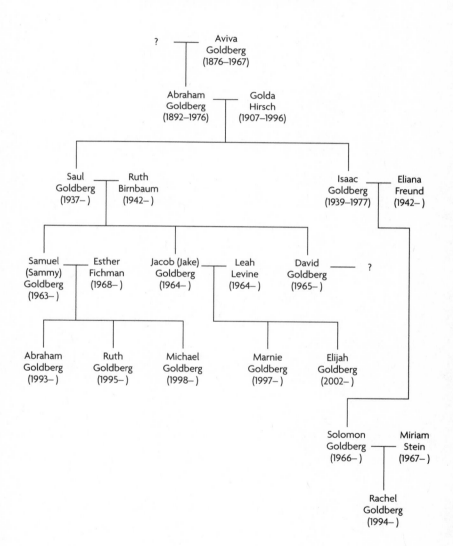

In memory of my grandfather Israel Goldberg.
(1892–1965)

"Character is destiny."
— Heraclitus

"Who is it that can tell me who I am?"
— Shakespeare, *King Lear*

PART ONE

Lower Canada College, Montréal
1977–1983

1

AS A CHILD, I never understood how concrete was actually made or what distinguished good concrete from bad. But my father was apparently something of a small legend in a city that relied on concrete to keep its two and a half million people housed and moving and safe, at least most of the time. Whenever there was a major job, the managing contractor sought him out, which was a rarity in his business, as far as I could tell.

Declan McFall was tall, over six feet, and broad. He'd left school when he was fifteen and started in construction; by the time he was in his early twenties, he had worked his way up to foreman in a subcontracting company, with as many as a hundred men under him. He often worked for the Italians, building expressways usually but sometimes skyscrapers and, when nothing else was going on, the odd parking garage.

The most I could gather during my childhood years, usually from my friends whose fathers worked with mine, was that Declan had a secret and celebrated way of mixing and curing cement and distinct ideas about the right temperatures and humidity levels at which the mixing should be done, and even the best time of day for it. If my father had possessed this talent alone, it wouldn't have been enough to get him more than steady work, and it certainly wouldn't have earned him a reputation that went beyond eccentric.

What I think Declan owed his success to, and what endeared him to his mostly Italian bosses, was that he wasn't only a deep thinker when it came to cement mixing and concrete making: he had a gift for determining the most economical way to manage the entire concrete supply chain. From specifying the raw materials to laying out the details of the mixing process, from purchasing the fuel for the trucks to plotting their routes and organizing the labour, Declan was constantly coming up with suggestions to improve the margins of any company fortunate enough to have him on their project. It was almost mystical the way he approached his job — despite the fact that according to the standards of many people in white-collar jobs, Declan would have been working at the absolute lowest level of creativity and ingenuity.

Occasionally, my father would take me out to the job he was on if it was especially interesting or he was particularly proud of his contribution. In the early seventies, when I was still a child, Declan got to work on the biggest construction project Montréal ever saw: the Olympic Stadium. The massive concrete oval, resembling a giant spaceship, consumed three years of his life as he worked to complete Mayor Drapeau's twentieth-century monument to himself, athleticism, money, and Montréal.

Declan never spoke about the work "interruption" that lasted from the spring of 1975 until the fall, when workers walked off the Olympic Stadium job, but the following spring, as everyone raced to finish in time for the 1976 Summer Olympics, he brought me to the construction site almost every month. Declan would introduce me to the other men on site, and once, he introduced me to the owner of the contracting company his smaller company was working for. This man was small and dark, with excellent manners. He bent down to shake my ten-year-old hand and said to my father, "What a handsome boy you have, Declan. With your brains and his looks, you'll have to watch out."

Even at that young age, I thought it was a strange thing to say because my father was a handsome man. He was black Irish: jet-black hair, lightly tanned skin that never seemed to burn in the sun, and wide-apart eyes dark blue like the deep lake in the Laurentians we would sometimes go to for a week's vacation in the summer. He was the kind of man who looked good in cement dust. It made him appear even bigger and stronger, not weak or tired. As for me, I always assumed I was completely nondescript: brown hair of a shade difficult to describe, unremarkable blue eyes. Even at that age, I knew I was smaller than the other boys in my class.

It wasn't until later that I read about the controversy surrounding the building of the stadium: owners reproving workers for deliberate slowdowns and actual sabotage, unions decrying equipment shortages and harsh working hours and conditions, the widespread presence on-site of alcohol and drugs. The Big Owe, as Montréalers soon came to call it with a mixture of civic pride and embarrassment, ended up ballooning to a billion dollars, which took Montréal taxpayers thirty years to pay off.

Declan never spoke about any of this, but as I grew older and asked him about his work — was it true what people said about construction in Montréal being run by the mafia, that it was all corrupt and building standards were second-rate — he didn't get angry. He smiled and said, "Sean, my work puts food on the table. I'm building this city, as right as any city councillor. Have a little pride in your father, will you?" He tousled my hair in a way that said the conversation was over, more powerfully than any words could have achieved.

My mother, Mary, was also Irish, but petite, at five foot two, and as luck would have it, it was she who passed down to me the genes for height, the same genes that led some of my elementary school classmates to unimaginatively rechristen me "Sean McSmall." It was also Mary who passed on to me her love of books. When I turned four, she taught me how to read. Each night before I went to sleep, she would lie down in bed beside me and we would read a Dr. Seuss book. I would have to read the first page, and then she would read the rest. The next night I had to read two pages, and she would finish. This would go on for as many nights as there were pages. By the end of each evening's reading, I was ready for sleep and would close my eyes soon after my mother kissed me good night. My father would sometimes come to kiss my forehead while my mother and I were reading, but he would never say anything.

One night, after this bedtime ritual, as I was falling asleep with the scent of my mother's perfume on my pillow and my sheets, I overheard my parents in their bedroom, on the other side of the wall.

"How's his reading coming along, Mary?" My father worshipped my mother, and he always deferred to her when it came to my education.

"He's picking it up quickly. He'll be reading without me by the time he's four and a half."

"I'm glad you're the reader in the family, Mary. I wouldn't have the patience to teach him. And judging from his size, he's going to need book smarts."

I don't remember my mother's reply. I must have fallen asleep. But from the very beginning, I knew I wasn't cut out for my father's life. Everyone in construction was big and loud, always making jokes, only some of which I understood. They worked as hard and cheerfully as Clydesdales until all their heavy lifting and the grease in their homemade lunches caught up with them in their fifties. Either rheumatoid arthritis weakened once-strong arms and wrists, their backs went out one day when they were lifting bags of cement mix, or they collapsed of a heart attack in their small, invariably immaculate backyard gardens.

I was lucky that Mary was a reader. She always had a book beside her, and she read throughout the day, whenever she could catch a moment. It might have been while waiting for the potatoes to boil or the wash to be done. At the time, I didn't think much about what she was reading, but later, in high school, I learned enough to recognize that her bookshelves were filled with literary classics. Victorians. Twentieth-century Americans. Nineteenth-century Europeans and Russians. Mary was the only mother, among those of my friends, who read Russian novelists.

WHEN I WAS beginning grade six, it was Mary who encouraged me to apply to Lower Canada College, the prestigious private boys' school on Royal Avenue, only a few blocks away from where we lived in a small duplex on Westhill in Notre-Dame-de-Grâce, just below Sherbrooke and just above the train tracks. She practically forced me to apply. Don't get me wrong: Mary was never able to intimidate physically. She got her way through sheer force of will, which is something that people with less physical stature often have to cultivate. Whenever she asked me to clear my plate or take out the garbage, there was something in her voice that led me to conclude there was no alternative. As a result, I never once tested her resolve. Not even when I was a teenager and I might have credibly blamed a moment of insane rebellion on rampant hormones. She had an almost hypnotic quality when she looked at me with her pale green eyes. I took it for granted as a child. It was only later, when I came to know the Goldbergs and began to work for them, and as Mary's influence over me began to wane in comparison, that I came to appreciate the rare nature of her almost supernatural ability to always have her way.

2

ONE AFTERNOON IN the early fall of grade six, when I had just walked the eight blocks home from school and sat down at our dining room table, my mother offered her "suggestion" about my future along with a tall glass of milk and a warmed-up slice of her homemade apple pie.

"I have picked up an application for you for grade seven at LCC," she said in her soft voice that always sounded more beautiful to me than any musical instrument. After the milk and pie had been placed in front of me, she added, "You're going to apply." She didn't say anything else, but after I had finished my afternoon snack and gone up to my room to do my homework, the application in its neat brown envelope was waiting for me on my small desk.

My father had not yet arrived home, and my mother hadn't mentioned anything to him about this potential new direction for my life, but it was understood between Mary and me that I would not speak of it to my father, at least not yet, and that I would most certainly not ask for his help. This was because books and education were my mother's domain and because we both knew Declan would disapprove, just as he had less than two years earlier when my grade three teacher told my parents that I should skip grade four.

"YOUR BOY IS gifted," Mrs. Macdonald had said across the old-style teacher's desk during our parent-teacher meeting. She stated it as if there were not a doubt in the world, with the same earnest elementary schoolteacher conviction that the German teacher had possessed nearly a century earlier when pronouncing little Albert Einstein intellectually hopeless. "He's bored in class with all his worksheets," Mrs. Macdonald said. "He's reading at a grade seven level. He's not just good in math and science or English and social studies: he's gifted in every subject. That is, in every real subject." She was diligent enough to add that I wasn't great in gym. I always tried my best, but, to use her kind parlance, I wasn't "overly gifted" in athletics. "When children get bored, they start to do poorly. Your son deserves the best chance."

My father didn't usually attend parent-teacher meetings, but Mrs. Macdonald had written a letter home asking both my parents to attend what she promised would be a "special meeting." That was why Declan was there in person when he heard his son declared "gifted" and the educational institution's official recommendation that his son should skip a grade.

I knew from the times he had taken me along to his work that my father had a way with the simplest words and gestures when he was outside the house and talking to other men. "Morning, Jim" with a nod of his heavy head or "Good to see you, François" and a wave of his large hand. "How's the family, Fred?" as he made his way past men hard at work. And, contrary to how most people greet each other, Declan always stopped and waited for the reply. When he said hello, it wasn't with a false sense of cheeriness.

Sometimes he smiled and sometimes he didn't, but underlying it all was a deep seriousness and sincerity. Judging by how the men responded, smiling, eyes lighting up, they appreciated him.

Despite his practical if limited volubility at work, Declan barely spoke at home. A grunt from him could easily function as a comment, and a glance would convey a week's worth of emotion. It was as if he used up all his simple eloquence at work and had little left for us when he came home. Evenings were usually quiet. He spoke slightly more on weekends. But on the twenty-minute walk home from school on the day we met with Mrs. Macdonald, Declan couldn't stop talking. He didn't hold back with me walking beside him. He spoke about me as if I wasn't there, almost like Mrs. Macdonald, who had spoken about me in the third person the whole time.

"Sean might be the most gifted boy in the world. He just might," Declan said without any irony. "But he is not skipping a grade. He's small as it is, and if he skips a grade, he'll be even smaller. When the other kids hit puberty, Sean will still be playing with toy soldiers. He's not great in gym now. It will be too much for him." And on it went for twenty minutes until we reached the front door of our house.

I'd like to say that as we walked, I was oblivious to everything or fell back so that I couldn't hear. But I kept pace with my parents and listened, fascinated, to every word. At a certain point, without realizing it, I stopped taking it personally and, without appreciating what I was doing, began to analyze my father's arguments and the way his feelings were getting in the way of his logic. I also remember feeling proud that my father loved me enough to go head-to-head in an argument with my mother, an argument that he knew, even before he opened his mouth, he was going to lose.

And he did.

My mother didn't say a word in response on the way home, but, when we reached our doorstep, she turned to my father and looked up the ten inches he had on her. She reached up and brushed his dark hair from his face, smoothed the lines on his forehead with her fingers.

"I love you, Declan, and I know you love Sean. We're going to do what's best for him. Sean is going to skip grade four." Then she stood up on her toes and kissed him gently on the mouth. And here my six-foot-tall father, like a very young child playing hide-and-go-seek who thinks nobody can see him when he closes his own eyes, closed his eyes so that I wouldn't be able to see him losing. From that day on, both my parents looked at me differently. My mother with even more pride, and my father with what I only realized later was just a trace of apprehension.

IN THE MONTH that followed my mother telling me I was applying to LCC, I filled out the forms and gathered copies of my report cards. I wrote the required essay about who I was, what I'd done in my accelerated elementary school career up to that point, and why I wanted to attend LCC. I sought and received two reference letters from my current teacher and Mrs. Macdonald. My mother double-checked the application checklist to make sure I'd included everything required and proofread my essay. I never told any of the friends I'd made after skipping grade four, not Michael, Eli, or Stephen, that I was applying — I was worried they would laugh at me — but I did make an exception for Jane. After swearing her to secrecy, I asked her to look over my application.

Our parents were neighbourhood acquaintances, we both went to Willingdon, and Jane and I had played together in elementary school ever since she'd moved onto our street four years earlier, even though she was a year older and tall for her age. We played together innocently as if boys and girls playing together were the most natural thing in the world. We rode our bikes together everywhere, went swimming at the outdoor pool in the summer, and walked to the neighbourhood candy store, where we pooled our change and split our chocolate bars and bubblegum. In the winter, if I wasn't playing hockey with my father, we'd sometimes go skating together and come back to either her house or mine for hot chocolate.

After I had skipped grade four, we ended up in the same grade and the same class, and when I told her I was applying to LCC, she said, "That will mean we won't go to the same school together let alone be in the same class."

I remember thinking that what she said was true, but also that it wasn't the kind of thing Michael, Eli, or Stephen would have said. But Jane wasn't feeling sorry for herself or worrying about our friendship. She said it without sentimentality, simply a fact that occurred to her. The way she said it made it somehow profound. As if the future paths of our lives were altering as we stood there and spoke. She followed this up with, "I will miss you, but if that's what you want, I'd be happy to look at your application." That was Jane at eleven. She was very good in English, far better than me at the time, and perhaps far better than I would ever be.

JANE'S REACTION WAS so simple compared to my father's. I never quite kept my application secret from Declan, but I never quite told him either, not over the dinner table when he asked me about my day, and not when he started to take me out to the park near our house to play pickup hockey at the outdoor rink the city set up each year as soon as the winter set in.

We would join the other men and boys who came out to play, and each time the ritual was the same. All of us would skate around the rink, solipsistically stickhandling the puck if we were on our own or casually passing it to each other if we were there with a friend, taking lazy shots on an empty net, trying our best not to get in the way of the other skaters. Some of us were bad, some were relatively great, at least by local neighbourhood standards; most of us were ordinary. Eventually, somebody would skate over to centre ice and drop his stick and skate away, turning self-absorbed circles on his blades.

Once the first stick was dropped, without a sound, without a call to play, we'd all stop whatever imaginary miniature games we had been playing and skate over to centre ice, ceremoniously dropping our sticks. The pile of sticks would grow, and, when it was complete, the man who had first dropped his stick would skate back over and stand in the middle of the pile. He'd bend down, reach for the sticks, and start tossing them randomly, one at a time, to either side of the blue line. As we saw our stick being thrown to one side or the other, we'd skate over and pick it up and join that team.

Sometimes I would end up playing on the same team as my father and other times on the opposite team. I liked how it felt to play on Declan's team, but I liked it better to play on the other side, where he couldn't protect me as much. I was already small, even in those days, but there was no checking, so I never felt like I was at much of a disadvantage because of it. Pickup hockey was all about speed and soft hands, passing and receiving, scoring deftly without slapshots. Declan wasn't fast, but he had soft hands and an ability to somehow turn an awkward skating style into effective puck handling and scoring. It was always fun to watch him lumbering down the ice, twisting and turning with obvious effort, somehow making it past more skilled teenagers to the other end of the rink.

Once he got within fifteen feet of the net, he almost always scored. I, on the other hand, was the opposite. I was relatively fast but clumsy with the puck. It bounced off my stick when people passed to me, and more often than not, the puck went wide when I tried to pass or score. But I enjoyed the games, enjoyed playing with other boys and men and testing myself against players with more natural skill and ability. And even though we rarely spoke to each other on the ice, even when we were on the same team, it was time with my father.

We were walking the six blocks back home from the rink after a game the evening before my application was due when my father let me know he had the slightest idea what was going on.

"Do you have your application all done, Sean?" He didn't look at me as he spoke. He stared straight ahead as he lifted one heavy foot in front of the other. It was only half a question. He knew my mother, and he knew me.

"Yes, Dad. It's done. Mom helped me." My badly kept secret was out in the open.

Declan nodded, pleased that I had acknowledged the truth, even though he had already known it. We walked together in silence for another block, down the slight hill toward Sherbrooke. I hoped that our conversation was over. But as we waited for the light to turn green, Declan asked in a low voice, again without looking at me, "Are you sure it's what you want?"

I didn't answer right away. I didn't want my father to think I was giving him a snap answer. I wanted to leave him with the impression I was giving his question the weight it deserved. I didn't want to appear so insecure that I was overeager to defend my mother's decision. I waited until we had crossed Sherbrooke and walked one block west, then I took a deep breath and answered in as thoughtful and certain a voice as I could manage: "Yes, Dad, it's what I want." I didn't mean to, or at least I didn't deliberately think about it, but I took his hand as I spoke. Declan nodded and held my ten-year-old hand tightly in his. He kept holding on to me as we walked the rest of the way home, relinquishing his grip when we were about to walk through our front door.

I was both fascinated and frightened by the prospect of LCC, but I didn't want my father to feel even worse than he already did about me going. LCC was beyond me, as unknown as the Monkland Tennis Club across the street from it, a narrow green world of unimaginable privilege nestled between the massive field belonging to LCC and the nondescript apartment buildings that fronted Monkland Avenue. Once, in passing, some friends and I had tried to look through the tennis club's fence, its vines heavy with leaves. We had managed to see several thin, tanned people dressed in white hitting balls back and forth, the *thunk* of the bright yellow ball so different from the scrape and swish of skates and ice, so much more restrained and predictable than the loud *thwack* of a puck hitting the boards. To our surprise, we'd seen others through the vines, equally fit and even thinner without their tennis shirts and shorts, lounging by a pool that was blue-green.

LCC was just as mysterious and forbidden, an oasis of privilege in a middle- to lower-middle-class neighbourhood. I had only been outside the school, walking down Royal Avenue past the not particularly distinguished two-storey brick building and its outdoor hockey rink with the old-fashioned wooden roof and open walls. Ironically, LCC looked far less impressive from the outside than my public elementary school, with the two storeys it had on LCC and its dark pseudo-Victorian brick façade. If the founders of LCC had allowed themselves any extravagance, it was in the playing field across the street, as wide as a city block and nearly as long.

LCC made a bigger impression on those of us who weren't its students than did the Monkland Tennis Club because, unlike the tennis club, LCC was reserved for children, which is what we were. I knew that the adults who gracefully hit their bright yellow balls back and forth with dependable thumps or lounged timelessly around the pool were separated from me by age and experience in addition to their wealth and so I never compared myself to them. But I had seen LCC students waiting at the bus stop and riding the bus. They were like us public school children in so many respects that the subtle ways in which they were different stood out. It wasn't just their uniforms: the grey flannel pants and white shirts, the rep ties and navy blue jackets that set them apart just as clearly as we were defined by our corduroys and jeans with patches on the knees.

LCC students looked like they had somewhere mysterious and wonderful to go, even when they weren't getting picked up after school but were only waiting for the Monkland bus that would take them to other buses and from there to their homes around the city. They were always laughing, looking relaxed, as if life were just a game of tennis to be skillfully played and enjoyed, as if there were no risk of real consequences, no possibility of failure.

When LCC and Willingdon Elementary students ended up together on the bus, we never mixed. We kept to ourselves like two separate gangs. We watched the LCC kids out of the corners of our eyes, trying to make sense of their uniforms, the privilege they carried lightly like their backpacks. They rarely looked at us. I assumed they thought of us as interlopers, somehow inferior.

THE SPRING DAY I received my LCC acceptance in the mail, my mother danced with me in the kitchen. When my father came home from work and she told him the good news, "Well, congratulations then," was his response. There was no hug. My mother couldn't stop talking as she served supper and cleared the plates. My father was more silent than usual. Later that evening, as soon as they thought I was asleep, my parents set to arguing with no preliminary skirmish. But even when they fought, my parents did not interrupt each other.

"Mary, how are we going to bloody afford it? The fees are ridiculous. I make a decent living, but it's not like we have our own personal gold mine."

"Don't be silly, Declan. He's going on a full scholarship."

I could sense my father's body slump. "That's even worse."

"How so, Declan?"

"He's already different enough because of his height. The effect will be bigger because he skipped that stupid grade. Everybody will know he's there on charity. It will make him smaller in everyone's eyes."

My mother was silent. When she spoke again, her voice was softer. "That's a mighty stupid thing to say, Declan. There's nothing to be ashamed of that would cause us to turn down a full scholarship to LCC. It's not charity. Sean earned it. He's very bright. You should be feeling so proud. Besides, how is anybody going to know? They all dress the same."

"Mary. They will know the first time he invites them over after school. The first time they tell each other what their fathers do. Where they live. Where they go on vacation."

"Oh, Declan." I could tell by my mother's voice that she had wrapped her arms around my father and was holding on to his thick neck. I imagined the embrace included a chaste, reassuring kiss on the lips. "He's our boy. He has both of us in him. He will be fine."

3

BEING ACCEPTED TO LCC on a full scholarship was a major mile-stone in my childhood, but the trajectory of my life was only really altered when I met David Goldberg on the first day. In a way, that must have been what my mother had in mind when she told me to apply to LCC, except she was too sophisticated to ever say it. She knew it would have offended my father above everything else. The old "It's not what you know but who you know" way of looking at the world. If I hadn't gone to LCC, I would have turned out all right, certainly by my father's standards, but at LCC, expectations were automatically raised.

I met David Goldberg in gym class on the first day of school. We had gym every day at LCC, and the first day was no exception. There were twenty boys in the class. This was the old LCC, over a decade before the school took the first tentative steps to going coed. So, while the boys didn't feel the need to compete for the attention of any girls, they did compete because it was simply in their nature to do so. And they all knew each other, having attended the LCC elementary school.

Our gym teacher, Mr. Waters, was a forty-five-year-old Old Boy. He didn't come from money but had gone to LCC in grade seven on an athletic scholarship then was accepted to McGill on a football scholarship. He took a sabbatical from the McGill Redmen and full-time higher education in his second year to play running back in the CFL. When after five underpaid years his bruised hips and battered knees began to hamper his ability to run as well as he needed to, he returned to university full-time to take kinesiology and education, and he ended up where he'd started, back at LCC, this time teaching gym.

In our first gym class of the year, we were taken outside to play touch football. Without appearing to give it any thought, Mr. Waters picked captains: "Goldberg, Flemming." The names meant nothing to me, but Waters spoke them like he was used to calling them out. Goldberg and Flemming, whoever they were, moved off to opposite sides and began to pick teams. At my old school, I was usually picked last or second to last because of my size and my less-than-sterling coordination. At LCC on that first day, I felt poor, small, and nondescript.

I adopted my most patient and world-weary smile while preparing myself to be picked last. I looked around, hoping to see a fat kid who might have asthma or a thin one who might be lame in one leg or blind in one eye. There was a heavy boy, but he was also tall, so I figured he would be picked early for his size alone. Even though we were only going to play touch football, he could always stand in the way. And as I was to find out in the game, this boy, whose name was Paul, was actually relatively fast, with very soft hands, despite his deceptive bulk.

The choosing of teams began as I'd predicted. The tallest, fittest, broadest boys, who stood with grace and confidence, were chosen first. The big kid went early with them, a surprising fifth pick. Then a funny thing happened with the sixth pick. One of the captains, a tall, thin, blond boy, actually looked me in the eye and smiled. Without thinking, I smiled back. "You, the new kid. On my team. By the way, what's your name?"

I was surprised and elated to be picked so early, but I had the presence of mind not to run over to my new captain like someone who had just been rescued from impending humiliation. I stopped smiling and said, "My name is Sean. Sean McFall."

The tall, blond boy smiled even wider. "Well, young Sean, Sean McFall, my name is David Goldberg. And now you're on my team." I walked over to David Goldberg's team, which was *my* team, and turned to watch the remaining boys being picked. The world appeared completely different from where I was standing. Now that I was looking at the still unselected players, I felt separate from them. And from my new vantage point as a middle if not early draft pick, I could see how David Goldberg would have seen me, trying not to look nervous but standing awkwardly. Hoping to be picked. Hoping not to be last.

Once everyone had been chosen, David Goldberg turned to me and whispered, "Have you ever played touch football before?"

My first instinct was to lie, not because I was a born liar but because I was embarrassed I had never played football before, neither touch nor flag. At Willingdon, our games were far less sophisticated: variations of tag and dodgeball. And because, even though I was only half a day into my new life as a private school student, I somehow already knew that in everything that was going to happen to me from now on, an excess of confidence was going to be required. For the rest of my life, I was going to have to give everyone around me the impression that I could do the job, whatever the job might be. David Goldberg must have seen the split-second indecision on my face, but he was patient. And earnest.

There was something about his cheerful, ironic, indomitable optimism that conveyed he would be more impressed by honest doubt than put-on confidence. And there was something in his eyes. Even in the bright sun, they were a dark blue I only later came to recognize as the colour of the sea. And they were strangely symmetrical, as if they would look the same whether they were right side up or upside down. "I've never played before," I whispered back with almost an intake of breath.

David Goldberg nodded as if that were the answer he had expected. "Fair enough. How's your coordination?"

Again, the temptation to lie. Again, manfully resisted. "Mediocre."

Another unsurprised nod. "Speed?"

I smiled. "Not bad." I was being modest. Speed was the only thing going for me. I had neither experience nor size nor anything approaching good eye-hand coordination. But for some reason that I never understood or questioned, I could run half decently.

David Goldberg grinned, and I could see that even though he was only twelve, he had laugh lines already at the corners of his impossibly blue eyes. "Speed it shall be." By this time, the other students on our team were becoming impatient at the delay being caused by the new boy. They had already gathered in a huddle, waiting for David. He jogged over with me at his side and passed out the flags. We were the blue team. Everyone leaned in, and David began to tell us our positions. He spoke fast, without hesitation. It was like he had already mapped out in his head which of us would play what. Big Paul was a linebacker, no surprise. I was named wide receiver.

At the time, I didn't know enough about football to wonder why David hadn't made me the running back, where my ability to catch would have been less important than my ability to run.

But later, when I began to work with him, I learned that he liked to challenge people to do more than they ever thought they could. By now, all the boys were looking at me with skepticism, but none of them was prepared to question David.

Mr. Waters blew the whistle, and David ran over for the coin toss. He nodded to me to wait for him. After he won the coin toss, he jogged back. He put his arm on my shoulder and pulled me close. "Here's the wide receiver position in a nutshell: you run, you get open, you catch the ball. I'll be throwing. Once you catch it, you hold on to it like it's the most important thing in the world. Run toward the end zone and try not to get flagged on the way. Got it?" I nodded and waited. There had to be more to it. There was.

"Each time we have possession, I will give you a pattern to run. Most of the time you follow the pattern. Sometimes you will vary it, but only rarely, only if circumstances warrant it. As you play more and get more experience, your judgment of when not to follow the play and create your own will improve."

I nodded again. He was making football seem very simple.

"You look smart, and if you are fast, you should be fine with everything I've just said. There's only the matter of catching the ball. The overall strategy I set for all of us is called 'the play.' Once you're open, I'll take care of getting the ball in your hands. When the ball comes, don't think about how you'll catch it. That's the most important advice I can give you. Don't think. I will get the ball to your hands. Then all you have to do is bring it close to your body and run while holding it as tightly as you can. Got it?"

I nodded.

"Okay. The first pattern is called a buttonhook." And he did something I had never seen anybody else do before. He sketched the pattern for me with his right index finger on the palm of his left hand. He drew it twice so there was no chance I would misunderstand.

We had first possession. We lined up. David pointed to where I was to stand. He crouched. A player in front, who I was later to learn was called the centre, snapped the ball to David, and the play started. The offensive linemen cleared the way for me with their bulk, and I ran through an opening. I ran toward the other end zone, two of the opposing team's players covering me. After I had gone twenty yards, I suddenly doubled back and ran toward my own end zone. I looked up at David and caught sight of him. His offensive linebackers were doing their job. David was open. His eyes found mine, and he threw the ball. I was still running and still telling myself not to think. For the first time in my life, I was not afraid of missing a catch. David had promised he would get the ball to my hands. I held out my hands, and the ball found them. I pulled the ball into my body as David had told me, and I had no time to be amazed that I had made the catch. I pivoted and ran back toward the opposing team's end zone.

When I had first changed direction and started running back toward my own end zone — the essence of the buttonhook — I had surprised and lost the two boys covering me. But now they were on to me again. I was fast and had pulled ahead of them when I saw another boy coming at me from the side and a little ahead. I found another burst of speed. So did he. I kept going, knowing he was closing the gap and would pull the flag from my hip. Seconds later, he did.

But, at the same time as he was pulling my flag, he was running into me with his right shoulder. He was heavier than me. As I flew through the air backwards, all I could think of was how hard it was going to be for my mother to get the grass stains out of the brand new school gym clothes she had scrimped and saved so hard to buy. I landed on my back, my head hitting the ground, and I slid in the grass, gasping for air. David was the first over, and he pulled me up before I realized the whole field was turning around me.

The boy who had hit me, who I would later learn was a talented athlete named Roger Macdonald, was frowning, looking puzzled, avoiding looking at me. "Sorry, Mr. Waters. Didn't mean to touch him. He's so small and fast. Must have misjudged something and grazed his shoulder. Couldn't stop running."

David stared at him. "If you were really sorry, you'd be apologizing to Sean, not Mr. Waters."

Roger looked over at David. He said nothing to me. This was years before the awareness of concussions. The accepted wisdom was to shake it off and get back in the game. I had caught my breath, but the dizziness was not subsiding. The field whirled faster and faster around me. But David continued to hold on to my arm, making sure I was steady. He held on to me as I turned pale and threw up all over our shoes. He remained beside me, holding me up, preventing me from falling down.

My career as a junior high school wide receiver had just begun and already I had been taught how touch football was played at a boys' private high school.

4

IN OCTOBER, DAVID persuaded Mr. Caine, our English and drama teacher, to stage *Romeo and Juliet*. A week later, David's audition convinced Mr. Caine that he should cast him as Juliet.

It was clear from the way Mr. Caine called David's name at the audition after school that he had low expectations. Not because David was auditioning and not because of his choice of part. After all, it was a boys' school and there were no girls. I think it was because Mr. Caine expected David to play it campy. As did all the other boys who had gathered to watch. Auditions were open, so the audience wasn't composed of only students who were trying out for a part. All the boys, especially the older ones, giggled like girls when David walked on stage. I had to work hard to suppress a laugh. As far as I could tell, the only boy who didn't laugh was Roger Macdonald, sitting in the back row.

David wore his school uniform, as he had to, but he'd put on a long brunette wig. He hadn't taken more than three steps before it became apparent it wasn't your typical cheap wig that costume stores sell for Halloween and fathers put on for a laugh to go trick-or-treating with their daughters. It looked like real hair. Our laughter started to subside when we realized David was wearing someone's real hair on his head. He was carrying a chair. When he walked slowly to the centre front of the stage, he walked as he normally did. He didn't try to walk like a girl. By this time the giggling had stopped completely. We were mesmerized.

David slowly put down the chair with its back to us and stood on it. He stared out at the audience and, without giving any indication that he saw any of us, began Juliet's balcony monologue.

"O Romeo, Romeo! Wherefore art thou Romeo?"

He didn't bother putting on a falsetto: that would have started us laughing again. He stage-whispered the scene, as if half asleep in a dream, so he could use as much of his real voice as possible and it wouldn't sound strange coming from someone who was supposed to be a girl. He spoke his lines naturally, without any attempt to affect a metre or to sound dramatic. He spoke the words in such a way that we understood the meaning.

When he concluded with "Take all myself," there was silence for a few seconds before we jumped to our feet, giving him a standing ovation.

Mr. Caine, a former British soldier who was known for keeping things close to his vest and who proudly never revealed the results of any auditions before everyone had had their chance, said in what sounded like a very loud voice after David's speech, "You've won the part, Goldberg. You've won the part!"

IT TURNED OUT that David acted as well as he played football. As rehearsals progressed, it became clear he was going to steal the show. David's athletic ability might have been one of the reasons why he wasn't teased for dressing up as a girl. He was good at sports, but he didn't think or care too much about the fact, just like he didn't seem to care that he was good at school. As I got to know David's brothers, I would realize that his oldest brother, Sammy, wasn't as good at sports in grade nine as he wanted to be, although he was better than most. David's middle brother, Jake, suffered through every single sport that LCC threw at him in grade eight with the determination that he assumed was expected of a Goldberg. But for David, everything was a game.

After the full cast was chosen by Mr. Caine, it became obvious that the best athletes were often the best actors. I found this surprising because I had always associated acting with being articulate and sensitive and sports with people like my father. Big Paul got the part of Mercutio and proved himself a witty friend and a skillful fencer, despite his bulk. As good a fencer as a linebacker. Roger Macdonald, gifted athlete and private school juvenile delinquent that he was, got a good part. And it was soon apparent, even in the early days when every boy was still learning his lines and holding copies of his script, that Roger would make an excellent Tybalt: physical and sardonic, with the right mixture of aggressive friendship and menace simmering just beneath the surface.

As I tagged along to rehearsals, carrying my knapsack so I could study while I half-watched and listened, I formulated my own theory of why athletes might make good actors. The first part of my theory was grounded in kinetics. On one very physical and literal level, actors move about the stage. They have to fence and box and — in the movies at least — ride horses and climb mountains. But even on the limited stage where their words and gestures serve to create an imaginary world, they move around a great deal, usually with more grace than awkwardness.

This realization led me to the second part of my theory, which was more psychological. Most of the athletes I got to know at

LCC had an easygoing manner. They had well-developed senses of humour. It was clear they didn't take themselves too seriously. They were "light of mind," as my mother Mary used to say of people who carried a halo of good humour. If they had darker thoughts inside, they never let them show. The only exception to this rule, as far as I could tell, was Roger. He went around with a permanent scowl on his otherwise handsome face. The thrust of this second part of my theory was that because athletes generally don't take themselves too seriously, because they are used to performing in front of others, because when they are on the football field or hockey rink they don't have time to blame themselves for mistakes made on the last play but have to jump back into the fray, they lack the self-consciousness and the resulting woodenness that ruins amateur acting. Their acting is natural in a way that technique can't ever quite account for.

As I watched rehearsal after rehearsal, I learned that as much as acting was about immersing yourself in someone else's character, it was also about revealing your own. And the more an actor tried to hide himself in the guise of an imaginary character, the more he revealed something of his true self. This for me was the great irony and beauty of drama. Underneath Paul's bulk was a slender, jesting swordsman and, more importantly, a loyal friend. He didn't have to work to pretend to be Mercutio. He just channelled the little bit of Mercutio that was already inside. And behind Roger's scowl was a boy who understood the importance of tribal loyalties but who remained insecure and who was, above all, a hothead. The most talented actors understood this instinctively. Mr. Caine didn't have to teach them.

For David, as with everything, the truth was more subtle. It would be too easy to say David had his feminine side; we all did. And somewhere deep down we all knew we did, even if, on the cusp of masculine adolescence, most of us were afraid to admit it. By playing Juliet, David wasn't competing for attention. He wasn't rebelling against his father, the way it was obvious his middle brother, Jake, always was, once I got to know him. And he certainly wasn't trying to live up to his father, like his oldest brother, Sammy. I'm not sure I can explain it any better than this, but in auditioning for Juliet and in playing the part so well, David was just being David.

David was also just being David when he spent time with me — at lunch in the cafeteria, walking to classes, or while trying to convince me to try out for a small part in the play. At that point, I hadn't spent any time watching rehearsals so hadn't yet developed my theory that acting was as much about revealing what was already inside you as it was adopting a new character. That would have made me even more nervous about auditioning. Despite my early success on the football field, thanks to David, I still felt ill at ease among my fellow students. I wouldn't yet have been prepared for them to see through whatever character I might have been playing on stage to that small, true part of me: a poor Irish boy whose father worked in construction.

But no, that wasn't my initial reason for declining to take David up on his suggestion. He was very supportive — he even offered to read with me after school to help me become familiar with Shakespeare's language. He was careful not to convey any prejudgments, but I got the sense he assumed I hadn't been exposed to Shakespeare, either at my former school or in my home. It was one of the very few times in our friendship that I would find one of his conclusions patronizing. In this, he would have been only partially right.

We had never come close to touching on Shakespeare at any point in elementary school, but my mother owned a complete set of Shakespeare, which I saw her reading from time to time, at night when all the housework was done. She never read to me from the actual plays, but sometimes she would tell me bedtime stories that I later learned — at LCC, where I learned so much — were based on Shakespeare. At the time, I thought she was making up the stories herself.

David's suspicion that Shakespeare was unfamiliar territory for me came close to why I refused to audition for a role. It wasn't the fear of revealing something of my inner self on the stage — at least not yet — and it wasn't the fear of having trouble with Shakespeare's language, although that was part of it. It was simply because I had not acted before and so was nervous about attempting something new on top of everything else at LCC. At eleven years of age, I had a limited capacity for trying new things.

The blue-and-grey uniform, with its white shirt and school tie, earned me instant respectability among adults and the irrational jealousy and suspicion of my old friends. The teachers all seemed to have mysterious and adventurous pasts, unlike the teachers in my old school, who apparently had done nothing before taking up their jobs in the classroom other than attend teacher's college. The ranks of LCC teachers boasted former soldiers, a retired professional football player, even an independently wealthy stockbroker who had retired at forty and taken up teaching mathematics to the sons of wealthy families for the fun of it. In the classes where we read the classics, we were addressed by our last names, as if in British public school.

Even in the late 1970s, the so-called Me Decade, there was still a belief that we had an obligation not just to make something of ourselves but to serve society. It was clear that we weren't being trained to make something as ordinary as money — that would come later and naturally by virtue of our parents' connections and the connections we were making with each other. We were being trained to do nothing less than to take on our adult responsibilities in making the world a better place. LCC instilled a sense of palpable importance in ourselves that my old friends found far more irritating than my uniform. The bricks and mortar of our respective schools were mere blocks apart, but we might as well have been in different worlds.

All this newness led me to resist auditioning for the play. David finally let me be, but I was surprised by how many boys did try out. Remember, this was the seventies. The idea of full-blown celebrity was still a couple decades away. Most early adolescents didn't hope to become famous for its own sake. Certainly very few, if any, of the boys who attended LCC harboured dreams of becoming a professional actor. Or musician. Or even something as mundane as a writer. It was only in retrospect, when I joined the world of business, specifically the world of the Goldbergs, that I realized drama was excellent preparation.

We didn't know anything yet about the adult world except what we picked up when we overheard our parents whispering about what went on in their lives and the insights we could glean from the anecdotes told by our teachers. These anecdotes were somewhat distorted and suspect, given they belonged to men who had chosen to spend their lives around boys, instructing boys in an adult world from which, notwithstanding any experience prior to joining the monastic life of a teacher at a boys' private school, they were now largely excluded.

Despite this lack of knowledge, the boys who tried out for the play knew instinctively that they were being trained to take on a part in the adult world. Their whole career at LCC was one audition after another, whether studying math or English or playing the team sports that seemed to have been invented only to teach us character. Each boy knew that following LCC, he would go to university and be well on his path to taking on the trappings of men of success, men of the world. Beneath their schoolboy confidence, their ability to laugh, they also recognized they needed as much training as possible. No boy, no matter how rich, no matter what he has inside him to begin with, starts off being an industrialist or a doctor or a banker or a politician — or a corporate lawyer for that matter. Each of us has to learn how to play a part.

Once, after a particularly boring rehearsal in which Mr. Caine spent much of his time showing his actors where he wanted them to stand and how to breathe, where David had winked at me during the part when he was supposed to be thinking about Romeo, I asked David the secret of good acting. By this time, I had worked out my own amateur theory of athletic self-confidence combined with revealing part of your true nature, but I was also interested in what Mr. Caine was teaching.

"Is there a key technique?" I knew Mr. Caine taught voice exercises, but most of the LCC boys already possessed strong voices in the same way the British upper classes possess the right accent. There was the projection of confidence, which could be achieved through proper breathing and posture and expression, and technical exercises to steady the nerves sufficiently before one pranced out on stage. That would prove important for boardroom meetings or sales calls or funding pitches. Even for delivering bad news to patients or exhorting masses of employees to do their best. But these were all technical skills, and I already knew instinctively that technique was a poor substitute for what went into making a great performance.

David agreed. "The real trick's believing. You've got to believe what's happening to you and what you're doing is real. You can only lie successfully if you believe it. There aren't any techniques for that, at least none that I know of."

I HAVEN'T TOLD you anything yet about the boy who played Romeo; his name was Hector von Faustenberg. His mother was Spanish and his father was German. They owned some "import-export" business. Not even Hector seemed to know what his parents actually imported or exported. Apparently they were good at it, because he was at LCC and was dropped off and picked up each day by a solemn chauffeur at the wheel of a silver Jaguar sedan. Hector was chosen by Mr. Caine in part for his looks, which he got from his mother: dark and romantic. But he could also act, judging from his monologues. Surprisingly to me, at least at first, he appeared to lack any athletic ability at all, other than running in the track and field unit of our gym class. But he turned out to be more than believable, at least for a twelve-year-old boy declaring his love for a girl being played by a boy.

Nobody ever said it to his face, but half the boys in the school, at least the ones who weren't in the play, were convinced that Hector was secretly in love with David, which was why he was able to be so convincing. One older boy even compared the situation to Mick Jagger's infatuation with Keith Richards, with a knowing attempt at a worldly smile as he flicked ash from his cigarette during recess. At the time, I didn't understand what he was talking about, but if this was ever the case with Hector, I never saw any real evidence. Had it been true, I'm not sure Hector would have acted on his feelings outside of the confines of the play. We were still mostly innocent back then, even as we moved from twelve to thirteen years old, or in my case, from eleven to twelve. It might have been different if Hector had stayed on at the school.

5

IF REHEARSAL FINISHED early, a few of us would sometimes wander down the street to the Kentucky Fried Chicken at the corner of Royal and Monkland. Even Roger, who didn't seem to have a lot of friends, would occasionally come along. We'd walk in a group in our uniforms, moving down the block like a pack of dogs, swinging our knapsacks, jostling each other, talking loudly.

From time to time, others would pass us on the street. If they were adults, we would politely form a single file and move over to the right side of the sidewalk, lowering our voices. Occasionally we would stop talking altogether. Any adult was a figure of authority to us. It came with the territory of private school. We would be respectful of younger children as well. But if we passed other children our own age who did not attend LCC, something took over in our brains, and we refused to cede the sidewalk. We pretended we didn't see them, and we made them walk around us, which they usually did. There was something about the children of the rich, a sense of confidence that went beyond the uniform when they did something as simple as walk down the street. The uniform didn't give them more confidence; it merely acknowledged what they already knew. If their characters are good, the children of the rich don't care too much about money because they take it for granted. They assume everybody lives the way they do.

Every rich kid in the twenty-first century wears jeans, running shoes, and sweatshirts when they're not wearing the sober greys and blues of their private school uniforms. They don't need anything as transparent and banal as a logo to bring attention to themselves. When they do dress up, it's the material and the cut of their clothes that gives them away. Because when it comes to clothes, the wealthy know a secret that most people don't: what matters is not how clothes look but how they feel. It's what's underneath the clothes that brands the wealthy far more effectively than any fabric stitched together by child labour in Bangladesh.

It starts with their hair (shiny enough but not too shiny), the haircuts that aren't too long or too short, the clear skin courtesy of the right diet and dermatologists. Then it's their builds: hardly ever fat, never too thin, usually not overly muscular unless they play a sport that requires hours in the gym. Their muscles toned instead from the right amount of running or biking or swimming or skiing but not so much as to bring out any fatigue or frustration on their faces. But even more than their hair or their skin or their conditioning, it's the way they exist in their jeans, running shoes, and hoodies that sets them apart.

In the early twentieth century, those who noticed such things — F. Scott Fitzgerald was an obsessive observer — called this quality of existing effortlessly in society "poise." Today, we've largely lost sight of it. Instead, a pushy exhibitionism full of selfies and self-promotion has taken over. But the rich, especially the truly rich, feel no need to advertise when they walk down the street. And even though we were still only boys, the LCC boys already had this quality. They walked with self-assurance. Youth or wealth on their own are compelling, but taken together they are irresistible.

On the late March day when Mr. Caine had the cast rehearse the scene where Mercutio is fatally stabbed by Tybalt, everyone's spirits were tuned to a higher-than-usual level of intensity as we walked to get our snacks. Roger was shoving Paul, even though he was much bigger, and Paul was shoving Roger in return. The two of them were at the back of the pack. David was at the front with Hector. I was just behind them. David was talking loudly to Hector about something, and so he didn't see the small group of other boys walking toward us. I recognized them before anybody else did. Actually, I was the only one to recognize them. They were from my old school. Just three of them: Michael Appleby, Eli Tredman, and Stephen Elias. There were five of us.

We were about two hundred metres apart and approaching each other on the sidewalk on which, at best, two boys could walk comfortably beside each other. Or one boy could pass another walking in the opposite direction. Eli, Michael, and Stephen noticed us. I was partially hidden behind David and Hector; they wouldn't have been able to make me out. Eli was even more slender then. Michael was downright skinny and still wore glasses, but Stephen was nearly full grown, even at the age of thirteen. While I had skipped a grade, he had failed one. In grade six, he had got into more fights than the rest of us combined, and unlike most kids, he actually enjoyed them. The three of them were openly looking at us as we came closer. Our gang of boys hadn't yet noticed them, or else we were pretending we hadn't, and I found myself wondering who would make way for whom. Would we change our arrogant custom and walk politely onto the grass on our right and cede the right of way? Would Michael, Eli, and Stephen step onto the street on their right and let us pass?

As we cut down the distance between us, both groups of boys slowed their pace just a little, and conversation died out. Each of us began to walk a little taller. We threw our chests out and our shoulders back. One hundred metres became fifty metres and fifty metres became twenty-five. At this point, Michael recognized me. He smiled and waved. I waved back. Strangely enough, nobody else seemed to notice, not even David; if anyone did, he didn't let on. Twenty metres. And then fifteen. Everyone slowed.

At the last possible moment, when our two groups were less than one metre apart and it looked like we would crash into each other, David veered right onto the grass as did Hector and then I and Paul. At almost the same time, Eli stepped onto the street, quickly followed by Stephen. But Michael hesitated, and although he moved over to the edge of the sidewalk, he remained on it. As for our group, it was Roger who didn't step onto the grass. Like Michael, he stayed on the sidewalk, but unlike Michael, he didn't move to the side. He continued to walk down the middle of the sidewalk as if Michael wasn't there. Even still, if Roger had walked in a straight line, nothing would have happened. All of us would have kept walking, and we would have passed each other narrowly but without incident. But Roger didn't let it go at that.

As he and Michael passed each other, Roger leaned left and hit Michael with his shoulder. When their shoulders connected, Michael spun backwards and nearly lost his balance, partly because Roger was heavier and more muscular and partly because of the surprise. Michael recovered and didn't fall. All of us stopped. All of us except for Roger. He took another four or five steps. When he noticed the rest of us were still, he stopped walking and turned around.

The two groups of boys looked at each other. The Montréal spring air felt hot on my face, and Michael's face was red. He

didn't know whom to look at, but he noticeably refused to look at
Roger. Roger looked at a point above Michael's head, and when
Stephen started smiling at him, Roger pretended not to notice.
I had seen that smile before. But Stephen didn't move. Not yet.
Eli looked at Roger and then at me, and David caught Eli's eye.
They seemed to both be coming to the same decision. I could have
sworn they nodded at each other.

David tried to make eye contact with Roger, but Roger ignored
him. It was then that David stepped forward and said to Michael,
"Look, I'm sorry."

Michael appeared less aggrieved at this, but Stephen stared at
David. Still smiling. Eli kept his face blank.

"For my friend," David added as if it might not have been
obvious.

"That's nice, thank you," Stephen said, smiling through every
word, "but it's not your apology to make." He spoke slowly. He
was calm. Not a word expressed in anger. Definitely none in any
way approaching fear.

After he finished speaking, he looked over each of us in turn.
He took in our faces, our arms, upper bodies, legs, the way we
held ourselves, how we balanced on our feet, and then back up
again to our eyes. Even though he was only thirteen, he was like
a general assessing the condition and position of enemy troops.
Through it all, he never stopped smiling. I had seen him do this
before, in the playground or at the park or on the street with
other boys. I knew he had trained himself to keep smiling as he
measured the likely strength and skill and, most importantly, the
will of those he was about to fight. He had taught himself to smile
no matter what he concluded from the size and muscle tone and
height and what he saw in the eyes of other boys: a flicker of fear,
a numbness, a determination to fight and to win.

Stephen found himself in a lot of neighbourhood fights in the course of each year, ever since he had been the biggest kid in grade one, and even more after he'd failed grade four. He won most of them. To his credit, he never stopped smiling before a fight. I don't think he had ever studied psychological warfare or read Sun Tzu, but from an early age, Stephen had known that most battles are won before they ever begin. Unless an opponent was supremely confident, Stephen's large body and wide smile could be intimidating. His smile signalled that unlike most boys, Stephen enjoyed fighting, loved it without reservation, desired it.

Michael was the opposite of Stephen in many ways. He didn't like to fight, and if he practiced anything he practiced not ever showing his anger and frustration. Michael was reasonable. That day, he shrugged his shoulders and said, "Let's go." He even half-heartedly began to walk away, but he stopped when neither Eli nor Stephen moved. Eli was looking pale and serious, and Stephen kept smiling. Stephen was looking at Roger alone now. Roger was making his best effort but was finding it hard to meet Stephen's gaze.

"You're going to apologize to my friend," Stephen said. His smile didn't wane. He could have been asking Roger to pass him the salt at dinner. It was almost as if he had said, "Please." I had nothing to compare it to at the time, but now I know that even though Stephen had not yet turned fourteen, he was speaking the way confident men speak when they know they don't need to try to persuade anyone because who they are and their words are enough. He was calm, and he was also speaking the way he spoke to his dog, a German shepherd, when the dog didn't listen to him, which was rare.

Stephen had once explained to me that dogs and people were very similar, and you had to treat them the same. Reliably. Predictably. It was all about conditioning, follow-through. In giving Roger a command, I'm sure that Stephen knew how he would respond. Having fought so many times, and having sized up so many boys before, he knew exactly what Roger was going to do. And he desired Roger to do exactly that.

Roger looked at Michael then back again to Stephen. Roger was trying to appear affronted. Supercilious. But I had spent sufficient time around Stephen and seen fear in other boys' eyes on enough occasions to know that Roger was uncharacteristically and unusually afraid. Stephen had three inches on him at an age when every inch counted, and at least forty pounds. And while some of it was late childhood fat, most of it was muscle. Roger's eyes flickered over to David as if looking for guidance, but David's eyes remained blank. It was then that Roger looked again at Michael, turned his gaze back to Stephen, and said, "Fuck you."

Stephen's smile never wavered. If anything, it grew wider. When he spoke, his voice was low, as if speaking to himself, and his eyes closed halfway, although I don't think he was aware of it. "I hoped you'd say that." And he started to walk toward Roger. They were about two metres apart. At this point, Roger could have done one of three things: he could have blurted out an apology, which would have disappointed Stephen but would have stopped him. He could have turned around and run. Or he could have done the third thing, which I suppose his nature dictated he had to, and that was to swing his fist at Stephen's face.

Stephen moved quickly for a big kid, and he had the advantage of knowing what Roger was going to do even before Roger did. He blocked Roger's right fist with his arm and then swung low and punched Roger in the stomach. When Roger bent over, Stephen punched him twice in the face. His head snapped back, and when it came forward again his nose was bleeding.

The next minute was a long one. Stephen stood with his fists clenched and elbows slightly bent. One foot forward. Roger wiped his nose with his arm and looked at Stephen. He was asking himself if he wanted to go through it again. David was watching it all but not saying a word. He, like Stephen, knew what Roger was going to do. The rest of us waited, wondering what was going to happen. Nobody made a move to help Roger.

Even after what had just happened, it all could have ended there. It should have, and it would have with any other boy except Roger. But Roger was Roger, and he couldn't help himself, so he said, "Fuck you" again.

Stephen swung.

When his fist hit Roger's face, we all heard a loud crack, and we knew he had broken Roger's jaw. Roger went down. It was then that I saw David shake his head and walk over to Roger. I could see on his face that although David disapproved of Roger's behaviour, he disapproved more of what Stephen had done to an LCC classmate, no matter how justified.

I was sure Stephen would break David's jaw as well, and I was torn. I wanted to support my new friend, but I also didn't want to completely abandon my old friends. As I was making up my mind, the boys on each side of the divide began to walk toward each other, trying to pick out someone who was their own size, guided as they walked into a fight by their adolescent codes of honour and individual senses of self-preservation. There were three of them and five of us, but Roger was out of it now, and David was stepping in. Paul stopped moving forward when David did something quickly with his hand to wave him off. I was beside David and so ended up in front of my old friend Michael. Hector paired up with Eli, and Paul as the extra boy chivalrously held back.

I waited a split second, and by then Stephen was in front of David. This time Stephen didn't wait for David. He swung first, but David was ready. He blocked the fist of the larger boy and hit him under the chin, rocking his head back slightly. Stephen looked stunned and then angry in a way I had rarely seen, and then he went for David. And I saw David do something surprising. Stephen was angry now, and he was fighting, but what David was doing was different and new.

David had his fists up, and his arms were moving, and he was moving in and out, and he was balancing on the balls of his feet. Stephen appeared to be wrestling half the time, and when he threw punches he would swing, and he looked slow in comparison. David was throwing quick combinations, and with each punch he would turn his shoulder and throw his body into it, all the while almost floating on his feet. Although he was fighting, it looked like dancing to me, like something he would have done in the play. It took me a few moments to realize that David was boxing.

The closest I had ever come to boxing was seeing it on TV. Declan loved to watch boxing on the weekends, and I would sometimes watch it with him even if I always felt I was somehow infringing upon his space, even though he never said anything to suggest he would have preferred to watch it alone or with his friends rather than his small son. I had never seen anyone box in real life before, and certainly not a twelve-year-old. The odd time I had seen fellow students fight at my old school — even Stephen, in retrospect — they mostly wrestled and grabbed each other, occasionally swinging an unconvincing punch from the side. But David boxed.

Stephen mostly kept missing David, but even when he connected, David managed to be at the far end of Stephen's fists so that his force was spent and his blows would glance off David's body. But when David landed a punch, it was full of momentum. I could see Stephen was becoming frustrated because he stopped smiling. As the fight went on, Stephen became less angry at David, not more, and this was disappointing to me. Even though David was my good friend, I wouldn't have minded Stephen's anger with him. I wouldn't have minded if Stephen had become angry with me for deserting my original friends. That would have been easier to take than what I saw in his eyes. Because what I saw in his eyes as his anger wore away was something worse, and that was fear.

I had never seen fear in Stephen's eyes. He wasn't afraid of David or of what David might do to him. As he fought David, Stephen was coming to the awful realization that in all his fights, he had never faced anyone who knew, really knew, how to fight. And for the first time in his life, he was beginning to doubt himself, to think that maybe he was not so good at fighting as he had previously thought. All of this was revealed in a few seconds, and then he was back to focusing on David. Soon Eli and Hector were fighting. Michael and I had come across each other in the action seemingly by accident, but in retrospect it must have been by mutual design.

I had never got into a fight in my life, even though I knew it was the kind of activity that my father expected of me in certain circumstances. Mary had forbidden it. She'd taught me always to use what she called my wits. "I know you're strong, Sean, even though you may not be large, and I know you could fight, and could do it well if you wanted to. But you have to save your strength for other things. You are going to have bigger battles, and if you start too early, well, you might never get a chance to fight them." I didn't understand what she was talking about until much later when I started to work for the Goldbergs and I began to see how adults fought with each other outside of war: across boardroom tables with money and lawyers. But I always listened to and respected my mother, so I stayed away from fighting.

That day, Michael and I just looked at each other before he slowly took off his glasses and put them in the back pocket of his jeans. I waited for him to be done, like a man waiting for his opponent readying his pistols for a duel, and I wondered if he'd be able to see me clearly enough to hit me. Then he half-heartedly raised his fists, and I raised mine, and we threw punches in each other's general direction without really trying to make contact. We both understood we were supposed to live up to the examples of David and Stephen, but we were also both hoping it would all be over before either of us had to hurt the other.

Halfway through, as Michael and I went through the motions of our reluctant combat, I realized we had an audience: David's older brothers, Sammy and Jake. Jake just a year older, in grade eight, and Sammy two years older than David, in grade nine. Like David, Sammy was very blond, but he was heavier, not fat but muscular because he was always working out. His head was big, just slightly out of proportion with his body. Jake had dark blond hair and was slight. They both had what I had come to know as the Goldberg eyes, blue and symmetrical. That day, I heard Sammy before I saw him.

"Get in close, Davey! Neutralize the advantage of his longer arms!" Sammy was bouncing around in his excitement, almost shadow-boxing, sounding like a cornerman and trying to show David how it was done, although it would appear David didn't need any instruction. Jake was standing to the side, still except for his arms, which he didn't seem to know what to do with. At first, he stood with his arms crossed, then he uncrossed them and put his hands in his pockets before repeating the sequence. It was as if the sight of his brother fighting with someone fully grown just down the street from his school made him uncomfortable. Sammy kept offering advice. David was as intent on his fighting as he was in everything. I was only able to notice these things because Michael and I weren't really fighting.

Sammy was engaged and cheering, but I could tell from his stance and his smile that he wanted to see how his little brother "handled himself," and he was not unpleased with the results as they were unfolding. Jake, on the other hand, with his arms wrapped around his own body, looked like he was thinking about himself, as if he were wondering how he would fare on the childhood battlefield against someone of Stephen's size. Strangely enough, it was Jake, despite his seriousness and introversion, despite his decision to stay above the childish fray, who looked younger than his age, which would have been thirteen, while Sammy in his childhood exuberance looked older than he was at fourteen. Perhaps it was the weight he had on Jake. Maybe it was the way he wore his school uniform. The rest of us looked like kids in private school. But Sammy, only in grade nine, yelling ringside advice at his twelve-year-old brother, looked like an adult. He wore his tie and blazer over his white shirt with more gravitas than the rest of us. For us it was very much a school uniform. But Sammy had already made it the uniform he would wear when he became an adult.

PEOPLE WILL ALWAYS strive to differentiate themselves, even when they are conforming, and when their options for doing so are limited, the way they choose to show their character will be subtle and may even appear superficial and trivial. Sammy wore a full Windsor knot in his tie that bulged around his already large neck. Jake wore his uniform pressed without a wrinkle. David didn't care, and whenever he could, as was the case today, he left his shirt untucked. Most students would have been asked by our teachers to at least tuck in their shirts. But our teachers went easy on David, partly because he was the youngest son of Mr. Goldberg, the wealthiest parent at the school, and partly because he was David.

The battle between who our parents were and who we were as individuals played out in many ways, and I thought David wore this tension and expectation lightly. But still, the major distinguishing factor for most of us at LCC was our parents and what they did. It placed a burden on many of the students in a way that my old friends wouldn't have understood. For all the kids in my neighbourhood, what our fathers did was inconsequential, in the sense that it didn't matter to us. Eli's father had been a bus driver but was now a poet. Michael's father was a university professor. Their professions were far and away the most exotic in our neighbourhood. My father was in construction. Stephen's worked at a garage. None of this meant anything special to us, and yet we understood every one of these paternal jobs, at least sufficiently that we didn't have to think about them. At LCC, what everyone's father did mattered, in the sense that it helped us define and place every single boy, even though in grade seven we rarely knew what these adult jobs actually entailed, aside from the doctors. I never really knew what a corporate lawyer did, not before I studied law and became one.

As with all the other boys at LCC, the difference between them and me was rooted in what our fathers did. But it was also based on other things, like the cars they would receive as gifts for their sixteenth birthdays. The designer drinks, the drugs. And how they wore their school uniforms.

It's a myth that school uniforms completely iron out the disparities between the rich, who have too many clothes, and the poor, who have too few. As my father, Declan, knew, you can still tell the difference. You just have to look more carefully. When it comes to their school uniforms, the rich are more casual, more cavalier. They don't worry if their pants get stained or accidentally torn. They know, without having to think about it, that their parents will buy them new ones. They don't always do up all the buttons on their shirts, at least not the top one. And they don't always perfectly tighten the knots of their ties. It's an affected sloppiness that the children in my neighbourhood would never have dreamed of adopting.

This attitude at LCC was paired with a casual intelligence. The rich kids were not all smart to begin with, but they knew enough to know they didn't have to be, and they didn't worry about whether they were or not, at least not outwardly. They appeared relaxed, as if they knew they'd eventually find a place in the family firm. But I have to be careful not to paint them all with the same brush: some were serious even in grade seven, usually the doctors' children, because they already knew they'd have to reach a certain level of capability if they were going to follow in their fathers' or mothers' footsteps. And yet despite all this privilege, there was an irony inherent in the location of LCC, in the midst of Notre-Dame-de-Grâce: the children who went to LCC were the interlopers in our neighbourhood. LCC was an island of privilege in a lower-middle-class sea of semi-detached homes.

HALFWAY THROUGH MY lacklustre fight with Michael, I sensed, rather than saw, that our small audience had grown to three. I didn't know where my neighbour and former close friend Jane had come from, but she was now watching us from across the street. Since I had started at LCC, Jane and I were spending less time together. Like Jake, her arms were folded, but the resemblance stopped there. Jane was staring at us the way you might watch wild animals in the zoo, with a mixture of interest, perhaps even admiration, but also detachment and a certain condescension that I don't think even she would have been aware of.

While Sammy was twitching and Jake was struggling not to, Jane was completely self-possessed. Looking at us as if we were silly and yet worthy of a sort of respect at the same time, possibly slightly dangerous yet not to be taken too seriously. I remember glancing at her and then back at Michael. Part of me now wanted to fight harder, to try to hit him for real and make him bleed with the power of my fists. But I am happy to report that a better part of me was embarrassed, and I redoubled my efforts to look busy in a way that would not have any consequences.

AFTER IT WAS over and the LCC boys had won, if you counted the bleeding noses and split lips and didn't count Roger's jaw, which ended up being fractured, not completely broken, we walked over to Kentucky Fried Chicken to celebrate our triumph. David was up front, like a winning general after a battle. Sammy came over to us and made an effort to shake each of our hands momentously and to tell us we had acquitted ourselves with honour. Jake separated himself as he walked and tried to smile. As soon as Michael and I had extricated ourselves from our hesitant battle with quiet and embarrassed glances of understanding, I'd looked around for Jane, wanting suddenly to see her. But she was gone. For a second I doubted myself, wondering if she had ever really been there, but I had forgotten about her by the time we reached the restaurant.

I knew the various meanings of the word *irony* thanks to Mr. Caine, who had explained them in English class. Knowing something before a made-up character made me uncomfortable and impatient. It was like cheating on the part of the writer, and I wanted to skip ahead to where our levels of knowledge evened out. I could have lived with that, but worse, dramatic irony seemed unfair to the unknowing character. It put him at a disadvantage to me. Verbal irony was a bit too close to sarcasm for my liking: even then it struck me as weak. I knew enough about situational irony from Mr. Caine's lessons that, as I bit into my greasy chicken, I thought how ironic it was that the rich kids were the ones who really knew how to fight. It was supposed to be the other way around. The poor kids were supposed to be the tough ones, the ones the rich kids lived in fear of. The poor might not have money and more than one car and big houses and fancy vacations, but they were expected to hold their own with their fists. David had just disproven that. Here too the rich could win.

I was happy that Michael and I had never really hit each other. That was how we managed to remain friends and why I wasn't really forced to choose sides on that day. I think Eli filed the whole experience away for later when he finally became a writer and spent his time trying to make sense of and describe things that are difficult to understand let alone explain. Later, he had a fight scene in one of his novels that seemed a bit too familiar. Stephen ended up getting charged with assault under the youth criminal act and just narrowly missed spending three months at a juvenile detention centre. The judge took a liking to him, and he got off with a warning to avoid fighting in future. He did this in the brave and quiet way some teenagers give up on an acting career when they realize their talent won't carry them far beyond their high school play and so they go into finance. David became even more of a hero in our grade seven class, adding boxing and perhaps even street fighting to his already recognized talents for football and acting. Only later, when I was invited over to the Goldbergs' house for the first time, did I discover where David had learned to box.

6

THE AUDITORIUM WAS full on opening night. Mary loved theatre and had insisted on arriving early. Declan had refused to come. He prided himself on disliking highbrow culture, and he still hadn't become used to the idea of his son attending private school. He hadn't set foot in the place once, managing to avoid parent-teacher night. Ever since the first week of school, when he had asked me what it was like, he had never spoken to me again about LCC.

At the end of that first week, Declan had asked if I wanted to throw a baseball around at the park. I had a lot of homework, and I didn't really want to go. But he was my father, and an invitation from him, no matter how informal, was not one I ever entertained declining. So I went.

We walked up the slight hill to Benny Park, where we threw the ball back and forth for about ten minutes before Declan spoke. He had just thrown the ball to me, and I had caught it. My father always threw a ball well — hard and fast — but even then, when I was eleven, he still held back.

"So, Sean, how's the school?" Ever since my mother had first come up with the idea that her son should apply for a scholarship to LCC, my father had refused to say the school's name. It was always and would forever remain "the school."

I threw the ball back to him, and as it flew through the air, I mumbled, "Fine."

He threw back to me. Faster and harder. I caught it. David's football lessons were having an effect. Declan waited until I had it firmly in my glove before he spoke, as if he didn't want to distract me. "That's not an answer, Sean. I'm your father. I deserve an answer." He didn't say it with petulance or anger. If anything, he spoke more softly than usual, just loud enough to be heard across the sixty feet between us.

When I threw the ball back to him, it went high. Declan jumped. A big man, he had an awkward grace when he moved, and he looked like a baseball player on TV leaping for a high line drive. He seemed to hover there for a moment in the air before landing with a spring. Before he had time to fully plant his feet he fired the ball back to me, like a shortstop throwing to first base before the hitter made it halfway.

I wasn't sure if I'd be able to properly talk and throw at the same time, so I held on to the ball for a moment after I'd caught it. "Sorry, Dad. It's different. Everybody seems smart. There are no girls. The teachers are interesting. I played football this week. I think I made a friend." I had to raise my voice a bit, but I was careful to be serious and brief. I didn't want my father to know that I was enjoying LCC. That flag football, despite the tackle, had been fun. That David might turn out to be a good friend. That aside from Roger, who didn't seem to like anyone, the rest of the boys were welcoming me into the fold. I threw the ball then and hoped my father would leave it at that. Which he did. We tossed the ball back and forth for another fifteen minutes, but my father no longer seemed to be enjoying himself. He went back to throwing softly and didn't ask any more questions.

Each time there was a reason for Declan to come to "the school," he somehow had to visit a construction site or attend a meeting, even when the meeting was at the Monkland Tavern. The production of *Romeo and Juliet* was no exception. But Mary wasn't letting his absence ruin her mood. She was pleased we had arrived early enough to be almost first in line. When the doors opened, we had our pick of the auditorium. Mary took us down to the fifth row centre. From the look in her eyes and the way she stood straight and smiled, you would have thought she was attending a premiere at Place des Arts. I was happy to see her so excited, and in some hidden place I was also ashamed that she was taking it so seriously. For a short moment, I regretted coming, and for a longer moment, I was worried she would sense my discomfort. As people began to arrive and take their seats, I noticed David's two older brothers. Sammy and Jake both waved to me and staked out a stretch of four seats several places to our right in the same row, just in from the aisle. Sammy sat on the aisle, and Jake sat three seats over. They each put an arm protectively over the back of the empty seat beside them. I thought maybe they were waiting for dates.

Mary looked around the auditorium. She had worn her best dress for the occasion and a relatively new pair of shoes. She wasn't dressed anywhere near as expensively as many of the other mothers. But, unlike how Declan would have sat in that private school auditorium, Mary looked comfortable and relaxed. She looked every bit as if she belonged with all the other mothers whose children were paying full fees. At one point, she reached over and squeezed my hand in an encouraging and slightly conspiratorial way, as if I were one of the actors in the play and she was telling me to break a leg.

There was no reason for me to feel nervous, but I knew she was still wishing me luck as all the families walked in and took their seats as though they and their ancestors had been attending LCC for centuries. The women with their expensive haircuts and diamonds; the men looking well-groomed in a way that my father and his friends would never be — the well-cut clothes, the costly shoes, the hearty handshakes and confident laughs as they greeted each other. The men all looked like doctors or millionaires to me; the women I assumed were socialites or the accomplished wives of diplomats. They were dressed to attend a party at an embassy rather than a school play.

While everyone came in and took their seats, Sammy and Jake stared straight ahead at the stage like unhappy soldiers on watch. As 8:00 p.m. approached and the seats around them began to fill, Sammy, agitated, stood up and looked around, but Jake didn't move. Jake looked at his older brother at one point and then resumed his forward stare. Finally, as the lights began to flash off and on, signalling everyone to take their seats, and the loudly talking crowd began to hush, I saw two tall people walk slowly down the aisle and approach Sammy's row. Sammy jumped to his feet, and even Jake stood up, as if he were welcoming someone important.

A big, blond man in a dark suit and tie accompanied by a younger-looking blond woman were taking their seats. The big, blond man, who I now assumed was Mr. Goldberg, reached over and tousled Sammy's hair — blond, somewhat wavy, and combed straight back like his own. He nodded at Jake. Mr. Goldberg let the tall, blond woman, who I thought must be Mrs. Goldberg, go ahead of him into the row of seats. She sat down beside Jake and gave him a warm smile. I couldn't see the expression on Jake's face because he was turned away from me, but I saw him nod in return in a limited way.

As they took their seats, Mr. and Mrs. Goldberg didn't look around at anybody else other than their two sons. Their body language didn't suggest arrogance or lack of interest. It was almost as if they moved in their own bubble, as if they possessed that rare human quality of being able to walk down a crowded street or move through a full room with a sense of being alone. After giving his mother that small nod, Jake looked away. Sammy didn't take his eyes off his father. Mr. Goldberg sat down.

As Mr. Goldberg sat down with the smooth motion of a diver entering the water, I had the strangest sensation. It was if the whole audience had its eyes on him, and when he sat, he sent out a wave that rippled through the auditorium. The lights dimmed and the curtain rose and my mother's face came alive in the darkness. I could see her green eyes reflecting the light from the stage, almost like a cat's eyes taking advantage of the smallest source of light to shine, and then we were pulled suddenly into Shakespeare's make-believe world of Verona.

Even though we were witnessing nothing more than the efforts of junior high school amateur actors who would go on to become doctors and lawyers and CEOs of companies or owners of their fathers' companies, and even though the chances that any of them would go on to become professional actors were almost nonexistent, the innate talent that can be found in any children, under the magical workings of inspired artistic direction, suspended our disbelief from the moment that Robbie Jeffries, grade eight student, came on stage and began to speak the solemn opening words of the chorus, "Two households, both alike in dignity ..."

From there, the action moved quickly. Caine had cut some of the chattier scenes and some of the minor characters to bring us an action-packed play that would run just under two hours. Even in the late seventies, our fragile attention spans were already beginning to fray. Masked balls, sword fights, and balcony scenes bled into each other in quick succession. Caine had opted for the sparse sets that would have been common in Shakespeare's time, and he let the actors and the language carry the play.

In the two short scenes that led up to Juliet's first appearance, I glanced over at the four members of the Goldberg family in the audience. Jake stared straight ahead, still serious, but with the slightest hint of a smile turning up the corners of his lips despite his best efforts to appear solemn. In the coming years, I would learn that the only times Jake smiled around his father (and I'm not even sure he was aware of it) were when he anticipated some coming discomfort for him.

Mrs. Goldberg, like Mary, was fully engrossed in the play. She looked and dressed like the type of woman who enjoyed the theatre. For his part, Mr. Goldberg was impassive. His head was larger than Sammy's, but still it was handsome, with his large nose and heavy chin and swept-back golden hair. His face appeared brighter than the rest of the family, as if it were glowing. I leaned forward so I could see Sammy. He, too, was leaning forward with his chin cradled in his hands, like a teenager worrying. He kept glancing quickly from the stage to his father. And it occurred to me that neither David nor his brothers had told their father what part he was playing. I tried to remember if I'd seen Mr. or Mrs. Goldberg carrying a program that would have listed the cast, but I couldn't remember seeing anything in their hands.

When Hector came on as Romeo in the first scene, I could see Mr. Goldberg shift in his chair, Jake's slim grin widen slightly, and Sammy look stricken. I shouldn't have been able to see all this in the darkness, but the Goldbergs were only a few seats over, we were close to the well-lit stage, and Mr. Goldberg seemed to be giving off a golden glow. Judging from the way Mr. Goldberg moved in his chair and Mrs. Goldberg reached out to take his arm, neither of them could believe that David hadn't been cast as Romeo.

But it was when David appeared in the third scene, dressed as an aristocratic Venetian girl of about twelve or thirteen, that Mr. Goldberg straightened up and the strange light coming off his face brightened. I watched him carefully. His brow furrowed, and he began to frown. Mrs. Goldberg looked up at her husband, and she squeezed his hand. For a few frightened seconds, I was worried Mr. Goldberg would stand up and storm out of the auditorium in disgust. Sammy couldn't bear to look at either his father or his youngest brother playing the part of a girl. He had lowered his eyes and was staring at the back of the chair in front of him. But Jake was sitting up straight and glancing back and forth between his father beside him and his younger brother on stage.

"O Romeo, Romeo! Wherefore art thou Romeo?" David as Juliet looked out from the stage with such innocence, and his voice was so young and so pure. I'd read somewhere once that bishops in the Middle Ages would sometimes castrate choirboys with beautiful voices so their voices would never change, and before I had time to be embarrassed of the thought, I was thankful that David had been born in our century, Jewish, and rich. He laid his head on the piece of wood that was standing in for the edge of his balcony and looked up at the dark ceiling of the auditorium. In that small gesture, he ceased to be David and became Juliet.

I could tell by the way Sammy was anxiously watching Mr. Goldberg more than the play and by how Jake was trying not to smile that they expected a sign of disapproval from their father. But by the end of Juliet's first speech, Mr. Goldberg's forehead had already unfurrowed, his jaw had unclenched, and his shoulders had come down. The initially troubled expression on his face was replaced by something almost beatific, as if he were in the presence of God. By the time the first stolen kiss between Romeo and Juliet came, I knew there was no danger of a relapse on Mr. Goldberg's part. David as Juliet and Hector as Romeo could have kissed full-on and he might still have been willing to suspend his disbelief. But still I was relieved when the two boys, one of whom was pretending to be a girl, engaged in what was clearly an air kiss. But I have to give them credit. They both put their twelve-year-old hearts into it.

From then on, Mr. Goldberg's attention never wavered, and whenever David was on stage, Mr. Goldberg leaned forward just a little in his chair, unable take his eyes off his youngest son. When Hector drank the poison and David pretended to lick the remnants from his dead lips before stabbing himself, I swear I saw a handful of tears running down Mr. Goldberg's cheeks.

When the curtain came down and the lights came on, Mr. Goldberg stood up to his full six-foot-two height and began to clap loudly and shout, "Bravo, bravo!" The other parents clapped politely. But when Mr. Goldberg went on standing and clapping and shouting, "Bravo," he must have emboldened some of the other parents and grandparents because a few well-dressed, sober men and then a few women stood up. Before long, the LCC production of *Romeo and Juliet* was enjoying a standing ovation.

Sammy jumped to his feet once he saw what his father was doing. Jake stayed sitting until the whole auditorium was standing. And Mrs. Goldberg stood once she saw the whole room was going to rise. On stage, David was bowing and watching his father and smiling and enjoying the applause. He was holding Hector von Faustenberg's hand, and Hector was beaming.

IT WAS THE last time I would see Hector looking so happy. A month later, his parents' import-export business mysteriously took a wrong turn. Over lunch one day in the cafeteria, Sammy said something about Hector's parents becoming "overextended." He said it in a whisper, as if afraid that if he spoke too loudly it might happen to his family as well. He also spoke in the overly formal and elaborate way people reserve for talking about things they don't really understand. Whatever it was, Hector's family could no longer afford the fees at LCC, and less than a month after his triumph as Romeo, Hector left LCC. He was there one day and gone the next. Overnight, despite the exoticism of his last name, von Faustenberg, and his theatrical exploits, we all seemed to forget he had ever been part of our school.

Years later, I still remember three things about Hector. His role in the play. His sudden, unceremonious departure from our school. And the bit of information that he imparted to me about the Goldbergs while he was still at LCC. David had never told me what his father did to earn a living. Unlike many of the other boys at LCC, who found various ways to tell you what their fathers did, David never spoke about it. It was Hector who told me about how the Goldbergs made their money. He mentioned it casually in passing, over lunch in the cafeteria one day when David was home with the flu. Although the mysterious business of Hector's parents must have paled in comparison, Hector told me about the Goldberg family gold mining company without a hint of envy, only admiration. When I made some harmless joke about how the family name was appropriate to what they did, Hector laughed like I was the wittiest person in the school, even though I'm sure he'd thought of it himself and heard it many times before.

AFTER THE PLAY was over and the actors had come on stage and smiled and bowed repeatedly, receiving their due applause, we were invited to have refreshments next door in the gym. I wasn't sure at first if Mary wanted to stay, but she grabbed my arm firmly, never once worrying about whether her soon-to-be twelve-year-old son wanted to be seen arm in arm with his mother. She held on to me in a grown-up way, like I was her escort for the evening. I only really remember how she held my arm in retrospect because at the time I was mostly thinking about whether the Goldbergs would stay for the tea and cookies. When the boys in the play came out from backstage, changed out of their costumes but still in their makeup, with their bronzy base and dark eyeshadow and bright lipstick, they were treated by their parents like conquering heroes, and I remember being surprised that in my new world, talent on the stage seemed to be recognized as warmly as talent on the playing field.

Mary walked into the gym with all the other families as if she belonged there, even though she knew nobody, but I, who had played in that gym a number of times by now, walked in as if for the first time, as if I were seeing it through my mother's eyes. Mary knew that the best way to feel at home in a setting like this was to have food and drink in hand, so she walked up to the table that had been set up, took a cup of tea and a biscuit, and ensured I had some as well. From there she scanned the room, and so did I.

Everyone seemed to be gathered in happy groups: some were just families, others were extended groups of parents who knew each other, and many others were made up of students who had broken off into little clusters of their own. I was wearing my uniform, so I looked exactly the same as the other boys. Now that the play was over and we were all standing in the gymnasium, I paid more attention to my mother's clothes. She had dressed for the occasion, but I am ashamed to say that in the bright lights of the gym I considered her outfit in the context of what the other mothers were wearing, and I found it wanting. It wasn't that Mary's clothes were shabby, far from it. They were out of style, their cut was just a little off, and I was thinking of this when David appeared and introduced himself.

Mary was delighted to be shaking hands with such an accomplished Juliet, and she was proud when David introduced himself. "Good evening, Mrs. McFall," he said with the self-assured manners of the young who are practiced at introducing themselves and shaking hands. "I am David. Sean and I are best friends."

At this, any concern I had about my mother's clothes went away. David could have introduced himself simply as a friend of mine. Or he could have said he was my best friend, which would have implied that our relationship was unequal, that he was the best friend I had because he was the only one, while he had an infinite number of friends. But he had described a state of harmony and reciprocity. It was only later, as I got to know David better and heard the stories about his grandfather Abraham — his *zayde*, as he called him — that I would appreciate David's education outside of LCC and the long and deep schooling he had received in the art of shaking hands and putting people at ease.

From the way Mary smiled and shook the hand of this boy in front of her, the self-declared mutual best friend of her only son — I say self-declared because although I had always secretly thought of us as and hoped we were best friends, neither of us had ever brought up the topic, we had just gone on being friends — it was as if being introduced to David had become the new highlight of the evening. But there was more to come. Taking Mary's arm the way she had taken mine, but with a little more grace, David said to both Mary and me, "Come, I'd like to introduce you to my parents."

Before I had a chance to be nervous, David had guided us across the crowded gym to his parents. Unlike Mary and me, who had been standing near the food table and against the wall, David's parents were standing in the centre of the gym, amidst a large group of parents. Even from a distance, Mr. Goldberg was giving off that strange glow, or so it seemed to me, and he was speaking. As we got closer, I realized he was speaking loudly, and as we came up to him, it was clear he was talking about the American president. Mrs. Goldberg was listening to him with the absent-minded devotion some women reserve for their wealthy and powerful husbands. A slight smile was parting her lips even though the subject had no inherent humour.

"His first term might be only a year old," Mr. Goldberg was saying, "but already he's sowing the seeds of his defeat. When he appears on television in his cardigan and tells Americans that not only will they pay more for less oil but that it's their moral responsibility to do so, he comes across as a scolding schoolteacher who thinks he knows more than he does. He may or may not be right, but just because something might be right, people don't necessarily want to listen, and nobody likes to be lectured. The Americans will tire of him long before the next election."

He spoke slowly, not quite ponderously, but as if he knew his audience would be patient and would listen to him for as long as he was speaking, and he spoke definitively, as if there were no other possibility than the one he was advancing. As if he wasn't just a man in Montréal sharing an opinion but someone who had inside access. This was the first time I heard Mr. Goldberg speak. Only later did I learn how much he despised politics and politicians. Perhaps others in the room knew him better, or thought they did. Everyone around him nodded.

It was clear that Mr. Goldberg was just warming to his topic, that he had remaining evidence of his conclusion to share. But when he saw David, with his crazy makeup, Mr. Goldberg's large, golden face lit up. And seeing the glow, every other well-dressed parent standing around him turned around, and when they saw David, they smiled and the group of them parted so that none of them were standing in the way of father and son, and by extension me and my mother. And then, with everyone looking on, David walked us up to Mr. and Mrs. Goldberg and introduced my mother and me.

"Father, I'd like you to meet my friend Sean and his mother, Mrs. Mary McFall." I had never heard anyone actually call their father "father" to their face, and it was only the second time in my life anyone had called my mother "Mrs." in front of me. It gave me a strange feeling, as if I were both grown-up and still young at the same time. I noticed that David didn't add the adjective "best" to describe our friendship this time, but I knew this was because we were now standing in front of too many people and David didn't want any of them to feel that his connection with their sons was anything less.

Mr. Goldberg nodded and took my mother's hand in his huge one and said, "Mrs. McFall, it's a pleasure to meet you." He turned to me and said, "Young Mr. McFall" as he took my hand, and he turned back to my mother with a smile. "I've heard a lot of good things about your son from David." My mother smiled. It was the first time Mr. Goldberg had spoken to me and the first time anyone had called me "Mr."

And then Mr. Goldberg looked at me again as he held on to my hand, firmly but not too firmly because he knew I was just a boy and he didn't have to bother to intimidate me, but still he sized me up as he looked into my eyes. Now that we were out of the darkened auditorium and I was seeing him full-on in the light,

I could see that his eyes were flat and blue and perfectly symmet-rical, like David's. I realized that all three Goldberg sons had their father's eyes, but none to the same degree. Mr. Goldberg's eyes appeared to be the original model. In addition to their strange shape, they were vaguely reptilian, the way they both stared at you and moved around the room. And although this is going to sound ridiculous — because I was only a boy in a school gym meeting the father of my friend — I had the strange sensation that Mr. Goldberg's eyes had looked on the world for a long time, and he was looking into my soul the way he would look into the earth for something valuable that he could extract and take away and by so doing add to his considerable store of wealth and power.

Mr. Goldberg was charming. He glanced between me and David, assessing in a few seconds the value of our friendship, judging whether I was worthy of his son, looking already to the next thing. It reminded me of being x-rayed once after I had fallen heavily on the ice during those pickup hockey games with my father.

Mr. Goldberg blinked slowly, and his heavy eyelids came down over his strangely shaped eyes and rose again, like he was taking a photograph of the inside of my brain, and I could almost feel the flash going off inside my skull. In the end — what could only have been seconds later but which felt like forever — Mr. Goldberg finally let go of my hand and smiled at me, and his whole face glowed.

Mrs. Goldberg had been looking in another direction, but she turned back smoothly at our approach and greeted me and my mother graciously. In that quick moment of introduction, I noticed the deepness of her voice and how she looked at my mother and me differently than Mr. Goldberg had. I remember thinking that she didn't look like a version of anyone's mother.

She had a sleek, enhanced, just slightly off-balance look. And then happily the conversation turned to the play and to David.

We chatted about the production — wasn't David wonderful, and wasn't Hector great as well — and about the school — was Sean enjoying it, yes he most certainly was — and before the conversation had a chance to finish naturally or die out, Mr. Goldberg was politely ending it in the way that I would learn before too long the rich do so well: "Well, Mrs. McFall, I should let you go. I don't want to monopolize you and young Mr. McFall tonight. I'm sure there are others you wish to speak with." He was so polite about it, it sounded like he was doing us the favour and it was Mary and me with whom everyone else wanted to spend time. "It was wonderful to meet you. And good to meet you too, young Mr. McFall. No doubt I will be seeing you again, perhaps up at our home."

And before we knew what was happening, Mr. and Mrs. Goldberg had moved off to the cakes and tea. But I was pleased to see that David was still with us, that he had stayed behind so that we did not perceive his father's ending of our brief audience in the LCC gym as overly abrupt. David did this so skillfully and solicitously that it wasn't until years afterward that I realized we had been dismissed. By then I knew not to take it personally, and given how the introductions had just gone after the play, it was clear I was being slowly welcomed into the family as one of David's friends, perhaps even really as his best friend.

7

THE FIRST TIME I took the Goldberg private jet, I was surprised. Surprised I'd been invited along on the family trip to Curaçao in the winter of grade eight and also by how small the cabin was. It wasn't only my first flight on a private jet, it was my first time on a plane. I'd mentioned this to David with some embarrassment in the weeks leading up to the trip, but he just laughed it off the way he had done when he'd taught me how to play touch football and then chess later that year.

I didn't know what to expect. For some reason, I'd assumed the Goldberg plane would be a reconfigured Boeing 747 with a long aisle of seats and a dining room and sleeping area in the back with queen-size beds, the kind of plane used to jet around the world by an oil-rich sheikh. But it was like getting into a very nice large car. The inside was beige, with soft leather seats and expensive-looking wood accents. There were only seats for eleven passengers, four rows of one seat on each side and beyond these an extended seat against the left side in which three people could sit comfortably. Whenever Mr. Goldberg got bored of the conversation, he stood up, went back to the long seat, stretched himself out, and fell asleep.

There was no stewardess — we didn't call them flight attendants then — but the chief pilot, Jean-Guy Laflamme, took good care of us. Jean-Guy was a quiet, efficient, forty-something Québécois who'd been hired by Mr. Goldberg after serving for ten years as a fighter pilot in the Canadian Air Force. Jean-Guy was very kind to me on my first flight, showing me with a minimum of fanfare how to pull the seat belt over my shoulder and adjust it. When we were airborne, he gave control of the plane to the co-pilot and served me soft drinks and chocolate bars as if I were minor royalty.

But my surprise at taking my first flight on a private plane was nothing compared to my surprise at being allowed to go in the first place. You can only imagine the fight between my parents when I came home from one of my visits to David's house in the early fall of grade eight and told them I'd been invited by the Goldbergs to fly down with them on Christmas break to their house on Curaçao. This was the next big step in being welcomed into the family, after being invited over to the Goldbergs' home. I had first been invited there in the spring of grade seven, shortly after I had met Mr. Goldberg at *Romeo and Juliet*. I found out later, from David, that none of the Goldberg sons was allowed to invite a friend over before Mr. Goldberg had met them first outside of his home, "on neutral ground," as he put it. And the first time I was invited over to the family home, it was Mr. Goldberg who drove us.

SOME OF MY classmates took the bus home after school, but many of the students at LCC were picked up by their mothers who "didn't work outside the home," as their sons reverently put it, or else by their largely mute, tentatively smiling nannies who could be trusted to drive one of the less expensive family cars. But only the very wealthy, like the Goldberg boys, were occasionally picked up by their fathers. It was only the fathers who had so much money that they didn't have to work at all or the fathers who owned their own companies and who didn't have to schedule their lives according to the timetables of other men who could afford to pick up their own sons. On the first day I was invited to the Goldberg house after school, just a week after meeting Mr. Goldberg at the play, it was Mr. Goldberg himself who drove. Sammy, who was just a few months shy of his fifteenth birthday, sat in front, beside his father, and I sat in the back, between David and Jake. After that first visit, I would be invited over after school at least once a week, and we usually arrived there in Mr. Goldberg's white Mercedes.

Driving with Mr. Goldberg in his Mercedes was a different experience from driving with my father. Like many women of her generation, Mary had never learned how to drive, but Declan had a Mustang that he washed with devotion every Sunday in front of our duplex. Despite the car's eight cylinders, and unlike many of his friends from work, Declan always drove slowly through the streets of Montréal, and he drove just barely above the speed limit each summer when we took our one-week vacation at a small cottage in the Laurentians. Declan drove as if he expected to be pulled over by the police at any moment, even though he wasn't a teenager and his car wasn't bright red but dark blue.

I never really noticed how my father drove until I started to drive with Mr. Goldberg. And then I began to be aware that Declan drove the way he spoke, sparingly, despite the power of his car. He wasn't tentative, but he was careful, always looking in his rear-view mirror, keen to obey the speed limit, suspicious of the behaviour of pedestrians and cyclists, as if they might jump out in front of him, testing his reactions, his ability to stop instantly. He was even more quiet than usual when he drove, only speaking if my mother asked him a question or if he had to ask us one.

If my father drove cautiously and laconically, Mr. Goldberg was the opposite. He drove smoothly, but much faster than my father. He was always several kilometres above the speed limit as he made his way up and down the curved, sloping streets of Westmount. He never seemed to worry about the police. When he saw them, he waved — something I had never seen my father do — and they waved back. He spoke loudly and often when he was behind the wheel, and also unlike my father, Mr. Goldberg seemed to know everybody and every building in Montréal. Sometimes he would take the long route home after school, driving along Sherbrooke in the direction of downtown before turning up Greene, and other times he would continue downtown to pick up something he had forgotten at his office.

"Do you see that man getting out of that car?" he might say as we waited at a light on Sherbrooke in front of the Ritz-Carlton hotel. "That's Michael Cranbrooke, Minister of Natural Resources. We met last week." Or, "See that building?" as he stopped in the middle of Peel Street. Ignoring the blocked cars honking their horns behind him, Mr. Goldberg rolled down his window, stuck out his arm, and, apparently unashamed of pointing in public — my mother Mary had always taught me not to — he directed our attention to a miniature Gothic castle complete with turrets and battlements. "That's Seagram House, the old headquarters of the Bronfmans' company. They live within spitting distance of us." Later, I would learn what Mr. Goldberg thought of the Bronfmans themselves. A drive with Mr. Goldberg, even the short one from school to his house, was never boring. He volunteered information, telling us who was who or what was what. Once, when a tall, well-dressed, serious-looking man crossed the street in front of us, making an effort not to look anywhere around him except straight ahead, Mr. Goldberg said, "See that man?" We all looked. "He owes me money."

As a boy I thought that perhaps Mr. Goldberg simply had more words than my father, just like he certainly had more money. My father rationed out his speech while Mr. Goldberg seemed to spew out words as if he had an inexhaustible supply.

DAVID LIVED ONLY a fifteen-minute drive away from LCC, down Royal to Monkland then onto Cote St. Luc and across the Decarie Expressway and up the western slope of Mount Royal on the swiftly ascending road that became the Boulevard, but it was like entering a different world. Suddenly you were in Westmount where the houses were grand, leaving behind any apartment buildings, and then you drove up one of the side streets that curved and cut steeply upward and you were there near the top of the western side of the mountain where you could see out over the city.

The Goldberg house on Sunnyside Avenue looked like it belonged to a British aristocratic family, built to resemble a castle: stone, turreted, with a heavy oak door and surrounded by a barrier of majestic oak trees. Within the miniature city of Westmount, built against the mountain where wealthy families had sold off parcels of their land to make even more money, parcels on which other families had built so that some people barely had a backyard, the Goldbergs had a large garden in the back, a grass tennis court, and a pool set into stone where Mr. Goldberg and his sons swam, and where I spent many weekends in the summer after grade seven.

When you looked out the second-storey windows at the back of the Goldberg house, you could see the whole city below. The tall steel and glass buildings and bridges and cars looked like toy buildings and bridges and cars, and the people looked like ants. The South Shore stretched out into the hazy distance, and although the city was busy, there was no noise at this height.

When he was home, Mr. Goldberg walked the inside and the grounds of his house like a lord, as if the property had been in his family for generations. And, true to their separate natures, the three Goldberg sons exhibited different attitudes to their childhood home. Sammy took the same unstated pride in the house and the grounds as his father did. You could see this in the way Sammy walked through the sliding glass doors at the back to the pool, walked slowly up to the diving board, and dove in, cutting through the air gracefully and entering the water without a splash, as only the rich or those who have trained for years to dive manage do. Jake slunk around the house as if he were embarrassed to have it as his address, and he was always awkward around the maid and the gardeners and the other men who seemed to be continually working on the outside of the house. David acted as if it all didn't matter, as if the house weren't there.

David acted the same way when he came to visit my little house and we sat on my small balcony in our tiny, narrow backyard. He could see all our neighbours. He always complimented my mother on our tidy rows of red and white geraniums even though it was my father who'd planted them, and he seemed to take as much pleasure in my family's efforts to civilize our little yard as he did in his own extravagant landscaped garden with its ever-present gardeners and flagstone paths.

The strangest thing about the Goldberg house, which I didn't consciously think about until much later, was that it was a house largely without women. There was Mrs. Goldberg, of course, but she always seemed to be out at one of her volunteer events or shopping. And Rita, who I first thought was a babysitter but who turned out to be the live-in maid, glided through the house without calling attention to herself. The boys were everywhere. Mr. Goldberg was large and loud. In retrospect, I can't help thinking the Goldberg house, despite looking like a castle, was halfway between a barracks and a monastery without a vow of silence.

The first time David took me to his house, a week after I had met his father, he tried his best to be nonchalant about it. Had I been in his shoes, it would have been hard, showing my castle to a boy from the lower part of NDG. I think David felt something of this because instead of showing me his garden or even his bedroom, which I would learn later had a view of the city and the river, David took me down to the basement, after the requisite after-school glass of milk and a plate of Peek Freans cookies.

The old wooden beams in the original ceiling had been left exposed, but the rest of the basement had been redone. There was no TV, as I would have expected. When David saw me looking around for one, he told me that his father didn't believe in television — Mr. Goldberg hated acronyms and insisted on always spelling everything out — at least not for entertainment. There was one in Mr. Goldberg's study, but it was reserved for news. Mr. Goldberg watched the evening news, and he read five newspapers a day: the *New York Times*, the *London Times*, the *Wall Street Journal*, the *Jerusalem Post*, and, so he didn't lose sight of what was happening in Canada, also the *Globe and Mail*. But he wasn't going to expose his boys to "the banal temptations of Hollywood sitcoms and soap operas."

After David explained away the absence of the TV, he took me over to a door set into a wall at the far end of his basement.

He opened the door, ushered me into darkness, and, after a few seconds longer than it should have taken, he turned on the lights. This was the reason David had brought me downstairs.

He turned to me and said, "You asked me once where I learned to box." He smiled and bravely waved his arm around like a young impresario, with that cheerful, ironic, indomitable optimism with which he approached everything. "It was here."

The room contained a full-size boxing ring, at least to my untrained just-turned-twelve-year-old eyes. Later, I found out it was a real boxing ring in every respect, from the standard-issue canvas floor to the ropes and the dimensions, down to the exact inch. Outside the ring on one side, six seats had been bolted to the polished concrete floor. Four sets of well-used but still brightly golden gloves hung neatly on the wall, one for each male Goldberg, the name of their respective owners spelled out above them on a wooden plaque so there would be no confusion. And over to the left in a small alcove, hanging at rest, a speed bag and a heavy punching bag.

David ran his right hand along the top rope of the ring. He didn't look at me as he spoke. He kept his eyes on the empty boxing ring. Now that he was getting into the details, his tone was neutral, perhaps even deliberately nostalgic. "My father had this built when Sammy was born. In the beginning he taught us himself. He used to spar with us, and then when I turned eight, he began to referee little matches and even tournaments between the three of us. Three rounds. He'd move between our corners, giving us advice, standing behind us in alternate rounds. When Sammy turned twelve, he hired a trainer." By the way David said "trainer," I knew he wasn't talking about an instructor down at the Westmount YMCA.

David never asked me to box with him, and I never did see any of the Goldbergs sparring with each other in the ring, so I had to imagine it. As I grew up and started working at their company, occasionally the image of the boys fighting with each other in the ring, egged on by their father, would appear in my mind. Each time the image came, unbidden, it was hard to be rid of. I think in some way David knew what he was doing when he brought me down to the basement. He wanted me to better understand him and his brothers and his father, and he wanted this to happen in a way that would stay with me forever. The funny thing was that Mr. Goldberg never let any of his boys play organized hockey, even though Sammy had begged for permission every winter until he was fourteen. Mr. Goldberg thought hockey was too violent. He didn't want any of his sons to lose their teeth.

8

WHEN MR. GOLDBERG invited me to accompany him and his family on that trip to Curaçao, I only told my mother at first, knowing that if I didn't get her support before approaching my father, it would be hopeless. I was frightened of bringing up the topic with Declan without first strategizing with Mary. Provided she said yes, of course.

She did, but even Mary did not immediately grant me permission. She was silent when I told her about the invitation, and she didn't ask me any questions for a few seconds. This surprised me. I had expected her to say, "Of course." And I'd been half hoping she'd also say, "I will talk to your father for you." But instead, she said nothing, and when she asked me her first question, it wasn't about where we were staying or how we would get to Curaçao or even for how long. It was, "How do you spell it?"

I was stunned for a moment, and I'm embarrassed to admit I thought my always-under-control mother had lost her mind.

"The island you're going to, Sean. How do you spell it?"

I let out a nervous breath and spelled it out for her. "David pronounces it 'Kurasow,'" I added. I could tell by the way she nodded that she was going to look it up in the second-hand set of Encyclopedia Britannica she'd insisted my father buy for me once I was accepted at LCC. I tried not to show I had noticed she hadn't used a future conditional tense to describe my upcoming trip. As hard as we both knew it was going to be to get my father's approval, there was no doubt in her mind that in the end I would go.

Her second question seemed equally bizarre at first, although I understood it by the time I had finished answering it.

"Who invited you?"

"It was David," I said, but when I saw the disappointment flash across her face because of what she thought she'd have to ask me next, I followed up quickly with, "But Mr. Goldberg also mentioned it to me when I was over at their house yesterday." My mother's small shoulders relaxed. But the slight wrinkle on her forehead above her nose didn't smooth out immediately, and she looked away without replying. It was as if deciding to let me fly away with the Goldbergs to a remote island was a bigger decision than urging me to apply to LCC in the first place.

When she turned back and smiled at me, it was only with her mouth. She looked into my eyes as though trying to memorize their shape and colour. And when she said yes, it was as if she were trying to convince herself. "As far as I'm concerned, you can go." Yet she stopped my smile when she added, "But for something like this, we have to speak to your father. It's not going to be easy, so I want you to start off and stay calm and let me finish." She grabbed onto my twelve-year-old shoulders, which were starting to widen but were still more bone than muscle, and said, "But you'll have to be the one to start the conversation, and the request itself has to come from you. Understand?"

I nodded, and I couldn't help noticing my mother's eyes were still serious. Then she relaxed her hold on my shoulders and let

me go. "Tonight, over dessert. I will make your father's favourite
apple pie."

I KNOW MY mother made an apple pie that evening, but I don't
remember a thing about what else we ate for supper or what we
talked about during most of it. My throat was so dry I could
hardly swallow, and I was so nervous that I worried I wouldn't
be able to speak when the time came. I remember Declan was
more talkative than usual. He was excited about a job he'd just
started, a new piece of highway in a city that loved big infrastructure projects. But I wasn't listening to his monologue. He asked
me a couple of typically general and brief questions about my
day. I responded in monosyllables, which normally would have
annoyed him, but he was in such a good mood that he didn't
seem to notice. My mother didn't speak much. Halfway through
the meal, she mentioned she'd made his favourite dessert. This
made me feel like I was about to throw up, but I managed to get
through dinner without incident.

I helped my mother clear the table, as I usually did, but I was
dizzy as I stood up and nearly had to sit down again. I put the
plates down a bit heavily on the yellow linoleum countertop in
our kitchen and stumbled back to my seat, nearly knocking it over
as I sat down. My father gave me a funny, indulgent look and
took a final gulp of his second beer. He leaned back in his chair
and smiled at me. I felt a terrible sense that I was about to betray
him. I nearly called the whole thing off. I thought up an excuse
I could give David: that I'd asked my parents if I could go with
him to Curaçao but they'd said no, that they'd planned a surprise
winter vacation. As these thoughts were flitting through my mind,
my mother returned from the kitchen with two heaping plates of

warm pie and lumps of vanilla ice cream. She placed them before my father and me and returned to the kitchen to get her plate.

Mary began to eat deliberately and with small, precise movements. She didn't look at me but looked across the table at my father. He was oblivious to her gaze. He closed his eyes as he chewed. My mother watched him. I was frightened to see her watching him with a mixture of love and what could only be described as pity. I waited for a signal from my mother, even though I knew when it was going to come. Mary waited until Declan had finished his last bite of pie before she pushed her plate gently to the side and nodded to me to begin. I was sure my voice would fail me, but, after my mother had gone to so much trouble with supper and dessert, there was no way I was going to let her down.

The first words out of my mouth were surprisingly clear. My voice didn't waver. I didn't shake or sweat. My nervousness went away as I began to speak, and I surprised myself with my calmness.

"Dad?"

"Yes, Sean?"

"I need to ask you something."

"Yes?"

I wanted to glance at my mother for some sign of encouragement, to draw on her strength, but I knew this would signal prior knowledge.

"I've been invited to go on vacation with the Goldbergs this year. On their winter vacation. They leave just after Christmas, so I wouldn't miss it." I had debated with myself whether I would provide all the information that my father needed to make a decision in my opening or whether I would let him tease it out of me in cross-examination. I'd settled on the latter because I knew if I told him everything right away the blood would rush to his large, handsome head and he'd make up his mind against the idea, and once he did there'd be no changing it.

My father looked down at his plate and then reached for his beer. Both were empty. He glanced at Mary, who was studiously looking at me. "And where are the Goldbergs going?"

"Curaçao."

"Kura what?"

"Sow. Kurasow." I said it out loud and then spelled it for my father and waited for him to continue. When he pushed his chair away from the table and leaned back in it, I knew this wasn't going well. His smile was gone, and I could see something terrible in his eyes. As with Stephen during the fight, I wouldn't have minded anger, but this was worse. It was the slightest of fears. Later in my life and career I would see many emotions in men's eyes, and I would conclude that fear is the worst. I would see it often across the boardroom table, occasionally across my desk and in the hallways, despite every effort to hide it with a smile or a joke. Fear of humiliation. Fear of losing money. Fear of losing one's job, one's place, one's sense of self-worth. It's especially unsettling when you see it in your father. Declan tried to catch my mother's eye, but she remained focused on me. Although she was pretending she was hearing this for the first time, I'm sure my father suspected that my mother already knew.

"And where is it?" After his initial surprise, my father's tone was now flat.

"It's in the southern Caribbean. Part of the Dutch Antilles. Forty miles off the coast of Venezuela." I pre-empted every question in a monologue. "The Goldbergs have a house there. The whole family is going. They go a few times a year. Sometimes one of the boys is allowed to invite a friend. David asked me. He'd already cleared it with Mr. Goldberg. It would be for one week.

It would be on the family plane. I'd only need to bring some light clothes and a bathing suit. Everything else would be covered." The last sentence was embarrassingly not my own. It was Mr. Goldberg's.

Sensing that I was losing my father, I decided I had to defend my friendship and my friend. "David is a really nice guy, Dad. Down to earth. Not conceited." It sounded stupid even as I was saying it.

Declan said quietly, as if he were disappointed in himself that he had to disappoint me, "Sean, if your friend doesn't have to act like he's rich, there's a good reason for it."

I wanted Declan to react loudly. I wanted him to tell me there was no way I could go, to get up and storm away from the table. But he didn't. Halfway through my short litany of answers to the questions he never got to ask, he stopped looking at me. He stared across the table at my mother.

This was when my mother was supposed to join the conversation, jump in with unbeatable arguments about why the trip was a good idea: it was a gift and it would be rude to refuse; I was being given an opportunity to see a new and exotic part of the world; David was my best friend; I would get to exert some measure of independence; it was a trip we'd never be able to take as a family. She was too smart to say that being a guest of a family like the Goldbergs could only help me on my way to university and a career. But as she looked at my father's helplessness, I could see her mind changing. Not about whether I should go but about her role in the conversation. Despite the plan she had outlined for me, in which I would start with the request and she would finish, she held her tongue.

She looked across the six feet of our dining room table and stared back into Declan's eyes. She was telling him it would be okay, he had nothing to fear, he was not losing his son.

My father turned away and nodded in my direction. "You can go." With those three words, I moved a little further away from my family and a little closer to the life I was being prepared to lead.

When I said a bewildered thank you and stood up to give my father a hug, I thought he was going to refuse to look at me and dismiss me with a wave of his hand. But instead, he stood up quickly before I had time to reach him, and he embraced me tightly.

9

THE FIRST THING we did when we landed in Curaçao was to visit the island's synagogue, even before we went to the *Landhuis* Goldberg. Mr. Goldberg's property manager Gerrit — Dutch and tall — was there to greet us at the airport and hand over the keys to Mr. Goldberg's vehicle. When we walked out into the small airport parking lot and the humid island heat washed over us, I was outwardly impressed and secretly horrified to discover that the brightly painted gold Land Rover parked in the no-parking zone in front of the doors was for us. Mr. Goldberg wouldn't have driven anything so garish in Montréal, but the vehicle itself redeemed the colour. This was in 1980, back when Land Rovers were still tall and ungainly and beautiful.

Sammy, Jake, David, and I climbed into the Land Rover as Mr. Goldberg got behind the wheel. Mrs. Goldberg hadn't come because of some issue with one of the charities she chaired. Mr. Goldberg drove efficiently, noticeably not as fast as he did in Montréal, taking the island roundabouts at measured speed. On that first day in Curaçao, I didn't know the names of anything — whether bridge or neighbourhood or beach — but it was a small island, and within a few days I knew everything. From the airport we took the narrow archway of the Queen Juliana bridge over Sint Anna Bay, and I had my first glimpse of Willemstad, the capital. In deference to their tropical surroundings, the row of Dutch canal houses that adorn every postcard of the city were clad not in European brick but in brightly painted stucco — baby blues and pinks and browns and bright yellows. Once across the bridge we dropped down into the heart of Otrabanda, the neighbourhood on "the other side." Mr. Goldberg parked. We all jumped out.

He walked ahead, at home on the streets crowded with a mix of tourists and residents. Mr. Goldberg walked with confident ease. Jake, David, and I were wearing the jeans and T-shirts in which we'd boarded the plane, but Sammy was wearing a white button-down shirt and Mr. Goldberg was wearing khakis, a white linen shirt, and a navy blazer. He looked like a yachtsman. His bulk moved easily along the narrow streets, and his hair seemed already to shine a shade brighter in the Caribbean sun.

Mr. Goldberg moved quickly, so that Sammy, Jake, David, and I had to make an effort not to fall behind. Sammy kept stride beside him, Jake deliberately stayed back three or four paces, and David appeared oblivious to his father, staying further back, never trying to catch up. I didn't want to be rude to my friend's father who had so generously invited me, but I couldn't break ranks with David. Amongst the many Dutch, with their height and blond hair, Mr. Goldberg stood out. He looked at home, yet somehow exotic, if it's possible to look exotic in the Dutch Caribbean.

We turned onto a street with a high yellow wall enclosing a curious yellow building. David and I were about thirty feet behind when Mr. Goldberg stopped at a tall door set into the wall. He knocked twice, and before he had taken his hand away from the second knock, the door was already opening.

A small man with olive skin and a mustache greeted us with a smile, ushering us in with nineteenth-century manners. When we were through the door, he shut it firmly. He reached out to shake Mr. Goldberg's hand with a nod of his head and even the slightest suggestion of a bow. "Mr. Goldberg, it's a wonderful pleasure to see you again." And then he greeted each of us boys with a respectful handshake, solemnly, the way men greet the sons of very rich and powerful men, as if they are princes.

When it came to my turn, as the mustached man held out his hand he said, "Good afternoon, I'm Shimon Cohen," putting the stress on the second syllable of his first name.

I said my name, and Mr. Goldberg said, "This is David's friend." Shimon Cohen made another small bow.

"I will leave you now, Mr. Goldberg. But I will be in my office if you need anything." And then Shimon Cohen disappeared, leaving us in a small courtyard. Mr. Goldberg walked about twenty feet ahead and turned right. We followed him through another door into a strange, beautiful building.

The walls were bright white, and the dark wood pews on either side of the central aisle appeared even darker as a result. Up ahead, two white pillars framed a gold chandelier. The late afternoon sun was shining through the windows or, rather, the openings where windows should have been. The floor beneath my feet stirred my imagination. There wasn't one. There must have been a floor somewhere below, but I couldn't see or feel it. We walked on sand. Not a few grains sprinkled on a floor but thick sand that gave way beneath my feet without revealing a hard surface beneath. I wanted to take my shoes and socks off and walk on it the way someone who has grown up in a city and has never seen the ocean wants to take off their shoes when they first step onto a beach and see the sand and water stretching out before them.

At this point in my life, I knew very little about Jews. I had known the Goldbergs were Jewish, but it had never been clear to me what exactly that meant. I had missed David's bar mitzvah the summer before, just after we'd finished grade seven, because Declan had made us go on a trip to New York to visit a cousin of his. We'd never met her before, and Mary had thought it was mysterious that we should have to meet her on the exact weekend of David's bar mitzvah, but for once in his life Declan had insisted, and for once Mary had let him have his way.

Declan never explained why he didn't want me to go to David's bar mitzvah. I never asked. Although Declan would have been trying to make a point in having us go to New York on that particular weekend, I don't think it primarily had to do with David being Jewish because at home we didn't talk much about Jews. I don't think they really existed for Declan because he didn't work with any. Mary liked Jewish writers and admired any culture that prized education, but Jews themselves were still a foreign subject to her, even with all her reading. Although my parents never actively joined in, around some of their friends I'd overheard the usual double-edged compliments and jokes that were always accompanied by a knowing chuckle and a wink, and even a good-humoured hint of admiring envy: Jews were invariably smart, good with money, and who could blame them if they were a bit too focused on making their money and keeping it? But that was as far as it went.

Part of my confusion was that the Goldbergs didn't look the way Jews were supposed to, at least not in my limited experience and imagination. I don't know why, but I had always thought all Jews had dark hair, dark brooding eyes, and olive skin, and were on the shorter side. Like Shimon Cohen. But the Goldbergs confounded my expectations. They were all tall, blond, and blue-eyed.

Later I would learn that Abraham, the patriarch, had been over six feet. I knew that Mr. Goldberg was six foot two. Sammy was six foot one and, at fifteen, looked like he would continue to grow. Jake was almost six feet tall, and David was approaching six feet. They looked more like Vikings than my preconception of Jews. Ironically, I was the one who wasn't blond. And I wasn't tall. The only thing I shared with them physically was my blue eyes.

Without thinking of it, I had always assumed Jews had churches of their own, but I had never heard the word *synagogue* spoken, let alone been inside one. By the way Mr. Goldberg left us standing in the sand while he found a seat close to the front, bowed his head, and prayed, I knew we were inside a house of worship. But it was different than anything I was familiar with because Mr. Goldberg didn't pray silently or stay deadly still as I had seen my parents do on the few times we'd found ourselves in church. Any religion that my parents had was a private affair that happened outside any church walls and about which they stayed mostly silent in front of me. Here in synagogue in Curaçao, Mr. Goldberg swayed back and forth and muttered. I instinctively moved away, embarrassed by the possibility of overhearing Mr. Goldberg conversing with his God. David sensed my discomfort and moved with me, but Sammy and Jake waited for their father to finish.

I learned later that the Curaçao Synagogue would not normally have been open at that time, but Mr. Goldberg was a member and a donor, and whenever he came to Curaçao he had his pilots call ahead with his arrival time. Mr. Shimon Cohen would open the synagogue especially for him. The first thing Mr. Goldberg did every time he landed was go to the synagogue to pray.

AFTER SYNAGOGUE, WE went to the beach. We didn't stop at
the *landhuis* to drop off our suitcases or change. This, too, was
apparently a Goldberg family ritual. We drove up and down green
hills, along narrow, winding roads roughly bordered by stunted
trees with slanting trunks moulded by island winds. The ocean,
and what I later learned was called Knipp Beach, came out of
nowhere, shimmering below, glinting in the sun. When I first saw
the water, I thought maybe I was seeing a mirage.

We parked in the lot set on a steep slope and walked down the
stone steps to the beach after changing in the Land Rover. David,
Jake, and I were wearing T-shirts. Mr. Goldberg had taken off his
blazer, but both he and Sammy still wore their white shirts. Their
only concession to casual was they wore their shirts loose and
untucked over their bathing suits. I noticed that while Jake and I
carried nothing but our towels in our hands, Mr. Goldberg and
Sammy each carried a leather bag over their right shoulder. David
had a knapsack over his. The beach was untouched. There were
no buildings in sight: no hotels, no condos, no restaurants. No
sign of human settlement, no attempted dominance of the environment of any kind. As we stepped off the stone steps onto the
sand, a slight, smiling man came running up to us. "Mr. Goldberg,
Mr. Goldberg, I have your chairs!"

"Hello, Harrie! Thank you. Mrs. Goldberg isn't with us today,
but we have a guest and so we'll still need five chairs. The usual
place."

Harrie smiled and led us halfway down the beach where five
empty lounge chairs were waiting for us in the shade of a tree. "As
soon as I knew you would be arriving today, I saved your chairs
and your place!"

"Thank you, Harrie," Mr. Goldberg said and passed a few
American bills to Harrie. A chair on the beach at Knipp couldn't

have cost more than a couple U.S. dollars back then, but by the way Harrie smiled, you'd think Mr. Goldberg was giving him enough money for a year. Harrie wasn't going to get rich, but Mr. Goldberg always tipped him well, and Harrie always saved the best chairs for the Goldbergs in the best location: under the shade of the least stunted tree that grew in the sand on the edge of the narrow beach.

Mr. Goldberg settled himself in his chair, put on a khaki panama hat and a pair of Ray-Ban aviator sunglasses, and pulled something else out of his leather bag. I somehow knew it wasn't going to be a beach novel, but even I was surprised to see him unfold the *Wall Street Journal* and turn to the stock indexes. Papers still carried them back then. Sammy was wearing the same sunglasses and the same style of hat as his father, but in a slightly lighter shade. This time I wasn't surprised when he, too, reached into his bag and pulled out his own edition of the *Journal* and started reading with an expression of concentration similar to his father's. He held the newspaper the same way his father did, slightly raised, not down on his waist, so he was almost staring straight at it. Later, I learned from David that Sammy's favourite books were the James Bond novels. But he read them at night, when he was alone in his bedroom. In the presence of his father, he read the *Wall Street Journal*.

Jake never sat down. He threw his towel on the chair his father had just paid for and, without saying anything to anyone, went off for a walk. That left David and me. He turned to me and grinned as if having a father and an older sibling who read the stock prices on the most beautiful beach in the world and another brother who couldn't stand being around his family was the most normal thing. "Young Mr. McFall, shall we swim?" Ever since Mr. Goldberg had first greeted me as "young Mr. McFall" after

David's play, as he continued to do so from time to time, David sometimes did it as well, with a mock formality, as a sort of inside joke about his father.

I treated it like the rhetorical question it was. I had never snorkeled before and didn't expect to start that day, but David pulled two sets out of his knapsack and handed one to me. "Try it on now to get used to the breathing and adjust the mask so it's tight on your face." I did as he suggested and then was ready. "One more thing," he said as we started walking. "There's a band of coral at the edge of the water. When Sammy was still fun and would swim with me instead of reading newspapers, he called it the 'carpet of death.' It's made up of little pieces of dead coral that are hard on your feet when you walk on them. It's only in the first little bit, then you're free of them and the ocean floor is smooth. But there's always sand in the middle of the beach that remains relatively clear." We walked to our right for about thirty feet. "Here it is. Come." And David actually grabbed my arm and pulled me running into the water. Knipp wasn't one of those beaches where the water looks green from a distance but then once you're near it turns ordinary blue like water you can find anywhere. The water was equally green when you were in it. I couldn't understand how Sammy and Jake could resist it and asked David why they weren't swimming. "Heaven forfend, young Mr. McFall, that Sammy should actually go swimming before my father does and that Jake should enjoy himself at all."

At first it was hard to breathe through the snorkel, but David showed me how, and I mastered it quickly. He had been to Curaçao so many times that he knew where all the best reefs were at every beach. Knipp was no exception, and he took me to the right side of the beach. I was swimming and watching him and waiting to see something when he pointed ahead and I saw a large circular reef surrounded by swirling colours. As I got closer, I saw that the colours were bright blue and green striped fish and tiny silver ones that shimmered as they moved with the waves.

IT WAS ONLY when David and I were coming out of the water thirty minutes later that Mr. Goldberg stood up from his *Wall Street Journal*. He took off his white shirt, slowly rubbed suntan lotion on himself, and traded his Ray-Bans for a pair of swimming goggles. I was surprised to see he had a respectable amount of muscle for a man in his early forties.

Mr. Goldberg began to move down the beach, but unlike David, he didn't run into the water. He walked deliberately and powerfully, and as I watched him, I realized I had never seen him run. He strode patiently into the surf, his body powerful and glowing, neither his eyes nor feet apparently taking any notice of the sharp and bumpy coral beneath his feet. Unlike David, he didn't walk into the water where it was sandy but strode across the "carpet of death" as if the coral were the hot coals he wasn't noticing after a three-day motivational seminar. I thought Sammy would go swimming with him, but Sammy stayed on the beach, watching him over the pages of his paper.

When the water was up to his waist, Mr. Goldberg rinsed his bright green swimming goggles in the ocean, adjusted them on his face, and dove in. His motion was graceful and awkward at the same time. He was underwater for several seconds before he re-emerged, and, when he did, I saw he was doing a forward crawl. It was a heavy, ungainly thing, the kind of stroke from which you can tell the swimmer never took professional swimming lessons. For all Mr. Goldberg's wealth, his swimming stroke was more like mine and the opposite of David's. But even though it didn't look quite right, it was undeniably powerful. He swam determinedly but unhurriedly, a strange sort of elegance. And as he swam back and forth along the beach, you had the sense that he could keep it up forever.

When Mr. Goldberg came out of the water, still wearing his goggles, instead of obscuring his strange, reptilian, perfectly symmetrical eyes, the goggles amplified them. Not in terms of size but in the intensity of his gaze.

As he approached us, lounging on the beach chairs he had paid to rent, it was Sammy who stood up and passed him a thick white towel. He took it with a nod, but rather than drying his body he only dried his face and hands, brushed his golden hair out of his eyes, and then threw the towel over his shoulders. He sat back down on his beach chair.

10

AFTER A COUPLE of days, we settled into a pattern. Beaches and stock prices in the morning, followed by lunch at a restaurant — Mr. Goldberg didn't cook — then a short trip around the island and a late-afternoon visit to another beach. Supper was at another restaurant, usually back in Willemstad, but once at a restaurant perched on a cliff and another time on an open-air patio on a beach. I went to more restaurants during those ten days in Curaçao than I had been to in Montréal in my whole life up that point. The island was tiny: you could drive around it in two hours, and Mr. Goldberg made sure we visited everything worth visiting. The three Goldberg boys already knew the island as well as their father did, but they were good sports for my sake and pretended they were enjoying it as much as the first time.

On our drives to other beaches, Mr. Goldberg often took us to small museums or landmarks where we took in the exhibits or walked through caves or played with domesticated animals. But afterward in the golden Land Rover he would sometimes lecture us, presumably for my benefit because his sons had heard it all before. I like to think he appreciated having me as a new member of his audience for whom all his stories and opinions were fresh and new.

Our third day on vacation, we drove up the hill to *Landhuis* Knipp, high above the beach that I was growing to love. Mr. Goldberg looked at me in the rear-view mirror and said, "Young Mr. McFall?" Mr. Goldberg didn't always call me Mr. McFall, but he did now, as if he were a teacher and I were his student.

"Yes, Mr. Goldberg?"

"Have you ever heard of Tula? The slave?" In the front seat, Sammy turned around and grinned. Jake, on my left, looked away. On my other side, David appeared politely interested. It was clear they had all heard the story a few times before.

"No, Mr. Goldberg, I have not." I didn't consciously decide not to use contractions when I spoke with Mr. Goldberg. That's just the way my words came out. "Haven't" would have sounded disrespectful. Halfway through the conversation, I found myself enjoying the verbal formality. Mr. Goldberg seemed happy with my attention.

The golden Land Rover climbed the little mountain. When we reached the top, I could see we were at a beautiful yellow plantation house that had been turned into a museum about slavery. I had always enjoyed history and was looking forward to the exhibit, but when we all stepped out of the Land Rover, it was clear that Mr. Goldberg was not yet ready to go inside.

He pointed down below to where a wide expanse of flat, marshy land fed into the sea. "Mr. McFall, do you see below?"

"Yes, Mr. Goldberg."

"Salt flats. Imagine it's 1795. Almost two hundred years ago. On the one hand, it seems like a long time, far away. On the other, it's only two and half lifetimes. Every day, the slaves go out in the hot sun and gather sea salt by hand." Mr. Goldberg didn't look at me as he spoke. He stopped himself for a moment, and I wondered if he was comparing in his mind the work of those long-ago slaves to the work of the modern men who laboured for him and his family. "There's a slave called Tula."

I noticed that Sammy was hanging on his father's every word. Jake was admiring his shoes. David was listening intently and watching me at the same time.

"I'm not sure if Tula is a reader — maybe he is like Jake here who loves his books — and he reads about other economic and political systems or if he just gets it into his head one day. However it happens, Tula wakes up one morning and realizes he has grown tired of being a slave. He decides he's going to make some demands. So, like a union foreman" — said with surprising neutrality, perhaps even with respect — "he gathers his fellow slaves on this plantation, maybe he stands right where we are now, in this courtyard, and he asks for an audience with the landowner. His owner." As I was listening to Mr. Goldberg, I noticed he was using the present tense to speak about the past. It wasn't an unpleasant experience, having Mr. Goldberg personally give me this history lesson on the top of a mountain surrounded by other mountains. It was flattering that he would devote his attention to me, the young friend of his youngest son. I felt I was floating in the ocean and the surf was washing over me.

"Tula has just three demands." Mr. Goldberg looked at me now and proceeded to use his right hand to count off on the fingers of his left hand. "An end to collective punishment — one has to assume that when one slave does something bad, they all get whipped — one day of rest a week, presumably Sundays, and finally, the right to buy clothes from someone other than their master." Mr. Goldberg paused. "What do you think of that?"

I could hear a mosquito buzzing close to my ear. Mr. Goldberg was waiting for my response, Jake was still looking down at his shoes as if the answer could be found there, Sammy was smiling and waiting, and David was now looking out at the salt flats. He didn't seem to care what I answered or even if I had an answer.

"Tula's demands do not seem unreasonable to me, Mr. Goldberg."

At this Mr. Goldberg laughed, Sammy smiled even more widely, Jake actually looked up, and David turned back to me with a grin. It felt like I had passed some sort of test, although I didn't know what it was.

"You are absolutely right, although the people at the time are not necessarily all that reasonable. The landowner tells Tula to take his demands to the governor because what Tula is asking for is beyond his authority. This sounds like the landowner is paying attention, but he knows it won't go anywhere. It is the classic response of the man who is lacking in both physical and moral authority."

Mr. Goldberg looked out at the salt flats and the ocean and the hills, and following his gaze I saw a few other plantation houses, or *landhuizen*, as I had learned they were called, each built on high points, each visible to the others. Mr. Goldberg noticed me looking. He lifted his arm and pointed. "Each house is built on a mountain. But it's not for the view, as beautiful as it might be. It provides natural defence, and they can signal each other in times of trouble. Storm. Invasion. Slave revolt." His arm descended, and he resumed his story.

"Tula takes his owner up on the suggestion, and he goes from plantation to plantation. He is like Moses, gathering slaves along the way. While this is happening, he sends his demands to the governor. Naturally, they are rejected. As they must be, for this is

1795. The governor commissions a militia to put down what is now a full-fledged revolt. At the height of his rebellion, Tula has a thousand slaves with him. But they are not all capable of fighting. The number includes women and children. Small battles are fought, and miraculously the slaves keep winning. They start off hiding in caves, but after a few weeks they are bold and powerful enough to camp out in the open, on the beaches, at the edge of the ocean. For the first time in their lives, they feel what it means to be free. Up to this point, it could be one of our own Jewish stories where we had to put down the books we love and take up arms and fight for our freedom. Passover. Hannukah."

Mr. Goldberg looked back at the salt flats, at the glimmering ocean beyond. "But it is not the same. Not the same at all. For do you know how this story ends?" Here he took off his sunglasses and looked into my eyes. For the first time I had ever seen, his eyes looked tired. Bloodshot. But there was also something that made them look electric.

"I do not, Mr. Goldberg." Even if I had known, I wouldn't have said anything. I wanted him to finish the story that he so obviously wanted to tell.

"Unlike our Jewish stories of freedom, this one doesn't end well. Tula is winning, but he is betrayed to the authorities by another slave. In this it is like your story of Judas and Jesus. The most terrible villains in all our myths are those who betray, especially for money." As Mr. Goldberg spoke the last sentences, he quickly looked at his sons.

"Tula is executed in a public square in Willemstad, beside the wide green ocean. Because of his crimes, daring to be free in a society that cannot comprehend and refuses to allow such a desire, his punishment cannot be so simple as death by hanging or firing squad. They kill him slowly. With great deliberation. They want to make an example of him so that never again will slaves rise up and rebel on this little island so many miles from Holland."

Mr. Goldberg looked out at the ocean, collecting his thoughts. He put his sunglasses back on. "They systematically break almost every bone in his body. They do it in the exact way that will keep him alive as long as possible. The executioner has actually studied the matter of breaking a man's bones and has formed an opinion on how it should be done." Mr. Goldberg waited a few more minutes. Our faces became paler, even through our recent tans; our mouths dried out. We didn't speak.

"Do you know what the moral is of Tula's story?"

Another test, perhaps a trick question. Don't be so open about what you want? Don't revolt if you can't win? Be careful whom you trust? By the way David smiled at me, I could tell he didn't care whether I got the answer right. He was curious to hear what I had to say.

I waited so long to respond that Sammy looked anxiously at me as if I were straying into rudeness by not immediately answering his father. I was about to give up and tell Mr. Goldberg that I didn't know the answer when at the last possible moment I said, "Don't be a slave?" forgetting in my haste not to use contractions.

Mr. Goldberg's laughter was immediate. "Mr. McFall, you do impress me. That's half of it. One of the great ironies of Curaçao is that many Jews came to this island in the New World — fleeing persecution in the Old — only to take up slavery once they arrived. At least my people offered the world an innovation: free every slave in his seventh year. Nearly two hundred years after Tula, we may have outlawed slavery, and almost everyone where we live can afford a car and a television. But the world has always been and will always be divided into those who are slaves and those who are not." He looked at me, no longer as a teacher speaking

to a student, and not as a grown man talking to the young friend
of his sons, but I thought as something approaching an equal.
"Make sure you choose well." Mr. Goldberg waited for me to
speak. It was another test.

"And the other half, Mr. Goldberg?"

Mr. Goldberg smiled. "Don't ever forget what kind of world
we live in."

ONE DAY, WE drove further up the west coast of Curaçao, through
villages and over long, low speed bumps, past locals waiting for
the bus in open shelters with only rudimentary roofs and no walls,
and by houses in various states of disrepair until we turned off at
a place called Lagun. On our left was a dive shack and restaurant.
In front of us a parking lot. And to our right what looked like
a beach. Mr. Goldberg parked the Land Rover. We all jumped
out. The beach was narrow and tiny and bookended by rocky
cliffs about sixty feet high, the ocean was electric blue, and there
were small houses or motels built on top of the cliff. I knew they
were there because we had passed them on the drive in, but I
could hardly see them from the beach down below. This time, Mr.
Goldberg had come to swim and there was no preamble on the
beach in the company of the stock pages.

All the Goldbergs took their bags and strode to the beach.
They each grabbed a chair — at Lagun the chairs appeared to be
free — and dumped their bags. Mr. Goldberg unbuttoned his shirt
and dropped it on the ground. Sammy waited for his father and
waded in with him. I noticed neither of them was carrying a mask.
Jake didn't take off his shirt and wandered off on foot to inspect
the cliffs. David had his snorkel and mask, and I had the set he
had given me at Knipp.

As we walked down the narrow beach toward the water, we saw a man and what looked like his two young boys dragging a small rowboat onto the sand. As the two boys stepped away from the boat, I saw it was half filled with a tuna that must have been six feet long. Even though it had been pulled out of its element and was dead, it still retained an afterglow of the life and dignity that had recently been taken from it. It was a powerful, muscular fish, with a broad body and sharp tail. Its unseeing eye was sharp and black and filled with neither life nor pity. The children were excited and laughing, and the man who I assumed was their father was looking at his sons and the tuna they had caught together with unvarnished pride. But as I watched him closely, I saw that he was glancing back and forth between them as if he was afraid to rest his gaze for too long on either sons or fish. The scene seemed to make an impression on David as well. After we walked past, David stopped and turned back to watch long enough that I stopped as well and waited for him. From this angle, the tuna was barely visible; the two young boys had run back into the water, but the fisherman was sweating as he pulled the rowboat higher up the beach.

The ocean wasn't quite warm as I stepped into it, but it wasn't cold either. When the water reached my waist, I dove in shallowly, careful not to put my head in so deep that the water would get in my snorkel. Later David showed me how to spit out the water if that ever happened. David dove in as well and then called me over to him with a wave of his arm. "We're going there," he said, pointing to a spot about fifty feet out. I followed him. Up ahead, I saw something move, and David pointed further out in the water. Through the clear plastic of my mask, I saw a school of fish, bright blue, and I gave David a thumbs-up to show him I had seen them.

We swam slowly, stopping to watch another school of fish, these ones tiny and silver, glimmering in the light, turning this way and that like synchronized swimmers. David moved right and we swam together, watching the fish swim in and out of coral. Whenever one of us would see a fish, or a group of them, he would point, and the other would look in that direction and give a thumbs-up when we saw what the other had seen.

I enjoyed the feeling of floating, of being weightless. My body was half in the water, half out. Sometimes my ears were underwater and I could hear my breathing and it sounded deep and hoarse and sometimes my ears were above water and I could hear the other swimmers laughing and shouting. We saw a fish that was bright orange and gold and larger than most of the other fish. It was about a foot and a half long. Swimming slowly, lazily, it looked like a carp I had once seen in the tank of a restaurant in Montréal's Chinatown that Declan had taken us to on a special occasion. But this fish was bigger and wasn't bound by rectangular glass walls. I saw him first, and when I pointed him out to David, David's thumb went up, and we both felt the same need to follow him. Sometimes he would speed up, but only slightly, and so would we, and other times he looked like he was barely moving.

The golden fish moved into a wall of coral up ahead. The coral must have been growing against the cliff because as we approached it, we moved into the shade. Just when it appeared the fish could go no further, he disappeared. David and I waited for a few seconds, and when the fish didn't re-emerge, David shrugged and started swimming away. I remained in place, admiring the coral and the schools of small gold and silver fish that suddenly appeared. These little fish were swimming as one when they weren't hovering in place. I was enjoying watching them when they suddenly scattered in every direction as if a heavy rock had been dropped on them. When the water cleared, I saw that something large and brownish green had taken their place. It didn't move like a fish but unfurled itself as it swam, slowly and majestically. It was long and muscular, thicker than a man's leg.

I didn't want to turn my back on the creature so I started to swim away from it on my back, watching it as I moved away and looking for David. I lashed out, kicking my legs to frighten whatever it was, imagining how I'd hit its face if it got too close. I didn't see David anywhere. When I stopped kicking to see if it had swum away, it was still there, only about five feet away. It looked at me with its flat back eyes, and in my fear, my bladder let go. The thing looked at me a moment longer, and then, as if in disgust at my weakness, it turned and swam slowly back into the darkness of the cliff.

I resumed swimming backwards, not wanting to turn my eyes away from the cliff in case it returned, and I kicked and splashed as hard as I could. David couldn't have swum too far away from me and must have seen me not moving as fast as I wanted to because he swam over and grabbed my arm. The water wasn't deep, and when I stopped swimming, I found I could stand, and I tore off my snorkel.

David looked at me and shook his head. "You saw an eel?" I nodded, and he squeezed my shoulder and, without any of the malicious pleasure that many people take in seeing fear in others, said, "I'm sorry, Sean. I should have mentioned it was possible, but I haven't seen one for a couple years. It would have been a moray. They live in the coral by the sides of the cliffs."

My breathing was returning to normal, and I had the presence of mind to grin although my legs were weak and I didn't trust myself to speak. Later that evening, my encounter with the

moray eel made a good anecdote over a supper of fried fish on the
boardwalk at Jan Thiel. Sammy and Jake appeared to enjoy my
account, and Mr. Goldberg took it in with amusement and some
measure of what looked like approval. Only David seemed not to
be enjoying himself as he listened with a mixture of embarrassment and regret.

11

THE BREAK-IN HAPPENED on our last night in Curaçao. We returned to the Goldberg house at 9:00 p.m., after a typical day at the beach in the morning and a visit to the island's three-hundred-year-old Jewish cemetery in the afternoon. Mr. Goldberg turned off the alarm, and we kicked off our sandals and wandered into the living room. It was then that the lights came on, and two men were waiting for us. One was black and the other white, but we could tell that only from the colour of their hands because both were wearing masks. Bright pink pig masks with what looked like lipstick around the openings for their mouths. The black one, who was the taller of the two, must have had a sense of humour because he said, "Bon bini" in a low, amused voice and waited for us to respond. By this time, I knew "Bon bini" was the friendly way to say welcome on Curaçao. The four Goldbergs stopped. None of them moved or said anything.

I had never seen Mr. Goldberg look bored, but that's exactly how he appeared. Sammy tried his best to seem bored as well. Jake couldn't seem to make up his mind if he were more scared or intrigued by the situation, by how little control his father had over what was about to happen. David had gone very still, stiller than the others. I didn't know how to act or where to look. I had never been the victim of an armed robbery before. The men were definitely armed. I noticed their weapons a split second after the pig masks. They were each holding what looked like a rifle, although I couldn't tell for sure because I had only ever seen them in the movies. I waited to take my cue from the Goldbergs. Perhaps getting robbed at gunpoint came with the territory of being billionaires.

When he saw that Mr. Goldberg wasn't going to say anything, the taller robber waved his gun at us and said in English, "Okay then. As you wish. Please place your hands upon your heads, slowly, and sit down. Do not turn your back on me as you do so. I will not shoot to kill, but I will be happy to shoot you in the leg."

We all did as we were told. My legs were tired from swimming, but still I lowered myself slowly into an armchair. It felt strange to be ordered around by a pig with a gun. Mr. Goldberg spoke. He was not used to waiting to say anything. He looked at the pig masks and said, loudly and calmly, "*Trayf.*" It was more observation than accusation.

The taller robber said, "Pardon me?" We seemed to be dealing with polite robbers. Possibly even educated ones. Maybe it was the friendly culture of Curaçao, the moderate climate, that brought out the best in people, even violent criminals. But by the way the shorter one tightened his grip on his gun, you could tell he was angry. Perhaps feeling he had to take back control, the taller robber said to Mr. Goldberg, "Did you call us traitors?"

At this short burst of dialogue that was neither witty nor insightful, I couldn't help thinking of a Yiddish expression that David had taught me one day after Roger Macdonald had clumsily responded to one of our teachers who had accused him of something: *Afn ganef brent dos hitl.* On the thief's head the hat burns. David's generation didn't really speak Yiddish, but his *zayde* had, and Mr. Goldberg spoke it sometimes, mostly in the form of elaborate curses and swear words and colourful phrases, and so David picked up words here and there from his father.

The shorter pig seemed unbecomingly sensitive to the accusation. But of course that is not what Mr. Goldberg had said. He proceeded to explain, speaking more slowly than usual. "I said *trayf.* It means unclean. It refers to types of animals that Jews aren't allowed to eat. Pigs are at the top of the list." I was sure Mr. Goldberg didn't mean it to sound funny, but it sounded absurd, especially at the wrong end of a gun. And from someone who didn't hold to the kosher food laws.

The taller pig looked frustrated at this. He clearly wanted to change the subject of his choice of masks and return to his mission. "I'm afraid we don't have the time for this. Please open your safe. Give us everything and we will go. And you will be fine."

I tried to guess what Mr. Goldberg would say, but he never got a chance to respond because Sammy jumped in. With words, not deeds. I knew Sammy was trying to figure out a way to swing into action and save the day in front of his father. But it's hard to be heroic when you're sitting on a soft leather couch with your hands behind your head and two men are pointing guns at you.

"Why would you choose pig masks?" Sammy asked. "They look ridiculous." We all looked at Sammy. Even Mr. Goldberg turned his massive head to look at his oldest son, sitting at the other end of the couch. Sammy took this as a sign of encouragement. "Only a coward puts on a mask! Are you afraid to show your face?"

Sammy was trying to upset the robbers, goad them into a mistake, but he hadn't thought things through. The taller one shook his head, but the shorter one angrily lifted his left hand to his face. That was when the taller one and Mr. Goldberg both shouted, "Stop!" at the same time.

The shorter pig dropped his hand and grabbed onto his gun so he was holding it again with two hands. The taller pig nodded at Mr. Goldberg and then again in Sammy's direction. Mr. Goldberg was not used to anyone telling him when to speak let alone to whom, but he turned again to Sammy and said in an even, unruffled voice, "Samuel, as your father and as someone who has your best interests at heart, I must forbid you from speaking from now on." The rest of us breathed a sigh of relief. The taller pig nodded his still-encased head in thanks, and Mr. Goldberg nodded his in return.

The taller one reminded us why he and his partner were here. "The safe."

Mr. Goldberg said, "Of course. May I?" And he was already standing up, slowly but without waiting for permission. Even though he was about to give up the contents of his safe, he was reasserting his control over his movements and the timing of them.

"Please don't be hasty," the taller pig said, and again he was revealing his good manners. Mr. Goldberg slowly pointed down the hallway and started walking. He returned his hands to behind his head, but he was moving so quickly the taller pig had to keep up with him. They both disappeared into Mr. Goldberg's bedroom. We heard the taller robber say, "Please write down the combination on this sheet of paper. Then stand back, and I will open it."

Presumably Mr. Goldberg did so because we didn't hear anything for a few more minutes except for him saying, "I would appreciate it if you would leave our passports. It would save us some trouble."

And our now almost courtly armed robber replied, "Of course. We would be happy to." Then both men were back, and Mr. Goldberg was asked to seat himself again.

"Now we go," the taller pig said. "We cut your phone line before you came home. We will take your car keys and drop them where your driveway meets the main road. Please do not run after us." And then they were gone.

We all took our hands from our heads but remained sitting where we were for some time. Now that it was over, my legs felt weak.

Mr. Goldberg stood up first. His look of boredom was gone now. "I will get the car keys and drive over to the Weiremas'" — the family that lived over a kilometre to the east — "to call the police. But first, Samuel, some free advice from your father. If you ever find yourself being robbed by armed men again, don't ask them to take off their masks. I'd say don't even think about it, but that would be gratuitous. I hope, now that you've had a chance to let things sink in, I don't need to explain."

Mr. Goldberg turned away and, without looking at Sammy, without looking at anyone in particular, said quietly, "Don't ever be such a *dummkopf* again." Then he turned back to us and looked at David. "And, David, thanks for the *seykhel*." There was nothing for Jake. He was the deliberately forgotten son. I could tell by how Mr. Goldberg looked around the house on his way out that he was wondering how the two men got inside and reset the alarm so that it was on and had to be turned off as we came in. He must already have been thinking it was some sort of inside job, someone who had worked at the house before.

Sammy's face was red, and the moment Mr. Goldberg left the house, Sammy went to his room and slammed the door. Jake couldn't stop fidgeting and went out for a walk. David asked if I

wanted to go for a swim. It was too far to walk down the mountain to the small beach that came with the Goldberg *landhuis*, but
the Goldbergs had an infinity pool.

On the way, I asked what *dummkopf* meant. I had correctly
assumed it was Yiddish. David hesitated and looked away. "It
means stupid. Literally, dumb head."

"And *seykhel*?"

This time, David waited even longer to respond. "Smarts.
Maybe even cunning. It's a particularly Jewish word. Related to
survival." Our flip-flops were making slapping sounds on the concrete path between the house and the pool.

I didn't understand. David hadn't done or said anything.

"Last year, when there were a couple of robberies in the neighbourhood, I suggested to my father that he take our real valuables
out of the safe. He agreed, and since then, all we keep there are
our passports and a bit of cash: no more than two, three thousand
dollars. And we keep photocopies of the passports elsewhere. If
we were ever robbed, as we were tonight, we could open up the
safe and the robbers would think they were getting something. We
keep the five gold bars my father insists on carrying around with
him everywhere sewn into our mattresses. Each of us has one in
our beds. Even you."

That night, even after the swim, I had trouble falling asleep. I
had never slept on a gold bar before.

THE SHORT, BARELY noticeable argument my parents had when I
returned home made me forget the one before I left. It was made
worse by the fact they had reversed their roles. My mother was
horrified that armed men had pointed their guns at her only son
when I was too far away for her to do anything to protect me.

Mary wasn't one for regrets or second-guessing, but by the way her mouth twisted and she ran her tongue along the edge of her bottom lip when she found out what had happened, I assumed she was wondering for the first time if it had been so smart after all to have me fill out the application for LCC.

When he dropped me off at my house, Mr. Goldberg apologized to my parents for the fact I had been caught up in an armed robbery at his vacation home. My parents were too polite and too respectful of his wealth and generosity in inviting me along to be concerned in his presence. But when he left, Mary grabbed me and started yelling as if the robbery had been my fault, even though she was also asking me if I was all right and if I had been scared and whether this sort of thing happened often to the Goldbergs. It was Declan, despite all his original misgivings, who came to my rescue.

"Mary," he said as he put his thick arms around her and gently pulled her toward him, "it's okay. Sean's okay."

My mother pushed him away. "I know he's okay, Declan. But he might not have been." I felt sorry for my previously optimistic and steadfast mother. An armed robbery on a small island thousands of miles away had instantly changed a confident woman into someone who couldn't help imagining the worst. And my father, who all along had feared losing his son to another family and a different class, was the one left defending me.

"Mary, you can't stop living because something bad happens." And because Declan had said everything he needed to, he left it at that and left the room. My mother looked at me and burst into tears. I hugged her until she stopped crying.

PART TWO

McGill
1983–1990

1

MCGILL HAPPENED TO all of us in a blur of classes and studying and drinking. None of the Goldberg boys drank at home because Mr. Goldberg didn't — except for the obligatory sips of that sickly sweet Manischewitz kosher wine on Jewish holidays — but they more than made up for it at McGill. It was the perfect place for the Goldbergs because they wouldn't stand out. Every second student was a millionaire or the son or daughter of someone famous, or so it seemed. The effect was that everything was equalized.

In retrospect, it seems foolish that neither David nor I applied anywhere else. Our marks were high, and we'd attended LCC. David had his last name going for him. If they had wanted to, the Goldbergs could have gone to Princeton or Yale or Oxford, but they weren't the kind of rich people who defined themselves by what university they attended, and for all I know, Mr. Goldberg didn't want his sons out of his sight for four years. David's grandfather Abraham had graduated from McGill, as had Mr. Goldberg's late brother, Isaac, and even though Mr. Goldberg himself was a university dropout, he was a McGill dropout. There was never any real choice for Sammy, Jake, and David.

I, on the other hand, could have gone anywhere I wanted on a scholarship, including the Ivy League, if Mr. Baylor, our guidance counselor, was to be believed. Just by applying to university, I was already going further than my parents or my grandparents, so there was no legacy to uphold. But of course, even though the pressure on me was much less, over the course of six years of high school, including a grade twelve prep year that my old friends at Willingdon wouldn't have understood, my destiny had become somehow tied to that of the Goldberg boys. At least it had in my mind. So I applied to McGill alongside David.

Although I wasn't officially a member of the Goldberg family, like David (and like Jake and Sammy before us), I had been promised a job in the family business before I first stepped foot on campus. Knowing that we would each have a job when we came out of McGill gave all four of us confidence and faith in the future that carried us through listening to the lectures professors read blandly from their notes and having to skim so many books each week that any meaningful retention beyond the day of the exam was impossible.

But I had Goldberg expectations and standards to meet. I couldn't coast through my classes. Mr. Goldberg had been very clear about that when he promised me a job upon graduation. I had to do "reasonably well," which he never bothered to quite define and which he said to me without smiling and without any trace of irony, one night after supper at his house. This was in marked contrast to what Mr. Goldberg expected of his sons.

Mr. Goldberg had distinct ideas of what constituted excellence when it came to his sons working in the family business, but those expectations didn't extend to university. The advantage of this attitude for David and his brothers was that Mr. Goldberg was flexible about what they could study, as long as it led them into the family business sooner or later. That was why Sammy could take business, Jake could get away with completing an undergraduate degree in mining engineering — like his beloved grandfather over half a century before — and David could blaze his own path. He took economics. It was a strange, impractical choice, at least for a Goldberg, because in many ways the dismal science, as economics is known, was closer to philosophy than to business, more suited to observers and analysts than men of action. He minored in theatre, which was a program of the Department of English.

When David told his father he was going to major in economics with a minor in theatre, I thought Mr. Goldberg would be angry, despite his tolerant attitude to his sons' academic choices. If not for studying economics, then for studying theatre. Economics would have been bad enough for Mr. Goldberg — he thought economists were halfway between academics and voodoo doctors. As for theatre, Mr. Goldberg had enjoyed going to see David's high school plays. I think he even felt *naches*, that peculiarly Jewish word that means pride in one's children in a culture that takes pride in one's children to great extremes. Yet somehow, without him ever saying anything on the topic, we all knew that in Mr. Goldberg's eyes, theatre was primarily for children. But Mr. Goldberg smiled indulgently and his eyes crinkled when David told him what he was planning to study, as if one part of Mr. Goldberg admired David's youthful rebellion and the other part knew that eventually David would grow out of it.

Sammy never would have thought of studying anything other than business, although from the moment he applied to university he knew he wasn't going to stay long enough to earn the degree. This was at least partly why at family suppers during Sammy's first year, whenever Mr. Goldberg asked Sammy what he had learned at school, he would rarely actually let Sammy finish his chronicle of whatever management theory he had been exposed to that day. He'd interrupt his son's account with anecdotes about *his* day.

Everyone in the Goldberg family and all of Sammy's friends — and I think the majority of his professors — knew that Sammy would be gone from McGill by the end of his second year, if not before. It was understood, the way it's known that certain people are going to achieve whatever they set out to and others won't based on how they carry themselves when they walk into a room. Mr. Goldberg knew it too, although, as far as I could tell, he and Sammy never discussed it. Mr. Goldberg knew it because everything he did his oldest son did too.

Mr. Goldberg had been accepted at McGill, in business, but had dropped out after his second year, in 1960, to join the family company that bore his name. According to David, Mr. Goldberg's father, Abraham, had been disappointed, but he had also understood that his first-born son wasn't meant for university. What Mr. Goldberg thought of Sammy's university destiny, I don't know for sure. But I'd say his thinking was in keeping with how he saw his oldest son generally: one part affection because he recognized the most unsophisticated part of himself in Sammy and one part contempt because Sammy tried too hard to be like him. If we all knew from the beginning that Sammy would drop out before he graduated, we also knew that Jake would not just graduate but would do so with flying colours. He was the most unusual McGill engineering student I ever met: he spent more time reading than drinking. He read all his books carefully, from cover to cover, and went to all his classes.

An undergraduate degree (or less) was fine for the Goldberg boys. But for me, an honorary member of the family who was invited over to the Goldberg house every second Friday night for Shabbat dinner and down to Curaçao on family trips during major school holidays but who was not bonded by blood, an undergraduate degree was an insufficient ticket into the family business. Mary had made me miss the Goldberg trip to Curaçao I was invited on the year after the robbery, but starting in grade ten, she let me go again every year after I'd assured her the Goldbergs had improved their security and Declan had intervened with a laconic observation about lightning never striking twice in the same place. Declan turned out to be right: there never was another incident, at least not while I was there.

On one of the trips to Curaçao, in our first year of university, Mr. Goldberg made it known, after a day of swimming at Knipp Beach, that I was expected to study law after I graduated from McGill. Mr. Goldberg never took the trouble to explain why law and not something else. It was clear from the way he would bring up Ira Levin's name when he was speaking of his company — almost always in the context of "Well, as Ira says" — that Mr. Goldberg had nothing but respect for Goldberg Limited's most senior lawyer. After earning my undergraduate degree, I was expected to study law at no less a faculty than McGill's, and to gold medal in it, or to come within spitting distance.

As with David, Mr. Goldberg never suggested to me what I major in for my undergrad, but he had somehow made it clear, without ever saying anything, that it should complement law. So I took history with a few business courses.

Although Sammy had already determined, before he walked through the Roddick Gates, that he wouldn't be graduating, he seemed to enjoy his first-year finance courses, and despite himself, he uncharacteristically began to study. Once, in that first semester, Mr. Goldberg found Sammy absorbed in a heavy finance management book while David and I played a game of chess nearby. Mr. Goldberg watched his oldest son for a few minutes, which was a long time for Mr. Goldberg, and then said, as if he had all the time in world, "Samuel, do you know what happens to those who get As in university?"

Sammy looked up from his reading, startled, and shook his big head. Mr. Goldberg went on, with the timing of a dry-witted comic: "They become professors." Sammy nodded and looked up at the ceiling as if Mr. Goldberg had just said something particularly profound and he was giving it due consideration. And he probably was because Sammy as a rule didn't do irony, at least not where his father was concerned. But Mr. Goldberg wasn't finished.

"Do you know what happens to students who get Cs?" Sammy looked confused. Mr. Goldberg smiled. "They donate buildings." And Mr. Goldberg gently slapped his oldest son on his back, which made Sammy relax and smile.

GETTING Bs or Cs might have been fine for the Goldberg boys, especially for Sammy, but I had to earn straight As so I would be accepted to McGill's Faculty of Law. Earn As I did, without missing out on the social life that David was always at the centre of.

The summer before we entered McGill, David began to grow out his blond hair so that by the time we finished our first year at university it was down to his shoulders, and by the beginning of our second year he sometimes put it in a ponytail. He always wore a black leather bomber jacket in the fall and spring, and midway through our second year he started to wear a long, grey fur coat in the winter. The fur looked thick and rough and bulky, and I always thought it was wolf, but I could never bring myself to ask him. As we walked through the door of a party one night, someone told David that he looked like a Russian prince. It might have been part of an act for David, but if it was, it was a good one. The difference in our student lives was that after staying out until 3:00 a.m. drinking, David was able to sleep in late while I had to get up early to study.

IT WAS AT one of the parties we were always going to that I first saw Solomon, at the start of our second year.

We were at someone's apartment in the McGill ghetto. It was after midnight, and we were all drunk when a new guest appeared. Perhaps it was because we were all sprawled on the couches and on the floor, and he was the only one standing, but all our eyes turned to him as he walked in. Or perhaps it was because we were drunk and the guest who had just arrived was fresh. The effect was similar to whenever David entered a room with his height and his long blond hair in a ponytail.

The student who had just walked in also had height, the big Goldberg head, and the golden hair, but, unlike David's, his was cut medium length. I knew immediately that he was related to David in some way because he had the same Goldberg eyes: flat, slightly reptilian, and symmetrical. His features were a little softer than those of the three Goldberg sons, but his eyes were a slightly darker blue, and there was something harder in them. Yet even with these minor differences, he could have been David's younger brother. He surveyed the youthful human wreckage spread across the room, smiled, and said, "Bring on the beer" in a loud voice as if he, too, were drunk. Everyone laughed then went back to making solemn pronouncements and witticisms.

But David, who was sitting at the feet of a woman regally ensconced in an armchair — a fellow student I recognized from one of his theatre classes — pulled himself up and stood and reached out to shake the hand of the new arrival, as if he were assuming the duty of representing all of us in welcoming him to the party. The other student — I somehow knew he was a McGill student and not a friend of a friend invited along to a college party — looked at David's hand for a few seconds before deciding to shake it. And when he did, he said in a quiet voice, "Cousin. I'd ask what brings you here, but I can see for myself."

The two of them were almost the same height, but Solomon was just the slightest bit taller. This caused me a measure of conscious disappointment. And then, without waiting for a response, the newcomer disappeared into the party, leaving David standing alone. Even in my drunken state, I remember thinking I had never seen anyone leave David so abruptly before, not even Mr. Goldberg.

We took a cab home together at 3:00 a.m., and on the way I asked David whom he had shaken hands with at the party. By this time the alcohol was starting to wear off and fatigue was setting in. David leaned back against the headrest, his eyes closed. He opened them and looked out at the darkness as the taxi left downtown and took us up along the slope of the mountain toward the summit on the western side and David's home. "That" — and he paused for the longest time as if it pained him to go on — "was Solomon."

The taxi driver let David off at his house, David gave me ten dollars to pay for his part of the cab ride, and then the driver took me down through the winding streets of sleeping Westmount to my parents' house in NDG. I was tired, but it took me longer than usual to fall asleep. I remember feeling ashamed as I lost consciousness, ashamed that for the first time I had met someone who seemed to have a Goldberg glow that was just slightly brighter than David's.

2

"THERE'S SOMEONE I want you to meet," David started off by saying one day after class early in our second year. We were about to walk over to the parking spot he rented in the McGill ghetto, just east of the campus.

Whenever we finished classes at the same time, David drove me home in the bright red 1953 MG convertible that Mr. Goldberg had given him when he turned sixteen. It had been Mr. Goldberg's before, a gift from his father, Abraham, when he himself had turned sixteen in 1953. It wasn't until David began to drive that I realized that the more expensive and beautiful the car, the more time it spent in the garage. The Goldbergs had a good mechanic. Hans Doterlein had recently emigrated from Germany, and he liked working on vintage British cars almost as much as he liked working on German ones.

The Goldberg fleet of cars needed constant care and attention, and I accompanied David on many after-school trips to Doterlein's garage. It was in my neighbourhood, near the train tracks just a few blocks east of my house, in an area crowded with garages and body shops. David frequently dropped off or picked up one of his family's many cars. Doterlein always greeted him respectfully, like a son or maybe more like a grandson, for Doterlein would have been in his late fifties, older than Mr. Goldberg at the time. After David introduced me to him, Doterlein greeted me unfailingly with the same measure of affection and respect, even though neither my father nor I brought in a car to him. The fact I was a friend of David's was good enough for him.

The MG was David's summer car, which he drove from May, when the snow and the salt that Montréal liked to pour prodigiously on its streets disappeared, until October, when it started to snow again. Mr. Goldberg, despite his wealth, didn't believe in spending money on winter cars, so David, like his two older brothers, had to make do with a second-hand BMW, which he'd purchased, from November to April.

"Actually, it's someone you already know — Jane."

I'm still embarrassed that it took me a few seconds to place her, and I had to say, "Jane?" as if asking David for her last name.

He looked at me as if I were stupid and said, "Jane Dunfield. Your neighbour?" When I still looked blank, he said, "You haven't moved, have you?"

It was only then that I remembered my childhood friend Jane had also gone to McGill, from Westhill, our neighbourhood high school, on a full scholarship. Although we still lived on the same street, our high school years had been lived separately. After I started going to LCC, we didn't have the same set of friends, we didn't go to the same parties. We'd see each other occasionally on our street and say hello, but by the time I was eighteen, the easy intimacy of our childhood had disappeared. And because Jane had stayed in the public school system and done two years of CEGEP instead of one year of prep school, she had just started at McGill, a year after David and me.

"How do you know her?" It came out too quickly, almost defensively. How would David know anybody from the neighbourhood where I had grown up, anybody other than me?

"We're in a play together. She's a theatre student, and unlike me she's rather good at it. It's her major."

"Please tell me it's not *Romeo and Juliet*."

David laughed. "Quite the opposite, actually. *Macbeth*."

"Not Macbeth and Lady Macbeth?"

David laughed again, pleased with himself. "The one and the same!"

I wasn't sure what would have been worse: David and Jane falling in love as Italian teenagers or else plotting together as Scottish spouses to murder Duncan and steal the throne.

"She mentioned the other day that she knew you, that you'd grown up on the same street. That you still live on the same street." David wasn't looking at me as he spoke. I wasn't sure where he was going with this. "When I heard you were both still practically next-door neighbours, I offered her a lift home. And she accepted. Here she is. The proverbial girl next door."

I looked up to see Jane waiting on the steps of the Arts Building. She was holding some books to her chest, and she appeared even more earnest and taller than I remembered. Perhaps it was because she was standing on the second step or maybe it was because I hadn't paid attention to her the last few times I'd seen her in our neighbourhood. She didn't just look taller. She looked grown-up and beautiful in a simple, unflashy way, and I remembered her beauty as a child, which had registered with me then in a different way. Even though she still seemed as serious as she had as a child, she was also smiling the same way she had smiled at me in grade six. Except now she was grown-up with long hair. And from the way she kept smiling while saying "Hi," first to David and then to me, I had the feeling that my two friends had been conspiring behind my back in setting up this meeting after class.

When she placed herself between us, putting her arms through each of ours while we walked to David's parking spot, I was even more confused. As we walked through the bright fall day, she turned first to David and then to me before returning her gaze to what was directly in front of us and said, "Do you know what was happening the last time I saw the two of you together?"

David and I both turned to Jane and exchanged puzzled looks as a funny smile started to play out across her mouth. As far as I remembered, this was the first time the three of us had been together. I tried to recall what great event had been unfolding when the three of us might have met. But I had nothing to go on. David had been my Westmount friend for over seven years. Jane had been my NDG friend when we were children, and I found myself feeling ashamed that I had let our friendship lapse, that Jane and I had grown apart from each other between grade six and university.

"Neither of you can guess?" A mocking tone had crept into her voice. She glanced at us again. "No?"

David and I both shook our heads. Not only was I embarrassed, but I felt I was somehow letting Jane down with my failure.

Jane squeezed our arms and pulled us closer to her. She quickened her pace and broke into laughter. "My two forgetful warriors!" I looked over at David, and he was obviously bewildered. At this point my embarrassment reached an acute point, but I also felt calmer and superior to David because it was then that I remembered, and he clearly did not. But of course he couldn't have remembered, while I should have, because the last time the three of us had been in the same place at the same time, David hadn't met Jane yet, while she had already been my friend for five years.

It was the day David and I and our classmates from LCC got into the fight on the sidewalk with Stephen and Michael and Eli from my old school, the school Jane had still been attending. Jane had been passing by and had stopped briefly to watch. And the way Jane had watched us that day came back to me: curious, questioning, mocking. Evaluating us boys fighting with each other and finding us perhaps mysterious and amusing but ultimately wanting and not worthy of her full attention.

By this time, David could tell from my face and the way Jane was playfully pulling my arm that I had figured it out, and he looked at me as if wanting to be admitted to the shared memory. I cleared my throat. "It was the day of the fight after rehearsal. The other boys went to my old school. Jane was watching us. For part of it."

David didn't laugh. All he said was, "I never knew you knew them. I'm sorry, Sean."

I said, "That's okay," and the three of us kept walking toward David's car. Jane fell silent now, not having anticipated that her memory, which was obviously still amusing in her mind, would cause David and me to become so serious.

When we reached David's red convertible neatly sitting in its small parking spot, he opened the door for Jane. I noticed she appreciated this, and it made me think they must be boyfriend and girlfriend when they weren't together on stage. After Jane got in, David pushed his seat forward and let me into the tiny back seat. I wasn't sure where to sit, behind David or behind Jane. I chose to sit behind him so I would be able to see at least part of her profile.

David was witty and relaxed as he drove us home. Jane seemed to find his company more than enough. She rarely glanced back at me and didn't seem to notice the way other drivers or people on the sidewalk would turn their heads to watch our car go by. I felt like my father, Declan: words hard to come by, stuck in my throat like dust.

DAVID'S TIME AT McGill was a lot like his time at LCC. Charmed. Successful. Fun. He had to learn a few drama techniques the first year — no matter how talented, your high school drama teacher can only take you so far — but starting in his second year he starred in every production he tried out for: *Macbeth*; *Hamlet*; *The Importance of Being Earnest*; *Betrayal*. He did them all: Shakespeare, the nineteenth century, the moderns. Even musicals. I can still see and hear him as Freddy Eynsford-Hill in *My Fair Lady*. I was not surprised to learn that his singing voice was as good as his acting one. I went to every production. And more often than not, Jane was there too, not with me but on stage with David, usually playing opposite him. These plays were not easy for me to watch, seeing the two of them together in their make-believe worlds. But I never once seriously thought about not going.

Afterward, we would go out together for drinks, usually with the whole cast but occasionally just the three of us, and Jane would be equally friendly to both David and me, sitting close between us in a booth if we could get one, taking our arms in turn, first lightly touching his shoulder and then mine in the course of conversation. I found this confusing because ever since that first day I'd seen her with David, I'd assumed she preferred him.

These after-theatre drinks were the same each time. Even though the three of us were sitting practically on each other's laps,

I would try my best not to feel that somehow Jane was closer to David than to me, just because she had spent the last few months in rehearsals and the last two hours up on stage with him either falling in or out of love. I'm ashamed to say that sometimes I even found myself counting how many times Jane unconsciously touched one of us — on our shoulders, our backs, our arms. It was my way of keeping score, seeing who came out ahead each night. But the two of them had the shared experience of the theatre, and even on nights when Jane's long fingers grazed my arm or shoulder more often than David's, I felt again like I was the last person picked for the football team. Except this was worse because I wasn't on the football team at all, wasn't on the playing field or the bench. And because, for the first time in my mind, I had cast David as my rival.

ONE NIGHT AFTER a play — I think it was actually *Betrayal* — we had gone off to one of those snug, interchangeable bars on Crescent Street that David liked for some reason, I think because they played a lot of jazz and David was going through his jazz phase at the time. We crowded into a corner booth with Jane sitting between us as she usually did, leaning first against me, then against David, apparently giving us equal time. She was laughing at our silly jokes and venturing some of her own when David got up to go to the bathroom and made an awkward production of it. It was uncharacteristic of him.

Jane had been leaning against me, and, when David stood up and looked down at us, she moved slightly away from me so that she was sitting up straight. David was drunk — at least he appeared to be; he was a good actor, after all — but he noticed Jane shifting in her seat and, with only the slightest slur to his words, said with mock seriousness, "Oh no, don't move away from Sean on my account. I might not be back for a while." He made it sound like he was going off to war and Jane shouldn't even think about waiting for him because he probably wouldn't return. Even though we were only a few feet away from him, he waved at us, half royally, and concluded with the self-mockingly arch, "Please talk amongst yourselves," then walked off, trying his apparent best to remain steady and upright.

I was slightly drunk, but curiously Jane was looking more sober by the second. She was also very quiet, and after some time I said to her, "What do you think he meant by that?" I was surprised when Jane moved further down the booth and looked at me with something approaching pity in her eyes. I stared back.

"You really have no idea?" she asked finally, and I was reminded of just one of the reasons I liked Jane. Most actors, even when they're young, have trouble shutting off their work. They either can't distinguish between what's going on only on stage or they don't even try. They never stop acting. Even in their most personal moments, when they're afraid or when they're falling in love, they can't help falling back on their training to amplify what they're feeling and how they're transmitting those feelings. They always give you the sense that they, too, are aware and watching themselves act. But Jane was different. She left her acting on the stage. She never, as far as I could tell, manufactured an emotion or a gesture in her real life. So now, as she was talking to me, half drunk, in a small bar, she was genuinely surprised. And although she was nineteen and beautiful, she looked exactly like my childhood friend with whom I used to play on the street. I shook my head.

"Oh God," was all she said and looked away, and before too long she took another sip of red wine. I must have looked even more bewildered because she put down her glass and turned back and said, "It may be 1985, but I am *not* going to kiss you first, let alone ask *you* out."

I suddenly wasn't drunk anymore, but I still didn't understand what we were talking about. How had the conversation moved from David heading off to the bathroom in grand fashion to her telling me she wasn't going to kiss me first? Or ask *me* out? And then, very gradually, I thought I was beginning to understand. And by how Jane reacted to my next few words, as fragmented and incomplete as they were, I realized that up until then I had been misinterpreting everything.

"I always thought ..."

"Yes?"

"I always thought you and David were ..."

"David and I were what?" I looked around. Jane was practically shouting at me, but nobody in the small space had yet noticed. Thankfully, the jazz quartet's concentration had not been broken. Perhaps Jane wasn't really yelling and it only sounded loud to me.

"Were ..."

She let me hang out there for some time, but when she saw that I couldn't finish my sentence, she eventually said, "Friends?" And I remember thinking what a weird word. It sounded strange to be hearing it from Jane.

"No. More."

Jane laughed. "Oh, I'm pretty sure I'm not David's type. Why would you ever think that?"

Because David was tall and blond and talented and rich? And because I was everything he was not? But I didn't say it because I realized how stupid and self-pitying it sounded to me, and how infinitely more stupid and insulting it would sound to Jane. Instead, I did the far better thing. I kissed her.

And miraculously, she kissed me back.

A WEEK LATER, when Jane's parents were away and I was over at her house, we spoke about our first kiss the way people do. We talked about the time it had taken us to get to it, not just the months at university after being reintroduced by David but the almost decade and a half before that, when we were nothing more than childhood friends and before that, only neighbours. We agreed it was good that we hadn't come to it earlier, because then it might not have lasted. And we realized we were both grateful to David for bringing us together by making his dramatic exit to the bathroom of a Crescent Street bar. I tried to sound nonchalant, as befitted our relaxed mood, and asked Jane whether she had ever wanted to go out with David, perhaps when they were starring together in a play. "Don't the leading man and woman always fall in love? Isn't that part of Broadway mythology?"

Jane laughed. "You really don't know, do you? That's the power of acting. David likes you and respects you too much as a friend to ever try to make a move. Loves you, probably. And besides, even if that weren't the case, all I ever wanted was you."

She looked up at me and laughed again, not unkindly but as if I were really stupid. "Since I moved onto your street and first met you. When I was seven." And then wisely I stopped asking my questions, and we stopped talking.

I NEVER TOLD David that Jane and I were "going out" as we put it so quaintly then, and I'm not sure if she ever did, but I think he just knew when he returned from whatever he had been pretending to do in the bathroom and Jane was leaning against me. She didn't move back and forth between us anymore that night, but did take David's hand and squeeze it briefly when he sat down, as if gently signalling that now they were clearly only friends.

But afterward, on the days when David was giving us a lift home and we walked together to his car, she still took both our arms and walked between us the same as before. We continued in our shared friendship, and as far as I could tell, David was very happy for both of us, and I think his feelings were genuine.

A few days later, when David and I ran into each other at the McGill library and Jane was in class at the other end of campus, all David said was, "Your Jane is lovely," and I nodded in agreement.

3

IF JAKE TOOK his studies seriously, and if Sammy studiously avoided them, David was both indifferent to his studies and enjoyed them in an easy way that neither Sammy nor Jake could, even though Jake loved school. David took whatever courses he wanted, doing generally well while not appearing to care about his grades. He didn't seem to pay attention to what was required to earn a degree and somehow managed to accumulate the credits required for an economics degree with a minor in theatre.

Our attitudes toward our degrees mirrored our attitudes toward business and Mr. Goldberg: I was diligent and serious and set on studying law. Sammy ended up dropping out because he was impatient to start making money and to make his mark. After his early interest in finance, he soon found his professors dull and many of his fellow students pretentious in their pursuit of knowledge, the way they used academic jargon and posed in class, covering up their ignorance with studied questions. He found ways to convey his evolving opinions to his father. Sammy knew Mr. Goldberg had completed two years of university before dropping out. Sammy bested him by dropping out after only one.

David neither rebelled nor conformed. He continued going his own way. And as for Jake, if Mr. Goldberg had dropped out, then he was going to get the highest marks ever achieved by any Goldberg. In his final year, when Jake was on his way to earning a 4.0 grade point average in mining engineering, the same major as his beloved *zayde* Abraham, he got a job offer.

It was Friday night, and we were having supper at the Goldbergs'. David and I were in our third year. By then I had grown used to the Goldbergs having family arguments in front of me. The arguments were never about money on its own, but during our university years they were almost always about what the Goldberg sons wanted to do to earn it, right away or eventually.

OVER A YEAR earlier, in the middle of his third year, Jake had shared, albeit *sotto voce*, at a family Friday night dinner that he was thinking of doing his MBA when he completed his undergrad.

Mr. Goldberg's eyelids lowered before he responded. "Jacob?"

"Yes?"

"I know Samuel took business for a year and David is *studying* economics, but do you really think a graduate degree in business is the right thing for you?"

"Yes. I do."

Mr. Goldberg waved his right hand in dismissal and then held up his index finger. "There's only one MBA worth having, and that's the GMBA." He waited for Jake or any one of us to say something. Not surprisingly, it was Sammy who took the bait. He always played the straight man to his father. David didn't bother, and Jake knew better. But Sammy fell for it time and time again.

"The General MBA?"

"The Goldberg Master of Business Administration, Samuel," Mr. Goldberg said, nodding his heavy blond head and not looking at him. "Don't you boys ever forget it. You get the best education in the business right here," he said as he pointed at the centre of the table around which we were all sitting.

And, then, as if the idea were just occurring to him and he was pleased with it because in his view it summed up all his thoughts and was perfectly suited to his audience, Mr. Goldberg said to his oldest son, "Asking a professor to teach you about business, Samuel, is like asking a monk questions about women. It's something they've both only read about in a book." He smiled proudly, like a child.

BUT THIS LATEST argument around the dinner table was far worse. With less than two months to go before the end of classes, Jake had announced, over Rita's excellent chicken matzo ball soup, that he had been offered, and was thinking of accepting, a junior consulting role with McKinsey upon graduation. McKinsey with its fabled hundred-hour workweeks, ridiculously high client fees, and intimate access to CEOs determined to restructure their companies in their image.

After making his pronouncement, Jake lifted his spoon to his mouth, and, taking in his soup without a slurp, he swallowed thoughtfully and looked at nobody in particular. Mr. Goldberg, normally self-composed, glanced around the table: at Sammy, who shrugged, spilling some of his spoonful; at David, who had resumed eating; at Mrs. Goldberg, who tried hopelessly to give her husband silent advice through a slow shake of her head; and at me. I put down my spoon and returned Mr. Goldberg's gaze.

I knew what he was thinking. Mr. Goldberg bit off a piece of challah and chewed it thoughtfully before saying, "Why a consultancy, Jacob?"

"Calling McKinsey a consultancy is like calling a Rolls-Royce a car." Jake's analogy sounded rehearsed, but after having seen the Goldbergs in action many times, I knew that Jake was going into this latest skirmish with his father the way one of my favourite history professors said French Navy captains went into battle against Lord Admiral Nelson: not attempting to win but determined to show they could die well.

Mr. Goldberg was unfazed by Jake's challenging response. "It's of no matter to me whether it's a Rolls-Royce or a Bentley. You'll be paid to go into other people's companies and help them make more money."

"That's the point."

"I don't get that point, Jacob. You have your own company to help run. Why would you want to help other people run their companies so they can make more money?"

"I don't see it that way. I think about it as solving problems. As learning."

Mr. Goldberg's eyelids fell just a little. "You think we don't have enough problems to solve here? You think it's child's play to pull metal out of the ground more efficiently than anybody else, to get thousands of people not just to work for you but to do their best? Teaching the Goldberg way of doing business to the people who work for us? Being the best and the cheapest in the world? You *think* this is so easy that you want to head off and help others run their businesses the way we do? So they can get better and compete with us and make more money?"

"Dad ..." Jake closed his eyes for two seconds then reopened them and went on. I noticed it was the first time he'd called Mr.

Goldberg "Dad" in the conversation. "I don't have to work with any gold mining companies while I'm there. I'll learn a lot. I don't want to do it for more than five years. Think how much outside knowledge I'll bring back to our company."

Mr. Goldberg's eyelids fell at this, and his eyes narrowed. He didn't say anything, and for a moment I thought he was going to stand up and leave. But then he said, "You don't think I have enough outside knowledge? You think I have to send my son to work for others so I can get more outside knowledge? And by the way, I don't care whether the knowledge is inside or outside."

Jake closed his eyes, and I was afraid for a few seconds that he was going to pass out. Instead, he said, so softly that we all had to strain to hear it, even Mr. Goldberg with his sharp hearing, "*Zayde* would have let me go. I think you should too."

Mr. Goldberg's eyes widened.

"I wasn't going to be the one to bring your *zayde* into it, Jacob, but since you've brought him up, why not. Your *zayde* started this business in 1913. As a Jew in Canada in 1913. I'm not sure if you've noticed, Jacob, but there aren't a lot of Jews in mining today. There were fewer then. Back then, nobody would have hired your *zayde* as a mining engineer. He would have never had the chance to work for someone's else's company, so he started his own. And he did it all on his own. No connections. No advantages. No capital. No consultants. No outside knowledge. No nothing." Every short sentence came to a full stop.

"He had no outside knowledge from other companies. He never worked for any other companies. And neither have I. Everything I've learned about other companies I've learned by buying them, not by working for them. Everything I learned about this business, I learned from your *zayde* — my father — just like you'll learn from me if only you'd stop to listen instead of chasing after your so-called outside knowledge. We know more about gold mining than anybody else in the world, Jacob. That's why none of *my* sons is ever going to work as a consultant. Not as long as I have anything to do with it."

Mr. Goldberg glared at his middle son. Jake still said nothing. His eyes darted to each of us, but I doubted if he was really seeing anything.

When Mr. Goldberg spoke again, his voice had returned to normal. He attempted to look kind, but he smiled thinly. "Do you know what a consultant is, Jacob?"

"No." Jake couldn't bring himself to look at his father.

"It's somebody who borrows your watch." Pause. "Tells you what time it is." Pause. "Gives it back to you." Pause. "And then charges you for it. None of my sons is *ever* going to work as a consultant to make money for other people. I don't care if it's McKinsey or your friends working out of their garage. Frankly, I can't believe you would even ask."

Jake said nothing. He had just been reminded yet again that he was engaged in an argument with his father that his father would not let him win. Mr. Goldberg waited a few minutes in vain for Jake's reply. And then, perhaps unsure whether Jake's silence was a sign of weakness or silent rebellion, and no doubt wanting Jake to categorically admit defeat, Mr. Goldberg pressed on with what he must have thought was his advantage, delivering his *coup de grâce*. His tone was matter-of-fact, his voice low, and he actually broke off a piece of challah as he started to speak. "Jacob, we can talk about it all we want, but you're not joining a consultancy. You're not working for other companies." He put the piece of challah in his mouth, chewed a bit, and resumed speaking with his mouth still half full. "We all know that if you ever do, so help me God, I will disown you."

I remember at the time thinking what a funny word it was, "disown," with its implication of ownership. And how nonchalantly Mr. Goldberg had spoken it. I couldn't bring myself to look at Mrs. Goldberg, who remained silent, but I looked around the table at the three Goldberg sons. Sammy's big jaw had fallen, and his mouth was hanging open. He was staring at his father with something approaching horror, and although the effect was unintentionally comic, I understood his reaction. Because every single thing that Sammy did was designed to emulate his father, I'm not sure he would have been able to conceive of a worse fate. Mr. Goldberg must have known this because in all the time I knew him, he never came close to threatening Sammy in this way.

David was a different story. I don't think Mr. Goldberg ever worried about how David might feel or react to one of his threats, or promises for that matter. In the time I'd known them, Mr. Goldberg had always somehow treated David like an equal. He never spoke to him as a weaker child. And, perhaps as a result, although I saw no evidence of this until much later, I think David was the only one who had the power to make him truly angry. That was because Mr. Goldberg never felt sorry for David, the way he felt sorry for his two older sons: Sammy because his desire outstripped his ability, and Jake because in Mr. Goldberg's eyes he was turning his back on his family.

With that, Mr. Goldberg assumed the matter was firmly closed. We all did, which was why Jake's next words surprised all of us, perhaps even himself. "I'm sorry, but I've already accepted their offer." And then, not waiting for his father's reply, Jake stood up and left the room.

I expected one of us to come to Jake's defence or at the very least for David to run after him, but David looked down and toyed with his food. After an awkward moment, we all returned to eating our soup in silence. Despite Jake's defiance, Mr. Goldberg had not stopped eating his. As I finished my soup and started on my roast chicken, I had no doubt that David was going to speak, that he was just biding his time. I waited until the end of the meal for him to say what he had to say. I waited until dessert was served and eaten and the empty plates were taken away by Rita, and by that time I thought I was going to be waiting forever. During all that time, it never occurred to me that I could be the one to say something, I who was not a real member of the Goldberg family.

It was only when Mr. Goldberg finished dessert and was about to stand up that David said, "Dad?" and I knew that my confidence in David had not been misplaced.

"Yes, David."

"You shouldn't be so hard on him."

It wasn't much, but if anybody else had spoken so directly to Mr. Goldberg, his eyelids would have lowered and the person who had so dared would have received an earful or a disdainful silence. But David had always had a special dispensation to speak to his father. Mr. Goldberg smiled magnanimously, as if indulging the idealistic and perhaps idiotic sentiments of the young. But he couldn't leave it there. "Do you know why I'm so hard on you boys?"

"No, Dad."

"Because if I'm not hard on you first, with a father's unconditional love and affection, the world will be hard on you, hard on you without an ounce of care. And you won't be prepared. Not even with all your advantages."

Later that evening, when we were alone, David took pains to explain to me that he hadn't run after Jake when he left the room because that would have made things worse for Jake in Mr.

Goldberg's eyes. And although he hadn't been successful in convincing his father, at least not outwardly, David had said his piece and felt confident that it would have some effect down the road, that his father would take his words into account the next time. As to whether Mr. Goldberg would carry through on his threat to disown his middle son, David had nothing to say.

THE MCKINSEY OFFER was rescinded less than twenty-four hours later. When their HR department phoned Jake, they were very apologetic. It turned out that the mining and metals practice he had been invited to join was just about to go through a restructuring that the hiring manager had been unaware of, and his role had been eliminated. They offered to pay Jake a year's salary in severance for his trouble, and to avoid a lawsuit. Jake was so disappointed he could barely speak or look Mr. Goldberg in the eye for a week. He didn't accept the money, although I think I would have, at least then. I might even have sued. But Jake didn't need the money.

4

IN THE BEGINNING of our university careers, Mr. Goldberg went
to David's plays, but with each passing year he became less and
less comfortable in his seat. By the end of our second year, he
started fidgeting before he sat down. He became how I had imagined he would be at that first production at LCC, where David had
played Juliet and I'd expected Mr. Goldberg to be scandalized.
Not that David played women's parts anymore. There were more
than enough women in university theatre classes to go around.
But David's interest in drama, tolerated when he was thirteen,
was increasingly troubling to Mr. Goldberg now that David was
halfway through university and approaching twenty-one.

I didn't have any of Mr. Goldberg's misgivings about David's
acting. As I proceeded through my pre-law studies in history and
business, I allowed myself to be mesmerized by David's plays and
fellow actors. He was undeniably set apart by his talent, but he
wasn't the only one. More than twenty-five years later, I don't
think I've seen better Duncans and Lady Macbeths, Witches and
Poloniuses anywhere, not even in London and certainly not on
the screen. I'm not talking about technique that can be learned

but rather raw talent. I'm not sure if it was the youth of the actors or the times — the innocent mid-eighties — or, most likely, my young, impressionable age, but there seemed to be an oversupply of dramatic talent at McGill. We were all young and overconfident and determined to succeed in our chosen professions and to conquer the world.

The would-be lawyers in my classes were no different in that respect than the would-be professional actors, just not as creative or expressive or as dead set on beating the career odds. I didn't waste any of my time thinking that most of the theatre students would eventually give up on their quest after one failed audition too many and end up in accounting or management, or perhaps sales or politics, where they could put their gifts to good use. But even then, I knew David was special. Just like Jane. There are some people who you just know will succeed in their chosen profession, and I would include Allan Keyes — and to a lesser extent my old childhood friends, Eli and Michael — in that exalted category.

Eli and Michael were going to McGill as well, and I would occasionally run into them. I didn't yet know Allan personally, didn't yet know what he was destined for politically, but we all knew of him, and we all knew he was the finance minister's son. I watched him from the periphery as Michael and Eli were drawn into his orbit. Although we had already grown apart after six years of separate schools, I was in the cafeteria the day Eli and Michael helped Allan launch his political career with a bid for student council, and I was also in the sparse audience when Eli gave the poetry reading that caused him to abandon his literary dreams, at least for a while, until he found something worth writing about.

As I watched the three of them from afar, it was clear that Allan was sweeping up Eli in his gravitational pull, but I could already see that Michael was going to chart a different course, choosing to remain aloof so he could preserve his objectivity and right to comment. Jane knew Eli and Michael too, from the neighbourhood and from the Department of English, where she took theatre and Eli took his literature and writing courses. Both Eli and Michael would eventually find their respective ways and become who they were meant to be, but Allan found his political talent early at McGill, and, as with David and Jane's acting, it was obvious to all of us. My mother called this kind of self-evident talent a "gift," and I remember her telling me when I was a boy that I had my own gifts and had a "responsibility to use them," at a time when I had no idea what my "gifts" might be. I think she meant it as a lesser form of destiny.

TOWARD THE END of the first semester in our final year, David played Mark Antony in Shakespeare's *Julius Caesar*. His rendition of the ironic "I come to bury Caesar not to praise him" speech was pitch-perfect. Afterward, when he had taken his bow, changed into his jeans and T-shirt, wiped most of the makeup from his face, and emerged flushed from the changing room, I saw him approached by an older man who had been sitting in the front row. They spoke for about ten minutes, and then the man passed David his card and shook his hand a little too warmly for a little too long.

Later that evening, we went out for beers with much of the cast and their entourage. After Jane had gone down to the other end of the table to talk to a first-year actor who she thought was talented, David leaned over and, with a degree of pride that he rarely allowed himself, told me that the man was a casting director who worked both sides of the Atlantic with all the famous

Italian-American and Italian directors: Coppola and Scorsese regularly, and on occasion Bertolucci and Zeffirelli. He had been in town visiting family and, on a whim, had decided to take in a play. Impressed with David, he had invited him to Hollywood for a screen test. He was convinced that David had the right amount of presence and talent to make it in movies. "They want to bring me out for a week in the spring." If anybody else had told me that, anybody else other than Jane, I would have been skeptical, not necessarily of the teller but of the talent scout or agent's flattery. But because it was David, I knew the praise and attention were well deserved.

At the same time David was being courted by Hollywood agents, Jane was being wooed by theatres in London. Even then, in the beginning, Jane and I somehow refrained from ever talking about the future. We knew it was there in front of us, waiting for each of us after graduation, but we didn't know how we would both fit into it together. I was going to study law and then go to work for the Goldbergs. Jane never had any desire to appear in movies. All she ever wanted was to act on the stage.

I WASN'T THERE when David told Mr. Goldberg he was going to LA for his screen test, but he told me about it afterward. He let his father know he was going two days before he left, but only after the plane ticket and hotel had already been booked.

According to David, Mr. Goldberg didn't raise his voice or become sarcastic. He said little, offering only to fly him out on one of his two private jets. When David refused, Mr. Goldberg asked if he could introduce David to a couple producers that he knew, which was a surprise to David because Mr. Goldberg never travelled to LA and had never spoken about any Hollywood connections. We all knew that Mr. Goldberg hated Hollywood. This paternal offer was also politely refused. David left on his own, on a commercial flight, the day after acing his last exam, for the 300-level course Money, Banking & Government Policy.

A WEEK LATER, David was back. We weren't yet using email, so I didn't hear from him while he was gone. He called me on Sunday morning to go for a run on Mount Royal. He picked me up, and we drove over to the parking lot at Beaver Lake in silence. He didn't speak about his week in Hollywood until we'd left the man-made pond behind us and were jogging toward the summit. When he did speak, he didn't look at me. "They want me to audition for a role in a movie. Either Coppola or Scorsese."

I glanced over at him. He wasn't celebrating; he was a man intent on his jogging. He didn't have a congenital fascination with the glamour and beauty and talent of Hollywood. I've never stopped being surprised by how even the most wealthy and powerful can become children in the presence of celebrity. But David wasn't like that. He already had all of it. When it came to Hollywood, David was simply an aspiring professional having trouble believing he had just got his break.

"In addition to the screen test, they've seen me in *Macbeth*. And *Caesar*. Professor Roberts must have sent a tape. I think the screen test was just an excuse to get me out there." Professor Roberts was David's favourite professor and director. I was happy for David and proud of him; although I had never known anybody before who had been invited to Hollywood, I was not surprised.

It was just a regular Sunday on Mount Royal. David was just an ordinary guy out for a run. But he still wasn't meeting my eye. I could run faster than him for short distances, yet he could run

seemingly forever without losing his breath. He usually kept to
a moderate pace, but today he was running fast. He still wasn't
looking at me. And then, as we passed the rolling hills that people
spread themselves out on to worship the sun in summer and that
children tobogganed down in winter and moved onto the wide
dirt path shared by walkers, joggers, cyclers, and the occasional
horse-drawn *calèche*, I understood his refusal to celebrate.

When I asked, "What does your dad think?" I knew it was the
obvious question. But David seemed relieved that it was now out
in the open, that he would be responding to a question rather than
volunteering information about his father. I realized it had always
been this way with David. Unlike Sammy, who never missed an
opportunity to openly admire his father, or Jake, who always
found a way to deliberately omit Mr. Goldberg from conversation, David neither brought him up in conversation nor shied
away from the subject when someone else did.

David looked at me and said, "What do you think?" and in
that question, thrown back at me, he reminded me of Jake. It
was a classic Jake response, never to answer a question about
his father. David must have sensed this, because he went on to
answer himself. "He's upset. Actually, I think it's the first time he's
ever been really angry with me." This seemed incredible, knowing
what I already knew by this time about Mr. Goldberg. But I also
knew that with David, the usual rules didn't apply.

"Didn't he offer to fly you out?"

"Yes, but that was just his way of exerting some level of control. He hates Hollywood. Hates everything about it. Thinks acting's for women and children."

I didn't have to ask the question for my own benefit, but knew
I had to keep prompting him. David wanted to talk but didn't
want to do it voluntarily. "But I thought he enjoyed your acting?"

David looked at me again and turned back to the path, which was growing crowded. "My high school plays, yes. My university plays, less so." He laughed. There was no bitterness or rancour.

David slowed his pace a little. We ran in silence, and then I asked, as I was supposed to, "Why is that?"

David laughed again. Not only was his laugh still not bitter, there was actually affection in it. "In high school I was a boy, a *yingele*. Now I am a *man*, and only a few months away from officially starting in the family business." He had allowed himself an imitation of his father's voice, but, like a good actor, he didn't overdo it, and he stopped there. Again, I filled in the blanks, saying what had to be said so that David didn't have to be the first one to state it, so he could just confirm.

"And Goldbergs don't go to Hollywood, they go into gold mining?"

"Exactly." And David laughed again. "At least the male Goldbergs, which is all we have. Somehow, I think if I had a sister and she wanted to be an actress, my father wouldn't be so against it. He wouldn't be all for it, but there'd be less pressure on a daughter to go into the family business."

We jogged together without saying anything until we were almost at the summit. When I was a boy, Declan had taken me for walks on the mountain. Like men of his generation and trade, Declan didn't jog. He didn't work out. He spent every day engaged in some form of hard labour, and he didn't have to sweat out his intellectual anxieties or pursue a semblance of physical perfection at a gym. But we used to walk together for hours on the weekends. Sometimes Mary would come.

Declan wasn't one for history or geography or explaining to me what I was seeing as we walked. But Mary was. It was Mary who told me during one of our walks that Mount Royal had once been a volcano. For years afterward, when I was still a boy, I would step softly on the paved footpath, with both anticipation and trepidation, because I expected the mountain to erupt at any small step. When Declan, Mary, and I reached what I always thought of as the summit, and the path ended in a small circle of asphalt, I assumed with the confidence of a boy that we were standing on the mouth of the volcano that men like my father had mightily sealed one day so that families like ours could safely take our Sunday walks.

It was at this exact spot that I asked David what he was going to do. He nodded and motioned back toward the path, indicating we should start our descent. He didn't say anything until we were halfway down, and then he spoke, very matter-of-factly. "I'm going to go for it."

I was happy for him. He was in an enviable and rare position. He could try to make it in Hollywood, but if he failed, he wouldn't have to settle for a life of waiting tables or teaching drama to children in church basements. There was always a billion-dollar family business to return to.

A WEEK AFTER our conversation on Mount Royal, David called to tell me the Hollywood opportunity had dried up. "The casting director told me they've decided to go in a different direction. It happens more often than not. Like a novel or screenplay getting optioned. Most never get made."

"Is that true of both the Scorsese and Coppola movies?"

He said, "Yes," and stopped. This time, I didn't prompt him, and he went on, his voice the same as always except a little quieter. "After rehearsal today, Professor Roberts called me aside. He acted normally during the rehearsal except for the fact he kept looking at me, more often than usual." Said without arrogance. "But when he started speaking, he was so angry he was shaking. He usually speaks in well-ordered paragraphs, and he could hardly put a sentence together. He was actually spluttering. And swearing." Pause. "About my father." David stopped again, incredulous for what seemed like the first time in his life.

Silence, and then a few words. "He said my father was behind it." And then more silence. I said nothing. David went on, trying at nonchalance, at reflection: "I don't know how Professor Roberts knows this, he must be more connected than I thought. Apparently, my father knows some money men — that's what they call them — who finance a few big producers."

Neither of us should have been surprised. Jake's coveted offer from McKinsey had been rescinded immediately after Mr. Goldberg had spoken to the managing partner. But despite this, it was difficult to believe that the same thing was happening to David. I had always assumed he had special dispensation, the Goldberg family version of diplomatic immunity.

David was speaking objectively now, as if he were talking about someone else. I think Roberts's outburst gave David the licence to sound reasonable, above the fray. "After he calmed down, Roberts told me not to give up, that he knew people in London who might be able to get me into British films or TV or at least onto the stage. I think in the end he felt embarrassed about swearing and calling my father crazy. He realized that despite everything, he was still talking about my father. Roberts gave me a big hug — something he's never done before — and said, 'Whatever you do, Davey, don't give up on your dreams!' I swear he had a tear in his eye, a real tear, not the dramatic ones he sometimes manages to coax forth." David actually laughed.

I was quiet for a while before I asked, "So what happens now?"

"Now I do what I think I've always known I'd have to do."
No dramatic pause. No deep breath. Certainly no sigh. David
even mustered up a smile. "Now, young Mr. McFall, I will put
away childish things and go into the family business."

DAVID'S FINAL PRODUCTION was fewer than two weeks away,
and I wasn't sure how he would be able to focus or motivate himself. But he did. He was cast in a good role for his swan song. He
received a standing ovation for his Lear. I still don't know how he
did it. The part itself is nearly impossible to play for most actors
without enough real age and experience and self-awareness, even
accumulated disappointment, in which to anchor their technique.
But there wasn't a second on stage that you would doubt David
was indeed Lear: Lear with all his age and pains and vanity, his
anger and confusion.

By this time, Mr. Goldberg wasn't attending most of David's
performances, and he wasn't in the audience for this one. It was
his loss. He missed the last and best performance of his youngest son's dramatic career. As for David, he never brought up
Hollywood or acting again. As far as I know, he never spoke with
his father about what had happened. He carried on, just as before,
but without the acting. And the day after he graduated, he cut his
hair short — businessman-like — and was officially welcomed
into the family firm, like his brothers before him. Sammy, who
had already been working at Goldberg Limited for five years, was
oblivious to this change. I think Mr. Goldberg pretended to be.
But after David cut his hair and started working at the company,
Jake started to treat him differently — every time he looked at
David from then on, it was with a doubled sort of regret.

5

AS DAVID'S ACTING career was prematurely winding down, Jane's was taking off. Hollywood agents had been sending her flowers and inviting her out for drinks since the middle of her third year, but she was having none of it. She had her sights set on the stages of London's West End. When the call came to act in London, it nearly tore us apart.

WE HAD BEEN spending the weekend at the Goldberg country house in North Hatley. Jane and I had been up most of the night, unable to fall asleep. She was lying on my shoulder when she lifted her head, leaned over me, and looked into my eyes. "Come with me to London."

When it first became clear that Jane was going to London to pursue her career, it had occurred to me in a moment of insanity that she would have been better off with David. A billionaire was more equipped to handle a transatlantic romance; a private plane would come in handy. I didn't want to sound harsher than I intended, even as I was careful to whisper because David was sleeping in the bedroom next door. "I can't. I need to work for the Goldbergs."

"Why? David is lovely, but there are people like the Goldbergs all over the world. I'm sure we could find someone to take their place in London. Besides, you're not even working for them yet, and you can study law in London."

"I need to study here. I need to stay close to them." Jane's style of acting was one of great restraint, and she wasn't given to dramatic gestures, but here she rolled her eyes. I asked, "Why don't you stay with me in Montréal?"

"And, what, act for the CBC?"

"You could still travel to act. Your base would be Montréal. You'd be close to New York."

I knew I was stretching geography, and she didn't even pretend to think about it. She frowned. "I don't think that would work. I need to be at the centre of it all. London. At least when I'm starting off."

"Well, that's the same with me and the Goldbergs."

Jane moved away from me and lay on her back. She was too polite to accuse me of preferring the Goldbergs in Montréal to sleeping with her every night in London, but it was a testimony to her skill as an actor or to the closeness of our relationship that the accusation hung in the air. When she finally spoke, it was so quietly I nearly didn't hear her. "It's not the same."

I was fully awake now. "What do you mean?"

"Acting and gold mining, they're not the same."

I wanted us to continue arguing just so I could hear Jane's voice. It was the first time I realized I might lose her, and it was better to hear her voice than not to, even if we were fighting.

I was preparing to respond to her assertion, to tell her that she could act anywhere but that I only knew of one gold mining company and it was run by my friends, but she pre-empted my comment when she said, "Working for the Goldbergs is not the same. Remember what Mr. Goldberg did to David's acting career?"

As she had known, there was nothing I could say in reply to this. There was nothing else that Mr. Goldberg could have done to his son that would have been worse in her eyes. After a while, we both turned away from each other and eventually fell asleep. Jane left for London a month later.

SHE DIDN'T LEAVE "for good," as she put it, and we didn't break up. With the confidence of youth, we set ourselves up for not just a long-distance relationship but a transatlantic one. We resolved to do this for at least the next three years, as long as it would take for me to finish law school and for Jane to see how her career would evolve. The Goldbergs gave me an office job in their company every summer, and rather than spending my money on beer and spring break trips to Florida, I saved it for flights to visit Jane.

My week-long jet-lagged visits to London were all the same. I'd watch Jane in whatever play she was in, and then we'd go to the flat that she shared with two other actresses. Each time I arrived, they would be solicitous and giggling and would leave us the flat, and we'd make love until the early morning. Each time, we would avoid conversation about anything important for as long as possible until, inevitably, one of us would bring it up. Jane would ask me to move to London, and I would ask her to move back to Montréal. Each of us would politely, and sometimes not very politely, refuse. We would distract ourselves from fighting about it by taking in ancient statues at the British Museum or paintings at the National Portrait Gallery, or sometimes we'd take a day trip to Oxford, and in these ways our short days and nights together would too quickly elapse.

I would return to Montréal disappointed and jet-lagged, trying not to fall asleep in my law classes; Jane would put on her makeup and costumes and take to the stage, resulting in glowing reviews. Neither of us wanted to give up what we wanted. Somehow, three whole years passed this way, and we stayed together even though most of the time we were on separate continents. Then I graduated from law school.

After sitting for three years beside intelligent and driven men and women who wanted to either rule the world or change it, I graduated at the top of my class. Later, at Goldberg Limited, Chief Legal Officer Ira Levin told me the old law school joke: "Do you know what they call the guy who graduates last in his class in law school?" He waited a few seconds before delivering the punchline: "A lawyer!" It was Ira's way of reminding me that not all lawyers were created equal and that it was incumbent upon me to be not just a good one in the service of the Goldbergs but a great one.

It was at McGill's law school that I learned how to write unimpeachable contracts and argue winning briefs in moot Supreme Court cases. It was also where I learned all the tricks of debating and the deep dark secret at the hearts of most of the men and women who are sworn to uphold the law — that which side is right depends on who is paying your legal bills.

Throughout it all, I managed to demonstrate the patience that Sammy had no time for, that was easy for Jake because he loved school, and that David didn't think about, but that for me was an effort because all I wanted to do was graduate so I could work full-time at Goldberg Limited and join my friend, making my mark and earning real money. Jane flew back for my graduation, joining Declan and Mary in the audience at Salle Wilfrid-Pelletier. Mary wept as Declan sat stoically in the one suit he owned, holding her hand.

A FEW MONTHS before taking my bar exam, I'd flown to London and was ringing Jane's doorbell. She opened the door to her flat, and as I reached out to take her in my arms, she spun me slowly around and pushed me against the wall of her narrow hallway, holding on to my shoulders at the same time.

"Sean." Her eyes were shining. I thought she must have landed a big part in a big play.

"Yes?"

"I'm pregnant."

I was too surprised to think. We seemed too young. "I thought you were on the pill?" It sounded stupid as I was saying it.

"Yeah?"

I shook my head. "Are you going to keep it?"'

"Of course," she said as she moved slightly away from me. "Never any doubt. And the baby's not an 'it.'"

"Right. What about us?"

"What about us?"

I felt dizzy. My mouth was dry. Then I backed away from the wall and, like someone I imagined in an old-fashioned novel, got down on my knee and asked Jane to marry me.

She said yes.

LATER THAT NIGHT, after we'd made love, Jane turned toward me and rested her hand on my chest.

"You don't have to marry me, you know."

I put my hand on top of hers. "I know."

"Okay."

We were married six weeks later in a small ceremony in Oxford. David was my best man. I flew Declan and Mary over, and Jane's parents were there as well. We showed off London to our parents in the days before the wedding, and for our honeymoon we took a train up to the Scottish Highlands, where, for a week, we hiked the hills and slept in castles after making love each night with the energy and optimism of the young. It was only after we were married that I learned Jane wasn't quite ready to move back fully to Montréal.

ONE MONTH AFTER our wedding, when we were sitting outdoors at the café in Kew Gardens, Jane was ready to tell me exactly what being pregnant and getting married meant for us.

After three years, Jane had proved to herself that she could succeed on the London stage and realize the promise of her talent. She had reached an understanding with herself and, by extension, with me. She would take six months off to be with our baby in Montréal, then find us a nanny and return to London and the stage. She would spend six months of the year acting in London, where I would regularly visit her and bring our children — we both wanted more than one — every two weeks for a long weekend and always on holidays. The other six months she would spend with us in Montréal. The nanny Jane found for us was named Louisa. She had two children of her own back in the Philippines, but she took care of our children as if they were her own. Louisa travelled with us when we went to London, and she stayed with us when Jane came back to Montréal. We lived this way for twenty-three years.

MY MOTHER LOVED Jane, and I believe Declan did too in his own undemonstrative way, but I'm sure they wondered if we would stay together after we graduated from university and she moved to London. I also think that even after we were married, they still saw her as the little girl who had moved in across the street a few years after they had bought their house. But they were always respectful of our life and our decisions, and they rarely asked about how things were between us, at least not directly. But one night, after I'd been in law school for six months and had just come back from my second trip to London, and I was refusing to shower because I could still smell Jane on my body, my mother said to me at dinner, after she'd served the mashed potatoes, "And how is Jane?"

I answered, perhaps a little too quickly, "I think Jane is fine."

Declan raised his eyebrows and said nothing, but my mother said, "You think, Sean? Or you know?"

"I think, Mom. I think I know."

Mary looked down at her plate, taking small forkfuls of the fine supper she had made, and without looking up at me she said, "And you, Sean? What about you? How are you?" Slight pause. Almost apologetic tone. "With, you know, your Jane being so far away?"

I remembered feeling like a little kid again. Angry and needy at the same time. Answering, "I *think* I'm fine." Impatient with the question but at twenty-two years of age still wanting my mother to put her hand on mine and tell me it would be all right and wanting my father to squeeze me in one of his tight hugs. But ever since LCC, hugs from my father had grown few and far between, and after I had started at McGill, even my mother had begun to treat me with a peculiar deference, as if I were somehow now beyond her yellowing collection of Victorian and European novels and her ability to teach me things. And so, when I insisted I was fine, all my mother said was, "If you say so, Sean." We didn't speak much more during the rest of our meal.

To her credit, my mother never said another thing about Jane and our long-distance relationship, neither the partial outsourcing of the raising of our children nor the fact that Jane lived away from us for six months of the year. Not surprisingly, Declan never mentioned it either, but he would have found it both puzzling and expected. It was just another way I was different from him. They both took their grandparent duties seriously. Mary doted on each child, and Declan was quietly amazed and then outwardly delighted every time one of his grandchildren wanted to climb up on his lap and wrestle with him. I was lucky to have them nearby.

We had Dylan, named after a favourite uncle of Declan's, and Bridget, named for a great-grandmother of Jane's. We could have stopped there, content with a boy and a girl — what Mary excitedly told me was called a "millionaire's family" before she blushed because she knew that with my legal degree and my job with the Goldbergs, I was well on my way to becoming one. But five years after the birth of Bridget, we had one more, a daughter whom we named Fiona.

Jane always came home to Montréal to give birth, and she always took six months off before returning to an even bigger and better role in London. Dylan and Bridget and then Fiona got used to travelling the five hours to London from Montréal, and when the trips were short, we dealt with our jet lag by keeping to our Montréal time zone while in London. Each time we made the flight, I silently thanked the Goldbergs for paying me well enough to make it all possible.

PART THREE

Goldberg Limited
1990–2010

1

BEFORE I STARTED my first year of university, I had been promised a job at Goldberg Limited by Mr. Goldberg, chairman, CEO, and majority shareholder. First it was a part-time job after my BA while I attended law school and then a full-time job upon graduation with my Bachelor of Laws. It wasn't a blank cheque from Mr. Goldberg; it was understood that the fulfillment of this promise was contingent upon my graduating what the Americans would call *summa cum laude* but which we Canadians prosaically just call graduating with straight As.

While Mr. Goldberg liked to remind us that nothing in life was a given, especially the opportunity to be part of running a gold company, my successful graduations were predictable given how hard I studied. I did graduate at the top of my class, both in my BA and in law school, but despite Mr. Goldberg's promise and my successful academic career, I nearly didn't ever start full-time at Goldberg Limited.

TWO WEEKS BEFORE I was supposed to start my full-time job, David met me downtown and took me out for a beer at Gert's, the McGill student pub. He ordered us each a tall draft, clinked glasses, and said the traditional Jewish toast, *L'Chaim* — to life! He followed that up with, "To the newest illustrious member of the firm, young Mr. Sean McFall," while smiling and winking. I thought it was presumptuous of him, but at the time I didn't know to what extent. The way David smiled at me that afternoon reminded me of when I had first met him. David had aged well; he was still blond, happy, charming, and confident. Only bigger.

As I was thinking how much he had grown, he did something that reminded me of a twelve-year-old boy. It wasn't how he took a big gulp of beer, burped, and didn't bother to excuse himself. It was the way he leaned in toward me like someone about to engage in a childish conspiracy. I could smell his beery breath and tried not to let it show on my face. "Now, I'm sure you're excited about starting your new job. But before you do, I have to let you in on a little secret."

Several thoughts crossed my mind. Was this where David confided that his father was a tyrant who yelled at people in the office? That wouldn't have been a surprise — I had always assumed it was the case. Or was this where my friend gave me the man-to-man talk about working in a corporation, where I might think everyone worked as a team but really they were all ready to backstab their rivals at every opportunity? Or was this where David, with a sheepish grin, confessed that Goldberg Limited practiced a reverse form of discrimination, where the minority oppressed the majority to make up for millennia of anti-Semitism? Any of these scenarios would have been preferable to what David did tell me, although at the time I thought he was joking and didn't properly appreciate that what he was delivering was a warning.

"Now don't be put off by what I'm about to tell you," David began, speaking thoughtfully, taking a long sip of beer before continuing. "The company is a great company." David always referred to Goldberg as *the* company. Never by its proper name, which I always assumed David thought sounded pretentious given how it was his own. And never *our* company, which is the way he and his family encouraged all the other employees to refer to it; I assumed he thought *our* company sounded too arrogant when spoken by one of its controlling shareholders.

"You will enjoy being part of it, but my father has some old-fashioned ideas." He took another sip of beer and swirled it around in his mouth so forcefully that I thought he was going to tell me that his father secretly liked to drink beer. "One such idea is what people have come to call the Honesty Test." I must have made a strange face, although it was probably the beer. Even after seven years of university, I still hadn't developed a taste for it. "The test has another name, its proper name, but nobody can remember what it is. Everybody just calls it the Honesty Test, although not in front of our family." And then David was silent, as if he didn't know how to go on.

I decided to help him out by saying, "Because it tests your honesty?"

At this David brightened and said, "Exactly," as if I had done him a great favour and he hadn't noticed I was gently making fun of him. I believe he would have left it there, and together we would have had a shallowly profound student conversation over beer at Gert's, but he felt responsible for me, and so he forced himself to continue. "There are a lot of questions on the test, and, well, it's important you answer them in the right way." He stopped again and stared into his glass. In the decade I had known him, I had never seen him so awkward, so at a loss for words. In retrospect, we must have both led charmed lives and had a charmed friendship because this was the most difficult conversation we had ever had. As it was happening, I didn't know why David was having so much trouble. He always knew exactly what to say and how to say it, and, more importantly, what to do.

Wanting to help him out again, I said with an encouraging smile, "The right way of being honest?" I think now he realized I was making fun of him, which he normally didn't mind, but that day he looked miserable, and I didn't know enough about what he was talking about to make fun of him in what might have been the right way.

"Exactly. There's a strong, how shall I say, *law and order* orientation."

I didn't know what to respond to this, so I thanked him and changed the topic. Less than a week later, I took the test and nearly failed.

A FEW DAYS after my conversation with David, I was called by Rob Goldstein, the aptly named head of Goldberg HR, to come in to do the test at the Goldberg offices. As David had said, the Honesty Test had a proper name, but even though I spent two hours with that test, I still can't remember it. Later, I learned that other companies used the same test, but that knowledge didn't help me at the time or afterward.

It looked harmless enough initially, like one of those mindless multiple-choice quizzes they give you in high school to test your knowledge in a way that will take up the minimum of your teacher's time in marking. I turned the cover page, not knowing what to expect despite David's awkward attempts to prepare me and not being concerned in the least.

The first question was easy: *Have you ever taken anything more valuable than office supplies from your place of employment?*

The only part-time office job I had ever had was with Goldberg Limited. I had never taken a pen home from there or anywhere else, not from school and not from the depanneur on Monkland where I had worked part-time in high school. I circled "No" and thought David had been overreacting. But as I circled "No," I remembered that once when I was very young, four or five, Declan had taken us on a week's vacation in Maine.

WE HAD STOPPED at a fruit stand in one of the small coastal towns, and I had helped myself to three cherries while my mother was carefully placing peaches and plums in clear plastic bags and weighing each bag before settling on the amount she wanted to buy. I had kept the cherry pits in my mouth and spat them out only when we were walking away from the stand and said nothing of this to either Mary or Declan. But that night as I tried to fall asleep, a deep, fearful, adult realization came over me: *I had stolen.* Even though it was only three cherries, I had taken fruit without paying for it, without telling my parents, and I had spat away the evidence.

I couldn't enjoy the rest of the vacation. I would forget what had happened during the day while Declan was playing with me on the beach or in the cold ocean, as we threw a ball around and collected snails, as Mary watched us protectively in between pages of her book. But each night, as I lay in bed, I was sure the police were going to come to that small motel on the highway and take me away.

I PAUSED BEFORE going on to the next question. I had, in fact, stolen something. It hadn't been from a place of work, and I'm not sure how much three cherries would have been worth in Maine in the early 1970s. But the memory caused me to pause and to question my honesty.

The next question was more complicated. *When using a vending machine, have you ever received more change in return than was due, and, if so, did you pocket the extra amount of change or did you leave it for the vending machine proprietor* — this was the word the test used — *to pick up when he next made his rounds?* I paused again. I didn't remember it ever happening to me. The closest I had come to it was when I had found a twenty-dollar bill at the local pool where my friends and I spent most of our summers.

I FOUND THE bill at the bottom of the shallow end. When I pulled it out of the water, I was surprised to feel that it was still intact, more like a piece of material than paper. I hadn't even thought of pocketing it; I had taken it straight over to the lifeguards' office and handed it over. The lifeguard on duty, a teenager who seemed impossibly tall and sophisticated at the time, looked at me like I was lacking some essential mental capacity and took the bill from me gingerly. He thanked me for turning it in and suggested I check in a few days. He said if nobody came to claim it, I could keep it. Two days later, when I stopped in to ask if anybody had come to assert their right to the twenty-dollar bill that had been found at the bottom of the pool, not one of the lifeguards remembered me, let alone seemed to know what I was talking about.

ENCOURAGED BY THIS memory of my probity, if also my naïveté, I answered with a clear conscience that I had never received extra change from a vending machine. I felt proud and relieved, as if my assumed morality on this question somehow made up for my more juvenile theft of the cherries.

I remember the vending machine question because I thought about it whenever I went to a vending machine for years afterward and because it was the last simple question on the test. From then on, the Honesty Test became highly problematic, and I finally understood why David had been so apologetic and had had so much trouble explaining it to me.

Because the next question was this: *Have you ever thought about robbing a bank?*

On its own, the question was innocuous. It was obviously designed to determine whether a potential employee had ever seriously considered robbing a bank. And if that was the intent, I think I could have truthfully answered that no, I had not. But the fact of the matter was that I had *thought* about robbing a bank. Just not seriously.

We lived a few short blocks away from a bank branch, and as a boy I had thought more than once about tunnelling from my basement to the basement of the bank, where I assumed they kept the vault. In grade six, I hadn't yet met the Goldbergs, and it was a couple years before the armed robbery at the Goldberg *landhuis* in Curaçao, but that year I read a biography of Jesse James and how he and his well-mannered gang would rob trains and banks. While I never seriously wanted to grow up to be a bank robber like Jesse or his brother, Frank, I did wonder what it would be like to walk into a bank and demand money. I thought about it at first from a purely pragmatic point of view: how could it be done? And then I found myself wondering, what would it *feel* like?

I never felt guilty about this, the way I did for years afterward about stealing those three cherries. I always felt I was simply exercising my right to use my imagination. But as I stared down at that black-and-white question, I found myself faltering. There was no middle answer that would most closely relate to my reality. I had thought about robbing a bank, but only in the imaginative sense, the way you read a book or watch a movie and put yourself in the shoes of a character. But I hadn't ever *really* thought about robbing a bank, not the way the creators of the test were thinking.

I could have easily answered "No" and gone on to the next question, but something held me back. It took me a full minute of reflection to recognize that I was offended by the presumption of the question, by the erroneous conclusion that would be reached about me if I answered truthfully. But I was even more offended that anybody, let alone my future employer, would dare to ask me about my *thoughts*, as if they had a right, as if any of my thoughts alone could be wrong.

I stayed motionless for twenty minutes, and I thought about putting down my pencil and walking out, withdrawing myself as a candidate. But in the end, I concluded that if I walked out, I would be letting David down, and I really did want to work at Goldberg Limited. So after all that thinking, I very quickly circled "No." But that was the first question on the Honesty Test where after I answered I felt like a fraud.

If I had trouble with the bank robbery question, the next question was even worse: *If you knew your mother stole five dollars from her employer, would you report her to the police?* At first I thought I had misread the question, so I read it again. Then I thought it must be a joke. Then I thought it was a trick question. Surely nobody would turn their own mother over to the police for much, let alone such a petty theft? This had to be one of the questions planted to separate the moral wheat from the chaff, the truthful, honourable would-be employees from the flamboyant liars. Anybody who answered this question in the affirmative would obviously be disqualified, the way you automatically failed your driving test if you ever went up on the curb.

I knew that I would never report Mary to the police for anything, short of perhaps premeditated murder. But the thought of Mary stealing anything, let alone murdering anyone, was beyond absurd. I knew without having to think about it that if my mother ever stole anything, she would have had a very good reason. She would have been desperate. She would only have done it to protect Declan or me from starvation or some comparable disaster. I would never turn her in.

I was about to circle "No" when a reverse sort of panic seized me. What if this question was not a trick question; what if there really was no room for interpretation? What if the test symbolized the hard, unyielding line on law and order that David had tried so uncomfortably to warn me of? What if the ethical standard at Goldberg was set so high that they expected their employees to turn in their own mothers?

For the second time during the test, I was paralyzed by indecision and now also by a growing sense of resentment at what was expected of me. It was only thinking back to David's embarrassment in the McGill student pub, his uncharacteristic inability to articulate what he was trying to tell me about the Honesty Test coupled with his wish that I should approach it properly and pass it, that caused me to quickly and shamefully circle "Yes," I would indeed turn in my mother. My face turned red, I silently begged forgiveness of Mary for telling this blasphemous lie and betraying her in my mind, and I put my head in my hands for a few minutes before I was able to go on.

But the last question was the worst. As I read it, I pictured the man who had come up with it coldly chuckling as he proceeded to type it out. It was Kafkaesque. It was uncompromising in its starkness, its lack of irony, its almost Orwellian deceitful clarity and triumph.

Have you ever lied?

The test creators had waited until the test was nearly over to ask the fundamental question, the one that called into question all that come before. Everything up to this point had been rehearsal.

Here I paused for even longer than I had at the question about whether I'd turn in my mother. I stood up and walked around the small room, grew warm, and closed the exam paper. I looked at my watch and found I had spent over an hour and a half on the test. I sat back down, reopened the exam paper, and read it from the beginning to the end. In checking my answers, I found I had answered more truthfully than not, but I had lied over twenty-five percent of the time. Surely the examiners would figure this out. Undoubtedly this final question, like the one about turning in your mother, was another trick question. Who had ever been alive who had never lied? There couldn't be anyone. What about white lies? Or harmless lies by omission? The question had to be ironic. Nobody could ask this question with a straight face.

I was about to circle "Yes" when I realized that if I did so, then whoever was marking the test would have to go back through it, and all my answers would be suspect to them. Clearly the honest thing to do would be to answer that yes, of course I had lied, on isolated occasions and without major negative consequences. But then if I had lied, I was by definition not honest, and I wouldn't get hired. I was damned if I did and damned if I didn't.

In the end, I thought back again to David's inarticulate advice, his obvious discomfort, and I perjured myself a final time and answered that I had never lied. I left that little room thinking that not only would I find out in a week's time that I hadn't been hired, I would be branded a liar in the eyes of the Goldbergs and, most importantly, in David's eyes, and because of this test, I would lose both the job I had wanted before I even started it and my best friend.

WHEN ROB GOLDSTEIN phoned the next morning, I had to hold myself back from apologizing for failing the test before he finished saying hello. And when he said congratulations, I had passed the test — whose proper name I still don't remember — with flying colours and asked if I could start the following Monday, I felt only a strange sort of hate, the likes of which I had never known before the Honesty Test. For the first time, I hated the Goldbergs — not David, but the Goldbergs in general — for making me write the test, I hated myself for guessing right about how it should be completed, and most of all I hated myself for completing it the way I had. I felt that I had lowered myself, and I resolved that one day, when I rose to a suitable position of power at Goldberg Limited, I would convince Mr. Goldberg — for I assumed the test was required by him and not by David — that it should be retired. Or, failing that, I was confident that if David succeeded Mr. Goldberg, he would abolish the test as one of his first acts as CEO.

I like to think David was pleased that I passed the Honesty Test so I could formally join him full-time at his company, but we didn't see each other for a few days following the test, and when we did, we didn't speak about it. The first few times we saw each other afterward we were quieter than usual and seemed to find it difficult to meet each other's eyes. What do two friends do when one knows the other is a liar, and one knows the other's family turns people into liars? I never mentioned it, and after a while, things between David and me returned to the way they were before. It wasn't until much later that I appreciated how ironic it was that I had to lie in order to go forward and eventually learn the truth.

2

THOSE WHO DON'T work in business, particularly big business, tend to believe all corporate people are loud and boisterous and only think about money. But the reality, as with many deeply held beliefs, is different.

Many corporations are full of quiet men and women who have egos they can manage, people who know how to keep their tempers in check. This is because most people know you don't get to the top of a corporation by making enemies. You have to play the long game, outlast and outwit your enemies. Many of them take a patient and political approach where they keep their cards close to their chests and don't stab their rivals in the back until they absolutely have to.

The internal political manoeuvring found at most corporations is even less apparent in a privately held, family-owned corporation, or even one like Goldberg Limited that was publicly traded but family controlled. This is because everybody in a family-owned company who is not a member of the family knows that no matter how good they are, no matter how smart or hardworking or valuable, they're never going to get the top job. They might go far, they might run a division and get paid very well, but they're never going to run the company. And this knowledge tends to attract a certain kind of person — quiet, low ego, usually introverted — at least in the larger, more established family companies. These senior executives tend to be foils to the family themselves, who are naturally not bound by the same low-key conventions of behaviour. While his middle and youngest sons were different from him, whenever Mr. Goldberg walked into a room you knew he was there. He lit it up with his golden glow.

It's in the smaller family-owned companies where non-family egos tend to run wild. Companies are like dogs this way: the smaller ones are full of bark and bite, always willing to take offence, on the hunt for insults. But the larger ones are quieter and more docile, more reflective, run by thoughtful executives. One such executive was Ira Levin, chief legal officer at Goldberg Limited.

Ira was forty-something with well-coiffed hair, immaculately tailored suits, and bushy black eyebrows. He had been Mr. Goldberg's lawyer for years. The Goldberg corporate legend was that a thirty-five-year-old Mr. Goldberg had needed a Montréal lawyer to write up a contract on a Saturday for the purchase of his cottage in North Hatley. The problem was that every Jewish lawyer that Mr. Goldberg reached out to was observing the Sabbath. Except for newly minted lawyer Ira, who answered his phone on the first ring.

THE FIRST FEW months in any job are frightening and humbling because everybody around you knows more than you do: how to act in meetings, what happened last year, where the bathrooms are. It was Ira who taught me everything I needed to know about working for the Goldbergs, at least in the beginning.

On my first day of work, Ira took me to Schwartz's for lunch. We could have gone to Ben's Delicatessen downtown with its signed photos of celebrities covering the walls — Ben's was still open then and was closer to our office — but Ira liked tiny Schwartz's on St. Laurent because it was not as fancy and all the waiters knew him. We went early to beat the line that always ran outside past the homeless who sat on their flattened cardboard boxes on the street, and we ordered our smoked meat sandwiches and cherry Cokes as soon as we got a table. Ira didn't speak to me until he finished half his sandwich. Every few minutes, he wiped the fat dribbling down his chin with a napkin, but he wasn't in a rush.

"Sean, you're going to work with Mr. Goldberg and the boys, but as a lawyer you're going to report to me. Because I'll be responsible for you and because I want you to be successful, I'm going to share a few things."

"Thank you."

"Did you ever read Clausewitz's *On War?*"

I'd heard about it in one of my history classes but hadn't read it. I shook my head.

Ira nodded in a worldly way, as if to suggest that nobody read anymore, not even young lawyers. "Clausewitz was a Prussian general who fought Napoleon. After Napoleon's defeat, Clausewitz wrote a book in which he tried to set down everything he'd learned during the Napoleonic Wars. At one point, Clausewitz says you can divide an army's leadership into four kinds of officers." And Ira proceeded to punctuate every subsequent point with the stab of a pickle. "The first kind is stupid and lazy, and Clausewitz says you kick these guys out of the army. The second kind is stupid but hardworking, and these officers are needed, so you keep them busy. The third kind is intelligent and hardworking: these officers are very valuable. They form the core of your officer cadre. But the fourth class of officers, the *crème de la crème*, if I can use that expression, is intelligent *and* lazy. These are the ones you invest time in and promote. They will become your greatest generals. Do you know why?"

I shook my head.

"It's because they don't just do what they're supposed to. They're motivated to find simpler, better ways of doing things."

I nodded.

"Mr. Goldberg has three sons. Lucky for him — and us — none of them is stupid or lazy, *kenahora*, may the evil eye stay away. But to best help them, you need to figure out where each of them fits." Ira knew I was closest to David, but he also knew I was loyal to all three brothers. In large part this was because they were David's family, but it was also because I liked them. I was tempted to ask Ira where he thought I fit into Clausewitz's categories. But I knew that he would have said one of two things. If he was feeling uncharitable, he would have said I wasn't an officer but an aide-de-camp, an adviser to officers. If he was feeling generous, he would have put me in the third category: intelligent and hardworking.

Ira ordered another cherry Coke. "Next piece of advice. This one applies to conversations both inside and outside the company. It's particularly important in the early days of your career." Ira slurped noisily. "Never be the first one to speak in a meeting. Always listen carefully before you say anything. Make sure you know where everybody stands before you open your mouth. People naturally want to oppose each other — men are a bit like dogs that way — so don't signal your position too early and don't reveal your vested interest, if you have one. Generally, try not to have one, but sometimes it's unavoidable. Napoleon planned each battle to a certain extent, but he never over-planned; he waited until he was halfway into it before committing his best troops. Only then could he see where his enemy's biggest weakness was and only then could he know exactly where to throw his greatest concentration of force."

I nodded, and Ira seemed pleased with my quiet agreement.

"Now I want to get to the important stuff. Where you and I stand in relation to the family." Ira leaned back in his chair. "The Goldbergs are family, and we all work in the same company. But everyone knows that you're" — he pointed at me — "David's man. And I," — he jabbed at himself with his thumb — "I'm Mr. Goldberg's man. It's important we both acknowledge that up front and never lose sight of it." At the time, I didn't really appreciate what Ira was saying. I heard the words. I understood them intellectually, but I didn't yet have enough experience with the Goldbergs to make sense of what Ira was really trying to tell me. I do remember wondering why Sammy and Jake didn't have their own "man." But Ira didn't explain, and I didn't ask.

Ira stared at me from under his bushy black eyebrows. "One final lesson. Don't ever forget it. It's the most important one. The longer you stay here, the harder it will be to remember." Ira pulled his napkin off his lap and folded it. "As high as you rise at Goldberg Limited, as powerful as you become, as trusted as you think you are ... don't ever forget this: you will *never* be a Goldberg." Ira watched intently for my reaction, which I hoped was suitably impressed, and looked at his watch. He took a final slurp of cherry Coke. It was time to get back to work.

In my early years with the company, Ira taught me a lot about corporate law. But it was during this conversation that Ira shared with me almost all the core tenets of his wisdom. It was Ira who opened my eyes to the militaristic majesty of business and to the position that each of us who was outside the Goldberg family occupied in relation to them. Every subsequent conversation we had was a variation on the themes he'd expounded on that first day. As we got to know each other better, Ira increasingly let me make my own way and gave me less and less advice. It was not until much later that he confided the essence of his long-term strategy. Even then, I still didn't fully appreciate what he was telling me until it was too late.

3

THE FIRST TIME I saw the original mine — the one Abraham had founded and that formed the foundation of the Goldberg wealth and corporate empire — I was sitting in the back of a Jeep, squeezed between David and Jake. I had just started working full-time at Goldberg Limited, and the sun was rising.

Sammy was in the front passenger seat, and Mr. Goldberg was driving. Not only did Mr. Goldberg like to drive, but he also liked to come across as a man of the people. So, while he permitted himself a white Mercedes in Montréal, it was a Jeep up at the mine, and it was only on vacation in Curaçao or Europe that he drove his really flashy vehicles. A golden Land Rover on the island and a silver Bentley in Europe. Closer to home, he liked his image of the relatively frugal, penny-pinching CEO.

Although Mr. Goldberg didn't give many media interviews, this down-to-earth persona was featured in more than one gushing profile in the *Globe and Mail*. "The gold baron who drives a Jeep" was how my childhood friend turned journalist Michael Appleby once phrased it. And it was a great talking point whenever Mr.

Goldberg was bidding for another company, selecting a supplier, or negotiating — or more likely breaking — the rare union that we inherited with an acquisition. Everyone sitting on the other side of the table knew he wasn't wasteful.

We had left Montréal at 4:30 a.m., and after we landed at the private airport that Abraham had built in northern Québec, we drove for about fifteen minutes along a bumpy dirt road, emerging at the top of a hill with a clear view of the valley below. Several hundred metres below us and about a kilometre away, with the sun starting to rise behind it, was the original Goldberg mine. It was called Springtime, in commemoration of the season in which Abraham had made his first trip to the region and in tribute to his mother, Aviva, whose name meant spring. In the weeks leading up the visit to the mine, David had told me a little about his great-grandmother Aviva, the Goldberg family matriarch. She had emigrated with her husband from Poland near the end of the nineteenth century. Her husband had died soon after arrival and just before Abraham was born. Alone in a new country, Aviva taught herself English while working two jobs so that Abraham could stay in school.

I ALREADY KNEW by this time that Mr. Goldberg paid close attention to names. "Names are destiny," he told me once while driving us back to his house after school. I don't remember what had set him off. He might have been complaining about how successive Québec governments kept changing the English names of well-known streets into French ones. Mary had once explained to me that when the English conquered Québec a couple hundred years earlier, they had replaced the French names of streets with English ones. Yet when Burnside became de Maisonneuve or Dorchester was renamed René Lévesque, Mr. Goldberg didn't seem to think rewriting old wrongs was any sort of excuse.

Mr. Goldberg didn't say anything about the apt family name he had inherited or the first name he had been given. He focused only on the names he had chosen for his sons. "Why did I give you boys biblical names? It's not just because we're Jewish. It's because I want you to have biblical destinies. I want you to prosper and multiply like grains of sand on the beach and grow tall and smite our enemies — in the courtroom, in the markets, on the seas, on the stock market, in the boardroom, in this vast, empty country that doesn't know how lucky it is to be situated at the top of the continent, sitting across the American empire while it is still strong, separated from its enemies by oceans on two sides and a wilderness of ice on top. Samuel. Jacob. David."

Mr. Goldberg paused after each name; at the mention of their respective names, his three sons reacted. Jake stared out the window. Sammy, sitting in the front seat as usual, turned to his father and waited on his every word. David winked at me. "Warriors. Judges. Prophets. Kings." Each word enunciated slowly. "Imagine if I had called one of you Bob? Or Jeff? Or Stu? What would you have amounted to?" Mr. Goldberg looked at me in the rear-view mirror.

Mr. Goldberg had met his general objective of choosing biblical names for his children, but the intent of his particular choices was not readily apparent. I knew by this time that Samuel meant "God has heard." One of the last ruling judges of the Old Testament, he anointed both Saul and David. I knew Jacob meant "supplanter," and this was because Jacob had cheated his brother Esau out of his inheritance. And I knew that David meant "beloved." I knew all this because I had looked it up. The choice of David's name was the only one that made any sense to me as far as Mr. Goldberg was concerned, but I could only assume he had his reasons. Funnily enough, I didn't look up the meaning of my own name until much later. I think this was because I expected my name to mean nothing, at least compared to the Goldbergs, certainly nothing biblical. But I eventually learned, when I took the trouble to look, that Sean is an Irish version of John, from the ancient Hebrew Jonathan. It means "God is gracious" or "God has given." Jonathan was the oldest son of King Saul and a close friend of the future King David.

But it was only from Solomon, years after I had got to know him, when he was sitting opposite me in a booth at a hotel bar in Europe drinking moderately, that I learned Jonathan's fate. "Do you know the story of Jonathan, Sean?" Solomon asked. That was typical of Solomon, to ask questions out of nowhere. Questions to which he alone seemed to have the answers. "He died in battle with his father, Saul, and his two other brothers. Fighting the Philistines, of all people. Saul is wounded by an arrow and doesn't want to be captured alive, so he asks his armourbearer to kill him. When the man refuses, Saul falls on his own sword. The Philistines cut off his head and strip him of his armour. Jonathan dies too, with less detail devoted to describing how. David is heartbroken. But then he becomes king."

As for his own name, to most of us he was always Mr. Goldberg. When you start off knowing someone from the disadvantaged position of youth, general inferiority, or weakness, it is not easy to shift the terms of that relationship, even when you grow older, become an equal, or grow stronger. So it was with Mr. Goldberg when I started working at his company. He had long been an adult to my child, and he was the father of my friend, so I had always called him "Mr." without thinking of it, and I continued to do so. But after I began working at Goldberg Limited, I was surprised to see that we all called him Mr. Goldberg. Except his sons.

As for their first names, Sammy preferred Samuel because that's what his father preferred. We all called him Sammy. Jacob insisted on calling himself Jake as an act of rebellion. Although David liked to sometimes be called Dave by his friends, because it was more familiar, I always called him David. Mr. Goldberg hated nicknames or even abbreviations of names. He insisted on calling everyone by their proper names, even his sons, and even others when they preferred Bob to Robert or Steve to Stephen. One executive, a thirty-year veteran in the mining business who was hired to run finance, always introduced himself as "Jim." When Jim was about to send his first email to employees, Mr. Goldberg demanded to see a printed draft and crossed out "Jim" at the bottom, replacing it with "James." The executive came to see him and explained to Mr. Goldberg that he always went by "Jim." Mr. Goldberg insisted on "James." After they had gone back and forth on this two or three times, the executive stood up and said quietly, "Fuck this. I'm done." He turned and walked out of the room. Mr. Goldberg accepted his resignation without comment.

MR. GOLDBERG MIGHT have paid attention to the art of naming, but I thought his father, Abraham, must have lacked the talent. The mine didn't look anything like spring, and nothing in my upbringing had prepared me for the sight of an open pit mine reflecting the early morning sun. Nothing had readied me to see its stark beauty.

It was an immense gap in the untouched landscape, a circular labyrinth descending deep into the ground, a static whirlpool carved into the beige-grey rock. I knew, even at that distance, even with my still-limited knowledge, that the trucks I saw on the road built against the walls of the rock must have been oversized, but they appeared so small I was reminded of ants working on an anthill.

But, most of all, the open pit mine, with its layers and grooves — which I later learned were called benches — carved into the rock and tapering to a level spot at the bottom, made me think of the inside of a wasp's nest that I had seen once under the roof of our back porch.

The day Declan found it, he told us to stay inside while he went out, as dusk fell in a humid Montréal summer, with a can of wasp spray. After I had come home from school, Declan had taken me along to buy the can and explained he had to spray the nest after dark when the wasps were sluggish.

I watched through the screened window in our kitchen as Declan lifted the spray can, pressed the trigger, and soaked the nest. One or two wasps — I thought of them as sentries — came out to engage Declan in battle and protect their home. But it was no match. Declan stopped them in mid-flight with a burst from his can, and they fell to the ground. Their gold-and-black-striped bodies bounced off the floorboards of the porch, making a light crackling sound as they hit the wood. The rest died inside.

The next morning, Declan woke me up early and took me to the nest. He reached up, gently took it down, and let me hold it. It was light and delicate. He cut it in half with his Swiss Army knife to let me see inside, but first he shook out the dense clump of dead wasps gathered at the bottom. They were all dead except for one larva that was still twitching. Declan threw the dead wasps and the still-alive larva away into the grass, and he gave me the nest to keep. It was a delicate, almost translucent thing the colour of dulled gold and made up of layers of light material, tapered at each end.

At the Goldberg mine, I couldn't help seeing the small yellow-and-black trucks carrying dirt and ore out of the pit as hardworking wasps. The image stayed with me, and I was reminded of it each time I came to visit.

Mr. Goldberg stopped the Jeep to survey the massive operation that he owned and controlled and that lived and breathed at his command. He took it in like an emperor reviewing the action in the arena, as if he knew he could stop it any time, throw the men out of work, turn it off. Usually so talkative, he said nothing for a moment. On later trips, I learned this was a ritual for Mr. Goldberg. He would stop at that particular point and look down with his sharp eyes. Even at that distance, he would notice things: too many trucks or too few, trucks that were moving too quickly or too slowly.

After about ten minutes, Mr. Goldberg restarted the Jeep and took us down into the mine. We drove slowly, in ever diminishing circles. It took longer than I expected When we were halfway down, I was struck by how foreign and familiar the mine was. I felt at home as if I had not just seen the mine before but had been down in it. When we reached the bottom, we didn't stop. Mr. Goldberg took the trouble to smile and wave at every driver whose truck we passed, and they all waved proudly back. Whenever Mr. Goldberg knew a driver personally, he shouted at them through the open windows, "Bonjour, Michel" or "Good to see you, Angus," and sometimes he gave his favourites thumbs-ups or pumped his fist.

When he was ready, Mr. Goldberg drove us up out of the mine and over to the administration building where the mine manager was waiting. He snapped to attention when we arrived, as if Mr. Goldberg were a four-star general. It was here that I began to learn the lesson that most men, no matter how competent, want to be led. They want to please those they consider more powerful than themselves. They want to be appreciated and valued by those they consider their superiors.

The mine manager ushered us into his office, and here began Mr. Goldberg's third ritual on any visit to the mine.

He began with the simple words: "So, John, how are things?" The mine manager, whose name was John Malcolm, began to answer. Over time, I would see this was how all their conversations began, but I also soon learned that John Malcolm would rarely get to finish his response in full because after Mr. Goldberg had his answer, but before John Malcom was completely done speaking, Mr. Goldberg would ask another question or make an observation that might as well have been a question. It might be, "Why are there so many trucks in operation?" Or "I only saw a few trucks today." Sometimes there should have been more trucks and sometimes there should have been fewer, and each time John Malcolm couldn't answer correctly or couldn't answer at all, Mr. Goldberg was asserting his dominance, and he would share his views on what was going wrong and what could be improved. It wasn't until later visits that I realized there was no way John Malcolm — or anyone else in the Goldberg empire for that matter, because Mr. Goldberg practiced this particular brand of questioning on all of his employees — could win. There were always too many questions that Mr. Goldberg could choose to ask and never enough answers for one man to ever keep in his head. John Malcolm was a great mine manager, but there was always at least one question that he couldn't answer, and he always gave at least one wrong answer.

This constant and relentless interviewing of the men who worked for him, even and especially the most senior ones, demonstrated Mr. Goldberg knew what was going on and constantly reminded them that he was boss, that his judgment was irrefutable. Talking to the mine manager was also Mr. Goldberg's way of teaching his sons, as deliberate as a polar bear teaching its cubs how to hunt: this is how it is done; this is how you exert control and reaffirm your influence over your environment and over the men you pay to work for you.

Sammy would pay attention to where his father was looking when he was out in the mine, trying to guess in advance what Mr. Goldberg would remark upon when they were in John Malcolm's office. I would watch Sammy closely. I don't think he was ever aware that he would smile when he guessed right and grimace when he guessed wrong. Jake would look the other way, as if watching his father watching the mine was too much to bear. David might look at the mine or away, but even when he looked at the mine, he wasn't following his father's gaze. He was looking to make his own observations, which he would file away, sometimes sharing them with me. In addition to watching the Goldberg sons, I watched the senior manager being interrogated to study his reactions. They were the same almost every time.

"There was a truck idling at the bottom of the pit."

"Yes, Mr. Goldberg." John Malcolm smiled proudly as if he were a teacher and his star pupil had noted the intricacies of a particularly difficult subject. He looked like my teachers at LCC when one of their wealthier students exceeded their expectations. "We're trying out something new, where we do the shift changes in the mine instead of driving all the way back to the garage. Rather than bringing our trucks back to the men, we're bringing our men to the trucks. It's saving us forty man-hours per day."

Mr. Goldberg smiled. "Very good, John, very good." Whenever Mr. Goldberg smiled at work, he smiled like a boy, innocent and conspiratorial and expecting those around to smile with him.

John Malcolm smiled in turn. "Thank you, Mr. Goldberg."

"And the men, they are well?" This was Mr. Goldberg's way of asking whether the men were content with their pay, their working conditions, their foremen, their senior leaders, and therefore would not attempt to unionize. I think Mr. Goldberg lived in fear of this prospect because he knew it would have disappointed Abraham if the family couldn't maintain their direct relationship with the workers. He detested unions. He'd once told me that they were organized laziness.

John Malcolm replied, "Yes, Mr. Goldberg. The men are good. Productivity is high."

"Good to hear; let's keep it that way. New winter jackets this year. Make sure you can see the logo clearly. Put it on the left side of the chest. And on the back."

On the jackets that John Malcolm had ordered for the men the year before, the Goldberg logo hadn't been to Mr. Goldberg's liking. It was smaller than usual and hard to make out at a distance. The Goldberg Limited logo was simply the name of the family in an art deco–style black font, set inside a golden rectangle. It looked like a heavy gold bar.

4

HOW ABRAHAM FOUND what became the original Goldberg mine was legendary, at least in corporate mining circles. I heard the story first from David, but the official version would eventually be written down in a company-funded book, the type specially designed for the occasion by a well-known Québec artisanal printer and accompanied by colour photographs taken by a celebrated Québec photographer and captured in prose by the famous Québec journalist and my old friend: Michael Appleby. Michael didn't usually lend his name to corporate vanity projects, but that reluctance was temporarily discarded after the re-election of Allan Keyes as prime minister in 2008.

This was the election in which Michael got the prime minister on his cellphone saying disparaging things about Canadians. Old-fashioned and fair-playing Michael, still thinking of traditional print deadlines, asked for a comment but didn't immediately file his story. After Eli fictionalized the whole incident in his first book, *Sons and Fathers*, Michael took a sabbatical from his full-time reporting position and took on a few corporate writing projects with the express aim of making money. When he ended up returning to full-time journalism nine months later, I think he felt embarrassed by his brief sojourn as a corporate hack, and he never included the project for Goldberg Limited on his distinguished resumé.

ABRAHAM HAD JUST finished the third year of his mining engineering degree and had rented a car to drive up to Québec's north to look for iron ore deposits. It was early May 1913. It had been a snowy winter and a long, wet spring; the roads in the north were still muddy. Early on the afternoon of May 9, Abraham's car got stuck, halfway between Chibougamau and Mistissini. The more he tried to free the car, the more deeply his tires sank into the mud.

He had been working on extricating himself for four hours when Ahanu, a seventeen-year-old Cree from the Mistissini Nation, came across this tall, well-dressed blond man so hopelessly stuck in the mud. Ahanu was returning from a long but successful day during the annual spring hunt known as Goose Break. Ahanu was accompanied by three friends, and they each had a couple of geese draped around their necks.

Abraham didn't have any Cree vocabulary at this time, but Ahanu spoke English. Ahanu and his three friends cut down branches to put under the large wheels of Abraham's car, helping Abraham gain enough traction to drive onto a drier patch of road. The road ahead was still muddy, so Ahanu suggested that Abraham spend the night at his home. At least until the following day when warmer weather was expected and the roads would be drier. Abraham gratefully accepted and accompanied Ahanu and his friends to Mistissini. Ahanu's family prepared a feast, and Abraham was so welcomed that he ended up staying for a week.

Abraham and Ahanu found they had a shared interest in nature and books. By the time he was ready to leave Mistissini, Abraham had a hefty rental car bill, a small working vocabulary of forty-two Cree words, and a friend for life. He also had a good idea of where to stake the claim for what would become his first gold mine.

Ahanu had no desire to become involved in the mining business, so he freely shared his knowledge that for years, at an isolated site not too far away, the people of his community had been finding rocks with splashes of gold in them and taking them home as curiosities. Over the course of Abraham's stay, Ahanu showed him twenty such rocks displayed throughout the homes of several families. It was in this way that Abraham met many people in the community, and they got to know the young, tall mining student from Montréal with his good manners and earnest way of listening. Unlike some of the other white men from Montréal whom Ahanu's family had met before, Abraham wasn't loud or boastful or condescending. He was quiet and respectful, listened more than he spoke, and didn't ask any more questions than his new friends were willing to answer.

At the end of the week, Ahanu presented Abraham with a local Indigenous artist's drawing of a hunter stalking a caribou, which Abraham hung in his office and treasured for the rest of his life. Abraham didn't have anything of value with him, and so he told Ahanu that the next time they met, he would bring him something. Abraham didn't return for six months, but when he did, he brought Ahanu a new Model T Ford, which had just started to roll off the assembly lines five years before. More importantly, Abraham offered Ahanu a ten-percent equity stake in what was to become his first gold mine.

Recognizing that his future mine would be on the site of the Cree's traditional territory, Abraham entered into an equity partnership with them decades before it became fashionable or standard practice. But Ahanu was hesitant at first. He knew what it would entail and what the wealth could mean for him and his community; it took Abraham another six months and two more visits to convince Ahanu of the merits of such a partnership — and, of course, his father as well, for Ahanu would never have entered into such a business arrangement without the blessing of his father, who was the local chief.

Ahanu and his family remained near-silent minority partners of Goldberg Limited all through the rest of the twentieth century and into the twenty-first. In later years, when environmental activists liked to claim that all Indigenous communities were against development, Ahanu would make the occasional appearance in the media, always dressed in one of the slim Hugo Boss suits he loved, speak eloquently about what the mine had done for his community, and dispel the misconception that his people were oppressed. Ahanu left the actual business of running the mine up to Abraham and then his sons while Ahanu took care with his sons and daughters to build up businesses owned by his nation that started by serving the Goldberg mine and grew over time to serve other mines in the area.

THIS WAS THE lovely legend that Goldberg Limited shared with the world and captured for posterity in the approved history written by Michael Appleby. It was the kind of corporate origin story that, among other things, helped to make Goldberg Limited a darling in both Canadian corporate and left-wing circles. I had to wait years before Solomon and I knew each other well enough that he bothered to tell me the real story.

5

ABRAHAM HAD THE Goldberg Building built in 1933 at the height of the Depression. It was art deco, tapering in straight lines as it rose, designed by Ernest Cormier. Clad in white limestone, it shone like marble, and although it wasn't tall, at eighteen storeys, it made an impression.

Every Hannukah, the Goldbergs hosted a holiday reception for their employees on that eighteenth floor, the executive floor. In that first year of my career at Goldberg Limited, as in all the subsequent years, the employees who worked in the head office lined up and waited in the stairwell that led to the floor where Mr. Goldberg and his sons ruled over the company.

The employees started lining up at 11:00 a.m., a full hour before the Goldbergs were scheduled to take their places. At noon, the Goldbergs appeared at the top of the stairs, where Mr. Goldberg nodded and the line began to move. When the employees reached the top, Mr. Goldberg was standing there beaming, with his three sons beside him, like the head of a receiving line at a wedding. It was unlike most weddings in that there were no

women present in the receiving line but like a wedding in that a
very important, if unequal, union was being celebrated with every
handshake and with the handful of words that were exchanged.

I hadn't lined up right at 11:00 because I had work to do, and
by the time I reached the stairwell, the line stretched down seven
floors. I waited patiently and slowly advanced with the others,
and as I approached the Goldberg family, I saw their expressions,
but I couldn't see the employees' faces. I watched Mr. Goldberg
smiling, shaking hands heartily, and speaking to every employee
he knew for about ten seconds before, with a hearty, "Well, good
to see you. Happy Hannukah," he would pass them down the
line to his sons. Sammy was doing the same. It was clear the two
of them were working the crowd, conscious they were on display.
Jake was formal and stiff, clearly uncomfortable, as though he'd
rather be poring over geological reports or financial statements.
David looked relaxed, as if he were at home and not on the executive floor of his family business, greeting everyone as if they were
special, asking after them and their families. He seemed to know
something personal about each employee: where they had gone
to school or worked before if they were fairly young or new to
Goldberg Limited, the jobs they had held previously if they had
been with the company a long time, the names of their wives and
even sometimes of their children.

BUT AFTER I had passed through the holiday gauntlet, and after
Mr. Goldberg had smiled at me and asked me how such and such
a file was coming along, and after Sammy had made a joke about
some legal challenge, and after Jake had relaxed a little because
he knew that I knew how hard all this handshaking was for him,
and after David had shaken my hand with mock formality and

said something like, "Good afternoon, young Mr. McFall, so nice to see you at the firm. Thank you sincerely for all your many contributions," and made me laugh, I stood aside rather than mingle with the crowd at the tables of Hannukah snacks: potato latkes and sweet soufganiyot and the kosher wine that most others found tasted sickly sweet but that tasted to me comfortingly like grape juice. Instead of joining my fellow employees in their eating and merriment, I found a spot by the wall where I could now see the faces of the employees as they shook hands with the Goldbergs and watch how their expressions changed as they moved from one Goldberg to another. It didn't matter whether the employee was senior or junior, old or young, formal or informal, every single one had the same reaction to each of the Goldbergs.

In shaking Mr. Goldberg's hand, they were nervous and eager, excited and honoured that the great man himself was bestowing some attention on them. With Sammy they were pleased, taking in the resemblance to his father and sizing him up respectfully. You could see they were imagining what it would be like to have Sammy at the helm, to report to him, advise him. And then with Jake, they were as uncomfortable as he was with them. A tentative expression would cross their faces as they moved toward him, as if they weren't sure how to act, whether he would be more pleased with a firm handshake or a weak one, whether to be serious or jovial. They seemed to wonder what he thought of them, and inwardly they questioned why he was so unhappy as a scion of the Goldberg family, as someone who had more wealth than they would ever see. When they came to David, their expressions changed yet again. They became relaxed and happy as befitted the holiday occasion, and this time their expressions took on some individuality. David put each of them at ease so they could be who they were. And then they left David and mingled with the rest of their colleagues. The Hannukah reception that first year set a pattern for me that would follow for twenty more.

I must have seen Mr. Goldberg shake hands a hundred thousand times over the years. He was always on his best behaviour with his employees. But when he was outside the company, he fell into the habit that many powerful people fall into. If the person he was meeting with was also powerful or important to the fortunes of Goldberg Limited, then he assumed a hearty familiarity with them and took his time. But if they were not important to the success of Goldberg Limited, he looked as if he was in a bit of rush, and he wouldn't look them in the eye for more than the quick minimum of time necessary. Most people took this roving impatience of his for a form of great and unusual energy because Mr. Goldberg wouldn't be abrupt to the point of rudeness. He would smile at the person and make small talk, but the moment he turned away, his smile would vanish, and his symmetrical eyes would grow cold.

AFTER MY FIRST Goldberg Hannukah reception, David pulled me into his office and closed the door. "Well, now you know what it's like to run the Goldberg Hannukah gauntlet." He smiled and shook my hand in a mock-congratulatory way even though he had just spent nearly two hours shaking everyone's hand. I hadn't yet properly met Solomon, and so the years when I would run into him in December and he would say, "You must be coming from the Handshaking Holiday, otherwise known to the rest of the world outside the Goldberg empire as Hannukah," were still slightly in the future.

David had a sofa in his office on which he lay down with his hands crossed behind his head; I sat, facing him, in an armchair. He closed his eyes, and so I mostly closed mine, and we sat together in comfortable silence until David opened his eyes and said, in a voice that was clearly not his own, "The first thing you have to learn, young Mr. McFall, is how to shake hands." I'd heard David imitate his father many times before, and although David had just called me "young Mr. McFall" as his father liked to do, this was clearly someone else. And then David told me how his *zayde* Abraham had taught him and his brothers to shake hands.

THE FIRST TIME Abraham showed David how to shake hands, David remembered thinking that his *zayde* didn't have a miner's hands — they were long and pale with delicate fingers. David and his brothers were visiting Abraham at his house in Westmount, which was also on Sunnyside, when Abraham told them he was going to take them up to the mine. David was excited because he knew they were going to fly in Abraham's plane. He had a Twin Otter by then, but David had seen pictures of him in his original Tiger Moth on the walls of his office.

David was seven, Jake was eight, and Sammy must have been nine. Abraham sat them all down while he remained standing. David thought that his grandfather looked even taller than usual, even at his age, which would have been eighty. He didn't seem to have shrunk as he got older. And he'd kept his hair, although it was no longer blond but mostly a warm, soft grey.

Abraham began with the Yiddish word for grandchildren. "*Ainikles*, listen carefully. I'm going to teach you one of the most important things you're ever going to learn. And that's to shake hands. Okay?" He often said "okay" to them when he wanted to make sure they were getting his point. Even as a child, David knew that for an adult, especially one as successful as his grandfather, this recurring inquiry was an unusual custom to follow with young children. David knew that his *zayde* couldn't have ever started and grown a gold mining company without a certain innate toughness, but the way he would ask his grandchildren if they were okay before he proceeded was a sign to David of Abraham's infinite gentleness. "Sammy, stand up." Unlike his oldest son, Abraham had no compunction against using the shortened versions of people's names. Sammy jumped up.

Zayde Abraham extended his hand, and Sammy took it. Sammy must have heard somewhere that people judged you on the firmness of your handshake because he squeezed Abraham's hand like he was trying to milk a cow, and he had this funny expression of concentration on his face. Sammy was big at nine, and he was strong, but Abraham didn't appear to be put off by his efforts.

"Good to meet you," Abraham said.

"Good to meet you too," Sammy replied.

Then it was Jake's turn. The sequence was repeated. If Sammy's handshake was too strong, Jake's was too weak, too tentative. And his eye contact was poor, as if he were shy, even though he loved his *zayde* as much as his two brothers. But just as Abraham had said nothing more than "Good to meet you" when he shook Sammy's hand, he said the same words when he shook Jake's. Then it was David's turn.

Before his *zayde* had time to extend his hand, David extended his as he stood up. And before Abraham could say a thing, David looked into his *zayde*'s blue eyes and said, "Pleased to meet you." And then he took his grandfather's hand and shook it firmly, but not so heavily as Sammy had done.

Abraham smiled, clapped David on the shoulder, and turned to his brothers. "Always extend your hand first, if you can. The one who shakes first is in the position of power. Look the other person in the eye. Don't look away. Don't ever look down. Shake firmly but not too hard. A weak handshake is always worse than one that is too strong, but too strong is nearly as bad. A weak handshake means you're uncertain. But too strong is a sign you're insecure. When you're meeting men at the mine, as you will, always reach out and shake their hands first. Don't wait for them. When you're over at a friend's house and you meet their parents, don't just say, 'Hello.' Don't say nothing, God forbid. Look them in the eye and reach out and shake their hand. Okay?"

The next lesson was about asking. Not asking for help from a position of weakness, but practicing the owner's art of getting other men to do what you wanted them to do. Ever since David and his brothers could remember, Abraham never spoke to them as if they were children. He treated them like grown men. "The first thing about leading men is that you never order a man to do anything." At this, Sammy looked confused. "Whenever you do, the man being ordered loses something of his self-respect. Over time, that has an effect. It corrodes his spirit. It creates resentment. Many men are so used to taking orders that they've forgotten that underneath it, all they want is to be free. But they do. You always say please. And you always ask. 'John, could you please do this or that at the mine?' You need to make sure that the man hears the question mark at the end of your sentence. Okay?" And then he would have his grandchildren practice.

But he didn't leave it there. "When you have to ask a man to do something, don't summon him to your office. Go to his office if he has one, to his desk or truck or other place of his in the mine if he doesn't. Going to him is a sign of a respect, a sign that you judge him to be important. And whoever is asking for something is always the one who has to go to the other. Make small talk, but

not too much. Get to the point quickly. Explain what you need
help with, but don't make that the main point. The main point is
why you need this man to help. So, 'I'm expanding the mine, and
I'm going to need someone to manage it. It's got to be you because
nobody knows the mine as well as you.' The man you're asking
has to feel that he is the best person in the world for the job.

"In these situations, you have to resist the temptation to sell
them on the prospect, to make it sound easy or too attractive, as
if they will be getting something — an experience, an honour, a
promotion — for nothing or next to nothing. This is the worst
thing you can do. You never want to make what you're asking
sound *easy*. If you make a job sound easy, then it means it's not
special, and if it's not special, then the man you're asking for help
will conclude you don't think *he's* special. A man wants to feel
free and important and good at his job. You need to make whatever you're asking sound difficult. Like this: 'It's going to be a
long project, with many extra hours, time away from your family.
It's not going to be easy. This is why I'm asking *you*.' And nine
times out of ten, the man you're asking for help won't be able to
wait until you're done before he will say yes. He may even shout
it out." Then Abraham shared something else with David and
his brothers, and he didn't elaborate or try to explain. All he said
was, "But if you really want to motivate someone, don't ever tell
them exactly what to do: tell them what you need in the end from
them, but let them figure out how to get there for themselves."
And then he moved on to the third and final lesson of the day.

Abraham's final lesson that day was about saying thank you.
"This is the most important lesson I will ever teach you. Nothing
else in business comes close. Whenever anybody does a favour for
you, does work for you, holds the door open for you, gives you
advice, teaches you something, you say, 'Thank you.' You say it

quietly, and you say it sincerely. 'Thank you.' You speak slowly, and you look into their eyes. 'Thank you.' If it's a big thank you, you shake their hand as well. You say it in a way they will never forget, so they realize that at that moment in time they are the most important person in the world, because they have done something for *you*. Okay?"

The Goldberg grandchildren nodded. "Okay," Abraham said, "enough lessons for today."

Sammy and Jake got up to go, but when David stood up, he extended his hand to Abraham and said, very seriously, "Thank you, *Zayde*." But he winked as he said it, so Abraham would know David wasn't sucking up to him. Abraham burst out laughing.

By this time, Sammy and Jake had left the room. Abraham put both his old man's hands on David's shoulders and pulled him close, and David could smell his breath. It didn't smell bad, like old people's breath. It smelled like tobacco and peppermint. "There are three things you have to learn, *Davele*: how to shake hands, how to ask another man to do something for you, and how to say thank you. There are many other lessons in business, but these are the three most important ones I can teach you. You know them now."

Abraham made that lesson about saying thank you come to life a year later. David, Jake, Sammy, and Solomon had been up at the mine with him for the day. They had a meeting with the mine manager, a tour of the latest expansion, rides in the trucks with the men, and lots of discussion about things David was only just beginning to understand: labour, downtime, productivity, extraction, cyanidation, reliability, global prices, logistics. Abraham didn't leave his young *ainikles* with a secretary to watch over them and a book or a board game to keep them occupied while he worked, he let them tag along for all of it. At the time,

Abraham's work seemed the opposite of work to David; it looked like nothing more than talking, and most of that was taken up with asking questions. But David knew it was somehow still important.

At 8:00 p.m., Abraham got everyone back on the plane for the ninety-minute return flight to Montréal. He hadn't woken the four young Goldberg grandchildren up too early that morning, and he had seen that they were well fed over the course of the day, but still the day had been long, and they were all tired. Sammy had fallen asleep soon after takeoff, Jake looked like he was falling asleep over one of the books he was reading, and both David and Solomon sat on either side of Abraham on the long seat at the back of the plane, leaning up against his shoulders, slipping slowly into sleep, when Abraham suddenly stirred from the production reports he was reading and called out.

"Matthew?"

The co-pilot came back immediately. "Yes, Mr. Goldberg."

"Can you please tell Stephane" — Stephane was Abraham's favourite pilot — "that we have to go back to the mine?" Abraham sounded wide awake and unstressed, but adamant. David noticed that his grandfather was not ordering the pilots to return but was asking them.

"We're just about to land, Mr. Goldberg, but we can return." Matthew didn't ask why.

"Thank you."

David was awake by now and clearly thought something terrible must have occurred back at the mine that required his grandfather's presence. Sammy was still asleep, and Jake looked at Abraham over the top of his book, not saying anything. Only Solomon seemed calm, taking the abrupt change in plans in stride. David felt the plane bank sharply as Abraham turned to him and

Solomon in turn and said, with only a slight note of apology, "Remember in the cafeteria, when Cook Lefebvre served us pie?" David and his cousin nodded. "Well, I forgot to say thank you." Jake's eyes widened. Abraham pulled David and Solomon closer to him and started stroking their heads. By the time they arrived back at the mine, it was close to midnight, and all four boys were asleep. Abraham let them sleep while he went to see Cook Lefebvre, who was working the night shift. Abraham didn't wake his grandsons until they landed back in Montréal at close to 3:00 a.m.

"THAT WAS A late night," David said, "but usually Abraham coddled us when he took us up to the mine. Big meals. Lots of treats on the flight. Sometimes card games on the plane. He taught us how to play pinochle." David was smiling and stretching out on the couch. But then his smile wore away as a new thought took over. "Travelling with my father was different."

THE FIRST TIME Mr. Goldberg took his sons up to the mine, he woke them up at 3:00 a.m. There was no reason they had to be up so early. They had their own plane. They could have left at any time. Just like they could have had breakfast. But Mr. Goldberg rushed them out of the house and into the car. He drove, of course, up to the private terminal in Dorval where the Goldbergs kept their two planes and helicopter. The boys were hungry and complained; Mr. Goldberg gave them half a Mars bar each. They were in the air at 4:15. The boys kept falling asleep on the flight, but Mr. Goldberg kept waking them up. At one point he kicked Sammy in the leg. Mr. Goldberg punched Jake in the arm to wake him up, probably because he knew it would offend him. But Mr. Goldberg was gentle with David. He rubbed his head.

When Sammy asked why they couldn't sleep, Mr. Goldberg responded with, "You need to be thinking about the big day you have ahead of you."

"What's to think, Dad?" Sammy said without a trace of irony. He was still sleepy, which made it come out even more deferentially. Mr. Goldberg could be cruel with Sammy, partly because Sammy tried so hard to be like him. Mr. Goldberg said, "Not much in your case, Samuel." Sammy must have not been too deeply asleep, or perhaps he was already becoming attuned to Mr. Goldberg's insults, because when Sammy realized what his father had said to him, he looked hurt and embarrassed. Then he looked away. He didn't respond. Mr. Goldberg turned away in disgust.

Mr. Goldberg turned back to address his sons. "You're going to the mine. You never go anywhere without first understanding what you're about to see. Never. Understand?" And then he proceeded to tell them, in his own fashion, about the mine and the men who worked there. Who managed the mine and what his name was and his wife's name and how many children he had and where they were going to university. He told them when the mine was built and how much gold it produced in the course of a year and how much an ounce of 24-carat gold was currently worth on the market. David knew, even at that young age, that it was amazing, the number of facts about the mine that Mr. Goldberg seemed to have at his command, but even then, he began to suspect that for his father, knowledge was a different thing than for his *zayde*.

6

IT WAS ALMOST a year after my first Hannukah reception that I had my second encounter with Solomon. As I was coming out of the lounge at the Montréal airport, Solomon was coming in — whenever any of us at the company travelled on our own, we flew commercial and always economy. Mr. Goldberg thought the cost of a business class ticket was a personal affront. Solomon was in the early years of his career and didn't yet have a private jet. Even later, when he acquired a corporate fleet in one deal, he sold them off to finance another.

It had been a long day, and I didn't notice him at first. I hadn't seen him since that party at McGill more than five years earlier, and David had never told me anything about him other than his name. Jake told me later, in passing, that Solomon was their first cousin on their father's side. Solomon and I had just walked past each other, and he must have stopped because when I heard "Young Mr. McFall" and turned around, he was waiting for me. He was carrying a small leather briefcase over one shoulder and holding his jacket over the other. We were both in our mid-twenties then, but looking at Solomon, I was reminded of the expression on

David's face when he picked me for his team on my first day at LCC. Calm. Amused. Pleased with everything, including himself. Solomon's hair had never been as long as David's, and, like David, he now wore it short, but standing face to face, I recognized him. It was his smile and the Goldberg eyes.

I could have been rude, walked away out of some sense of loyalty to the Goldbergs I knew. But as on that first day at LCC when David summoned me over to his team before he even knew my name, I walked over to Solomon. Even though I was nearly fifteen years older than when I'd met David, I found myself again happy that I was being chosen. "Solomon."

As we shook hands, he smiled again. And then he said, in that half-serious, mostly mocking tone that reminded me of David, "I hear congratulations are in order." He looked like he was about to continue, so I didn't say anything, and he added, "For becoming my cousin's *consigliere*."

I didn't know what to say to this. Anything I chose would either be impolite to Solomon or a small betrayal of the Goldbergs I knew, so I smiled without commitment. But inside I, too, was now amused. We didn't talk much that day. Solomon was running late for his flight, but he asked, still smiling and drawing out his words, "So, how *is* life at the dark, fluttering heart of the Goldberg empire?"

At the time, I didn't yet know the story of Solomon's side of the family, but even in the course of our short conversation, I felt I was starting to know Solomon. I said without thinking, trying only to sound witty and neutral, "Still beating."

Solomon stopped smiling and nodded. He lifted his hand to the side of his head and gave a funny wave, halfway between a wave and a salute, and said, with that mock-serious way of speaking, "So long, Mr. McFall. Until we meet again." And then, not waiting for my reply, he turned and was gone, leaving me alone, feeling proud and slightly ashamed, as if I had again passed some sort of test but betrayed, in a small way, both David and myself in the process.

THIS WAS THE first of many random meetings with Solomon all over the world, but usually in mining or financial capitals: London, New York, Johannesburg, Brisbane, Toronto. In airport lounges and hotel bars, even though neither of us drank much. Each time we met, our conversation lasted a little longer, and over time Solomon began to tell me his story and that of his family. It was not apparently thought out, and it certainly wasn't linear, and I had to often wait months to hear the next chapter.

Each time I saw Solomon and he asked me to have a drink with him, I hesitated, wondering what David would think, knowing for certain what his father would. I have always been a risk-averse person — a trait that only deepened with my study of the law — although in my defence, I was never the kind of hand-wringing lawyer that Mr. Goldberg called "an old woman." Yet despite my natural risk aversion, I found myself nodding and acquiescing every time Solomon asked me to sit down with him. I never once refused, because Solomon so obviously wanted to talk, and because he reminded me of David. But a more open David with a family history that he actually wanted to share. I also never refused because each time Solomon told me part of his story, I found myself wanting to hear more.

I SAW SOLOMON every year at the four-day Prospectors and Developers Association of Canada conference in Toronto.

Everybody in the industry was there. The Goldbergs were always the most restrained, attending only the sessions they needed to in order to advance their interests, spending most of their time in the closed-door side meetings that make these events worthwhile, avoiding the drunken parties that went on late into the night.

Each time I saw Solomon, he always extended the same greeting as when he'd first walked past me in the Montréal airport. "Well, if it isn't young Mr. McFall. How are things these days at the dark, fluttering heart of the Goldberg empire?" After a few years, Solomon added another question to his friendly, ironic catechism. "And how, if I might inquire, is un-plain Jane?" The question always made me smile.

Solomon was my age, but he always had the ability to talk to me as if I were younger than him, to make me doubt myself, even with the simplest questions. I assumed that his style of communicating wasn't totally negative and that he also had the opposite ability of inspiring men with confidence.

Despite my position in Goldberg Limited and how far I had travelled since growing up in NDG, Solomon always made me feel out of my depth, like my first day at LCC. Whenever I ran into him, I found myself waiting to be asked the same set of questions. Whenever he asked me anything about his family or the company, I would try to be as noncommittal as possible. After my first witty reply that the heart of the Goldberg empire was still beating, I settled for a benign, "Things are good."

And then Solomon would continue with the same questions. "And my favourite uncle, he is keeping well?"

And I would give my same answers. "Keeping well."

"And my dear cousins?"

"Also well."

Here Solomon might take a sip of his drink. He was famous in hard-drinking mining circles for being a man who drank moderately. In this, he was like his uncle and his cousins from whom he was estranged. After university and after they took up their roles in the company, the Goldberg boys cut back on their drinking, and they never drank in front of Mr. Goldberg, unless it was the few ritual sips of Manischewitz on the eve of the Sabbath or High Holidays. None of them, not even David, ever explained to me why nobody in his family really drank. I always thought it was because they didn't want to give up any little bit of their power, their self-control, even to alcohol, even for just a few hours.

FOR REASONS I didn't understand until much later, out of all the third-generation Goldbergs, and arguably even of the second, Solomon was the closest to a self-made man of any of the family since Abraham. All I knew at the time was that, unlike David and his brothers, Solomon didn't seem to have a father. I had Jake to thank for that information.

A few weeks after I met Solomon for the second time, I found a way to ask Jake about him. I knew I wouldn't get the whole story from Jake and David's side of the family, but I wanted to know where Solomon fit into the Goldbergs. Rather than asking about Solomon directly, I asked Jake about Solomon's father. Jake didn't look surprised when I brought up the subject.

"Easy answer," was all Jake said. "Solomon's an orphan." And then Jake looked at me as if daring me to follow up with another question, and of course I didn't. I decided to rely on Solomon to tell me the story eventually.

SOLOMON WASN'T IN the family-owned business; he had had to start relatively small, making modest bets with what his father had left him, buying junk deposits or old mines that were believed to be depleted and bringing them back. In one of his earlier investments, a gold mine in BC that had opened before the Second World War, Solomon practiced crowdsourcing before the term had been invented. His initiative didn't get written up in any books, but he made the mine's original surveys public and successfully ran a competition for outside geologists to help him figure out where gold might still be found.

For these reasons, and unlike the other Goldbergs, Solomon had the pure, unapologetic confidence of the self-made man. Solomon hadn't started with nothing — he was like many successful entrepreneurs who turned their father's initial wealth into something far grander. He founded Iseli Gold, named after the first letters of his parents' first names, Isaac and Eliana. But he didn't have the corroding self-doubt that lurks at the centre of anyone who is even remotely self-aware and who finds themselves born to money. This doubt often expresses itself in the question *Could I have made this money on my own?* Ninety-nine times out of a hundred, the answer is no. I'm sure Jake knew the answer for him was no. David did his best not to think about it. Sammy probably never did. And I think Mr. Goldberg secretly thought about it all the time but tried his best not to answer it.

Solomon, on the other hand, earned some wisdom about himself as a result. He knew what he was accomplishing himself with his talent. But his wisdom wasn't only self-referential. He looked at everyone who worked closely with his uncle and cousins as if he knew something important that we didn't. It was more a blend of bemusement and concern than overt condescension. And this was how Solomon greeted his cousins whenever he encountered them. But on the odd occasions when Solomon saw Mr. Goldberg, at an event where he or Mr. Goldberg hadn't timed their respective entrance or exit properly, his detached mask slipped a little, and I saw something else. It was a look of patient hatred and amazement that Solomon first laid on his uncle, followed quickly by determination. Solomon had inherited the Goldberg eyes, and whenever he saw his uncle, his own eyelids would lower, and he would watch him like a smaller lizard watching a bigger one.

OVER TIME, AS he got to know me better and realized he had a listener, if not an audience, Solomon changed the way he was with me. His language became freer. But there was always a point to everything he said. He never quite lost his overall purpose. And, within the short span of a couple of years, without me really ever noticing it before it was too late, he slipped from ironically asking me how his estranged family was doing to making disparaging comments about them and then to telling me stories about them.

One day — I think we were in Melbourne — he said to me, "Sean, do you know what the difference is between starting your business from scratch and inheriting your father's?" I think I had my own views by this time, but I said no so Solomon could continue. "Five thousand years, more or less, the difference between barbarism and civilization. Working your way up in your father's business is like inheriting the family farm. Yes, you've got to wake up early and step in shit and learn the ropes, how to shovel out the stalls and milk the cows and slaughter the sheep, and you can lose it all if you're not hardworking or careful or lucky, but you have something to lose. You know that unless you really fuck it up, you're going to be able to feed your children at the end of the day.

"But when you start a business from nothing, it's like going out and hunting the woolly mammoth: you don't know if you're going to come home with something to eat at the end of the day or if you're going to get killed. There's no comparison. Most of the people in business, even the executives who make billion-dollar bets, perhaps especially them, don't have a fraction of the courage and business sense that the owner of the humblest franchise has. You're not taking any risks if the only thing at stake is whether your bonus that year is going to be a hundred percent or fifty percent. My uncle thinks he's tough; he may even be tough. But it's a second-hand toughness. It's an inherited toughness, like our family money. You can do something with it, but you always know in your heart that you didn't earn it."

This was a favourite theme with Solomon, the difference between the man who starts with nothing and the man who inherits his father's business, and it was one he returned to again and again, in different cities, on different continents. "My grandfather built a company. My uncle conquers companies. It's a totally different skill set, a totally different way of looking at the world. One is pure creation, making something out of nothing. You have a vision, and you go out and build it. My uncle, on the other hand, doesn't have a vision, unless it's to dominate the industry. He has surrounded himself with an entourage of advisers, investment bankers, acquisition artists, and corporate raiders, men who specialize in taking over companies and plundering them: firing their leadership teams, taking out the fat, and remaking them in his image. Of these, of course, it's Ira who's the greatest. He orders the others around as if he's pretending to be his favourite general." And then Solomon stopped, waiting for me to respond, to challenge him. But I remained silent, feeling like I was betraying Mr. Goldberg by not defending him, but not knowing what to say in his defence.

7

DURING THE YEARS of my career when I was running into Solomon in far-flung airports, I was travelling regularly to London. To see Jane, of course, but also frequently with David. Toronto might have remained Canada's mining capital after the hollowing out of the Canadian mining industry in the early 2000s and the reverse takeovers of any remaining companies in the decade after that, but London was the mining capital of the world. Although Mr. Goldberg had a thing about not watching his competitors too closely, he liked to get to London occasionally. David had no such compunction about spending time with competitors, talking to them, learning from them. London was never simply a city of plays or museums or restaurants for us. There were legitimate meetings to be had. But it didn't take me long to realize that for David, London was always about more than just business.

He loved London because he could shed the heavy mantle of his family name. The Russian oligarchs and new global exiles hadn't yet descended upon the city, but even then, London was already full of billionaires. David didn't have to keep up appearances, didn't have to be on his best behaviour in public as he was in Montréal, because in London, nobody was paying him special attention, nobody was judging him with the extra layer of harshness reserved for those who are much wealthier.

If we went to a restaurant in London and the food took too long to arrive or it was poorly prepared, David didn't appear to have second thoughts about mentioning the delay or returning it to the kitchen. He was polite in any complaint, just as he was polite in ordering anything, careful to start with "May I have?" rather than "Can I have" or, God forbid, "I'll have." But he wasn't worried that the server in a dark nightclub in a city of ten million people would go away with stories of serving a Goldberg that night and how he'd been "fucking rude" when he'd simply been standing up for himself in pointing out excessively slow service or an overcooked steak.

In London, thousands of miles from Montréal, David could let down, if only a little, the hair he had kept carefully trimmed since graduating from McGill. It was in London that David would drink and on occasion go dancing. The first time I saw him drink after the hothouse atmosphere of university, it was strange, like watching a teenager drink his father's alcohol. Then I got used to it. He wouldn't drink heavily in London, but he would have a few mixed drinks and go out to the best clubs. Sometimes he would drag Jane along at night, and, if I were in town, he might invite me as well. I didn't like to dance or to drink much, so I often sat at a table while the two of them danced. Not close, like lovers, but like good friends. To anyone watching who didn't know us, it would seem that David and Jane were the couple and I was the friend. Thankfully, by then this didn't bother me. I trusted both of them.

Sometimes David would go off on his own, disappearing for a day or two. One time, when he had stayed out all night, he was dropped off the next day by someone driving a silver Rolls-Royce.

I didn't recognize the man behind the wheel, but they hugged each other tightly as they parted. I assumed it was one of those wealthy friends that the rich seem to acquire so effortlessly all around the world. Whenever David disappeared like this, I never asked him where he had been, and he never volunteered; although I never asked Jane, I always had the sense that she knew more about it all than she ever let on.

ON ONE OF our trips to London, David suggested the three of us fly to Zurich the following morning.

Jane looked at him, and David said, "Just for the day. Maybe overnight."

"Why Zurich?"

"I want to show you something."

It was early in the week, and Jane didn't need to be on stage until Thursday. The meetings David and I were in London for had finished early, and Jane and I nodded at the same time. David always took the corporate plane to Europe, and so we took it to Zurich. The pilots had arranged a car for us when we landed, and when we got in, David said, in that polite but sometimes formal way that he had, "Driver, Baur au Lac, please."

When we arrived at the hotel, which had been owned and operated by the same family for a century and a half, David suggested we check in and meet on the outside terrace in fifteen minutes. It was there, in this luxury hotel on the shores of Lake Zurich, over a whisky and soda, that David said, "This is where it all happened." And then over dinner he proceeded to tell us how his grandfather Abraham had spent some of his time during the Second World War.

THE SECOND WORLD War was a period of great economic trial for the Goldbergs. By the time the war started, Abraham had been the owner and operator of a working gold mine for over two decades. He was doing well, but in 1940, the federal cabinet passed an Order in Council appointing a Metals Controller to manage the buying and selling of most metals in Canada, including gold. Prices were frozen at pre-war levels. In a great inversion of peacetime's laws of supply and demand, base metals were prioritized over precious ones because they were essential to the war effort. Companies that produced copper, zinc, and lead were given more freedom to invest in expanding their mines, while those that mined gold had great restrictions placed upon them and were only permitted to invest in the most basic of maintenance. While gold mining itself wasn't forbidden, because of the controls on capital expenditures for new equipment and how manpower was shifted into other mines, a number of gold mines across the country actually closed down. The war was a lost six years for the precious metals industry in Canada.

During this time, Abraham expended much of his energy maintaining the morale of his employees. Unlike the owners of other gold mines, who saw their workers being diverted to the mining of other metals, Mr. Goldberg retained his workforce and their loyalty, not by raising direct wages — which he was prohibited from doing by the wage controls decreed by the federal government — but by taking out corporate bonds in each worker's name that were paid off generously after the war. Unlike other owners dealing with a flat gold market — after increasing by fifty percent in the early thirties, gold prices remained relatively stagnant well into the 1970s before starting their great decades-long climb — Abraham had invested in the future.

The decades after the war were not easy ones. These were the years when growth came from volume and not margin. But during this time, and thanks to his patience and careful planning during the lean years, Abraham found a way to profit and grow. After building up large cash reserves in the thirties, Abraham was able to buy a number of the shuttered gold mines for cents on the dollar when the war ended, and he held on to them until the price of gold began to climb. And from 1940 to 1945, while his business was heavily restricted by the demands of the war, Abraham used the extra time on his hands for other purposes.

EVERY TWO MONTHS, starting in 1940 and continuing through the war's end, Abraham took a break from running the mine to fly to Europe on the Boeing 314 Clipper he had bought just before the war and somehow managed to retain when commercial fleets were pressed into wartime service. Abraham was a man ahead of his time, anticipating the golden age of air travel that would emerge in the post-war boom of the 1950s. The Clipper was a flying boat, built with a hull to land on water instead of landing gear, the first plane to fly across the Atlantic, albeit with a few refuelling stops, with room for passengers and luxury in the form of a dining area and lounge. At Pan Am, the same planes had four-star chefs. Abraham hired his own.

Abraham was an early adopter of aviation technology. In 1931, as he was approaching the height of his pre-war powers, Abraham had bought himself a plane. Characteristically, like many great businessmen who have the confidence and ability to learn new things quickly, Abraham bought the plane before he knew how to fly it, and he bought it both for business and for pleasure, which for him were one and the same. He wanted to be able to fly over his mine, to see it from the height of ten thousand feet, to have a sense of the land he was digging deep into, and to be able to visit parts of Canada that few people would ever even know existed. He bought one of the earliest Tiger Moths made by de Havilland, an old-fashioned biplane with double wings and open cockpit. Sammy showed it to me in the Goldberg hangar when we were teenagers. According to him, it still flew.

In 1940, the trip over the Atlantic was a long one, with at least one stop. Abraham wouldn't fly it all himself. He shared co-pilot duties with one of his company pilots. They flew overnight to Zurich by way of Iceland, laden with four leather suitcases. Three of those were specially reinforced with metal sides and a metal bottom, and each contained twenty gold bars. The fourth suitcase held sixty forged Canadian passports placed carefully between Abraham's pressed shirts and pants. Abraham and his co-pilot would fly over the North Atlantic, high above occupied France, until they reached their destination.

Once in neutral Zurich, insulated from the horrors of Europe by its range of postcard-perfect mountains and hidden bank accounts, Abraham was able to move freely. He was handsome, well-dressed, and looked German or Swiss. Most people who met him took him for a banker because of his clothes, quiet politeness, and the impression that he could keep a secret. In a sense they were right; he was a banker of sorts. In time, it was the nickname by which he was known by the Germans, the Swiss, and even some of the more ironic Jews: the Banker.

In 1943, gold was trading at U.S. $36 a troy ounce. With the average gold bar weighing in at 400 ounces, each bar was worth U.S. $14,400. And that was the price per Jew that Abraham and the Germans had settled on early in their negotiations. Nearly

$200,000 today. But as Abraham used to say, how can you put a value on a life? Abraham was happy to pay it, and the Germans he dealt with were happy to receive payment.

Abraham would meet "his" Germans, as he called them behind their backs, in one of the restaurants or bars at Baur au Lac, at the edge of Lake Zurich, with its view of the placid water and jagged mountains. The men he met with were high-ranking German diplomats or ss officers eager to make some money off the war. Each of the Germans involved pretended they were helping Jews flee Europe out of conscience. Abraham let them think he believed them. This little fiction helped to keep the conversations civilized, made it easier for Abraham to keep them from getting too greedy, and kept the price per head below $15,000.

Sometimes, the men Abraham met had women with them whom they would tell condescendingly to wait at the bar while they spoke business, and while these women sipped their drinks, they would watch Abraham with interest. He was tall and blond, and, as Abraham knew from the brief conversations he'd had with some of the women, more than a handful thought he might be a German spy or even a confidant of Hitler's. One admirer thought he looked like a kinder, handsomer Heydrich, which was considered a high compliment in certain circles at the time.

Abraham was a moderate drinker, but he drank heavily at these meetings. He said it put his Germans at ease. They would hand over the necessary papers, and, after the drinks, Abraham would invite these sellers of lives up to his room, where he would transfer possession of the gold bars.

Taken together, the golden contents of the three suitcases would buy the lives of sixty Jews. And the contents of the fourth suitcase would allow all sixty to travel out of neutral Switzerland on Abraham's Montréal-bound plane and to proceed with a minimum of fanfare through the very narrow doors of Canadian customs. Each of the passports was a carefully forged work of utilitarian art by Yitzhak Shmuel, a talented but unlucky Montréal portrait artist whom Abraham's wife, Golda, had taken on as a special project and rescued from poverty when he was selling his sketches for two dollars apiece.

Following the transfer of payments, things would move quickly. Abraham would be given an address. There would be ten rented cars waiting around the block from the hotel. He would jump into the first car and personally escort the rest to the address. With their motors and lights off, the cars would wait, lined up like a funeral procession. Except these cars were taking people not to the cemetery but to new lives.

At the address, Abraham would knock three times and give the password, which changed on each visit. The passwords were always the names of high-ranking Nazis. Heydrich, before he got assassinated. Speer, Goering. Bormann. Abraham couldn't help wondering more than once what would have happened if the Germans had ever run out of names. What would their logical, organized minds have done then?

Once the password was accepted, the door opened, and Abraham would be ushered inside. The central hallway was clear. He would quickly walk through it. The rooms in the rest of the house were filled with frightened people. Men, women, and children. Mostly families, with one, two, or three or more children. They would look at Abraham with wide eyes. By this time in the process, they knew who he was. They were grateful, but they were also afraid, not quite believing that this wealthy Canadian Jew would be able to get them to safety. Sometimes a father or a mother would reach out to him and touch the sleeve of his jacket or grab hold of his hand and whisper a frightened and astonished

"Thank you." Later, when they made it to Canada and stepped off the plane, they would invariably break down crying and embrace Abraham, but in Switzerland, they still felt very much at risk.

The man who answered the door at every house was always the same, a Swiss Jew; he introduced Abraham to each person. Abraham didn't have much time, and he was tired, but he walked through each room with infinite patience, shaking every hand and handing out passports without any indication that he was in a hurry. Then he escorted each family to a waiting car before jumping in the first car.

At the airport, the families were silent. They were sure their papers would be rejected, but Yitzhak Shmuel was good at his work. Not a single passport was questioned. During the war, Swiss airport officials saw many strange, not-quite-right papers, but the identity papers designed by Shmuel were impeccable. And, as Abraham Goldberg looked Swiss, with his expensive cashmere overcoat and his shining blond hair, there was no reason to question authenticity. Over the course of five years, Abraham made thirty trips. He saved eighteen hundred Jews.

Back home in Montréal, in the days and weeks following each of these rescue missions to Europe, Abraham carved out a day or two to forget about the war and his business and focus his energy and attention on his family. During these brief periods, Abraham would reflect with a subdued astonishment that getting Jews out of Europe was surprisingly easy: all it took was money and having to smile and joke and drink with Germans. Getting the refugees integrated into Canada was the hard part. It required brains and cunning and patience in a country where the official federal policy in respect to Jewish refugees was None Is Too Many. Nor was Canada particularly known for efficiently integrating educated immigrants of any kind. Abraham didn't have anything against dishwashers and taxi drivers, but he didn't want his saved Jews to end up in those jobs for the rest of their lives if they hadn't been doing them back in Europe. Few of them had. They had been doctors, lawyers, accountants, concert violinists, artists, writers, teachers, civil servants, industrialists, millionaires.

The first thing Abraham did was find them places to stay. Usually these were in one of the many apartment buildings that he owned across Montréal. They weren't palaces, but they weren't shabby. Each was clean, well-lit, and well-heated. Next, he ensured the children were enrolled in school and the parents signed up for English classes set up by Montréal's Jewish Federation. Abraham was empowering, but he didn't give his trust automatically. He continued to take a personal interest in the lives and success of the Jews he brought to Canada. He would stop in to the English language classes to sit quietly at the back. If he wasn't satisfied that the teacher was teaching well enough and, even more importantly, quickly enough for the people he had rescued, he would intervene with Jewish Federation management and have the teacher replaced by one better. He set performance targets for these classes: every adult student had to be highly functioning within six months.

As the adult immigrants learned English, Abraham paired them up with local mentors: Jewish business and professional and academic leaders with whom he had personal relationships. These men and women would hire the immigrants themselves or, if the new Canadians' interests lay elsewhere, they would coach them on the unwritten customs of the job application process in their new country. One of the best mentors was Chaim Eisenstein. He owned two clothing factories on Delormier. Heavyset, impeccably groomed, always well turned out in one of the fine suits his well-taken-care-of employees made diligently by hand, Chaim would

take his charges out to Schwartz's and teach them the ins and
outs of Canadian interviewing techniques over plates of dripping
smoked meat and between slurps of cherry Cokes.

"When they ask you to tell them a bit about yourself, they're
not really interested in you, at least not yet, if they ever are. They
want to know about the kind of work you did back home. And
so do not tell them your whole goddamn life story. Pick, at most,
three jobs to talk about, show progression, show off your accom-
plishments. And when they ask you what you want to be doing
in five years, don't tell them you want to be Canadian or still
employed or earning a lot of money or, God forbid, that you want
to be doing their job. Tell them you want to be 'adding more value
to the firm.' And whatever you do, don't give them a straight
answer when they ask you how much money you're looking for.
Either you'll guess too high, and they'll write you off as a grasp-
ing immigrant, maybe even a greedy Jew if they're not one of
us, or more likely you'll guess too low, and they'll figure you're
too dumb to know your own worth, and because of that they
won't value your worth. Tell them you're interested in the job and
you're looking for a salary equal to your qualifications, and, if it
comes to that stage, you'll be happy to consider their offer. Let
them be the ones to sweat."

For the professionals who needed certification, Abraham organized meetings with all the professional boards and ensured that
well-regarded local medical or legal or financial men were there
to walk through the certification board's door by their side so
nobody ever went in alone. A solitary immigrant with a strange
accent, awkward and unsure, or, worse, a refugee Jew, was easy
to dismiss.

Abraham ran all of this out of his own foundation. Nobody
save his wife, Golda, ever knew its name. He did not advertise

this work, never gave an interview about it. He quietly gave away over $25 million in the 1940s — over $300 million today — to save Jews from the Holocaust and to ensure they weren't disadvantaged when they came to Canada. Abraham was as proud of the fact that every educated Jew whom he brought in ended up succeeding in Canada as he was that he had saved them from the camps in the first place.

8

WHEN SOLOMON TOLD me the real story of how Abraham found
the mine, we were at a mining conference in Rio — as far away
from northern Québec as I could imagine. It was exotic enough
that I would have brought Jane except she was in London playing one of the Merry Wives. Solomon's wife, Miriam, had flown
down with him, but she was having dinner with an old friend
from university who was from Brazil. Solomon had asked me if I
would join him for a drink. After a long day of presentations and
private meetings near the beach and far from the *favelas* clinging
to the hillsides, Solomon was still fresh and warming to his favourite topic after mining: his family.

"If you believe the Goldberg Limited mythology and its press
releases, Abraham was a genius and a saint. Brilliant mining engineer and builder of companies. Leader of men. But also caring
and compassionate. A true hero who flies to Europe on clandestine
missions to free Jews, buys them with the gold he so inventively
and efficiently mines from the earth, and then resettles them in
Canada so they can rebuild their lives. Generous donor to charities but only on the condition there will be no publicity and the

recipients won't tell a soul. Devoted family man. How could anyone live up this legend? And best of all, it's all true. But it's also limited. Because if Abraham had been half as smart as we all think he is, he would have realized the true nature of my uncle." Solomon refused to call Mr. Goldberg by name. If he had used his family name, I think he would have refused on principle to use the honorific, the "Mr." that Mr. Goldberg wore like a knighthood, and not because they were technically family. "He would have taken steps to limit my uncle's power and greed and to protect my father and my mother. But he never did. And you know that story of how he found the mine?"

"Yes?"

"It didn't quite happen the way it's come down to us in the oral history of Goldberg Limited."

"No?"

"No."

ABRAHAM HAD NOT been driving along that particular road in northern Québec during that particular time of Goose Break at that particular time of year, when it was likely he would get stuck in the mud, all as a matter of coincidence. Actually, Abraham was driving a car with good tires, and he had to work hard to get himself convincingly stuck in the mud, He hadn't been driving around somewhat aimlessly looking for iron ore deposits. There was nothing aimless about Abraham, and he wasn't the type to waste his time searching for iron ore. He knew exactly what he was looking for.

He had heard the stories about rocks with traces of gold turning up between Chibougamau and Mistissini from one of his mining engineering professors at McGill. An old Scotsman, this professor had done some prospecting there in his youth before he had exchanged his youthful dreams of a lucky strike in the north for the more predictable and softer life of an academic. He joked regularly with his students that one day one of them would strike it rich and do him proud, but most of the students wrote it off as the nostalgia of a soon-to-be old man. Abraham was the only student who drove up north at the end of his third year.

He had studied geological surveys and had three good theories of where the gold might be coming from. But he knew the Cree were numerous in the area, and it was their traditional lands, and even at the age of twenty-two, Abraham knew that the best way to build a mine was not to push it or himself on a community but to first build a relationship with that community and have the community welcome his project and pull him in.

And so he managed to "accidentally" get stuck in the mud and to be rescued by Ahanu, who was not just any Cree but the son of the local chief. Abraham never let on what he was really looking for but instead let himself be befriended by Ahanu, who thought this tall, blond man from Montréal was free from the pull of materialism and gold and power and so told him freely and willingly where to find what he already knew was there. But in this way, Ahanu felt he was giving Abraham the gift of the secret of the land and what was hidden beneath it, and because Abraham never gave the slightest hint that he was looking for anything precious, Ahanu never felt the urge to prevent Abraham from taking what was rightfully Ahanu's and his people's. And yes, it was lucky that it was Ahanu, the son of the local chief, who happened upon Abraham, but as Ira liked to remind me over smoked meat at Schwartz's, Napoleon always said that a man makes his own luck.

Compared to what I would later learn about Mr. Goldberg and his dealings with his brother, Isaac, Abraham's original deception was an innocuous family footnote. The main point of the story, at least according to Solomon, was that even saintly Abraham was not above subterfuge in the interest of what he considered a good cause. And so, in these less than honest, but certainly not amoral, beginnings was the start of a lifelong friendship between the son of a Cree chief from Northern Québec and the Jewish son of a widowed immigrant who was about to finish his final year of mining engineering studies at McGill. After the find, most men would have dropped out of university. But Abraham started his mining business while finishing his fourth year.

When Abraham's second child was born, he named him in honour of Ahanu, which means "he laughs" in Cree. Because he was Jewish, Abraham called his son Isaac, which means "laughing one." In the Old Testament, Isaac was a fitting name for the son of nonagenarians Abraham and Sarah, who both laughed out loud when God told them they were going to have a son at their advanced age. As for where the Cree name Ahanu came from, Solomon never told me. Once Solomon introduced me to Abraham's imperfections, it was only a matter of time before he got to Mr. Goldberg's. Eight months later, in London, he took me back to the beginning.

ON ONE OF those trips to London, I'd stopped in to the British Museum while David was meeting an old friend from his McGill drama classes and Jane was in rehearsals. I was admiring the Elgin Marbles, their whiteness, their fleshy bodies and limbs so carefully arranged on their iron pedestals, still beautiful after more than two thousand years and despite their brokenness, when I heard that by-now-familiar voice behind me. "Do they let you out of the office to look at art?"

"Solomon." I knew what he was getting at, but I wasn't going to give him the satisfaction of saying anything. There was no real art in the Goldberg headquarters, unless you counted the oil portrait of Abraham. It loomed behind Mr. Goldberg's seat at the head of the boardroom table, the table with gold leaf on the edges in what we all called the Gold Room because of the gold walls. The paint was made with real gold dust from Springtime.

Abraham Goldberg, in the prime of his life, had sat for his official portrait in 1948. He was fifty-six. The Goldberg family resemblance was unmistakeable in the slanted, vaguely reptilian, symmetrical eyes; the long, slightly angled nose; the strong, square chin. Abraham's hair was still blond and thick at the age of fifty-six, as was his son's. The main difference between father and son was that Abraham was slim. The portrait, by noted Montréal painter Moe Wolfowitz, only showed Abraham's head and shoulders, but you could tell from his face that he was not heavy. He had a slightly hungry look in his unusually pale blue eyes.

Abraham had worn a dark suit and a gold tie for the portrait. Looking at it from across the room, you couldn't help noticing Abraham's hair was very blond, almost like it was giving off light. His Goldberg eyes sparkled and glistened, as if he were really alive and about to say something. If you took the time to stand up and walk over to the painting, even if you knew nothing about artists and their tricks, you could see that flecks of real gold had been skillfully painted into the hair. The effect was subtle, as if the hair was reflecting the sun. And if you looked into the eyes up close, you would see that the artist had very carefully painted a handful of gold flecks into the pale blue irises. When you stepped back a couple of feet, you appreciated that it was the gold flecks that gave the eyes their lifelike qualities.

IT HADN'T ALWAYS been this way, this lack of art, but it had changed after Mr. Goldberg took over running the company. It was like the Goldbergs under Mr. Goldberg had taken the Jewish admonition against graven images to heart. This was in marked contrast to Abraham, who had been a patron of the arts. Or, more accurately, he had been the loyal supporter of a patron of the arts. His wife, Golda, was a legendary arts supporter in the Montréal community. She was on the board of the Montréal Museum of Fine Arts, the Montréal Symphony Orchestra, and even the National Theatre School. But her board work was just the beginning. It was by her direct patronage that she distinguished herself.

She was an enthusiastic buyer of the work of young artists, before they were making any money and when every sale or commission meant the world to them. She had a fine eye. Every artist whose work she bought went on to a serious career, with work in the permanent collections of galleries in Canada, the U.S., and Europe. Golda's success was based in large part on her eye; but, after a few years, her talent for spotting talent became a self-fulfilling prophecy. If Mrs. Goldberg bought your art, other collectors and curators came shopping for your work. To her credit, in nearly fifty years of art patronage, Golda Goldberg was hardly ever wrong.

It was a love of art and a talent for taste-making that she shared with Solomon's mother, Eliana. One of Eliana's early purchases, when she was first starting out, was the work of an obscure Montréal artist named Miranda Mortinsky. Miranda faced the ultimate challenge for an artist: she was dead before Eliana bought her work. Up to that point, nobody had paid any attention to her. Eliana didn't let that stand in her way, and even Miranda became famous. After Miranda, Eliana took a liking to her son Lewis Mortinsky, an architect who had painted in his youth and who only took it up seriously again in his early forties.

Nobody was ever really sure if Abraham had originally appreciated the arts or if he just took to them over time, not to humour his wife but because he loved her. Abraham did show up by Golda's side at every art gallery opening, every performance of the Montréal Symphony (to which they had season tickets), and he didn't stand in her way when she wanted to fill their home with art. David told me that when he was growing up, his grandparents' house looked to him like the Louvre, with walls of paintings and corners filled with statues. His eyes didn't know where to rest. It was only in Abraham's study that the riot of colour and quantity stopped. I know this because, after his death, Abraham's study was packed up and reassembled at the Goldberg Building downtown when Mr. Goldberg took over and remodelled the interior and, in the process, designed a much larger office for himself. Abraham's study looked like one of those reconstructed rooms from Pompei, and it served as a sort of miniature museum of Goldberg corporate history.

ON THAT DAY, standing in the Elgin Marbles room at the British Museum, Solomon proceeded to tell me a childhood story about Mr. Goldberg that he had heard from his father. Both parents had tried to pass on their feelings about art to their two young sons: Golda, her deep love, and Abraham, his growing appreciation, which was grounded not only in his love for his wife but also increasingly in his humanism, his belief that any creation by a human being, whether in art or science or even business, was worth celebrating.

ABRAHAM NEVER WORRIED about Isaac being well-rounded. As a child, Isaac drew pictures of his family and their Border collies

— they had three at the time — or wrote one-man plays he would perform for the family after dinner. It was Mr. Goldberg, from the youngest age, who displayed no normal childhood artistic interests.

Isaac was studious, even in elementary school, but the young Mr. Goldberg couldn't sit still in class. He was already trying to figure out ways to make money. One weekend in grade four, he walked down to one of the stores on Sherbrooke and picked up twenty chocolate bars for five cents apiece, and then on Monday morning he sold them at recess for ten cents. Even at nine, Saul knew the difference between wholesale and retail prices. Whenever he and Isaac, who was younger by two years, walked to the store and each bought a chocolate bar, Saul would offer to take the first bite of Isaac's "to make sure it's not poisoned. That's the kind of selfless older brother I am." It was an offer that Isaac never felt he could refuse and one for which he remained grateful for longer than he cared to admit. Abraham did his best to civilize the young Mr. Goldberg, but he was born fully formed. According to what Isaac told Solomon — and not without a sense of brotherly admiration and affection — Mr. Goldberg as a child was wild, always running through the house screaming at the top of his lungs, scaring even the Border collies and jumping on Isaac. So Abraham thought he would expose him to music, and when young Mr. Goldberg was ten, Abraham hired no less than the Montréal Symphony's first violinist to give him private violin lessons.

Mr. Schimmelberg brought his own violin and a smaller one for Mr. Goldberg. He was a quiet man, slow speaking and slow moving, his formal clothing having seen better days. He seemed proud, embarrassed, and a bit nervous to be in Abraham's Westmount house. Later, Isaac wondered how he ever worked up the nerve to play on stage. But Abraham and Golda were large donors to the symphony; Mr. Schimmelberg didn't want the lessons to go badly. He gave the violin to Mr. Goldberg to hold. He asked him to just touch the wood, and then the strings. He showed him how to hold it under his chin and asked, "Would you like to play your first note?"

Mr. Goldberg put the violin on the coffee table, uncharacteristically gently, and raised his index finger. "Actually, I have a couple of questions."

"Yes?" Mr. Schimmelberg looked delighted, and his happiness wore away some of his apprehension. His rich pupil, even at such a young age, was so engaged that he was already asking questions, even before his first lesson, before his first note.

"Actually, I have three."

"Even better." Mr. Schimmelberg relaxed. He must have believed that with such enthusiasm, the lessons would go well.

"How much does the violin you brought me cost? How much does your violin cost? And how much do you get paid by the orchestra?"

Mr. Schimmelberg looked as if he'd been shot. Ten-year-old Mr. Goldberg acted as if he didn't notice the effect of his words. Isaac, who would have been eight and was watching the lesson curiously from another room, had to cover his mouth to stifle his laughter, and he was only half-successful because both Mr. Schimmelberg and Mr. Goldberg turned around. Isaac didn't remember how Mr. Schimmelberg answered the impertinent questions, but he did know that only four lessons later they were indefinitely suspended. Happily for Mr. Schimmelberg, Mr. Goldberg became a loyal donor to the symphony when he grew up, largely on account of his wife, Ruth.

But the first thing Mr. Goldberg did after Abraham's death, which was followed soon after by Isaac's death, was to have the

Goldberg corporate art collection appraised. A month after the appraisal, it was all gone, auctioned off by Sotheby's. It was the largest collection of Group of Seven paintings ever to go up for sale at the same time. Golda pleaded and argued with her son in the weeks leading up to the auction, but he refused to be swayed, telling her it had to be done to finance his new acquisition. Golda cried for a week after the auction and never forgave him. Solomon's mother, Eliana, had always shared Golda's passion, and following the Goldberg art sale, it was Eliana who took on the mantle of Goldberg arts patron. She had a few works of art of her own, but compared to what Abraham had collected, she was starting from scratch.

"MY UNCLE WAS always different," Solomon said as if it were obvious. "Abraham, for all his intelligence, couldn't see it, but even my father and my father's *bubbe* knew something was wrong with him from the beginning."

"What do you mean?"

"Every Saturday, Abraham would take my uncle and father to visit his mother, *Bubbe* Aviva. Abraham had bought her a house in Westmount after he started up his first mine — the one he named after her — and she lived there for the rest of her life. She had help, a maid and a cook, and later a nurse to look after her, but Abraham was determined she would never have to go to a nursing home, no matter how nice. He felt she had gone through enough for him. She had emigrated from Poland in 1892, and her husband died before Abraham was born.

"Whenever visiting Aviva, Abraham would make his sons put on nice pants and shirts, he even made them shine their shoes, and then they would walk down the hill from his house over to hers. She'd greet her son and grandsons at the door in her dressing gown, and her dressing gown was nicer than the fanciest dress from any fashion house. Her hair was always done, her makeup was impeccable, and she never smelled like of any of the other old people my father knew. Nobody knew what her secret was. My father thought that maybe she bathed every night in asses' milk. He'd read about that in a book once. Of course, it was probably that she wasn't much older than Abraham — she was sixteen when Abraham was born. She was almost like an aunt rather than a *bubbe*.

"She'd always hug my uncle first, because he was the oldest, and give him a peck on the cheek. Then — and according to my father, it never failed — she would take my uncle's face in her two hands and stare into his eyes. Sometimes her gaze would flick back and forth from one eye to the other. It occurred to my father more than once that she was measuring the distance between my uncle's funny-shaped Goldberg eyes and then looking into them, looking for something that only she knew might be there." This was the first time any Goldberg had ever admitted to me that he knew the Goldberg eyes were shaped in any unusual way.

"Other times, my father had the feeling that Aviva was looking at his brother to make sure it was indeed him, and that another child who looked like my uncle hadn't taken his place. This all took only a few seconds, and then she would smile, more relieved than happy, kiss my uncle again, this time on the lips, and turn her attention to my father. She would hug him and kiss him too, but there wasn't the same tentative, almost fearful ritual: she didn't look at him in the same searching way."

IT WAS ON that same visit to London that Solomon told me David was gay. This was fitting, as Solomon eventually told me everything about the Goldbergs. At least he was kind about it. Knowing I would be offended that David hadn't told me himself and embarrassed that I didn't know, Solomon preserved the fiction between us that I must have known all along, or at least had found out from David himself, and if not from him, then from Jane. As Solomon started speaking, I realized that Jane must have known from the beginning. She must have figured it out when they were acting together at McGill.

By this time, we had left the British Museum behind. We were at The Mayflower, one of Solomon's favourite pubs. Solomon didn't start off talking about David. He had been speaking about Mr. Goldberg, about how he was missing some of the basic human sensitivities in relation to others that most of us possessed. "It's like Mr. Goldberg and David being gay."

I pretended to act unsurprised. Solomon was conveniently staring out the leaded windows at the Thames. "What do you mean?"

"Well, David has always been discreet, ever since he was a teenager, but it's not like he took a vow of chastity or skulked around in the shadows. He's had a few relationships over the years. One was with a Hollywood actor. It's not like his father could have lived so long without ever noticing." Solomon took a sip of his drink, which I had long ago noticed was one of his favourite techniques to prolong the suspense he liked to create when it came to telling stories about his family. "In fact, I heard from a reliable source that Mr. Goldberg once walked into David's bedroom in Curaçao and found him in bed with another young man."

Solomon, seeing the look on my face, added, "They were both sleeping."

Still. "How did Mr. Goldberg react?" I thought he must have yelled and called David a *fagela*, a pejorative Yiddish word for a gay man.

"Well, that's the funny thing. He didn't. He stopped and stared and left the room, closing the door softly behind him. He went out for a drive and a visit to one of the museums about slavery that he so enjoys. When he came back later, both David and the man were gone. That evening, Mr. Goldberg asked Jake if David had been out with a friend the night before and had they both gotten drunk and had David offered his friend a place to stay. Jake, who had been reading inside for most of the day, looked at his father for a long time and then said yes, that was his understanding. Mr. Goldberg never spoke of it again."

The point of the story, Solomon told me as if he was worried I might miss it, was that Mr. Goldberg refused to believe the sight of his own eyes. "He refused to acknowledge something fundamental about his own son." I never did ask Jane about David being gay, nor did I ever ask David.

9

THE FIRST TIME I had to fire someone, I had been with the company three years. We had just taken over MineGold. I couldn't sleep the night before. I could barely look the man in the eye. After the third acquisition, it became a little easier, and I could do it without stumbling over my words or avoiding eye contact, but I'm proud that I never completely got used to it, and I never stopped losing sleep over it.

The day the acquisition closed, Mr. Goldberg took Sammy, Jake, David, and me to meet with MineGold's management team. Their offices were just down the street from us. It was a cold early December day. Mr. Goldberg walked ahead, Ira at his right side, Sammy at his left. Jake walked alone a few feet behind Mr. Goldberg. David and I took up the rear. Downtown Montréal was full of businessmen and businesswomen in suits, making their way through the brown slush that was already filling the Montréal streets, but the way the Goldbergs walked caused other men coming from the opposite direction to instinctively find the outer edges of the sidewalk. Mr. Goldberg, Sammy, and Ira were absorbed in a conversation about the meeting they were about to have and didn't look around them as they walked. The rest of Montréal and the people in it didn't exist for them. The weak winter sun was still bright at noon, and Mr. Goldberg's hair looked more golden than usual. Jake, having nobody to talk to, and preferring it that way, was silent. David was unusually quiet.

Mr. Goldberg walked into the lobby of MineGold as if he owned the place even though all he owned as of eight o'clock that morning were the physical assets of a mine in northern BC, the mine's intellectual property, and the labour of the people who worked at the mine and in their corporate office on floors thirty-two to thirty-six of the building we had just entered. He didn't yet own his new employees' loyalty, their discretionary effort, or their souls. When we got out of the elevator on the executive floor, the receptionist stood up behind her desk and greeted us. She might have been friendly and gracious to begin with, but she also knew she was auditioning for her job. She offered us coffee and water and brought us to the conference room, where the executive team of MineGold waited. As we walked in, they stood quickly to introduce themselves and shake hands. Mr. Goldberg was all cheer and business.

Even though Declan and I seemed to have less and less to talk about the longer I worked for the Goldbergs, I still must have been my father's son in some respects, because I still felt uncomfortable in boardrooms. The way the always too-large table took up most of the space. The high-backed chairs and heavy formality. The art displayed on walls and pedestals like spoils of war. How men wore their suits like light armour and lined up on opposite sides of the table seeking to outmanoeuvre each other. And, for some reason I cannot explain, I always felt uncomfortable introducing myself as we went around the table.

I made it through the personal introductions, and soon, mercifully, the meeting was underway. The CEO of MineGold and Mr.

Goldberg sat opposite each other in the middle of the table with the rest of us flanking them on both sides. The classic negotiation seating arrangement. We had bought the company, but the men across the table from us were still negotiating for their jobs. They looked calm, experienced, and professional, but most of them knew what was about to happen. Mr. Goldberg would have met the CEO during negotiations.

"So, how are you boys doing?"

I don't think Mr. Goldberg meant anything particularly condescending by calling the grown men across the table boys. It was the informal, down-to-earth way he thought North American businesspeople sometimes spoke to each other that he affected from time to time, but the men whose company had just been sold out from under them were happy to take it as a deliberate insult. The CEO himself was not unfavourably disposed to Mr. Goldberg. He had presented the proposed deal to his board with the recommendation to sell over the opposition of his own executive team. This CEO had only been there two years, and now the rumour was that he had been brought in just to get the best price for the company. The period of intense cost-cutting he had put MineGold through in the two years before the sale would bear this out. But the rest of his leadership team had grown up in MineGold and built the company from nothing.

MineGold's chief operating officer didn't wait for his boss to respond, as protocol would have demanded. "Us boys are doing fine," he said slowly, not a trace of good humour apparent on his face. "How about you boys?"

I'm not sure if Mr. Goldberg genuinely didn't notice the insult or chose not to. But his eyelids didn't descend, and he smiled without pride or guile. "We're fine. Since we're both fine, let's get down to business. This week, each of you will meet with my son Samuel and our chief legal officer, Ira. We want to learn more about you, about what you do, about how you think you could add value. Next week, we'll let each of you know if there's room for you in the company. But I have to warn you, it's not going to be easy. Our leadership team doesn't have any gaps. Any questions?"

If the MineGold executive team had had questions before, they certainly didn't have any now. A week later, Ira met with each of them and told them unfortunately there was no room for them in Goldberg Limited. All of them except one. Ira took a liking to their finance officer and thought he could help Goldberg Limited. He was offered the role of treasurer in the merged company. It was an easy decision for Ira because our long-standing treasurer was set to retire in the spring.

AFTER THE MINEGOLD meeting, on the walk back to our offices, Ira let Mr. Goldberg walk ahead, and he slowed down to walk beside me. The slush was heavier, but Ira bounced along like a teenager. "Sean, you're quiet. Why so?"

"I'm not sure."

Ira smiled at me. He read me easily, at least in the early years. "In order to build and grow a business, you have to take advantage of other businesses' weaknesses, other people's weaknesses. For one business to succeed," he said as he pointed up to the buildings around us, "others have to fail. Don't look at me that way. It's not evil or even bad. It's the way it works." That might have been true of my father's line of business as well — if one company got the contract for cement it meant that another one had not — but Declan was far removed from those calculations. Although society would never have recognized Declan as such, he was a craftsman, and in that respect, he was insulated from the deeper realities of business as practiced by the likes of Mr. Goldberg and Ira.

Ira continued to bounce along, the slush not encumbering him. It sucked at my feet. "I want you to head up the new combined legal department." He turned to me to gauge my reaction. I kept it muted. Undeterred, Ira continued. "But with every great opportunity comes great responsibility. We have four lawyers. They have five. We have to end up with six. Although our lawyers are probably better than theirs, don't assume this is true in every case. Pick the best. I know you care about people, but remember: not only is a takeover neither good nor bad ... it's nothing personal." Here he slapped me on the back, and I felt his heavy hand on my shoulder even through my cashmere winter coat. "It's just business." Ira's words made no sense to me because everything I had seen and heard from Mr. Goldberg had taught me that there was no such thing as "just business" in a family company. It was all personal for them.

But Ira wasn't done with me. "I'm going to be watching carefully how you go about this. So will the Goldbergs. They'll want to see if you have what it really takes. You don't really know what it takes until you've had to fire someone. The second-toughest decision you have to make as a manager is deciding whom to bring in to the company. The only tougher one is deciding to show someone the door." And then Ira added, as if he'd had to think about it, even though I knew he hadn't, "They don't call it 'firing' for nothing."

WE HAD JUST met with the MineGold executive team, but the following day we had to address the whole company. First, their head office in Montréal. Then we flew across the country to speak

with the workers at their mine in BC. We had to do three sessions at the mine to reach all the men as they came off shift. The
Goldbergs had to speak in public.

Mr. Goldberg could speak well to a crowd when he had to or
when he wanted to, which for him was the same thing. Unlike
most of us, because of his inherited wealth, from the time Mr.
Goldberg was a boy, he had hardly ever done anything he didn't
want to. If Abraham, who was by all accounts a wise man,
had ever had any regret, this would probably have been it. Mr.
Goldberg had no experience subjugating his will to anyone else's
nor to outside circumstances.

He didn't speak to large groups often, but whenever he did,
he spoke without notes. He hated the idea of written speeches,
hated the idea of getting up and adhering to a script. Having a
speech prepared for him was the same as acknowledging an inad-
equacy: it meant he needed someone else to help him organize his
thoughts and craft his words. In his view, a man should be able to
speak his own mind, and if anyone needed any help in this matter,
he was a weakling, an egoist, a faker. Mr. Goldberg spoke with
the power of his passion. He appeared sincere because he never
had to look down at a piece of paper. His words were his own.

Sammy copied his father's approach to public speaking,
although this was probably the one area in his lifelong imitation
of his father where Sammy deviated from his ideal. Simply put,
he cheated. Sammy would write out his main points on cue cards,
and he would review them surreptitiously before any speech. He'd
keep them in his jacket pocket and do his best not to consult them
while speaking, but he knew they were there if he ever needed
them. I aways had the impression that Jake hated public speaking,
and he would avoid it whenever he could. David, unsurprisingly,
was a natural. He didn't mind preparing, but he prepared in such

a way that what he delivered was never a "speech." He just spoke, and whether he was speaking to an audience of fifteen or fifteen hundred, it was like he was sitting down beside you, having a conversation over lunch at Schwartz's.

The best time to see the Goldbergs speak together was whenever they completed an acquisition. The day after the deal to acquire MineGold was signed and all the employees of the soon-to-be acquired company were still raw and angry, the Goldbergs swooped in to do their presentation. As I would learn, these presentations followed a pattern, and because of that, I can't remember the MineGold takeover and its attendant Goldberg speeches without them blurring with the other takeovers I participated in. The Goldbergs would begin in the corporate offices and then swiftly move on to the operating site or sites of whatever company they had just bought. After Mr. Goldberg, the three boys spoke in the order of birth.

Invariably, the employees in the acquired company were nervous. They had heard the rumours; they were familiar with the myths. It was widely known and accepted that the Goldbergs were highly intelligent. Their mines ran profitably. Their acquisitions always turned out well. They always seemed to buy the mines of others at the right price, at the bottom of the cycle, taking advantage of the inevitable upswing in prices. They never divested, although the conventional wisdom was that if they had done so, they would have made a healthy profit. There was never the wrong kind of gap between their physical assets and their market cap. Their share price was always higher than the industry's average. Goldberg Limited had good alpha, the investment community's rather poetic word for how much a stock's return outperformed the market.

The family was inevitably regarded as hard-nosed. Counters of pennies. Ruthless. The myths were legion. And these myths predated Mr. Goldberg's time at the helm. Tinged with traces of casual anti-Semitism, the kind that implied a grudging admiration for the family's financial acumen, these myths began at the time of Abraham.

In the eyes of the public, the Goldbergs were wealthy Montréal Jews who worked through Sundays and often on Saturdays. They knew the value of a dollar and kept wages in check. In the early days, when Abraham was starting up Springtime, employees practically worked for free. They kept operational costs so low that in some mines, in the beginning, there were no bathrooms. Miners had to go out into the woods. And while they evolved with the times as they grew the company, this early attention to cost management never left them. Hence Mr. Goldberg's famous quote from an extemporaneous speech to new employees at one of his early takeovers: "We run lean and mean. If other companies need a thousand people to do a job," — dramatic pause — "we hire seven hundred and fifty."

Afterward, Mr. Goldberg somehow made sure to work that line into every presentation, including the one on the occasion of the acquisition of MineGold. Just like he always managed to say, "If you work hard and you do the right thing, you will have a long career with us, and you will be rewarded." And then, not leaving anything to chance, wanting to make sure there was no misunderstanding, Mr. Goldberg added that day, as he invariably did, "If you work hard for us, we will work hard for you." Which was the other side of the mythic coin when it came to perceptions about the Goldbergs, and which more than made up for everything else in the eyes of most of their employees. It was an unwritten contract, a bond of loyalty between company and employee. I sometimes think it explained much of the Goldbergs' success. It was the kind of employer-employee relationship that became rarer in the 1980s and the 1990s as the world globalized and companies outsourced and downsized with regularity, doing whatever they had to do to reduce costs while keeping shareholders satisfied.

There were no reporters present, but somehow the quotes about employees working hard and doing the right thing by the company and the company doing the right thing by employees — I give credit for the successful PR to Ira even though he was a lawyer — made it into the next day's edition of the *Gazette*. As far as I could tell, the Goldbergs were no more ruthless in their business dealings than the owners of any other mining company whose business it was to take metals out of the ground as profitably as possible. If anything, they were better at it than most. And after working in business for most of my life, I've found there are few areas of human endeavour where success is looked upon with more suspicion (if not downright fear) as business. Because success in business is seen, rightly or wrongly, to come at the expense of someone else: competitors, employees, suppliers. Regardless of their reputation, in every first encounter after they had taken over a new company, the Goldbergs won their new employees over with their honesty and their passion.

That's not to say it was easy. The biggest fear in the heart of every employee whose company had just been taken over was whether they would lose their job. But despite their fears, new employees were never afraid to ask questions of the Goldbergs. On the day we acquired MineGold, one of them asked their version of "We all know that when companies take over other companies, they look for efficiencies. When do you plan to cut jobs?"

This question was left to David to answer, as it always was, because he was the most believable. He recognized the importance of getting it right, and, even more importantly, he understood that he wasn't just answering a question in a specific circumstance. He was responding to a lifetime of perceptions about him and his family even though most of the new employees had never actually met a Goldberg. But for every story about an employee who worked hard and was rewarded with a long career, there were two stories about employees who had been let go.

Despite the fact that many Goldberg employees were twenty- or thirty- or even forty-year veterans, there were still many stories of Goldberg employees getting fired because they didn't perform or because they weren't loyal or because the Goldbergs didn't like them, stories that didn't make it into the papers but made the industry rounds. The joke among fired employees was that, unlike at a public company, the Goldbergs would fire you if you walked in one day and they didn't like the colour of your tie. But that was an exaggeration. I never saw it happen. The occasional wrongful dismissal lawsuit made it into the papers with all its innuendo and conjecture, along with the standard Goldberg response of refusing to comment on matters before the courts, which only added to the mythology of the family's hard-line approach and the mysterious goings-on at the company that bore their name.

But the concept of never letting anyone go for economic reasons, which David was about to introduce to the employees formerly of MineGold, was an unfamiliar one for most of them. In the short time before he spoke, David read the crowd accurately, as he always did, because he was empathetic, and so in answering the first question about cutting jobs, he explained, "Thanks for the question. I know this may sound strange, but we have no plans to reduce jobs. As a matter of fact, we don't reduce jobs. We want your expertise, your experience. We want to grow. We need each and every one of you." David then paused for dramatic effect before delivering the Goldberg Limited human resources punchline that never failed to impress. "We have never, not once in our history since starting in 1913, laid anybody off for economic reasons."

Here the crowd murmured, as it always did; some shook their heads in predictable disbelief, others smiled because they thought they had caught a Goldberg in a lie — their worst fears were being realized, and now they could add "liar" to the list of names they would call the Goldbergs in private. Others, more reasonable and open, tried to remember what they had read in the papers and what they'd heard from friends. But for most people in the audience, this was when they started to really listen and wanted to hear more, and although David knew that the applause would soon be coming, he continued, as he invariably did, without a trace of arrogance or self-satisfaction, only passion and conviction.

"During every recession, even during the Great Depression, certainly every time the price of gold crashed, we are very proud to be the only miner in Canada that has not laid people off." After I looked into this, I found it was largely true. On one occasion, a couple years before I joined the company, during the gold crash of 1987, the Goldbergs had asked everyone in the company to take a ten-percent pay cut, but they had kept the team intact through recessions and precious metals commodities' down cycles. And although nobody was overly happy about earning less money, it was preferable to losing their jobs. The tough but fair decision only increased employee loyalty to Goldberg Limited.

It was then that David and, by extension, his family received the first round of applause that marked the turning point in this presentation, as in other presentations to follow. From there it was easy. The applause for how David answered the question of layoffs at MineGold started off quietly, and soon the whole room was clapping. David waited for the applause to die down, and then, like any speaker drawing energy from a supportive crowd, he continued, and with his next words he sounded like his father, more so than at any other time. "Here, in a nutshell, is our philosophy: We believe in working hard but in playing by the rules. In being the best we can be. We respect the competition, but we don't study them to death, we certainly don't fear them, and we never, ever follow them. When it comes to everything we do, whether with employees or customers, we believe in the meaning of a promise." Applause again.

"If you choose to work with us," David continued, "you'll work hard, have no doubt about that. Harder than you've ever worked before. But each member of our family will be working just as hard, if not harder. And we will have your back during both the good times and the lean times. This is our promise." And here David paused. "And, oh yeah, the chance to be part of the best gold mining company in the world!"

WE MIGHT NOT have ever laid off non-management employees for economic reasons, but coming in after each takeover and laying waste to the majority of the acquired company's executive and management team, as well as most of its lawyers, was always outside the Goldberg promise of magnanimity to their new employees as a whole. Most of the newly acquired employees who were not managers seemed to understand the necessity of this, and if they didn't, they never said anything about it to their new masters.

The first person I ever had to lay off was Alex Spenser. He had worked at MineGold for nearly thirty years, since graduating from McGill. He must have been in his mid-fifties. I was in my late twenties, and as I walked into the spare office we had reserved for these conversations, I noticed that Alex Spenser was handsome, well-groomed, wore a tailored suit and expensive polished shoes; he was sweating slightly — there was a sheen on his high forehead. I remember thinking it should be the other way around, that no one should fire anyone older than themselves.

The scene was made worse by the fact that Alex Spenser reminded me of my father. He shouldn't have done so, because he was different in almost every respect from Declan, but despite Alex's advantage over me in age and experience, in looks and wealth and even height, he showed me a wary deference when I walked into the room. He looked at me the way my father had looked at me the day I was accepted to LCC.

Alex stood up to shake my hand and waited for me to sit down before he took his seat. His leg bounced up and down. His nervousness made me even more nervous. I instinctively knew not to prolong matters, not to engage with small talk, and to get straight to the point. I could barely speak when I told Alex Spenser that we had to make some tough choices for the long-term good of the newly merged company and it was no reflection on him and his honourable contributions over the years, but, unfortunately, there was no role for him on the team. My voice wavered. I felt like a child.

Despite his expensive suit and shoes, his handsome face, Alex Spenser couldn't hide the dejection that came into his blue eyes and was expressed in the way his wide shoulders sagged as he slumped.

LATER THAT DAY, after I had fired two other MineGold lawyers and one of ours because someone in MineGold was better — and he had started yelling at me that it was a betrayal and I was a disgrace as a manager because I wouldn't protect my own team and that I was a young schmuck and even an anti-Semite — Ira invited me into his office for a drink. Canadian Club. Ira was an unabashed nationalist when it came to booze. "Booze" was what Ira called it, and he elongated the single syllable so that it became almost two. He sat serenely behind his desk with a bronze bust of Napoleon. The statue faced inward toward Ira, and I had the strange sensation that the two of them had been having a conversation before my arrival.

Ira knew I didn't drink much, but he handed me a double with no ice or water and asked, "How did it go?"

I thought it had gone horribly, so I said, with a measure of defiance in my voice, "As well as can be expected."

Ira nodded and said, "They don't teach you this in law school, Sean. There you're given to understand that law is a calling, like being a minor saint or at least a humble servant of God. It's pure. And abstract. And maybe it is in some places. But business is different." Ira glanced over quickly at Napoleon before turning back to me. "Business is war without bullets." Ira watched me carefully to see how his *bon mot* had landed. I denied him his satisfaction. He tried again. "To take some liberties with Clausewitz, business is the continuation of war by other means." Ira's bushy eyebrows wiggled for emphasis. "And don't forget that you're not just an ordinary soldier in an isolated battle. You're a staff officer. You have to think strategically. If you want to remain an officer, part of your job is to send men into battle with an encouraging pat on the shoulder, without losing your nerve or smile, knowing you can't protect them all. You have to lead your men, motivate them, steady them: but you never want to get so *attached* to them that it affects your judgment."

I took a sip and felt like throwing up. I had never been a fan of rye. As the years unfolded, I would stop drinking with Ira. At the time, I was still young enough to believe I couldn't refuse.

"Do you know what the Duke of Wellington once said about his men?"

"No."

"I think he loved them, in his way, and they certainly respected him and would run uphill toward enemy cannon at his word. But he was a hard Anglo-Irish bastard with a deep sense of what he considered right and wrong, and he was highly conscious of his class. He would get frustrated with his men whenever they lost discipline, either on or off the battlefield. He had a lot of rules they had to follow." Ira smiled, as if he were personally familiar with Wellington's approach to discipline. And then his voice dropped. "Whenever they didn't live up his expectations, he called them the 'greatest scum of the earth.' Apparently on more than one occasion. And he was a great general. Defeated Napoleon, although he only faced him in battle once, at Waterloo, and Napoleon was not at his best. After a battle, Wellington would lie down on the ground, put his hat over his face, and go to sleep. Like a baby." Ira took another contemplative sip before speaking again. His right eyebrow twitched as it often did when he became excited. He had saved what he considered his most valuable lesson for last.

"I've learned a lot from Mr. Goldberg. Of course, about the mining business — I was already a good lawyer when I joined, but I knew nothing about gold — but really about people. And that, as we know, is what it's all about."

I nodded as noncommittally as I could, and Ira took this as interest and went on. "Most people are fundamentally weak. They may talk a lot about freedom, but the truth is that most of them are frightened by it. What they really want is to bow down to somebody who is smarter, stronger, braver, sometimes even better looking or, believe it or not, more mysterious. This is why we invented God. But even God is not enough. People want to bow down on earth. They want give up their sense of responsibility, their fear, the anxiety that lurks at the centre of every human being about why they are here on this earth, in their job, what they are supposed to do with their limited time and energy, how they choose between competing priorities. They want to turn over this responsibility to someone else. Most people want to be led."

Ira paused and waggled his bushy eyebrows again and said with all the sincerity that he had or could muster at that moment, "You have to realize this, Sean. Once you do, people are easy to dominate. Any misgivings you might have about exercising power go out the window. People look for reasons to follow, not for reasons to be free, even when it might not apparently be in their own best interests. You have to treat them like they were born to follow you." Ira said nothing more; the meeting was over.

I wondered how much of what Ira had just told me he had really learned from Mr. Goldberg and how much he was projecting from his own worship of Napoleon. Regardless, as I left Ira's office, I was thinking that the philosophy Ira had just shared for my benefit might be easier for the Goldbergs to implement than for most people. They were already taller, richer, smarter, and better looking than the rest of us.

10

DURING ONE OF my early visits to the original Goldberg mine, as we wore our golden hard hats with the Goldberg logo, we watched miners go down into the ground to break and remove the rocks with the heavy gold streaks. Mr. Goldberg asked, without looking at me, "Do you know why people are obsessed with gold, young Mr. McFall?"

"No, Mr. Goldberg."

"Pure narcissism. People are obsessed with gold because they are obsessed with themselves, because gold reminds them of their deepest, most arrogant aspirations. Of all the metals, gold has the most human qualities: it is malleable and ultimately worthless, like the human body without the soul. It is frivolous, foolish. It is the worst of all the metals, at least in practical terms, because it has no real, functional use. Its main purpose, by far, is to make jewellery. We only ascribe value to it, a value that is completely arbitrary. Gold retains its value because of our fascination with it. This is why I sometimes wish my father had gone into mining a more respectable metal, like iron. In another way, gold is not like people at all, because it lasts forever. Gold is chemically neutral.

It doesn't react to air, so it doesn't tarnish like copper; it doesn't react to water, so it doesn't rust like iron. It doesn't degrade. It cannot be destroyed. It remains. Every little bit of gold that has been mined since the beginning of time is still with us. In this, gold is comparable to men's souls. And in this respect, gold represents man's highest, most selfish aspiration, which is to live forever."

I never forgot that speech. Mr. Goldberg was right. People are obsessed with gold. I can't tell you how many people — relatives, friends, business acquaintances — asked me about gold as a way to ask about the Goldbergs. There was always a preamble followed by a hinted request for bits of gossip about the family. I always declined. The four most popular questions about the Goldbergs, in ascending order of popularity, were: Do they really drink three grains of gold each day with their morning orange juice because gold is supposed to be good for your health in small quantities? Does the paint on their walls contain flecks of real gold? What are the Goldbergs really like? And, finally, What is it like to have so much money?

I always gave the same answers: No, the Goldbergs didn't drink gold powder with their morning orange juice. I didn't volunteer that none of them liked orange juice. Yes, there were real flecks of gold in the paint on the walls of the company boardroom in Goldberg headquarters. The Goldbergs were very, very smart. Then whoever had asked the question would nod wisely because they already knew the Goldbergs were smart, and we would both leave it at that as far as the Goldbergs themselves were concerned.

I never really responded to the question of what it was like to have so much money. I'd mutter something innocuous like I didn't really know, and I'd smile and wait for the questioner to move on. The truth was, the Goldbergs were schizophrenic when it came to money. On the one hand, making money meant everything to most of them. I always got the sense that David and Jake didn't really care about it quite so much as the others, but Abraham, despite his good deeds during the war, had worked his whole life to amass a fortune. As for the rest of them, making money was what they had grown up with. It's what they had been taught; taking care of their family business was what got them out of bed each morning. But when it came to spending money, it meant close to nothing, despite Mr. Goldberg's spending habits with his cars and at the mines. That is what it is like to be a billionaire. Buying a vintage MG or a house in Curaçao was like shopping for groceries or going out to dinner for the rest of us. I always wondered how that attitude — caring too much on the one hand and caring too little on the other — affected them. But in everything else, they were just like you and me. They had the same amount of unhappiness. I never shared that with anyone who asked.

But the real question that people wanted to ask me all along — real because it was based on self-interest and greed — would come eventually. It was not a question about the Goldbergs themselves but about the metal they mined. Everyone who knew I worked for the Goldbergs was curious about the price of gold.

ONE LATE SATURDAY night in March of 2003, I found myself with Jack Hastings, Jeremy Last, and Jane at the Savoy's Beaufort Bar. We were sitting at a small table in one of the recessed arches that were overlaid with gold leaf that shone brightly. David wasn't there, but it was one of his favourite places to drink in London, especially after the theatre. We all felt his presence, because he'd introduced us to the bar. Jane was close beside me in the loveseat, and Jack and Jeremy were sitting opposite, leaning in. Despite his semi-drunk state, Jack was shyly asking me where the price of gold was heading. We were just three days into the Second Gulf War and three years into the dot-com crash, and gold, after falling for two long decades and then languishing in the high three hundreds, had started to slowly rise again in 2001. That day, it was trading at U.S. $474 an ounce.

A few short hours earlier, Jack and Jeremy had marched with the reported million Londoners who took to the streets of their ancient city to protest the younger Bush's just-begun invasion of Iraq. It was very early days, and Bush was still launching his soldiers in waves across the desert and toward the Euphrates to destroy the weapons of mass destruction that the U.S. had assured their allies and the UN were possessed by Saddam Hussein. After marching all day and chanting anti-war slogans — but not so loudly as to unduly strain their voices — Jack and Jeremy had drunk hot water with honey, put on their makeup, donned costumes, and acted with Jane to generous applause in *Betrayal*, one of Jane's favourite plays. Jack had played audacious Jerry, cuckolding Jeremy's dour, squash-loving Robert with my beloved Jane's accommodating and willing Emma.

Now Jack and Jeremy were both mildly drunk on red wine, their just-concluded acting, and the demonstration they had participated in earlier that day. Jack's asking of the question itself that evening was gentle and self-deprecating, as it invariably was, and it was accompanied by a shy, apologetic smile, almost as if he and Jeremy had drawn lots to decide who would ask. At a suitable moment in our conversation, Jack began in his lovely, trained-actor's voice, "So, Sean, if you really had to wager, where might you suppose gold prices are going to go?" He sipped his wine and glanced over to the table beside us, nestled in an arch with its own gold leaf. And then his gaze returned to me, modest yet expectant. Surely as legal counsel to Goldberg Limited, I would know.

I took my time to reply, so that even though Jack and Jeremy would end up disappointed, they would know that what was coming next was considered, if not particularly enlightening. I was careful to speak evenly, without a hint that I was surprised or offended by the question. My reply to the question of where the price of gold was going to go was the same that night as it always was, although delivered as if I were choosing my words for the first time, as if Jack were original in his curiosity. "Well," I said with a laugh, "that's certainly the billion-dollar question."

At this, both Jack and Jeremy smiled, their hopes of getting a priceless answer rising. But I didn't like to see people getting their hopes up unnecessarily, so I moved quickly to dash them. "Truth is, nobody knows where the price of gold is headed. Not those of us who take it out of the ground, not the best gold traders in the world." Here their optimism faded, and they couldn't help looking crestfallen. At this point, I offered, as I always did, "We actually have a standard question whenever we interview people for our trading function." And then, despite the lateness of the hour, the wine, and the fatigue from their busy day, Jack and Jeremy perked up, revived by their common hope that even though nobody really knew where gold was heading, someone surely must, and, if anyone were to know, it would be someone who worked for the Goldbergs.

"We ask them where they think the price of gold will be next month." I took a long, slow sip of my drink before continuing. "If these would-be Goldberg traders tell us where they think the price of gold is heading, if they even attempt the most modest of qualified guesses, if they give any answer whatsoever other than *they do not know*," and here I paused, "then we do not hire them." Jack and Jeremy's expectations deflated like a balloon. Even those hardy souls who could act a major part in a Pinter play to glowing applause on a West End stage responded with genuine surprise and even a hint of hurt, despite the dissembling discipline of their profession. They seemed to believe it was a case of my refusing to let them in on an industry secret.

And then it was time for me to be human and self-deprecating again, and so I ended with a rueful smile and said, "If I knew where gold was heading, I'd be a very rich man!" And here I gave a mock toast and turned to gaze at Jane sitting beside me to show that indeed I was already wealthy beyond measure, and I waited patiently for the topic of conversation to change.

Judging from the look in Jack's and Jeremy's eyes when we resumed eye contact and proceeded to talk about something else, they didn't believe me. Most people didn't. A few of them gave me the benefit of the doubt. A still smaller percentage — genuine friends and distant relatives — assumed I was too stingy to part cheaply with such powerful knowledge, and they resolved to become even closer to me so that down the road I might trust them sufficiently to share my priceless wisdom.

In all my time working with the Goldbergs, there were only two people who never asked me about the price of gold: my father and mother. Declan because he didn't want to owe Mr. Goldberg anything, least of all anything to do with money, and Mary because I think she alone could sense deep down that for me the price of gold was only increasing by the year.

It wasn't at all apparent to me. Money seemed to come to me quickly and easily and relatively early considering my upbringing. It meant the usual things. The starter home in my old neighbourhood in my late twenties, soon after I started earning a corporate salary. Then a few short years later, as the annual raises and bonuses came and followed each other with rapid succession in my mid-thirties, and as more were promised, the house on Argyle in Westmount, halfway up the hill, within walking distance of the Goldbergs. Regular trips to Europe and the Caribbean with Jane and the children. Sometimes with David. Sometimes to Curaçao. Private schools. LCC had gone coed by then, so it was LCC for all three kids. A cottage in Magog, much smaller than the Goldbergs' but only a twenty-minute drive away from theirs. Saving more for retirement each year than the average Canadian salary. Paying income tax several times what the average family earned. Never having to draw up a household budget. Never having to worry about what was on sale at the grocery store.

Mary was proud of me as she saw the money flooding in, but she was always too polite to say anything. Declan had stopped knowing what to say to me the day I started at LCC. Because of this, I was careful in what I bought them. Tickets to accompany Jane and me on the occasional trip to places they would never go to themselves, like London or Paris or Curaçao or the Bahamas, where they would spend uninterrupted grandparent time with Dylan, Bridget, and Fiona. Overcoming their innate resistance to accepting such large gifts by telling them the children wanted them to come. Expensive but not flashy clothes for my mother. And plenty of books. There was nothing I could ever really buy for my father, so I never tried. Each time I brought my mother a present and didn't bring him one, I told myself that if he got really sick, with cancer, I would fly him down to the Lahey Clinic for treatment, sparing no expense. Then he would see the value of money. But his good health and natural strength only seemed to increase steadily by the year.

Declan's reluctance to ask me about the price of gold was in keeping with his attitude toward my university studies and my career. In all our time together, whenever I was over at my parents' for dinner or to sit in their small backyard drinking a beer with him, Declan asked me only once about my work. I was twenty-seven and had been practicing law for three years. He combined the question with one about me so that both flowed into each other without my really noticing. "How are you doing, Sean? How are you enjoying being a lawyer?" I only answered the second.

"It's fine, Dad."

He nodded, drank from his Labatt 50 that I always found hard to swallow but that he loved, and looked over at the rose bush he had planted when he and Mary bought the house. I realized then that Declan hadn't asked me anything of substance since my acceptance at LCC.

Mary, on the other hand, despite her reticence to ask me about the price of gold and perhaps to cover up her growing unease, was full of questions about everything else. In this respect, at least, nothing had changed from when I was a boy and she was my confident mother. What is it like to be a lawyer? What is it like to work with the Goldbergs? Do you ever have to go to court? Do you have to write a lot? Is it really difficult?

More than once, I wanted to ask her if this was what she had hoped for when she'd helped me fill out the scholarship application for LCC. Or would she have preferred, in retrospect, that I became a doctor? An engineer? A professor? Although we never spoke of it, I always got the sense from Declan that he thought words came easily to me and that I had chosen the law for that reason. Perhaps this helped absolve him of having any influence over my choice of career. Sometimes I think he was right, but other times I thought studying the law made me more of what I am, made me measure out my words and aim for detachment. Mary would never have spoken about it in those terms, and she would never have admitted it, but in the early years of my career at least, she was living somewhat vicariously through me. Declan, however, remained stubbornly self-sufficient as he got older. And for that reason alone, I never ceased to admire him.

11

FOR YEARS, THE Bald Rock mine in Northern Ontario — not one of ours — had produced gold at a steady if unspectacular rate. The stated objective of its parent company during the preceding decade — which made infinite sense as gold was climbing — had been to modernize the mine and double production. If they had stayed loyal to gold, they would have avoided their fate, at least for a time. But they overextended themselves with a highly touted adjacency acquisition in African copper in early 2007, just before the global financial crisis hit and the price of copper crashed along with the world economy.

While the commodity price of "Dr. Copper," with its metaphorical PhD in global markets and ability to foreshadow global trends, languished in 2008 as the world limped through the aftermath of the Great Recession, gold in its lovely counter-cyclical way was years into its decade-long climb after having bottomed out at U.S. $379 an ounce in 2000. That June of 2008, gold was trading at U.S. $930 an ounce. If Jack and Jeremy had gone out and invested $10,000 in gold right after our conversation in the

Beaufort back in 2003, it would have been worth $24,000 five short years later.

Despite the rising price of gold, the owners of Bald Rock had overpaid for their copper venture, and they found themselves the victim of terrible timing. Overleveraged, they began to shed assets. Goldberg, on the other hand, had a full war chest, and the first action we took after our acquisition of the distressed Bald Rock mine was the environmental assessment to seek government approval for its modernization.

We called it "modernization," but it was really more of an expansion. We expected the approval process to take a little over two years, but after the first year, things began to get complicated. A First Nation over a hundred kilometres away claimed their traditional hunting lands encompassed our mine. The government asked us for more studies. An approval that we had expected in six more months was now over a year away.

For the previous five years, regulatory affairs and permitting for all our mines had fallen under Jake's purview. He liked the attention to detail that was required and the way the work involved external stakeholders. And, for reasons that were not clear to any of us, least of all Jake, Mr. Goldberg encouraged him. Perhaps Mr. Goldberg was growing wiser. Perhaps it was just his way of recognizing that his middle son's passion for arcane detail and technical knowledge would benefit the company. Jake's dream of working for a time outside the family company had receded far into the past as he approached his mid-forties; and, as Mr. Goldberg moved through his late sixties, the two of them seemed to have reached an understanding. Jake did his job with minimal complaint, and Mr. Goldberg let him. But the old friction between them never really went away. Occasionally it rose to the surface as a result of the smallest thing.

One day toward the end of our weekly senior management meeting that Mr. Goldberg still ran like a family gathering around the boardroom table, Jake asked, "Dad?" It was only in the last five years that Jake had taken to calling his father "Dad." Before that, he'd called him nothing, just started sentences addressed to his father without any acknowledgement of their familial bond.

"Yes, Jacob."

"We have a problem at Bald Rock." Jake knew better than to open a discussion with his father this way. Mr. Goldberg hated to hear about problems. As he told us whenever we brought one to his attention, "There's no such thing as a problem, only a solution." Most of us who worked with him only had to hear it once.

Mr. Goldberg did not wait for him to continue but waded in with questions. "Is it production?"

"No."

"Has anyone died?"

"No."

"What's the so-called problem?"

"It's to do with the EA."

"You know I hate abbreviations, Jacob."

"Sorry. The environmental assessment."

"Why didn't you say so in the first place?"

"A First Nation is causing trouble for us."

"You mean Indians?"

"Dad, nobody's called them *Indians* for years."

"Your *zayde* did. The word *Indians* was good enough for him. And we know how much you admire him, Jacob."

"It's a different time."

"I make my own time, Jacob."

There was nothing Jake could say to this, so he continued, "They're claiming they've fished and hunted for generations on the land on which our mine sits."

"So?"

"The evidence seems to bear them out, and more importantly, the government is inclined to believe them. I'm getting a bit nervous."

"Jacob. How many times do I have to say it? Goldbergs may get *concerned* on occasion, but we never get nervous. What's your point?"

"They are asking for more studies."

"How long?"

"A year."

"A year from now or a year from when we expected the permit?"

"From when we expected the permit."

Mr. Goldberg's eyelids fell. Jake refused to look at the rest of us around the boardroom table.

Mr. Goldberg sighed. "We do have a problem, Jacob, but it's not so much with the mine."

Jake waited and said nothing.

"It's with you. The problem's with you. Do you know what your problem is, Jacob?"

"No, Dad."

"You don't sufficiently care about whether you win or lose. I don't know where you got this trait, because I, your father, hate to lose. I absolutely hate it. That's why I rarely if ever lose. But when you don't care ..." Unlike most of us, Mr. Goldberg almost always finished his sentences, but even Mr. Goldberg knew that sometimes what is not uttered has more power than what is, and occasionally he left a sentence hanging to emphasize a point.

"I've been to see the deputy minister," Jake said, "and she says her hands are tied. Public expectations are higher than they've ever been. I think international organizations are watching."

"Really, Jacob? Really? Is that the best excuse you can come up with? That you think international organizations are *watching*? Do you know what I *think*? Of the deputy minister and her international organizations?" Jake shook his head. "I don't *think* you want to know."

Jake smiled, just the way he had years earlier when he was waiting for Mr. Goldberg to discover that David had been cast as Juliet.

"They can go and fuck themselves." Every word was said slowly. Accompanied by a narrowing of the symmetrical Goldberg eyes. Mr. Goldberg looked around the table, at Ira first, then Sammy, then David, and finally at me, as if daring any one of us to defend the government, to contradict him.

"Yes, Dad." For a horrible second I thought that Jake was going to get smart with Mr. Goldberg and ask him if he should write his words down. I'm sure he thought it, but he didn't say it.

"Get me a meeting with the prime minister. Tomorrow." Mr. Goldberg stood up, and the meeting was adjourned.

MR. GOLDBERG HAD a disdain for politics, its arbitrariness, its ebbs and flows that were based not on rational market behaviour and the supposedly rational decisions of consumers but on the crapshoots of elections and the conflicted fears and desires of voters. Like many businessmen, Mr. Goldberg didn't think in analogies or metaphors, and he never saw or bothered to see the parallel between business and politics: that both depended, in their own ways, on selling something. Like most prejudices, I think this one was founded on insecurity, on the suspicion that politics, with all its verbal gymnastics, its sophisticated messaging and pandering to the crowd, was at its core a higher calling than business, or at least that higher stakes were involved. No matter how important or sought-after the product — even when it was gold — making or transporting or selling it paled in comparison to protecting freedom and democracy and a way of life, even though most stolid Canadian politicians might never speak about their work in such exalted terms. Nothing came close.

Mr. Goldberg's ideas about politics were conventional, that is, self-interested and predictable. They comprised the mantra of the businessperson and depended on adjectives. Like most business-people, Mr. Goldberg hated to be taxed, at both the corporate and personal levels. He wanted taxes to be *lower*. He disliked regulation: it was all the brightest crimson red tape to him. He wanted *less* regulation, and whatever was left over he wanted to be *streamlined* and *efficient*. He was for trade: the *freer* the better. Innovation? He wanted *more* of it. He was a conservative by head and heart and had voted Conservative in every election.

When it came to government, Mr. Goldberg was like some businesspeople who thought government should stay out of their businesses, except when they wanted something: a tax break, money for infrastructure, an interest-free loan, or simply the soft, compelling, flattering words about the superiority of his product, business model, or strategy whispered into the ears of another world leader on a trade mission. Mr. Goldberg saw no paradox in railing against the intrusions of government one day and asking for support the next. He saw it as all part of the great game that had to be played to succeed as a billionaire industrialist in what he had on more than one occasion described in private as a "medio-cre, negligible country that had the foresight and brilliance to be brought into existence at the top of a continent, separated by oceans from Europe and Asia, sitting in the shadow of a superpower, on a near-endless land mass that made it the proud geological inheritor of original elements like gold," just waiting billions of years for men of energy and vision like himself to harness the efforts of lesser men to haul this natural wealth out of the ground for a profit.

For Mr. Goldberg's sons, politics was just another messy, idiosyncratic aspect of doing business. Sammy was Conservative because Mr. Goldberg was. Jake flirted with the NDP in public — nobody knew what he did in the privacy of the ballot box — because he knew it would annoy his father, and David was a closet Liberal, partly because somebody in the Goldberg family had to support Canada's natural governing party, to hedge their bets, and partly out of conviction. Unlike Jake, for David this wasn't an act of rebellion. If it had been up to Mr. Goldberg, the family company would have donated only to the Conservatives, but before corporate contributions were outlawed, I convinced him we should donate equally to both majority parties, and that if Jake wanted to make the odd peace offering to the perennially losing NDP, it wouldn't be the worst thing.

Mr. Goldberg only put aside his feelings about politics when he needed to go to Ottawa to ask for something. When Jake couldn't convince the deputy minister of environment that the expansion of Bald Rock was more important to the country than the land claim from one of our country's more than six hundred First Nations, Mr. Goldberg told Jake to set up a meeting with the prime minister. We could have driven from Montréal, but Mr. Goldberg was in a hurry, so we flew. The airport of our national capital was as sleepy and quiet as ever, and the drive downtown, on the winding country two-lane road and then alongside the canal, was fast.

Given his views on politics, there was little chance that Mr. Goldberg would think any better of its practitioners. At Goldberg Limited, Mr. Goldberg was as absolute a ruler as the Sun King, and he had a monarch's congenital disdain for the government leader who serves at the fickle pleasure of the crowd. But he had a soft spot for our prime minister of the day, Allan Keyes. Mr. Goldberg had the innate respect that the man who has gone into the family business holds for any other man who has done the same, even if that other family business happened to be politics. This natural respect was even higher for one of the few sons who had gone on to outdo their father. Allan Keyes's father had been one of the best finance ministers the country had ever seen, but Allan had made it all the way to 24 Sussex Drive.

When we met Allan that day, he was almost a year into his second term, and it was widely assumed he would seek a third. He was only in his mid-forties, still blond, without any grey hair. After five years as PM, his popularity was unabated, and he had all the energy of when he had run in his first election for member of parliament. His adviser Eli — my childhood friend — was in the meeting, and it was good to see him again. I congratulated him on the publication of his semi-autobiographical novel *Sons and Fathers* and asked him when his next novel was coming out. The PM overheard me and said, "Don't encourage him. I need him to stick around a little longer to keep me out of trouble!" I took it as a signal that Allan would run again. Eli winked and smiled.

Usually so confident, Mr. Goldberg wasn't accustomed to asking anyone for anything, and he hated, on principle, to do it. He was ill at ease, sitting at the edge of his seat, then leaning back, and then leaning forward again. Even today, when he needed a favour, he couldn't bring himself to ask outright, so he had to do it in a roundabout way. And because he couldn't bear the thought that anyone could have more power than him, he couldn't even bring himself to call Allan "Prime Minister." But he knew calling him by his first name would have been poor manners, so he didn't call him anything.

"Thank you for seeing us today."

"My pleasure." From what I could discern, Allan had a lot of time for Mr. Goldberg, probably considered him and his family business a national institution. He respected the fact that the Goldbergs paid their taxes and didn't try to hide offshore as much of their taxable income as other Canadian billionaires regularly did. And he admired the Goldbergs wholeheartedly for how responsibly they ran their mines: Abraham had set such high standards for performance that Goldberg Limited had never been charged for any environmental violations. Allan was naturally respectful of everyone, regardless of power and position, and he would have shown Mr. Goldberg deference simply because of his age even if he hadn't had all that wealth behind him. But just as we all like and respect the same qualities in others that we take pride in when we find them in ourselves, Allan also respected Mr. Goldberg's power. And yet, although none of us saw the point of ever mentioning this to Mr. Goldberg, Allan's respect and affection for Mr. Goldberg didn't prevent him from being equally respectful and friendly to Solomon as Solomon had built a company on his own and remade his family fortune one acquisition at a time. Not only did they share the affinity of youth, at least compared to Mr. Goldberg, Allan probably respected Solomon even more because he was doing it all on his own. But from his own experience in scaling the pinnacle of political success in Canada, Allan knew that a good family name didn't hurt. Today, like any skilled politician, Allan sensed his constituent's discomfort and decided to make things easier for him.

"What can I do for you?" It was a graceful opening, but Mr. Goldberg didn't accept it fully because, despite Allan's politeness, it would have put him in a subservient position.

Mr. Goldberg's eyes remained neutral as he said, "It's actually what you can do for the country. There is a mine expansion we'd like to go ahead with, but it seems to be tied up with a certain deputy minister."

"Hmm." From the way Allan inclined his head in sympathy, I could tell he had been well briefed.

"I'm not sure that many Canadians would fully appreciate the fact, but as you and I both know, nothing stands still. And the markets are certainly no exception. The window that is open today won't necessarily be open tomorrow." And then, as if to make sure Allan appreciated the metaphor he had just employed, Mr. Goldberg added, "What looks like a good opportunity this year to meet growing middle-class demand in China could very well change the next."

Allan nodded. He didn't disagree.

"There will be serious consequences, not just for a Canadian company but for Canada, if approval is delayed. Two thousand construction jobs. Four hundred permanent jobs. Six hundred and seventy-five million in royalties and taxes over the expected life of the project. That's money for health care and education." Mr. Goldberg didn't usually throw around dollar figures, but he liked to do so when he went to see politicians. He thought politicians were fuzzy thinkers, obsessed as they were with words. "Words ultimately don't matter," Mr. Goldberg had once told me on the way to a meeting with cabinet ministers. "The world only really pays attention to numbers."

"Mr. Goldberg," — even our PM followed the convention of using the "Mr." where Mr. Goldberg was concerned, and Mr.

Goldberg couldn't resist a small, boyish smile — "as you know, the Environmental Assessment Agency functions at arm's length. The process must be followed and impartial conclusions reached based only on the evidence."

Allan sounded needlessly formal, and for the first time in my life I thought Mr. Goldberg looked confused, concerned, perhaps worried. Even when he was being held at gunpoint in that armed robbery in Curaçao, thirty years earlier, he hadn't looked worried. But Allan was only saying what he had to say for the record, and to remind Mr. Goldberg of the power of the state, even one as small and reticent as Canada. He continued before Mr. Goldberg had undue cause for alarm. "But as we also know it's not unheard-of for bureaucrats to occasionally drag their heels when you're trying to lead them to water." Here Allan was mixing his metaphors as he was famous for doing, both in parliament and interviews when he spoke off the cuff. "In fact, sometimes I think it's part of the job description. But I've always been a big believer that stubbornness should not get in the way of nation-building. I'll speak to the deputy minister this afternoon."

I remember thinking that this was how government relations were conducted by a billionaire, but I don't recall much more of the conversation. I think it was mostly Allan asking Mr. Goldberg about mining operations and economic conditions in South America and Africa. Like most powerful and successful men, Allan had a deep and far-ranging curiosity.

TWELVE MONTHS LATER, we got our permit, one day earlier than the original target date Jake had circled on the Gantt chart that he had put together to track progress and that so annoyed Mr. Goldberg, who cared only about results and had little time for process. When the permit came through and Jake delivered the news in person, Mr. Goldberg couldn't resist giving his middle son a triumphant lecture in my presence on how to influence government.

"Never take no for an answer, Jacob, and don't waste time with the bureaucrats but always go straight to their political masters." Mr. Goldberg disliked bureaucrats even more than he disliked politicians.

Through it all, Jake never interjected or attempted to defend himself. He listened to every word that poured forth from Mr. Goldberg in his childish enthusiasm and nodded at every "Do you see what I mean, Jacob?" as he waited for Mr. Goldberg to be done.

12

A WEEK BEFORE the news of our latest acquisition — a mid-sized gold mine in Ghana and our first foray into Africa — went public in the early days of 2010, I ran into Solomon in LaGuardia. He must have been mixing business with pleasure as his wife, Miriam, and their teenage daughter, Rachel, were with him. He said he'd join them in the lounge in a few minutes, skipped his usual greeting, and said, "I hear you're in the throes of acquiring."

I was taken aback. Our latest purchase had been well timed to take delayed advantage of yet another company weakened by the Great Recession, but it wasn't public information yet. Solomon smiled at my discomfort. "It's been common knowledge, at least among a few of us, since last Saturday." At first, I thought it was the investment bankers I had just been meeting with in New York. They were known for the unlikely combination of charging high fees and having loose lips. "You'd understand what I mean if you'd attended synagogue last week. I know Ira's a bit of a mentor to you. Or at least he thinks he is. And you could do worse, because while Ira may not be wise, he's certainly clever. But if you really want to know what's going on at Goldberg Limited, you should start attending synagogue. Shaar Hashomayim."

I'd been with Goldberg Limited for twenty years and known the family for over thirty, and in that time, I'd been to synagogue with the Goldbergs on only a handful of occasions: that first time in Curaçao and then for the weddings of David's brothers. As time passed, Sammy married gentle Esther and Jake married boisterous Leah. Jane and I were married early on. David never did get married. It's not something the two of us ever spoke about. It was just another way he remained different and separate from the rest of us even after he had given up on the acting dreams of his youth and shed his long hair and the fur coat he used to wear in university. It made him slightly mysterious in the eyes of his father and his brothers, and even me, but I'm not sure any of us thought much about it because he was still David, and when we did think about it, we all assumed he hadn't met the right person. That made sense to us.

"Why synagogue?"

I knew Mr. Goldberg was a generous donor to the Shaar Hashomayim synagogue on the lower slopes of Westmount but not necessarily a regular attendee. This was the story that Solomon told me, almost gleefully.

MR. GOLDBERG DIDN'T attend shul regularly, but when he did, he was devout, and it was noticed. Certain members of Montréal's elite stockbroker community, not all of them Jews, took out memberships to Shaar Hashomayim and attended every Saturday just for those rare glimpses of Mr. Goldberg striding into the sanctuary in the tailored dark suits that he bought annually on shopping trips to Jermyn Street. Draped over his broad shoulders and falling across his chest, Mr. Goldberg wore a thick white tallit, the ritual prayer shawl with fringes at the bottom. Mr. Goldberg's tallit had a deep golden border that matched his golden kippah, or skullcap, which always seemed just a little too small for his oversized head.

Whenever Mr. Goldberg was seen entering the sanctuary and taking his seat, along with his beloved wife, Ruth, every stockbroker and investment adviser in attendance paid heed. And when they left later that day, a little after noon, even though it was the Sabbath and the Montréal Stock Exchange would not open for two more days, they would be making discreet calls urging their clients to buy shares or up their existing position in Goldberg Limited on Monday morning at the opening bell.

This had had been a Montréal tradition among a certain set of stockbrokers for years. Ever since Morty Mazurski, a young Turk investment banker at Goldman Sachs, had happened to sit behind Mr. Goldberg and shamelessly eavesdropped on the gold industry legend while pretending to pray, it had been common knowledge among those who got paid to know these things that when Mr. Goldberg attended Sabbath services at Shaar Hashomayim, a major deal was about to go down. It had never failed, not once in thirty years. And so it was that at least twelve of the men who worshipped each Saturday had become multimillionaires on the basis of both their own investments in Goldberg Limited and the generous commissions they received from their clients for their impeccable advice.

But that hadn't always been the case, and Morty Mazurski deserved the full credit for rectifying this deficiency in the insider knowledge of at least one subset of Montréal's investment community. Back on a Saturday in April 1979, when David and I were still at LCC, a young Morty Mazurski had had the good fortune to be seated in row eleven, two spots in from the centre aisle, when Mr. Goldberg made his way to his seat, shaking hands as he went.

Even then, when Mr. Goldberg attended shul, it was always an event. People who had only met him once were flattered when he remembered their names and greeted them like old friends. More often than not, they wanted to shake his hand so they could tell their neighbour or friend they had shaken hands with the great Mr. Goldberg himself, that he had spoken to them, that he had paid them a generous compliment. More often than not, they were not disappointed. As he made his way to his seat near the front of the sanctuary, Mr. Goldberg always took the time to speak with whoever wanted to speak with him. Ruth was always at his side, waiting patiently, smiling, making small talk with another awed spouse when warranted, remaining silent when not.

When Mr. Goldberg had made his way to his row, he sat down just in front of Morty Mazurski. Although they didn't know each other, Mr. Goldberg had turned and smiled briefly in Morty's direction as he was taking his seat. Mr. Goldberg hadn't extended his hand, but Morty had always assumed that was because at that exact moment, Rabbi Cohen had been clearing his throat. As the service got underway, and as the Torah and the Sabbath prayer book were read from, and as everybody stood up and sat down at the direction of Rabbi Cohen, and as the congregation swayed and prayed and bowed their heads and touched the fringes of their tallitot in the ritual succession of prayers exalting the glory of the one true God, Morty noticed that Mr. Goldberg was more devout than anyone else around him. He kept his eyes closed the whole time, and he swayed heavily back and forth, bowing his head lower than anyone around him in the worship of his God.

The *parsha* that day was from the later, ever sweetening stages of Exodus: the Israelites passing out of their forty-year sojourn in the deprivations and incertitude of Sinai after their miraculous escape from Egypt and beginning their heady and life-affirming fight for control of the land of milk and honey, completing their transformation from slaves into soldiers and princes. To Morty Mazurski's surprise, Mr. Goldberg never stopped praying, not even when Rabbi Cohen was speaking and everybody else was listening to the service. As Mr. Goldberg kept praying with more physical passion than Morty had ever seen in another human being, Morty found himself desperately wanting to know what the great man was praying for. Although he didn't want to be rude, and although Morty's cautious wife, Mindy, pulled him back when he began to lean forward, Morty couldn't help himself. He leaned as close as he could to the bench in front of him and the swaying bulk of Mr. Goldberg. And what Morty heard on that April day, as Mr. Goldberg worshipped, was this:

"Dear Lord, when my lawyers go forth to Westgold with the hostile takeover bid this coming Monday, I implore you, Lord, to look favourably on Goldberg Limited and Saul Goldberg: grant me the courage and power to smite my enemies who will also be bidding; let my offer of $32 dollars a share, a 10 percent premium over the traded stock price, be the winning bid, and may the decision to take on $350 million in debt be as successful as I know it can and will be."

At first Morty was amazed. Mindy thought her beloved husband was having a massive coronary when Morty suddenly recoiled from his eavesdropping and fell back in his seat. But after several minutes trapped in an almost catatonic state, Morty recovered his composure. As Rabbi Cohen droned on in Hebrew, a small but fetching smile crept slowly over Morty's features. And after the service was over, and Morty and Mindy had made small talk at the Kiddush lunch, Morty couldn't help racing his

Mercedes up the south side of Westmount to his stone mansion, where he placed his first discreet call to his best and most trusted client.

One week later, when the shareholders of Westgold voted to accept Goldberg Limited's bid of just over three dollars' premium per share, the personal net worth of Morty Mazurski increased by the not insubstantial sum of three million dollars. And from then on, no stockbroker worth his salt would miss Saturday morning service at Shaar Hashomayim.

"DOES MR. GOLDBERG know?" As I asked the question of Solomon, I couldn't help wondering what would be worse. If Mr. Goldberg did know, that would make him an accessory to insider trading, and if he didn't, that would make him at least reckless if not downright stupid.

Solomon must have guessed from my face what I was thinking because he said, "That's not the point, whether my uncle is guilty of insider training or just plain stupidity. I actually don't think he's an insider trader. Nor do I think he's lacking in intelligence, at least not by conventional standards. But those considerations are relatively trivial. What I think is of most interest is the way my uncle chooses to commune with his God and what that says about the state of his immortal soul." And then Solomon proceeded to tell me about Mr. Goldberg's idiosyncratic reading of the Bible.

DESPITE SPEAKING TO employees after each takeover, along with his sons, Mr. Goldberg didn't do many speeches or media interviews. Most of his media appearances over the years seemed impromptu and were the result of quick scrums he'd ended up doing when he was coming to or leaving big mining conferences. He'd oblige the media for five minutes, and then Ira, who doubled as his lawyerly head of PR, would call an end to the scrum.

Luckily for the media, Mr. Goldberg seemed to be at a public event around the time we had just announced an acquisition and sometimes even the closing of a deal. He would graciously take a few minutes with the Fourth Estate when they swarmed as he was about to take his seat. Our Ghana deal was no exception. Reporters always wanted to know why we were buying and how we intended to create value where the previous owner and management team hadn't been able to.

The answer was invariably the same, almost boring in its predictability and simplicity, but still one that never dissuaded the business media from running it every time. "Why are we buying? Three reasons." The rule of three in media relations was something Ira had taught Mr. Goldberg early on. "One, we watch our pennies carefully, so our debt ratio is always low, and this means we can buy in the down cycles when others are selling. Two, we know the mining business like the back of our hand, and we see opportunities to make improvements that the seller might be missing. And three, the new production adds to our already substantial size, which will give us economies of scale and enable us to drive down costs even further."

After the formal, almost boilerplate opening that Ira recommended for every acquisition, Mr. Goldberg's pronouncements were always generously contrarian, the opposite of whatever other mining CEOs were saying at the moment and counter to the recycled wisdom being packaged and sold at a premium in every MBA program at every top-tier university in that particular year. When companies were tripping over themselves in the 1990s to outsource their finance and IT functions first to North

American service providers and then eventually to overeducated and underpaid university graduates in India, Goldberg Limited was still proudly managing all its support functions and services in-house. "I like to create and maintain jobs for Canadians. If that means I'm old-fashioned, then I suppose I'm guilty as charged," Mr. Goldberg would say with an unapologetic and endearing shrug of his heavy shoulders.

In this, Mr. Goldberg was swimming against the corporate tide, but he was also simply remembering what the inventor of the Ford Model T, for all his many faults, had believed and what most business leaders had never known or else had quickly forgotten. "Henry Ford was a garden-variety anti-Semite, but he paid his workers above-average wages because he wanted them to be able to afford to buy the car they built on the assembly line," Mr. Goldberg explained. "I want my employees to be able to invest in gold and buy nice jewellery for their wives."

Because of his reluctance to embrace the ubiquitous outsourcing trend, there were some analysts who dismissed Mr. Goldberg behind his back and sometimes politely in their reports. But productivity and efficiency at all our mines remained high, and on all the metrics that counted — return on capital; earnings before interest, taxes, depreciation, and amortization; and the prized-above-all total shareholder return — we consistently outperformed our peers and the market. While everyone was benchmarking their competition and making unimaginative consultants rich and tripping over themselves to adopt the latest fads, like lean production and Six Sigma, Mr. Goldberg would proudly assert his distinctive path whenever he was asked what he was learning from the competition: "I don't pay attention to my competitors. I don't think about them at all. When you're running a race, you don't turn around to see who might be gaining on you, because that's exactly when you lose your concentration and can be over-taken. Perhaps you even trip and fall on your face. I just run as hard and fast as I can."

Mr. Goldberg's lack of concern over the doings of his competi-tors extended to the governments of the day. Unlike other English business leaders in Montréal, Mr. Goldberg never seemed to lose any sleep over the referendums on Québec independence, not in 1980 when David and I were still at LCC and not during the close one in 1995 when we were both working in the business. "This is our home. You don't leave your home," Mr. Goldberg said on more than one occasion in reply to questions about whether he was thinking about moving the Goldberg head office down the 401 to Toronto. Privately, he dismissed separatist politics as no more than clumsy sabre-rattling to get a better deal out of Canada. "In Canada, we never let our politics get in the way of making money. The French may come across as more romantic than the English, but even they understand this."

Mr. Goldberg could be eloquent, sometimes almost biblical, in his extemporaneous speech in private and even in his rare public remarks. But often with the media he intuitively simplified his grammar, became pithy, sometimes even used sentence fragments. And he never said anything he didn't want to. When a bold reporter once asked what he thought about *Harvard Business Review*'s latest study on the well-documented third-generation curse of fam-ily-owned companies, Mr. Goldberg shook his head and laughed. "Never read business magazines. Too busy making money."

Was he a dinosaur, one bold reporter asked — not using that particular word but making his meaning impossible to miscon-strue — because he held to the antiquated notion of the family-controlled firm at a time when most companies were going public to raise capital and grow?

"The family is the primary unit of society. The family-owned firm that upholds family values — a sense of belonging, deep loyalty, reciprocal relationships — is in the best interests of society. At Goldberg Limited, we have the best of both worlds: we're publicly traded, so we can raise capital to invest in our company and acquire others, but through our dual-class share structure we're still, and will always be, family-controlled. This means we don't have to kowtow to short-term thinking and live in constant fear of quarterly results pressures. We can make the right investments that will provide superior returns over time. We build for the long term." The Goldberg family owned only twenty-five shares, but those special shares gave them fifty-five percent of the voting rights even though they held only twenty-five percent of the equity.

Asked to elaborate on what it meant to own and run a family firm, Mr. Goldberg waxed almost poetic. "There is a tremendous responsibility that comes when your family name is the company's name. We're not a faceless corporation. We have a name to appeal to or to take in vain. Customers or shareholders know where to find us when they want to. I'm still listed in the telephone book." And so he was. Mr. and Mrs. S. Goldberg, their Upper Westmount address and phone number listed plainly for everyone to see.

Mr. Goldberg treated all business journalists the same. He didn't discriminate in terms of whom he spoke with or didn't. He never froze out any journalists because he never felt he had to. No journalists had ever "burned" him. He had a healthy skepticism, but he never got nervous around them. There was one journalist, though, whom Mr. Goldberg trusted above others because Mr. Goldberg thought he understood business, mining in particular, and because he never misquoted him and never seemed to have an agenda — my childhood friend Michael Appleby.

From time to time, Mr. Goldberg sat down with Michael for twenty minutes or maybe even half an hour, sometimes even over lunch at Schwartz's. In one of those few in-depth interviews, Mr. Goldberg in the early 2000s commented on the great hollowing out of the Canadian mining industry that was taking place.

"Many of the big Canadian miners are selling out, are being taken over, because they have no long-term vision, because their shareholders are impatient for profit-taking. That's not us. We're still headquartered in Canada. We're not going anywhere. My father didn't start this company ninety years ago, I didn't grow it for the last thirty, and I don't run it today with my three sons to sell it and retire early. We don't sell companies. We build them, and we buy them. We are not motivated to be the biggest, even though we've grown in size. But we want to be around the longest." As Canadian miners sold out around him in the first decade of the twenty-first century, Mr. Goldberg's thinking quietly changed. By the time 2010 was approaching and I had been with the company almost twenty years, he couldn't see the harm in doing both.

We made acquisition after acquisition and added production and scale and employees until we were the second largest gold producing company in the world, with mines on four continents and thirty-eight thousand employees. Through it all, we remained largely private in our business and how we presented ourselves to the world, despite some concessions to the public markets and the need to raise capital through our dual-class ownership structure and Mr. Goldberg's well-timed occasional forays into the media. And although we didn't see it at the time, around and above us, circling like a moneyed vulture, was Solomon, patiently looking to pick off the weak and the dying, gliding in the air while we clawed furiously at the ground.

PART FOUR

Solomon
2010–2011

1

IT WAS LIKE one of the scenes out of a Russian novel, as I imagined them to be. Imagined because I'd never read one from start to finish, even though my mother had, and early in my career, Ira had tried to get me interested in Tolstoy and Dostoevsky. *War and Peace*, although Ira's hero Napoleon is the archvillain of that book. *Crime and Punishment*, despite its predominant grimness. Both lawyers' favourites, but after being introduced to Dr. Seuss by my mother, I had reverted to and developed a preference for nonfiction, one that had remained with me for most of my life.

It was the spring of 2010, and Mr. Goldberg was in his sickbed one morning, surrounded by his three sons and two advisers. But this was Mr. Goldberg, so his sickbed was his office, and the only concession he had made to his condition was sitting in one of the armchairs instead of standing up and pacing as he liked to do when he was thinking and speaking. The three sons were on the leather sofa. Ira and I were sitting in armchairs. Mr. Goldberg was about to go into the Mayo Clinic in Rochester, Minnesota, for major surgery, but he was holding court. Sammy, as usual, was prepared to hang on his father's every word, although Mr.

Goldberg hadn't yet started to speak. Jake was looking like he'd rather be anywhere else. David had a neutral, almost bored expression on his face. Ira was sitting at attention, clearly working, even though he was silent like the rest of us. I was waiting for Mr. Goldberg to begin.

"As you all know, I will be seventy-three in December of this year." Ira shot Mr. Goldberg a look as if to say, *But you don't look it, Mr. Goldberg,* and Mr. Goldberg returned the look with one of his own — appreciative and innocent — and glanced around the room. Nobody said anything. After a suitable pause, Mr. Goldberg went on.

"In all that time, I've been fortunate to have had excellent health. So now I've got a little something." He shrugged in his chair. "It's my turn. I fly down to Mayo in a few days. The doctors are confident they can remove the cancer." Mr. Goldberg was matter-of-fact. He didn't appear worried. His tone didn't change when he said the dreaded two-syllable word. If anything, he sounded nonchalant, as if sharing with us that he had made an appointment to have a troublesome hangnail removed.

Although Mr. Goldberg had given, and continued to give, millions of dollars each year to the Montréal Jewish General Hospital so that Montréalers could get the best possible care that our public health system allowed, he had entrusted the removal of the cancerous tumour in his lower right lung to a thirty-eight-year-old Jewish surgeon at the Mayo Clinic, which was known for its lung cancer treatment. Although Mr. Goldberg would gladly hire men of all nationalities and religions to dig for gold at his mines, he let only Jewish doctors touch his body. He'd chosen the Mayo not because he felt their doctors were innately more gifted than their Montréal counterparts at the Jewish General. He was simply playing the odds that the American clinics tilted in their

patients' favour, having found a doctor at the Mayo who special-
ized in this particular rare form of lung cancer.

The cancer itself had been a surprise. Prostate cancer had
become an increasing occupational hazard of being born a male,
and if I ever thought of Mr. Goldberg as having any cancer it
would have been that one. But this was a small tumour on his
right lung even though Mr. Goldberg had never smoked. And, as
he had reminded us on more than one occasion before his cancer
diagnosis, we mined gold, not the poisonous asbestos that was
somehow still legal to mine and export from Canada. Cancer was
a crapshoot, a genetic lottery with numbers drawn daily. When
millions of cells die and are replaced each day, the odds are that
something will go wrong.

Ira looked concerned, albeit in a professional way. Even
though we had all heard the news less than a week earlier from
Ira — Mr. Goldberg had told him first — Sammy was stricken. I
imagined he was wondering in his peculiar fashion if he would
react as stoically as his father if it were his body that was mal-
functioning. Jake hadn't yet learned how to react to his father's
imperfections, and David responded with nothing more nor less
than a healthy concern.

But Mr. Goldberg didn't want to leave us in suspense. "They
tell me I can expect a full recovery. But it will take time. After the
surgery, radiation *and* chemo." Mr. Goldberg spoke as if he had
won a special prize, being chosen to undergo surgery and both
sets of treatments. He looked at each of us. Jake flinched. The
rest of us were impassive. "I plan to be out of the office for two
months, less if I can help it." I noticed Mr. Goldberg didn't say
he planned to take two months off work. He undoubtedly would
hold meetings with his inner circle, read memos. "Enough time
for my hair to start to grow back." A strange comment from Mr.

Goldberg, as I'd never thought of him as vain. "In my absence," he added, and here Sammy sucked in his breath and held it, "I've asked Ira to run things."

This was the first time Mr. Goldberg had taken an extended absence and the first time he had delegated the authority for running the company to anyone. He had chosen Ira rather than one of his own sons. Ira nodded.

"Ira is here to support each of you. Please reach out to him as needed." And then, just as suddenly as it had begun, the audience was over. Mr. Goldberg stood up to leave.

All of us knew that Mr. Goldberg had made up his mind. He rarely changed it. But Sammy, maybe for the first time in his life, wasn't ready to let his father go. When Sammy spoke, his voice was soft and as neutral as possible, with only the slightest stress on the name of Goldberg Limited's chief legal officer. He even used the passive voice so as not to bring attention to his questioning his father. "Why is Ira being left in charge?"

Mr. Goldberg didn't pause to think. "Because it's my decision. And I've decided on Ira."

Sammy didn't pause to think, and I admired him for keeping the emotion out of his voice. "What about leaving me in charge?"

"What about it, Samuel?"

"Well, I'm your first-born son."

"And your point, Samuel?"

Sammy should have stopped there. He might have escaped unscathed. But he had to continue. He had to ask the question that he really wanted to ask his father, the question that had been on his mind for years. It didn't seem to bother him that he was asking it in front of his brothers, Ira, and me. I remember thinking that, even with his lack of intelligence, of self-awareness, he was very brave.

"Fine. You've chosen Ira while you're out sick. Why won't you ever make me CEO?" With that question, the air went out of the room.

SAMMY HAD ALWAYS resembled his father physically, but the resemblance had started to become exaggerated as Sammy reached his late thirties. If you looked closely, you might suspect that God was pulling a fast one on Sammy, as if He had decided to slightly accentuate in Sammy's face and body every notable physical characteristic of his father as a divine joke, because inside, Sammy was not quite the man his father was. In my view, that wasn't a terrible thing, but Sammy took the opposite view.

Like Mr. Goldberg, Sammy was tall and heavyset, a little taller at six foot three to his father's six foot two, and two hundred and forty pounds to his father's two hundred and twenty. This extra weight was mostly muscle and came from hitting the gym three times a week. Like his father, Sammy combed his blond hair straight back from his forehead, and, like his father, his hair was still thick. When Sammy was young and starting his Bachelor of Commerce at McGill before dropping out to work at junior-level jobs in the family business — his father was adamant that his sons were going to work their way up in the family business as he had — everyone in the business and some outside it assumed that Mr. Goldberg's oldest son would be the one to succeed him.

Whenever Mr. Goldberg took Sammy to visit the mine when he was a child, Sammy would greet the workers with respect. He'd look them in the eye and shake their hands, thanking them for their work. He was equally good with customers and investors, and whenever Mr. Goldberg let him speak on behalf of the company, the media loved him. Sammy was handsome in a way that looked good on camera and that the media favoured. He had the confidence and smile of a born leader. Like his father, he looked like an athlete, and like his father, when he wanted to, he could speak in sound bites that described complex aspects of the mining business in ways that business journalists appreciated because it made their jobs easy and made them look good.

I think Mr. Goldberg had always thought more highly of David than Sammy, and certainly more highly of David than Jake, from the time they were boys and their characters were becoming evident. But it took him some time to rule Sammy out as his potential successor. Mr. Goldberg never told anyone this, not even his wife, but I think he realized that Sammy was too much like him. And Mr. Goldberg, in a rare moment of self-awareness, and to his credit, knew that for this reason, Sammy should not be the one to take his place at the head of Goldberg Limited. I had never told anyone, not David and certainly not Solomon, but the only people Mr. Goldberg had consulted on this matter were Ira and me. He had wanted a second opinion from a younger man.

FIVE YEARS EARLIER, Mr. Goldberg had invited me out to the Royal Montréal Golf Club, which billed itself as the oldest golf club in Montréal. Many Montréal golf clubs hadn't accepted Jews as members when he was growing up and for some years afterward. For this reason, David, and I think Solomon as well, never took up golf. But Mr. Goldberg had no such qualms. I think he enjoyed playing the game that had discouraged members of his family from playing an embarrassingly short few years earlier. For him, it was a kind of revenge. It was the same way he felt about trips to England. He had no reservations about going himself, but he would tease David about his love of London and its theatre, and he would say to me, "Do you know that England once expelled all its Jews, Mr. McFall? 1280. King Edward the first." And then, as if an expulsion that had lasted for seven hundred years wasn't enough, Mr. Goldberg would quote Shimon Peres: "There is in England a saying that an anti-Semite is someone who hates the Jews more than is necessary." Mr. Goldberg would laugh at this and then say, "What do you think of that, young Mr. McFall?" and I would mumble something suitably lawyerly in reply.

We played the first three holes in silence. It was only then that Mr. Goldberg came around to what was on his mind. Mr. Goldberg hit the ball, a long drive that landed nicely on the green. He gave his club to his caddy and started walking. I ran up to walk beside him. Even though he was in his late sixties then, he walked fast, and I had to walk faster just to keep up.

As was often the case with Mr. Goldberg, as it is with men who have power, there was no preamble when he wanted to get straight to the point. "What do you think of Samuel?" Not looking at me. Eyes straight ahead, his heavy body moving quickly and gracefully up and down the hills, his slowly greying hair even more golden than usual in the sun.

I knew exactly what I thought of Sammy, and I was fairly confident that I knew what Mr. Goldberg thought too. The trick in responding lay in how to articulate my views in a way that was helpful to Mr. Goldberg but that also didn't unnecessarily hurt Sammy — or me — at least not too much.

I didn't look at Mr. Goldberg as I prepared to reply because I knew it might embarrass him. I kept my voice and my gait light. I walked quickly but not too quickly, and I spoke slowly, conscious of not placing any emphasis on any particular word.

"Sammy is very good with people. Very passionate about the business. He works hard and tries hard." Damning with faint praise. Highlighting effort, not results. Mr. Goldberg walked faster. He was always determined to be stronger, faster, more resilient than anyone else. Everything was a competition to him. On business trips, he would be the first to wake up, the last to go to bed.

I went on. "He values your opinion. In fact, everything he does is to earn your approval." At this, Mr. Goldberg nodded and slowed down just a little. I knew what Mr. Goldberg was really asking me, but I couldn't go there right away. That would appear too eager and insufficiently loyal to Sammy, who, after all, remained his oldest son.

In retrospect, it's not hard to see why I felt like I was part of the Goldberg family, even though I didn't share their last name. There were the Friday night dinners that I was invited to at least once a month. The Passover seders, the Purim parties, the lighting of the giant menorah on Mr. Goldberg's front lawn every Hannukah and the heaping plates of latkes afterward that the Goldberg maid, Rita, would fry up for us. The regular invitations to the *landhuis* in Curaçao and the country house in North Hatley. The time my oldest daughter, Bridget, hit her head when she fell off her bike and David, without hesitation, offered to fly her to the Lahey for a consultation. The relationship wasn't just one way. I was a triple outsider to the Goldberg family — by money, by culture, and by blood — but I wouldn't have worked any harder for them and wouldn't have felt any closer to them if we had shared a last name. I like to think I was trusted, but in feeling like a member of family, I knew I was in danger of forgetting the most important piece of advice Ira had ever given me. No matter how much I felt like part of the Goldberg family, no matter how much they treated me like I was, I never would be one of them. I would always be, at most, a trusted confidant. I tried to keep this in mind as we golfed and I answered Mr. Goldberg's questions about his son.

"What kind of a CEO do you think Samuel would make?" Mr. Goldberg continued to avoid looking at me. He, too, was keeping his tone casual. We were approaching the next tee. I didn't have a lot of time. I had to choose my words carefully. Mr. Goldberg already knew the answer to his question, or else he wouldn't have asked it, but I had to answer in a way that was both helpful and acceptable. Mr. Goldberg had asked the question the way someone who watched sports might ask his friend if he thought a certain player would show up in an upcoming championship final. I wanted to say that Sammy was too much like Mr. Goldberg in certain respects, while at the same time he didn't have the handful of essential qualities that would make him successful. I plunged in.

"Sammy is a wonderful person. He's good at many things. He builds relationships with customers and investors, even employees. He would excel in investor relations, marketing, maybe even in HR. But being a CEO is different. You have to make decisions, not just recommendations. I think he depends too much on you and your judgment to be able to fill the role." I stopped there. I knew I was speaking the truth, but while there would always be an element of risk in offering your opinion to a billionaire about the fitness of his son, I was telling Mr. Goldberg what he already knew. When we reached the tee, Mr. Goldberg looked at me. I could tell that he agreed, but he wasn't going to share in words his own thoughts about his oldest son. After making me complicit in his judgment, he nodded and hit another long and accurate shot.

SAMMY'S VOICE WAS still matter-of-fact, but he had a terrible look on his face when he asked why his father wouldn't make him

CEO. We all looked away, even Mr. Goldberg. He shrugged and exhaled. He looked at Ira. Ira returned his gaze as if he was trying to communicate telepathically. Mr. Goldberg, never at a loss for words or for anything, certainly not an answer to a question, looked around the room as if he were trying to pull an answer out of the air. Finally, he stopped, as if he had decided that any old answer would do. His reptilian, strangely symmetrical eyes were flat.

"You don't read, Samuel. A CEO has got to read."

Sammy waited a moment before saying, "But you don't read." It came out sounding like a question. The tone was incredulous.

"That's not the point, Samuel," and Mr. Goldberg continued as if he were letting Sammy in on a secret, as if he had decided not to hold back anymore. "Unlike you, I'm the son of the founder. I don't have to read if I don't want to read. And that's because I grew up in the company. The company was still young when I first began to go with my father to the mine and to the office. Despite our successes in buying other companies, we were still small compared to the mining giants. If they had bothered to notice us and to take us seriously, the big companies could have crushed us, any day. I helped to grow the business with my father, and then I grew it even more without him. I learned the business the way people learn a first language at home instead of a second language at school. For me, it's like breathing. I've never had to think about it. But you," and here Sammy leaned in, scared but still eager to hear his father's opinion, "you're third generation." Mr. Goldberg said this with some measure of pity but without contempt. "You're that much more removed from the beginning. And that has consequences. According to the people who study these things, it's under your generation where everything goes off the rails. Partly because you all think you're so smart. You have the beginnings of a fancy education, even if you tried to impress me by dropping out of it. But it's mainly because when you grow up third generation, you have it too easy. You get soft. It's not that you've forgotten the early days; you've never had a chance to know them. I don't blame you for all of this. Not at all. It's why I've tried to toughen you up. But it can't all be up to me. To lead this company, you have to find a way to be better than me. You've spent your life trying to be as good as me. The same as me. When you're third generation, that's not good enough."

When Mr. Goldberg stopped speaking, Sammy didn't know where to rest his gaze. He looked like a boxer about to lose consciousness. Having responded at length to the terrible question posed by his oldest son, Mr. Goldberg spoke ostensibly now to Jake, even though Jake hadn't asked him anything. "You, Jacob, you're smart. Maybe too smart. Maybe you were right and I was wrong and I should have let you go work for McKinsey." Jake looked stunned even though he was forty-six and the McKinsey offer was almost a quarter of a century ago, but the rest of us all recognized Mr. Goldberg's unusual admission of fallibility as no more than nostalgia and preamble.

"Don't look like that. I haven't really changed my mind. It's one thing to give advice. You need to be smart for that. And you are smart, I will give you that. Maybe I should have let you go because you would have made a good adviser. Maybe that's your true destiny. But advisers are a dime a dozen. It's a completely different thing to make the decisions. That takes a certain kind of courage. A sense of when to turn the thinking off and actually do something." Jake looked away from his father. "When I come back, I want you to give up being vice-president of regulatory affairs and focus on your board responsibilities. That's where I need you. You, Samuel, can stay in marketing. But you need to start working more closely with Ira." There was no mention of David and what he should or should not do. Sammy looked deflated and bewildered, like an aging prince awaiting the monarch's death or abdication. Ira's face was blank. He didn't look at anyone or anything. When Mr. Goldberg stood up, we all did.

2

EVERYONE HAD ALWAYS assumed that if any of the Goldberg sons were going to have a nervous breakdown, it would be Jake. When it wasn't, it came as a surprise because Jake had only become more introverted with age, and those who spent any time with the family couldn't help observing that Jake rarely made eye contact with his father, even as he got older and seemed to make a sort of external peace with him. This had started in adolescence, according to David, although I had never noticed it at the time. I was too busy trying to fit in, trying to impress Mr. Goldberg whenever he asked me my opinion.

I think it ended up not being Jake because Jake never tried to compete with his father or earn his approval, although he never quite got used to his father's scorn. Jake's advantage over Sammy was that he knew he was never going to be CEO, knew he would never be his father, in large part because he knew he didn't want to be, and so the realization didn't take him by surprise. Sammy, on the other hand, was the complete opposite.

From the time he was a boy, certainly from when I had met him at LCC, Sammy had modelled himself on his father. He dressed like him, spoke like him, tried to think like him. From the moment he woke up until he went to bed, he was trying his best to be worthy of his father's approval, and every day of his life, Sammy worked to prepare himself to be a CEO just like Mr. Goldberg: the way Sammy stood and looked at you and shook your hand and communicated his ideas with that deliberate, bluff confidence. Until it was too late, Sammy believed that, as long as he worked hard enough and applied sufficient willpower, he could become CEO. I think he believed in an imperfect way that it was his destiny.

When Mr. Goldberg told Sammy he wasn't going to be CEO because he didn't read, it was apparent that Sammy thought he had misheard, or perhaps his father was joking. But Mr. Goldberg's eyes betrayed no mirth. He must have thought his father was testing him, wanting to see how tough he was, wanting him to fight for what was his. Sammy reacted the way he thought Mr. Goldberg would have reacted if Abraham had told him thirty years earlier that he wasn't going to succeed him at the head of the family business. He became angry.

When Mr. Goldberg stood up, we assumed the meeting was over. But Sammy couldn't let go. He summoned what remained of his courage and told his father that the conversation wasn't over, that he was ready to be CEO and had been ready for years. I had never seen Sammy contradict Mr. Goldberg in anything, and I can't say that I didn't admire Sammy for finally standing up to him. But Sammy's words didn't sound definitive, the way he had intended them. Instead, he sounded unconvincing, his claims a formulaic protest, his voice unsteady. He would have been embarrassed to hear what we heard — his words came out like a whine, not the confident words of a grown man of forty-seven. He looked even more embarrassed fighting back tears.

Seeing his son like this, Mr. Goldberg could have said a thousand things. He could have tried to shock him into understanding, told Sammy he was mistaken, that he would never be CEO. Or he could have altered his approach and gone soft on him and held out hope, told him he wasn't yet ready, that he still needed more experience. But he said nothing. He walked over to Sammy, arms extended, and pulled his oldest son into a tight embrace. Sammy reached out, as if by instinct, and held his father even though it was clear he didn't want to. Sammy sobbed on the shoulder of the man he had dreamed of succeeding ever since he was capable of having such thoughts, while the rest of us stood and watched, unable to turn away. By the end of the day, Sammy had been admitted to the hospital.

IT WASN'T UNTIL late that night that we learned what had happened. We pieced it together afterward, based on eyewitness accounts. After Sammy left the office, he got into his favourite Porsche and drove out to the Dorval airport. On the way, he called Rejean Tremblay, his favourite pilot. Rejean was picnicking with his wife and youngest son on Mount Royal; but, when he got the call, he made his apologies to his family, dropped them off at home, and drove to the Goldberg hangar. Normally he would have taken a co-pilot as well, but like Abraham and even like Mr. Goldberg, Sammy had his pilot's licence.

They flew north on a clear spring day. Afterward, Rejean reported that Sammy behaved perfectly ordinarily on the two-hour flight up to Springtime, the original mine. He joked, sat up in the co-pilot's seat, asked after Rejean's four children. Rejean's youngest son was only eleven but was already quite the hockey player. Québec Major Junior was a certainty, and although Rejean thought it was bad luck to even think about it, coaches and scouts were confidently talking about little Michel going in the middle rounds of the NHL draft. Sammy had seen Michel play a few times and was bullish on his prospects. Up to that point, it was like any other trip to the mine, except that Sammy had phoned with less than usual notice.

Rejean was one year younger than Sammy and had been a pilot almost as long as Sammy had drawn his first paycheque from the business, which was when he was twenty. In the years of Sammy's bachelorhood, Rejean had flown Sammy and whomever his girlfriend happened to be to New York City for dinner or to the Bahamas for a weekend. More than a few times, he had flown Sammy to London for supper and a show and then back again, keeping his earphones on while Sammy entertained his date. The life of a Goldberg pilot was filled with unpredictability, which is why the paycheque was good. And, truth be told, most of his time was spent waiting to fly, either in Montréal or in other locations. Like the other pilots on the Goldberg Limited payroll, Rejean had flown fighter jets for the Canadian Air Force before being recruited to become a corporate pilot. Ideally, the Goldbergs liked their former fighter pilots to have combat experience.

Even when they landed at the mine and deplaned, Rejean couldn't tell that anything was out of the ordinary. Sammy told Rejean to wait for him and drove the car the Goldbergs kept at the hangar the ten minutes to the mine. Agnes Johnson, secretary to mine manager John Malcolm, saw Sammy walking quickly through the administration building toward the back doors leading to the mine. He didn't smile and say hello. He didn't stop to ask about her children. He was in a hurry, swiped his pass, and walked outside to the mine without wearing the mandatory safety gear, emblazoned with the company name. Agnes went to tell John Malcolm, because she knew he would want to know that one of the Goldbergs was visiting the site, especially if he was behaving strangely.

Sammy's failure to wear proper protective clothing was just the beginning. As soon as he left the office building, he broke into a run. By this time, John Malcolm was following Sammy, and he decided to chase after him. Sammy ran down the mine road, not bothering to drive one of the Jeeps, not wearing his coveralls, no golden hard hat on his head, no steel-toed boots on his feet. He was still the boss's son, a Goldberg, and so John Malcolm didn't try to stop him right away, didn't yell at him for breaking the safety rules. He ran after him, keeping him in sight.

Sammy ran for about five minutes before he said anything. The ground was wet and slippery. He was wearing loafers. When he started yelling, his breath was ragged. At first, John Malcolm couldn't make out his words. Malcolm began to run faster to cut down the distance between them. Only then was he able to make out clearly what Sammy was shouting.

Mr. Goldberg, Ira, David, Jake, and I learned about this incident on a conference call while the corporate jet was returning with Sammy to Montréal. The Goldbergs and I were all in Montréal, but Ira joined us over the phone from Florida, where he was vacationing. John Malcolm lowered his voice to the point that even straining to hear him, we couldn't make out what Sammy had shouted.

Mr. Goldberg asked Malcolm to repeat himself. Malcolm cleared his throat and raised his voice and spoke Sammy's words. "What he said, Mr. Goldberg, was that he was Samuel Goldberg, the first-born son of Mr. Goldberg — well, he used your first name — the first grandson of Abraham Goldberg. He shouted this again and again. And then he began to shout, 'All this is mine. All this is mine.'"

According to Malcolm, Sammy repeated those words as he was descending into the mine that his grandfather had built. Then Malcolm told us that after Sammy started yelling his name and where he fit into the Goldberg family, his running became erratic because he began to take off his clothes.

"Began to do what?" Mr. Goldberg asked.

"Take off his clothes, Mr. Goldberg," Malcolm repeated in a dutiful and embarrassed voice.

At first, Sammy tore off his shirt and tie. He stumbled out of his pants without taking off his loafers first. He fell down twice in the mud, as if he was drunk, but each time he got up. He was less than a tenth of the way down the road into the mine.

Gaetan McKenzie, one of the drivers, was coming up out of the mine with a full load of ore when he saw Sammy in his boxers running toward him. John Malcolm saw Gaetan in his large yellow truck and started waving his arms, yelling at him to stop. Malcolm was worried that Sammy would fall off the edge of the road and break his neck or that Gaetan would accidentally run him over. Sammy didn't look back when Malcolm started yelling. He kept running. He began to half-run and stumble. He was covered in mud.

When Malcolm reached Sammy, he expected him to scream or to push him away or to hit him, but Sammy became silent and stopped moving. Malcolm lifted him off the muddy road where he had fallen and pulled him close. He held him tightly even in his near nakedness. He had known Sammy ever since he was a boy.

Malcolm held Sammy until Gaetan reached them with his truck. Gaetan called on his walkie-talkie, and other men came in a pickup truck with a blanket. They bundled Sammy into their truck and drove him to the administration office, where they dressed him in borrowed clothes. The on-site nurse gave him a tranquilizer.

Malcolm called Rejean, and together they put Sammy back on the plane to Montréal.

WHEN SAMMY LANDED, it was David who met him at the airport. Rejean had called David from the plane to ask him to be there because he was confident Mr. Goldberg's youngest son would know how to take care of the oldest one.

By the time they landed in Montréal, Sammy had retreated into himself. He had wept hopelessly on the plane. Rejean hadn't known where to put him; he was afraid to leave Sammy in the long passenger seat because he might harm himself, but Rejean was more afraid to have Sammy in the cockpit because he might harm both of them. So he seated Sammy halfway back and turned around frequently to see how he was doing. He had put a blanket around Sammy's shoulders, and Sammy pulled the blanket tightly around himself like a child. He wept on and off the whole plane ride back, and Rejean kept hoping for it to end. It finally did, as they were landing.

David was waiting on the tarmac just outside the hangar with his car running. Rejean helped Sammy down the steps from the plane. David took his older brother in his arms. Sammy held on to him and started to weep again. David gently led Sammy into his waiting car and drove him straight to Montréal General, where David knew the head of psychiatry. Dr. Schleifer came straight away from a dinner party when David called. Sammy's wife, Esther, arrived at the hospital at almost the same time. She held her husband's hand as he walked inside, and then she waited outside Dr. Schleifer's office while he assessed Sammy. She held him tightly as he was admitted and sat vigil outside his room as he began to shout again, before the new tranquilizers took effect.

By then, Sammy's eyes were glazed over, and all he would say in response to any of the psychiatrist's questions was, "I am Samuel Goldberg, first-born son."

When David called Mr. Goldberg later that night to tell him that Sammy had been admitted to hospital, Mr. Goldberg seemed to be at a loss for words. When he spoke, his voice sounded deliberately unemotional. "I think this is the first time that a Goldberg has ever been admitted to hospital for psychiatric problems."

David, who was usually so sparing of his father's feelings, said, "Well, you know what they say, Dad."

"What?"

"There's always a first time."

Mr. Goldberg didn't say anything. He hung up.

I WENT TO the hospital as soon as David called. Ira was already on his way back from Florida. David slept fitfully on a chair outside Sammy's room all night, along with Esther and me. When Mr. Goldberg arrived the next morning to visit his first-born son, David had just woken up and gone to get coffee for us, but Esther had been wide awake for hours and was waiting for her father-in-law.

The Goldberg wives were a presence in their own ways, and they were important to their husbands — I'm sure Mr. Goldberg, Sammy, and Jake loved their wives, and David would have as well if he had had one — and their wives no doubt served as advisers to their husbands outside of the office. But when it came to the running of Goldberg Limited, the Goldberg women were not even supporting actors; they were extras. It was clear from how the family spoke about her that Aviva had played the major role in inspiring, and perhaps shaping, her son, Abraham. She had done so with her courage in emigrating to a new country and transcending the loss of her husband so soon after their arrival and before Abraham was born, and in working two jobs so he could stay in school. But after her, the Goldberg wives were not part of the main action. Running the company was the exclusive domain of the men.

All the Goldberg wives from Ruth on shared similar features. Esther was no exception. Tall, thin, and blond, and possessing an ability to wear clothes so perfectly that one was never sure whether it was learned or innate. A certain hint of insecure haughtiness that couldn't be completely hidden in public, even underneath an excessive politeness and considerable charity work. But at home, Esther had been the ideal Goldberg wife, dutiful and supportive at every Sabbath supper, every High Holiday, every family function, through every family squabble, standing loyally beside Sammy while he stood loyally at Mr. Goldberg's side. Esther never raised her voice at anyone: not Sammy, not their three children, certainly not Mr. Goldberg.

When Esther saw Mr. Goldberg, all six feet two inches and two hundred and twenty pounds of him, come down the hallway to where she was sitting, walking in his expensive but sensible brown shoes with the padded soles that he had taken to wearing since his illness, she didn't see her father-in-law, or the father of Sammy, or a billionaire, or a still handsome blond-haired man of seventy-two. Later, she told David and me that at that moment, Mr. Goldberg looked to her like a very large, very dangerous cat, a golden panther on the hunt. And when this golden panther stopped in front of her, Esther stood up. But when Mr. Goldberg reached out to hug and hold her, she wouldn't let him kiss her. She held her arms at her side and moved her face. When Mr. Goldberg was done trying to hold her, she gently pushed his arms away.

Until she opened her mouth, she didn't know what she was going to say, and when the words came, Esther was doubly surprised to find she wasn't crying and was instead speaking to her father-in-law calmly but directly, in a way she never had before. She told him that what had happened to Sammy was Mr. Goldberg's fault.

"My fault?"

"For not understanding him, for standing by and letting him worship you all these years, knowing he wasn't going to run the business, the only thing he ever wanted."

Mr. Goldberg might have been able to say something then, something to show Esther that he was listening, but he stared at her. It was evident he didn't know what she was talking about. That was when Esther dropped her calm, and for the first time in her life, she started to scream at her father-in-law.

At first, Mr. Goldberg smiled uncomfortably, as if at a crazy person. His eyelids didn't descend. He looked at Esther and smiled. She screamed, accusing Mr. Goldberg of caring more about himself than his son, of not exercising his basic responsibilities as a father to help his son be independent. A nurse called security. Mr. Goldberg's smile began to fade, and the blood drained from his golden face.

When Esther finished and reached up with a small, well-manicured hand to slap her father-in-law's face, Mr. Goldberg grabbed her wrist and shook it roughly. He said quietly, "Don't you dare ever raise your hand to me again." He dropped her wrist and turned his back on her. Then he looked at me as if willing me to say something, to take his side, to attempt to calm Esther down. But I was shocked. I looked up at him helplessly and said nothing. Mr. Goldberg nodded just a little, like he hadn't really expected much of anything from me, and began the long walk down the hallway to the elevator. I turned to Esther. I didn't know her any better than I knew any of the Goldberg wives, but I took her in my arms. She wept on my shoulder. Mr. Goldberg waited for the elevator and got on it without turning around.

AN HOUR LATER, I was walking through the hospital lobby to the front door when Mr. Goldberg came out of the small coffee shop. He fell into step beside me without speaking. It was mid-morning, and the hospital was crowded. As we approached the door, Mr. Goldberg pulled me aside. He didn't speak loudly, despite the background noise, but because of the way he spoke and how close he stood to me, I heard every word. He spoke the way rich people usually do, knowing you will lean in to listen and will wait patiently until they are done. As he spoke, nobody accidentally walked into us or even came close. It was like Mr. Goldberg had created a bubble around the two of us in the centre of the loud, crowded lobby. He began without preamble, not always looking at me as he spoke. There was no "Young Mr. McFall."

"After the war, my father brought more refugees over. Families where possible, but usually remnants of families. Everybody had lost someone. Children had lost one or both parents, siblings.

"They were all scarred, but most got on with their lives, started businesses, resumed professions after they picked up enough English. And most of them did well. Very few became taxi drivers. Fewer still became alcoholics or drug addicts. Something about Jewish genes; we don't usually go in for that kind of thing. And after living through the Holocaust, what's a lost job, a failed business, a career disappointment? After surviving, many of them felt luck was on their side. A few did commit suicide. But most got on, and a greater percentage than you might think did really well, making millions. But out of everybody who had lost somebody, do you know who had it the worst?" It wasn't a rhetorical question. Mr. Goldberg waited for my reply. I shook my head.

"The parents who had lost a child. It was a fate worse than death. It was a living death. Each night, they saw their child in their nightmares, which would have been bad enough, but each day too. The parents who had lost a child — and some had lost more than one — shuffled through the rest of their lives, the walking dead. I saw fathers who were irreparably broken."

Mr. Goldberg looked into my eyes. His were dry, but the skin around them was red; this accentuated their strange, symmetrical shape. Mr. Goldberg was quiet for a moment. He watched a couple wheeling in a young child in a wheelchair. The child was smiling. Mr. Goldberg smiled.

"I remember visiting one of the families. The father was a doctor. And not just any doctor. He had been the foremost heart surgeon in Warsaw before the war. But when he arrived in Canada, he had lost the supreme faith in himself that you need if you want to be a surgeon. He ended up becoming a GP because he couldn't operate anymore. One day, when he was meeting with my family at our office downtown, this man broke down crying in front of my father, in front of me and Isaac. We were still young children. He couldn't speak; he couldn't catch his breath. Without thinking, my father stood up and embraced him. Abraham used to hug us and run his hands through our hair, but I'd never seen him hold a grown man before. My father held this other man while he sobbed. As you know, my family is tall, but this man was even taller, broad-shouldered, heavier. He was a strong man. But there he was sobbing in front of my father and us children. I had never seen a man cry before, and it seemed like it went on forever before he cried himself out on my father's shoulder.

"In the car ride home, I asked my father why the man had been crying. I knew already that he had survived the Holocaust, but I'd never seen anything quite like that. My father always looked at me when he spoke, but this one time he kept looking out of the car as our chauffeur drove." Mr. Goldberg paused, and then he said, "Unlike me, my perfect father often used a chauffeur." He paused again, as if aware he had interrupted his story with an irrelevant detail.

"My father's voice was flat when he replied to me, as though he didn't want to permit himself any emotion. 'He lost his first wife and two daughters in the Shoah.' That's what my father always called it. Never the Holocaust. Always the Shoah. Always said slowly, quietly, with reverence, the way he pronounced the word *God*, even though the two words were opposites. 'He blames himself. He wishes he had got his family out of Poland sooner. He had more than enough money, but he didn't foresee what was going to happen. For the first few weeks, he saw them in the women's section of the camp, through the barbed wire. They would exchange glances; they were forbidden to speak. But after the first few weeks, he stopped looking at them. He deliberately avoided catching their eyes.' My father had stopped speaking. I waited for him to continue. When he didn't, I asked, 'Why?'

"Only now did my father turn around and look into my eyes. 'It was shame, Saul. He was ashamed. He was powerless to protect them.' And then he rubbed the top of my head as if to remind himself that I was still there, as if he were afraid I might disappear, and he looked outside the car again."

Mr. Goldberg looked over at the little boy, who was being wheeled into an elevator by his parents. "You can't always blame the father, but a father is supposed to be strong. His most important responsibility in his life is to protect his wife and his children. When a man can't do that, a man is nothing." Then he turned on his heel and walked outside.

SAMMY STAYED IN the hospital for three months. When he was discharged, he had lost a lot of weight. Mr. Goldberg flew him, Esther, and their children down to Curaçao for a month, where Sammy rested and recuperated at *Landhuis* Goldberg, swimming and reading the papers. He would occasionally join us for conference calls about the business. As he recovered, he gained his weight back quickly and even gained a bit more than before because the drugs his doctor put him on to manage his moods caused him to retain water.

All through Sammy's recovery, Mr. Goldberg mostly handled his oldest son with a gentleness that I hadn't thought him quite capable of, and after Sammy returned to Montréal but before he returned to work full-time, Mr. Goldberg threw him a big party at the Ritz-Carlton, Mr. Goldberg's favourite hotel.

When Sammy stood up at the party and addressed his friends and colleagues, he was tanned and healthy and confident. All of us were pleased to see this, especially when he showed he could joke about his experience. But afterward, whenever he was away from a crowd and he let down his guard, if you knew him and looked closely at his Goldberg eyes, you could see that he wasn't the same as before. You could see that the self-doubt that had always been there beneath the bluff, confident, deliberate exterior had won out.

3

THE MEETING WAS never public, never made it into the pages of the Montréal or national papers — even as a cameo in one of those long-form stories that print media do from time to time to assure themselves that they still matter.

In fact, this meeting over lunch in September 2010 at the Montréal Ritz-Carlton was only briefly witnessed by a man on his way to be seated at another table with a business client. The man who walked by was a senior partner at Evans, Landry, Steinberg — the firm retained by Goldberg Limited to do most of their legal work under the in-house direction of Ira Levin. But the briefly witnessed meeting, the ninety minutes that it took from first handshake to last, made it into the Goldberg family mythology by the end of the early fall day on which it occurred.

The two men eating lunch, who had been seen but not necessarily overheard, were cousins, but they had not spoken about anything remotely material for more than thirty years; on the odd occasion they had seen each other, it had been momentary and accidental in public spaces, never at a private function because those in mining circles and Montréal society knew not to invite them to the same event. This was a lunch meeting attended by two of the cousins of the separate branches of the Goldberg family, the two branches that had been separate since the deaths of Abraham and, soon after, Isaac. That the two men should now be seated together in the golden splendour of the Ritz-Carlton restaurant was nothing short of astonishing.

The man who saw and reported them, the sober-headed corporate lawyer and one of the original partners in the firm that bore his name, Moe Steinberg, found the sight so hard to believe when he first thought he saw them that he blinked, and then a few minutes later he worked up an excuse to walk by the booth just so he could confirm the first impression of his own eyes before he telephoned Ira Levin from outside the door of the men's room.

Moe Steinberg was never close enough to eavesdrop, so when he called Ira to let him know he had just seen Solomon Goldberg and the middle son of Mr. Goldberg engaged in what appeared to be a friendly, perhaps even a deep, conversation over lunch, there was nothing else to offer. But in Ira's subtle hands, that sight would be enough. I wasn't there, and so I had to gather the truth from several sources: Ira later that week, Jake a few days after that, and Solomon himself eventually. David must have learned about what had happened in a similarly disjointed fashion.

How the two of them had come to be seated together at Montréal's finest hotel, discussing whether Jake might wish to leave his family's company and join Solomon's firm, was never really properly answered. But that didn't stop anyone who heard about it from speculating. Most assumed it had been the result of a long courtship in which Solomon had reached out to his cousin through a well-placed intermediary, looking to establish contact, to test the waters. This preparatory work was understood to have taken the better part of a year, and that it culminated in a lunch was testament to Solomon's persistence and persuasiveness, not to mention his insight into family dynamics. But some also wondered why the two men had met in the Ritz-Carlton dining room, such a public place, and not in Solomon's office or in a private conference room at a less prominent location. Some used this question to belittle Solomon's intelligence. But those who knew him better, and I count myself among them, had a different interpretation. Solomon never did anything by accident. Solomon must have wanted to be seen.

Nobody who had a reason to know about such matters assumed that the idea for the lunch had been Jake's. By virtue of attending, Mr. Goldberg's middle son obviously had it in him to be a traitor to his father — this was the kind of heightened emotional and moral language that those who spoke about the lunch didn't hesitate to use — but among those who knew Jake, it was understood that he didn't have it in him to initiate such action. Even if he had once been capable of it, those who were familiar with the Goldberg family agreed it had long been beaten out of him.

Jake may have been susceptible, but he had never been stupid.

Jake asked Solomon what he had in mind. Solomon needed an executive vice-president of new mine development. Jake wouldn't have to deal with marketing or HR or existing operations. Solomon would ensure that he was supported in all those areas. He would have one job: build new mines for Solomon's company. And Solomon had big plans for the future, including, as he confided in Jake in circumspect but still unmistakable language, potential acquisitions in the next few years that could vault Solomon's company into becoming the largest gold company in the world by production. Of course, Jake wouldn't start off being part owner in a family business in the same way he was already, but as a senior executive and cousin to the founder, he would be given a generous allotment of shares to start and would be paid well. Annual bonuses and long-term incentives including stock options and straightforward grants would mean that over the next decade, he could become a very wealthy man.

At this point in the conversation, Jake apparently looked down at the tablecloth, and Solomon blushed, because Jake was already wealthier than he needed to be and probably had more money than Solomon. Anyone who later analyzed what they'd learned about the conversation characterized this comment to be a gross misstep by Solomon. It wasn't. Solomon knew exactly what he had to say to accomplish what he wanted.

"But we both know this is not about wealth. It's not about wealth for either of us, is it?"

Jake nodded and murmured, "No, it isn't." It had never been about the money for Jake, and that was the source of his greatest strength and his greatest weakness. It was the reason his father had never really understood or fully trusted him. Solomon was offering Jake a chance to matter, to make a difference. He was giving him a chance to do the work he loved and was good at. Choosing to work with Solomon would mean turning his back on his father. Jake was tempted, but he knew he couldn't say yes on the spot, not to his cousin, not to the enemy. Jake asked Solomon why he was interested in hiring him when he could have hired almost any mining engineer he wanted.

Anyone hearing the story came away impressed with Solomon. He was obviously keen to steal Jake away from Goldberg Limited, but not so overeager as to lie. He put down his fork, and all he said was, "Because you're very good." He could have stopped there, because it was true, but it would have been only half the truth, and Solomon was never a half-truth kind of guy. "And because I want to hurt your father." Jake remembered Solomon looking very calm at this point, and when he told me the story later, he said that for a second, the thought flashed through his mind that Solomon was a more sophisticated version of Mr. Goldberg. But the thought quickly passed because Mr. Goldberg would never have been so straightforward in the same circumstances, and afterward, Jake remembered feeling appreciative of Solomon's brutal honesty. Solomon knew that he might lose Jake with that honesty, but he also knew that if he didn't offer it, he could never win his trust.

They ended the conversation with reminiscences of their child-hood when Abraham was still alive and family gatherings were full. When they parted an hour later, they knew they had resumed their relationship as cousins regardless of what Jake came back with as his answer to Solomon's offer.

Seconds after Moe Steinberg had made his call, Ira was look-ing over Montréal's downtown from his office, thinking about what he might do with the information. When he sat down with Mr. Goldberg later that afternoon, he would have known exactly what he was going to say and how Mr. Goldberg was going to react.

"MR. GOLDBERG, I don't want to upset you, but I have to share some news." Ira had interrupted Mr. Goldberg and me when he'd knocked on Mr. Goldberg's door. I was sitting opposite Mr. Goldberg. When Ira came in, my eyes wandered to the large photo on Mr. Goldberg's desk of Abraham standing with his two sons, one on either side of him, when they were both in their late twenties. He, the young Mr. Goldberg, was smiling in the photo. Isaac looked serious.

Mr. Goldberg smiled. "But how could you ever upset me, Ira?"

Ira nodded. "I know, Mr. Goldberg, that's very kind. But this time, the news is bad. Very bad."

Mr. Goldberg didn't think he was the kind of person who got rattled by bad news. What could it be? Gold prices collapsing? A death at the mine? A strike, or as Mr. Goldberg liked to refer to any labour action, a "work stoppage"?

"Go ahead, Ira. I've never closed my eyes to bad news."

Ira looked like he was making up his mind. "I have a favour to ask first."

Mr. Goldberg was already getting impatient. "Of course."

"I don't want you to be angry with him."

"With who?"

Ira hesitated. "With Jacob."

Like any father who thought he knew his son, Mr. Goldberg would have wondered what his middle son could have done. Had he crashed his car? Had an affair? Both were unlikely, because Jake never drove fast or looked at another woman. Was Jake resigning?

"What did Jacob do?"

"Promise me first. I don't want you to be angry with your son."

"Fine."

Ira's eyebrows went up. "Jacob was seen having lunch today with Solomon. At the Ritz."

Mr. Goldberg's slowly greying but still golden hair was thinning from his cancer treatments, and this made his strangely symmetrical eyes even more prominent. His eyelids lowered until his eyes were no more than slits. He stood up to his full height and started screaming.

Ira stood there, looking concerned as he let Mr. Goldberg tire himself out. Then Mr. Goldberg pressed the buzzer under his desk, and his secretary, Linda, ran into the room. He told her to call

Jake and to tell him to be at the office the next day at 7:30 a.m. Ira offered to call Sammy and David. Mr. Goldberg dismissed me with a wave of his hand. Ira stayed behind.

I think it was during Sammy's illness that Jake first got it into his head that it would be okay to talk to Solomon. If Jake had met with Solomon at any time, Mr. Goldberg would have seen it as the greatest betrayal. But because Jake waited until Mr. Goldberg had gone down to the Mayo Clinic for the surgery to remove his cancerous tumour and as he continued to fly back and forth between Rochester and Montréal for radiation and chemotherapy, Mr. Goldberg saw it in an even worse light.

A NUMBER OF Goldberg employees were beginning to arrive when I got to the office the following day at 7:15. The most ambitious knew that Mr. Goldberg liked people who started early. A couple of middle managers said hello to me as we waited for the elevator. I said hello back, but, when the doors closed, I rode to the top floor in silence. When they got out before me and said, "Have a good day," I nodded without speaking.

Sammy and Jake were already in the boardroom. As was Ira. Ira was telling Jake he didn't want him to be surprised, that someone had seen him having lunch with Solomon but that he, Ira, had done his best to smooth things over with his father the day before. David arrived five minutes later. He nodded at his brothers, Ira, and me and sat down. Jake was pale. I was afraid for him. David said, "Don't worry, Jake. It's going to be okay."

When Mr. Goldberg arrived, he didn't look at any of us but closed the door softly and sat down. The gold boardroom walls shone more brightly than usual. The patriarch of the firm looked out on his son from the confines of the golden frame

surrounding his portrait. He looked as if he had something to
say. Uncharacteristically for him, Mr. Goldberg looked like he
hadn't slept or combed his hair. His mouth was tight. When Mr.
Goldberg didn't start speaking right away and didn't look in
Jake's direction, I knew this was going to be worse than the kind
of meeting in which Mr. Goldberg exploded and then moved on.
Mr. Goldberg might have lost weight from his illness, he might
have been tired, and his still-golden hair might have been thinning
from the chemo, but he still managed to look powerful.

"A man is distinguished by the company he keeps," Mr.
Goldberg finally began as he looked at Sammy, at David, then at
Ira and me, "and equally by the company he doesn't keep. And as
you know, our branch of the Goldberg family does not speak with
the other branch. We do not speak with them on the telephone.
We do not speak with them when we pass them on the street. We
do not meet with them in any boardroom. We do not serve on
committees with them. We do not support the same charitable
causes. We do not go to government round tables together. We do
not attend each other's weddings. We do not celebrate Passover
with them. We do not break bread with them, not even, and especially not, at the Ritz. This fact is understood by almost everyone in our family. And it is this way for many good reasons, but
it's mainly because the other branch of the Goldberg family will
use every weapon at their disposal not just to humble us but to
destroy us. And they do want to destroy us. They want to see our
mines abandoned and our company burned to the ground. They
want to see our employees unemployed and scattered. They want
to see us cast out of this building. Their efforts to achieve this
end are varied, and they include trying to flatter some of us, the
weaker and more impressionable among us, into believing that
they are wanted and appreciated, that they are *special*."

Mr. Goldberg spoke carefully. "If anyone in this company ever speaks with that man again" — he couldn't bring himself to say Solomon's name or even acknowledge the familial relationship in the presence of his own sons — "I will personally see to it that they are immediately and irrevocably cast out of this company. Out of this family. Out of our lives." David had once told me that Mr. Goldberg had always refused to say Solomon's name ever since his father, Isaac, had died. When his sons and Solomon were young, Mr. Goldberg would refer to him only as "that boy," as in, "You are not to see or speak to that boy." Later, as his sons and Solomon grew older, Mr. Goldberg acknowledged the passage of time and started to refer to him as "that man." Solomon was never his nephew or his sons' cousin.

Then, still without looking at Jake, Mr. Goldberg looked at the rest of us and said softly, "Is that understood?"

We all nodded, even David, although he looked unhappy. When David nodded, Mr. Goldberg said his final piece, and from the way he looked at Jake and the way he spoke, it was clear he had intended to finish with this from the beginning. "But there is one thing I don't understand, Jacob. What I don't understand, what I really fail to understand, is this: why do you persist in thinking about leaving our company? Why can't you let it go, especially when we all know you don't have the courage to leave?"

Jake, a grown man of forty-six, stood up and ran to the door. Before it closed behind him, we could hear him fighting to contain his sobs as he ran past Mr. Goldberg's secretary, Linda, and into the bathroom. The last time Jake had fled a room, it was just after telling his father that he had already accepted the offer from McKinsey. This time, David went after him. As his youngest son left his presence, Mr. Goldberg's eyes widened for just a moment, and then he regained his composure. When Mr. Goldberg was

satisfied that both Jake and David were out of earshot, he turned
to Ira: "I want you to go after Solomon." Now that Mr. Goldberg
was contemplating legal action, he had broken his unwritten rule
about never calling Solomon by his name.

Ira had been through enough of Mr. Goldberg's vengeful
moods that he just nodded and didn't question his intentions. All
he said was, "Did you have anything in mind?"

Mr. Goldberg's eyelids rose. "Harassment? Corporate espio-
nage? Possession of confidential information? Think of something."

Ira nodded, opened his book, and took a note. "You understand that any legal action against Solomon with reference to the
lunch would involve taking testimony from Jacob."

"I know. I want Solomon to understand that although I have
cancer and am in treatment, I'm up for a fight."

Ira closed his book and nodded again.

LATER THAT SAME week, I saw Jake down at Westmount
Park where our youngest children played rugby together on
Wednesdays and Saturdays. Jake's daughter, Marnie, was a talented
forward who scored in every game. That evening, Jake had trouble
keeping his eyes on the field. He didn't say anything about the meeting and instead told me about something that had happened ten
years earlier. That was a full fifteen years after his attempt to join
McKinsey right out of university.

"Do you know what my father said to me when I told him I
was thinking of going to work for another company to run their
geology department?"

I shook my head. I could guess, but I didn't want to say. I was
trying my best to listen to him while also watching my youngest
daughter, Fiona, play, hoping she would not injure herself. She

played a back position and was small like me, and fast. She wasn't quite as accomplished as Marnie, but she was good.

"I had just finished my master's in geology." Jake had done this part-time after joining the company. Given his father's views on higher education and graduate degrees, and the fact that his uncle Isaac also had a master's in geology, it had been nothing less than a sustained, quiet act of rebellion.

"I still wanted to work outside the firm. I wanted to test myself. I had gone to see him in his office. He was signing cheques for maintenance work at Springtime. I didn't sit down. I was too nervous. I told him quickly what I wanted to do. He signed a few more cheques without looking up. I waited for the thunderbolt to come. I might have been imagining it, but, after I was finished speaking, I thought he started to sign his name more slowly, carefully, as if he were signing very important documents and I was interrupting him. After some time, he lifted his pen from the paper and looked at me with fully open eyes, surprised that I was still there, and said, 'We're not going to end up like that other family. Not on my watch.'"

Jake didn't have to explain. I knew exactly what he meant. Mr. Goldberg never mentioned them by name, as if doing so was beneath him or else their bad judgment might rub off on him. They were always *that other family*. But that other family was the other wealthy Jewish Montréal family: the Bronfmans. In an unabashed display of a latent puritanical streak, Mr. Goldberg had made it obvious that he disapproved of how they'd gotten their start selling spirits during Prohibition. It wasn't so much the peddling of alcohol itself but how they'd cozied up to "unsavoury elements" to ship their product into the U.S. that seemed to get to Mr. Goldberg. But that was a minor quibble.

What really irked Mr. Goldberg and set him off on occasional rants was how in the mid-nineties, young Edgar Jr. had impetuously traded away his family's stake in Dupont Chemicals for an unpredictable film studio and then, five years later, flipped the quintessential global spirits business — a recession-proof business if there ever was one — for a minority stake in a French conglomerate with interests in water pipes and television. Billions of dollars of family equity were destroyed when the share price of the French company collapsed. One of the founder's original sons, interviewed years later over lunch, called what had happened under his nephew's watch "a family tragedy." For Mr. Goldberg, the lessons were obvious. "That family lost their way. They forgot what they were about. They gave away control." And the original sin: "They placed too much trust in the wrong son."

"But, after invoking the Bronfmans, my father seemed to have a change of heart. 'You know what,' he said, 'why don't you go ahead. I can hire geologists a dime a dozen. It's the people who really understand business who are hard to come by.'"

Jake's eyes went to the field, but I could tell he was having trouble following the game. He didn't look at me as he continued speaking. "Then he looked down and went back to signing his cheques. The audience was over. He wasn't worried. He didn't even think I was worth the effort to get angry."

I waited a respectful few seconds. "And we know you didn't go."

"I didn't."

"Why not?"

Jake took a moment to respond. "I was too afraid." His daughter had just scored, but I'm not sure he saw it.

It was now or never, so I asked him why he'd had lunch with Solomon, why he'd been ready to leave the company this time. I already knew from my own experience with Solomon that he was persuasive. Jake looked at me and then returned his gaze to the game. Both our daughters were on the field. Marnie wasn't scoring, but she was running fast, and this time Jake smiled as she took possession of the ball.

"As I was looking forward to meeting with Solomon, I told myself it wasn't just about getting back at my father. I was doing it for Sammy. Because he was never going to be CEO, because of his nervous breakdown, because of what our father had done to him. Part of me even thought I could somehow bring the two families together again, and maybe Sammy could finally become CEO of something, a spin-off, one of the mines as a stand-alone business. But that day, as I walked into the Ritz, I knew it was for me." Then Jake was silent for a while.

When Jake spoke again, he was incredulous in spite of himself. "The funny thing is, if I had actually gone through with it, my father wouldn't have just let me go. He would have had Ira sue both me and Solomon. Solomon for something and me for the noncompete he makes us all sign." This was the first I had heard that each of the Goldberg sons had had to sign a noncompete contract.

Jake looked like he was trying mightily to concentrate on the action on the field. Then he gave up and turned to me. "Do you know what my family's problem is?"

"No."

He looked back to the field, trying to find his daughter. "We don't relate. We litigate." And then, still without looking at me, "It's the only way my father knows how to deal with people who don't agree with him."

IT WAS ONLY later that I learned David had had it out with his father over Mr. Goldberg's treatment of Jake. I learned this from

Jake. For the first time that anyone could remember, the father and the youngest son shouted at each other. When David raised his voice, Mr. Goldberg was at first taken aback. But then he started yelling, and once he started, he couldn't stop himself. For his part, David never said anything to me about what had happened to Jake in that boardroom or what he and his father had said to each other afterward, and none of us knew what a turning point it would prove to be in how much — or how little — Mr. Goldberg listened to his youngest son. But after that argument, David started to show up for meetings with his father just a few minutes late, just late enough to be noticed, something he had never done before. And the next time I saw him alone, at the Westmount YMCA, and without any proper segue, David found an opportunity to tell me that he envied me.

"Envy me?"

"Your position. Your freedom."

We were both jogging on the treadmill, side by side, staring straight ahead.

"What do you mean?"

"You don't share a last name with the company."

"Yeah?"

"You can always leave if you want. You have that option."

It was early evening, following the after-work rush before people went home to have supper with their families, and the gym was quiet. There was nobody on the treadmills around us, and the sounds of the machines, our running, and the radio were serving as white noise for my thoughts when David said, "One day, I'll tell you the story of my family." I assumed David was going to tell me why Mr. Goldberg hated Solomon and why the two branches of the family had so much distance between them. After that, David started running in earnest, and we ran together in silence. I was still trying to understand how one of the Goldbergs, let alone David, could envy me for anything, and I stopped wondering about why Mr. Goldberg hated Solomon. Instead, I found myself thinking about my parents and Jane and our children.

4

EVER SINCE I had first seen Solomon at McGill and David had refused to speak about him, I had been curious about their estrangement and about what had happened to Solomon's father, Isaac. But it took me years to work up the courage to ask David about it, and it was only after Jake's lunch with Solomon at the Ritz-Carlton that I was finally ready to do so.

I waited until we were on one of our trips to London toward the end of 2010. It was somehow easier to ask the question when we were on a different continent. We'd just taken in Jane as the new Molly Ralston in *The Mousetrap* and were in the theatre lobby waiting for her before heading off to the Savoy's Beaufort Bar. I suppose I thought of it then because the last time I'd seen Solomon had been in London — at a bar in Heathrow — and we'd just watched a mystery. David enjoyed the theatre, especially when Jane was on the stage. He was happy and relaxed. I think part of me knew I'd be getting him with his defences down. In retrospect, it was a poor strategy to ask the question in the lobby while waiting, a transitory sort of time and place.

"I've been meaning to ask you this for a while."

"Yes?"

"Whatever happened with Solomon's branch of the family?"

David didn't look surprised. Slightly offended, maybe, but not surprised. He laughed a little, but it was not his usual laugh. It was half-hearted. "I was wondering when you might ask. It's only taken you twenty-six years." David pressed his teeth together in a sort of grimace, flexed his jaw, and opened his mouth as if he were about to answer me, but Jane appeared. She grabbed both of our arms and, with herself between us, pulled us along, just like she used to do in university. Whatever David had been about to tell me wasn't going to be said that evening, but David, ever the gentleman, refusing to leave any strings hanging by pretending he'd forgotten our abbreviated conversation, said, "I guess you'll have to ask Solomon."

We had our usual good time that night in the golden darkness of the Beaufort — talking about the long-running play, the other actors, the audience's glowing reaction — but David drank more heavily than he normally did. It wasn't until later that I realized it was the first time in our friendship that David had refused to answer one of my questions.

I DIDN'T GET to speak to Solomon until half a year later, in August 2011. As it happened, it was in London too, and this time we weren't drinking. Solomon had wanted to meet at the Kew. When I asked him the question, Solomon's reaction was the complete opposite of David's. Where David had been reticent, it was clear Solomon had been waiting for me to ask him ever since we'd first met. He didn't speak right away, only nodded as he collected his thoughts. When he did begin to speak, he told the story in a slow, understated way, without his usual irony and drama, without any of the slightly overdone heartiness that he seemed to reserve for every topic, even when he was asking me in mock-seriousness about his estranged family.

ABRAHAM HAD NOT been buried twenty-four hours when Mr. Goldberg set it all in motion. The Goldbergs were sitting shiva. It was 1976. A year before I met David at LCC. The summer of the Montréal Olympics. Declan had just finished building the stadium. From the moment of Abraham's death, Mr. Goldberg had wanted to sit shiva in his house, so that's what everyone did. It wasn't far from Solomon's parents' house. Isaac and Eliana lived just down from Sunnyside on the Boulevard, still in Upper Westmount but a little lower on the mountain and in a house that was smaller. Mr. Goldberg told his brother the shiva should be at his house because it was bigger. There wasn't an argument because on principle Isaac didn't argue with his brother.

In most of their conversations, Mr. Goldberg talked loudly, and Solomon's father, Isaac, nodded in agreement. Isaac's usual deference to his brother, when it was he who had not only the degree in mining engineering, just like Abraham, but also a master's in geology, while Mr. Goldberg had dropped out of McGill, was a constant source of frustration for Solomon's mother, Eliana. After almost every board meeting and family discussion — the Goldberg women didn't work in the company, but some of them had seats on the board — Eliana would berate Isaac on the drive home (if they were coming from the corporate headquarters in downtown Montréal) or the short walk home (if they had been at a more informal meeting at Abraham's or Mr. Goldberg's house).

Abraham had lived on the same street as his oldest son. His house was smaller than Mr. Goldberg's and even a bit smaller than Isaac's. Isaac, just as he did with his brother, would let his wife talk herself out. If they were driving, he'd put his hand on her knee; if they were walking, he'd take her arm and say, "What can I do, he's my brother."

This simple and never varying response to anything Mr. Goldberg had said or done would only make Eliana angrier. And then she would deliver her set speech. "As if that explains it. Have you not read your Bible? Don't you know anything about brothers, about families? Saul might be your brother, but he's certainly not your friend." This, in turn, only increased Isaac's gentleness toward both his brother and his wife.

Everybody in Montréal and many people from around the world seemed to be at the shiva. The first day was the most heavily attended. People who had known Abraham from the global mining industry flew in from Toronto, Vancouver, New York, London, Johannesburg, and Melbourne. The prime minister himself drove down from Ottawa with a two-person security detail. One went inside and one stayed outside. And there were senior representatives from the Israeli government and the Israel Defense Forces and the head of Yad Vashem in Jerusalem because of Abraham's work rescuing Jews during the Second World War and his steadfast support of Israel. Abraham's generous financial support of the Jewish state had — according to a well-placed source in the Israel Defense Forces who spoke to the writer of Abraham's obituary in the *Globe and Mail* only on the condition of anonymity — begun before its founding, had continued during the War of Independence, and lasted through every war afterward.

With all these people, Mr. Goldberg's house, big as it was, was still crowded. After the funeral, everyone had followed in their black limos from Paperman's Funeral Home to the Shaar

Hashomayim Cemetery on Mount Royal, where the Goldbergs had a family plot. By the time every person in attendance had thrown their shovelful of dirt onto Abraham's coffin and the Kaddish, the Jewish prayer for the dead, had been recited, the grave was filled.

The drive back to Mr. Goldberg's house, with a Montréal police escort, was less than ten minutes: out of the cemetery, across Côte-des-Neiges, and up to the top of the western side of the mountain. Shunning shiva tradition, in which the family of the dead person is supposed to sit and mourn for seven days and wait during this time for visitors to come to them with condolences and food, Mr. Goldberg had positioned himself at the front door so he could heartily shake hands with everyone. He was most interested in the mining executives and directors, and in politicians. Solomon and his parents were seated inside, in the living room, on the same leather sofa.

When the prime minister arrived, flanked by one of his security men, Mr. Goldberg practically dragged him off his feet into his study for a private tête-à-tête. Years later, Solomon could only guess at what they'd talked about — likely the desirability of speedy environmental permits for their latest mine expansion or the benefits of freer trade. Or possibly forewarning the prime minister about a potential "work stoppage" by the union at a mine they had just acquired. When Mr. Goldberg re-emerged in the front hallway, he looked fresh and keen, as he always did when he felt he had succeeded in making his point, but the usually energetic prime minister looked haggard and left soon after, without talking to Isaac.

The intense, jet-lagged Israelis who had flown halfway across the world to pay their respects, and whom Mr. Goldberg practically ignored, had situated themselves on either side of Isaac, politely but firmly elbowing anyone else out of the way. Isaac was fluent in Hebrew, and they were speaking enthusiastically about Abraham's wartime exploits: smuggling Jews out of Europe and into Canada during the Second World War, helping to smuggle arms into Israel for the War of Independence and afterward helping to broker deals for more shipments. Isaac was animated, and there was no mistaking the affinity between him and Israel's emissaries. It was Isaac who knew every detail of every story of what Abraham had done in every war.

Seeing that his father was in good hands, Solomon went to look for David. At ten and eleven years old, they were still children, so they had the run of the place and no formal obligations other than to let family and friends tousle their hair, pinch their cheeks, give them smothering hugs even though they would soon be teenagers, and tell them how much they looked like Abraham. And to let the wealthy and powerful outside the Goldberg family shake their hands and turn all serious and tell them how sorry they were at the passing of their *zayde*, who had been a great man.

On the way to find David, Solomon passed Sammy and Jake. Sammy was standing toward the back of the front hallway, like a smaller version of his father, who was at the front door again shaking hands and backslapping everyone as if he were in the company box at the Forum instead of sitting shiva for his father. Sammy smiled broadly at Solomon. It was meant to project friendliness and confidence, and for most of the world it was sufficient. But Solomon could already see through his oldest cousin.

Jake was in the kitchen, speaking to a second cousin from New York and looking miserable. He nodded at Solomon and continued to listen to the cousin, who seemed excited about something. Solomon couldn't find David anywhere amidst the guests and piles of food. Wanting some air without knowing why, he went out the back door to the garden. David was sitting on the deck and staring out into space, and Solomon had the sense he had been there for a long time. David looked up at Solomon when he saw him and said, "Cousin" in that gently mocking, pseudo-formal, but also affectionate tone with which the two boys greeted each other. David made Solomon smile.

Solomon sat down beside David, and even though Solomon didn't think they yet knew the word, and in a sense were too young to use it, he and David spent the next hour *reminiscing* about their *zayde*: the life he'd led during the war, saving Jews, helping Israel, how he'd taken them on trips to the mines, the way he'd taught them to shake hands and say thank you long before he ever tried to teach them anything about geology or technology. The way his words and actions implied that people always came first, and if you got the people part wrong, then the science and technology would never work properly.

IT WAS ONLY later, while listening to his parents fight about it, that Solomon first heard about the conversation Mr. Goldberg had initiated with his father late that afternoon when there was a lull in visitors. The lunch crowd had left, and the family was waiting for the next shiva shift to bring supper. Mr. Goldberg interrupted a conversation that Isaac was having with an old friend from university. Just as Mr. Goldberg had done a thousand times before, he barged in, shook hands, said hello to the other person, and then turned to Solomon's father: "Izzy, we have to talk." And Solomon's father, as he always did, smiled apologetically at whomever he was speaking with and said, "Sure, Saul." Because, as he had explained a thousand times to Solomon's mother, Saul was his brother.

According to the very detailed account that Isaac gave Eliana, Mr. Goldberg took him into his study and sat him down in the chair opposite his large desk. But he himself remained standing. Everyone in the family was tall, so this gave Mr. Goldberg the advantage. "Izzy, I've been considering things." Mr. Goldberg had no time for people who thought too much or who prefaced any of their comments with the words "I think" because he thought it was obvious that they were thinking and it appeared tentative. Just like he preferred his sons to be "concerned" rather than "nervous" about issues or potential issues in the business, he preferred to "consider" things rather than to "think" about them.

"I don't need to say it for our benefit, but I'll say it anyway. It's just me and you now, *boychik*." Mr. Goldberg actually smiled at this point. "We are the remaining stewards of the company. We have to consider the future. Our responsibility is to preserve the company for the next generation, our boys: Samuel, Jacob, David, and, of course, Solomon. We don't need to read a book to know that in a family business, everything starts to unravel in the third generation. Because cousins are not as close as brothers. Because fathers want their sons to run certain businesses or sit in particular chairs. Because with every passing year, there are more and more people in the family who sit around the table and want money from the business without wanting to do any work for it. When people grow up in luxury, they get lazy. It's a law of life. This is why we insist that our boys have to work in the business in the summer, that they don't get promoted too quickly, that they show us they know not to take anything for granted. If we go about this properly, as I know we will, together we can avoid the curse of the third generation." And here Mr. Goldberg stopped. It was one of the characteristics of his way of speaking, especially in key moments, that he wouldn't say everything he had to say all at once. He'd say enough so whomever he was speaking with would have to ask him to go on if they wanted to continue the conversation. It was the verbal equivalent of giving someone a chair but remaining standing.

Isaac dutifully asked, "What are you thinking of, Saul?"

"Well, Izzy, it's simple." By which Mr. Goldberg meant it was anything but. According to Solomon, in this respect, as in many others, Mr. Goldberg was the opposite of Abraham. Abraham had a gift for making the most complicated subject truly simple and easy to understand. He did this in every aspect of his life, whether it was explaining the workings of a gold mine to his young grandchildren or teaching them on plane rides up to the mine how to motivate men to work hard day in and day out and to give the Goldbergs their effort and energy, if not their gratitude and love.

After a long day in the mine, as the small plane took off into the darkness with Abraham and his grandchildren — David, Sammy, Jacob, and Solomon — on board, Abraham would make sure the boys had their seatbelts on, and he would speak to them like he was telling a bedtime story. His voice was deep and reassuring, as a *zayde*'s voice is meant to be. "Remember that people are not a means to an end: they are an end in themselves. And while some people are motivated by money, most want to be paid fairly to take care of their families. In our business, their biggest motivation is to stay safe so they can go home to their families in one piece. Okay?"

Abraham knew this long before mining and energy companies started to track recordable injury frequency rates. And he knew that most people are fundamentally altruistic: they care more about keeping others safe than they do themselves. "After that, they want to do an honest day's work. They want to belong to something bigger than themselves. They want to know their work is accomplishing more than making shareholders richer. They want to know that their work matters, that they are appreciated. This might be the most important thing. They need to know that what they're doing means something. Not just for the business but for you, personally."

All four cousins, including Sammy, listened attentively because what Abraham was saying resonated with them, and the fact that he was taking the time to teach them what he knew was a sign of his trust. Solomon listened carefully to his *zayde,* because Abraham was so different from both his uncle and, in another way, from his father. Solomon had known this instinctively from a young age, for as long as he could remember, even though he didn't understand it intellectually until much later.

"MY ZAYDE HAD two sons, and he gave half of his character to each of them," Solomon said, digressing from the main part of his story. "It wasn't like my uncle was everything my *zayde* wasn't. It was like Abraham was complete, whereas each son was half. My uncle got Abraham's drive without his compassion. My father got Abraham's intellect and passion without his drive, without his socially approved killer instinct that he kept so politely under wraps with his well-cut clothes and impeccable manners. My uncle may have got my *zayde*'s toughness, his desire, his ambition to build something and do something great. But it was my father who inherited his wisdom, his empathy, his need to serve and to help. Abraham wasn't naïve: he knew you have to help your friends and crush your enemies. It's my uncle who thinks only about crushing his enemies. My father got everything from Abraham that was gentle, but without his toughness, his calibrated ruthlessness, my father was never going to succeed. He was never going to be a match for my uncle. In the end, being what he was, I think my uncle couldn't help himself in taking advantage of my father, just as the strongest dog in a pack naturally dominates the weakest one."

THAT FIRST DAY of shiva, Mr. Goldberg continued his speech to Isaac. "We need to give our two families space so we don't crowd each other out. Consider it." Which was Mr. Goldberg's well-understood way of telling the opposing party in any negotiation that he had already completely considered the subject at hand. Through a process of instinctual evaluation and elimination of lesser alternatives, he had arrived at the correct answer, and the other party could either accept the wisdom of his reasoning and live with it or make the wrong decision and leave a deal on the table. But Isaac wasn't a pushover. He loved his brother for all his faults, and despite these faults, he still trusted him. But he didn't go along meekly.

Isaac reserved his judgment when he learned that his brother wanted to allocate operational control over specific mines to either his or Isaac's branch of the family and to tie this management oversight to financial risk and bottom-line profit and loss. Abraham had run the entire company as one with his two sons as they entered the business, and all three shared equally in the profits generated by the mines. When Mr. Goldberg explained his thinking in more detail, Isaac deferred his response and instead embarked on a detailed program of due diligence.

Mr. Goldberg proposed an even split, according to production. He and his sons would retain control over the original open pit Springtime mine, while Isaac and his son would assume responsibility for the underground Firehall mine in British Columbia — they were the two largest mines in the Goldberg portfolio — and the two sides of the family would evenly split the smaller mines across Canada that Abraham had picked up for cents on the dollar during or after the Second World War. Mr. Goldberg would take the ones in Québec and Ontario; Isaac would get the mines west of Ontario. Isaac delegated the due diligence for the smaller mines to some of his trusted advisers, but he took personal responsibility for assessing Firehall.

Isaac already knew the mine well, but he studied it as if he didn't know a thing about it. He visited the mine, spent time with the operators and the local First Nations communities, pored over plans and financial statements. And because he was a geologist and loved rocks — their firmness in the face of time and yet their fragility when faced with human intervention, their reticence, the way they kept their stories and treasures hidden to anyone but the ones most determined to unearth them — he spent time with the geological surveys that projected twenty more years of sustained production. In the end, Isaac was satisfied, and Eliana went along with the decision. Six months later, Isaac and Mr. Goldberg drew up the agreement that separated the corporate destinies of their immediate families according to Mr. Goldberg's original proposal.

ELIANA WASN'T A passive observer of anything, and this business deal was no exception. She understood her brother-in-law. "I'm not sure if you know," Solomon said, "but my mother's first date with a Goldberg was with my uncle."

I shook my head. Solomon continued.

"He and my father both took her to the exact same place on their first dates: Mount Royal. But Mount Royal was the only thing the two evenings had in common. My uncle apparently took her out first for an expensive dinner at Moshe's. He made small talk with all the waiters, used their nicknames, acted like he owned the place, and made big talk about himself. I don't think he asked my mother one question. After supper, he took her up to the lookout on Mount Royal in his MG and tried to put his hand up her skirt.

"My father didn't even ask my mother out until he knew that things between my uncle and her weren't going anywhere. He also took her to Mount Royal, but there was no fancy dinner beforehand, and when he parked, they got out of the car and walked around. He took my mother for a hot dog and fries at Beaver Lake and gave her a signed copy of one of A.M. Klein's books. He asked her a lot of questions about her family and her background, and when she asked him questions — about his education, his role in the company, his family — he had the good manners to provide concise answers and be slightly embarrassed. My mother's experience with my uncle should have helped her figure out what he was up to with dividing up the company, but because of what she thought of him, she was conflicted."

On the one hand, Eliana was suspicious of any of Mr. Goldberg's ideas or plans. On the other, she was excited by the possibility that her immediate family and Mr. Goldberg's could separate their interests and areas of responsibility in the family business. Although Eliana knew her brother-in-law was driven by ego and was a bully, she didn't suspect how far he would go. She didn't immediately shut down the idea of separating the corporate assets. Despite what she thought of Mr. Goldberg, she trusted her husband and his intelligence when it came to matters of rocks and reports. If her husband the geologist with his MSc from McGill looked at geological reports and pronounced them fine, who was she — also a graduate of McGill but an English Lit major — to disagree?

WHEN THE UNDERGROUND Firehall gold vein started to decline less than a year later, Isaac didn't believe what the geologists were telling him. He insisted on going into the mine himself to inspect it. It took him two weeks. By the end of the first week, he was barely eating and sleeping, and Eliana feared he was going to die of exhaustion. It was Eliana who figured out what Mr. Goldberg had done. But true to form, Isaac refused to believe it until he had reviewed all his samples at least twice.

At the end of that second week, when it was clear to him what must have happened, Isaac fainted in the Firehall mine and was bundled onto his bush plane and flown home. He regained consciousness on the flight but was so agitated he had to be sedated. Eliana had been called by the pilots and was there to meet her husband at the private hangar in Dorval. Isaac was still half asleep when he was carried off the plane. Eliana woke up Solomon, and together they carried him into the house. They undressed him and put him under the covers.

SOLOMON REMEMBERED HOW pale his father had been and how thin. "My father was thin to begin with, but he lost twenty pounds in that two weeks. He slept for eighteen hours, and when he woke up, he could barely speak. A day later, he had a massive stroke. He fell into a coma, and a week later, he died. My uncle never came to the hospital, not once. My mother left messages. He claimed he was travelling out of the country and couldn't make it back in time. The doctors put down stroke as cause of death. But my mother always said my father died of an old-fashioned broken heart. I never knew such a thing was possible. My mother also said my uncle would have never dared to cheat my father out of his birthright when Abraham was still alive. 'Your *zayde* wouldn't have stood for it, and Saul knew that. He waited until Abraham was gone, and then he took advantage of his brother.'"

"What exactly did Mr. Goldberg do?"

"He never admitted it, but there's only one possible explanation: he must have salted the core sample reports. He added gold to the rock when it wasn't there. Because suddenly the mine stopped producing at normal levels. Nothing else would explain it."

"Why haven't you or your side of the family said anything? Done anything? Taken him to court?"

"I had just turned eleven when my father died. After that, my mother didn't want anything to do with my uncle, didn't want to be reminded of him, didn't want to hear his name. A legal action would have gone on for years and prolonged the connection. It's not like we were living on the streets. My father was cheated out of an equal share of the business, but we still owned a major gold mine, as poorly productive as it was, and some smaller ones. We didn't have to sell our home. I didn't have to drop out of Selwyn House. I could still go to university. There was still more than enough money to live on. And as my mother never ceased to remind me, someone had once said that 'living well is the best revenge.' She was adamant about that. She drilled it into me every chance she could."

But Solomon didn't sound convinced, and then, seemingly for my benefit, he added, with the slightest of smiles, "Someone else — I don't know who — said that timing is everything."

And with that, Solomon was giving me — senior counsel for Goldberg Limited and best friend of his cousin David — notice that for the last quarter of a century, since his father had died from a broken heart, he, Solomon Goldberg, had not forgotten what his uncle had done, and that although he had been following his mother's advice and living well, he was also biding his time.

THERE WAS ONE other question I had to ask Solomon that day. I almost didn't, because I was afraid of the answer; but I was more afraid of not asking.

"Does David know?"

Solomon didn't blink. He looked at me a for long time before replying. Like every other Goldberg, he never seemed to be at any loss for words. "Either he knows and remains by his father's side or else he has no idea. I'm not sure which is worse."

I NEVER DID ask David about what Solomon had told me, although I wanted to test it with him, assess his reaction. I didn't because I feared his response, perhaps because I was still unsure of my own. But on one point I was certain: while I remained loyally open to the possibility that Isaac had somehow misread the geological reports and misinterpreted his brother's actions, I couldn't quite convince myself of it. I felt I had descended another rung below the level ground, and I began to look at Mr. Goldberg in a different light. As a result, I looked at everyone around Mr. Goldberg a little differently as well, even, to my slight shame, my friend David. From then on, whenever I saw David, I wondered how much he knew. I admitted to myself that he must have known, but I also convinced myself he was just waiting until he succeeded his father, and then he would find a way of making everything right with Solomon. And yet, for the first time, I began to contemplate life outside the Goldberg cocoon and, on occasion, in the safety of my own mind, to rehearse what it would feel like to leave it all behind.

As I was to learn a little later, Solomon still hadn't told me everything. He was still holding back. He had one more Goldberg story left to tell. It was the story of his and David's beloved great-grandmother Aviva and her husband — Abraham's father, who had died before he was born. But after telling me about Mr. Goldberg cheating Isaac out of his fair share of the company, Solomon went radio silent. He didn't tell me the final story for another year, after the bidding war for Aussie Gold was over.

PART FIVE

Aussie Gold
2012–2013

1

THERE WERE ONLY five of us gathered around the boardroom table early on that April day in 2012. Sammy was to Mr. Goldberg's right, and Jake was on the left. Sammy was always to the right of his father, but the idea that he was his father's right-hand man had been mostly wishful thinking even before his nervous breakdown. The two other people at the table were Ira and me. Ira sat beside Sammy, and I sat beside Jake, and the empty seat beside me awaited the arrival of David.

His favourite son was late for the second time that week, and Mr. Goldberg was trying hard to pretend it didn't matter to him. He even tried to make a joke about the erratic sleeping habits of the young. His mouth stretched to a smile, but it didn't reach his symmetrical, pale blue, almost reptilian eyes as he looked around at each of us. With his half-hearted attempt at humour, Mr. Goldberg was also attempting to conceal his embarrassment that David would not bother to show up on time even on this important occasion, and that the rest of us were there to witness his favourite son's blatant lack of filial respect. Ever since they had yelled at each other after Jake's lunch with Solomon,

there had been a new level of tension between them. Seeing his
father's obvious unease, Sammy attempted humour as well: partly
to defuse the situation and partly to deflect attention away from
his squirming father. "Didn't someone say punctuality is the sign
of a small mind? David must be trying to show how smart he is!"
But nobody laughed. We were too tense.

True to his character, Jake kept his counsel to himself. He
didn't try to make his father feel better, he just stared ahead as if
the room around him and the people in it were not real. Where
Sammy had inherited, even deliberately cultivated, his father's
inability to sit still, to let anyone finish their side of the conversation, Jake could sit and listen for hours. Jake's speech and movements had always been spare, and he never interrupted when
someone was speaking. He appeared to think before he spoke.
And while Sammy often spoke in a voice that was just a little too
loud, as if trying to convince, Jake's voice had only become softer
with age, sometimes so soft that you had to strain to hear him.

As Mr. Goldberg spoke, if you were seated at the far end of the
boardroom table with its gold-leaf edges, you couldn't help noticing the extraordinarily lifelike portrait of Abraham that loomed
over the room and his oldest son. In any gatherings around the
boardroom table in the Gold Room, it was like Abraham was
there with you, listening, taking it all in.

After five minutes of waiting, Mr. Goldberg said, "David is
late again" as he looked around the room without looking at any
of us in particular. He sounded more resigned than disappointed
or angry, as well as a little embarrassed. And then he lapsed into
silence as his anger returned.

When David finally arrived, he was a full fifteen minutes late.
All of us knew this because each of us checked the antique golden
clock at the back of the boardroom frequently. And each of us

checked our expensive watches because we couldn't believe it. By this time, Mr. Goldberg's smile had vanished from his face, and it was all he could do to stop himself from shaking.

As I watched Mr. Goldberg, I was reminded of something else I had learned from working with him and his family. I had learned by watching them but also by watching many of the men they worked with or fought against: friendly and enemy politicians, businessmen who were partners or competitors, union leaders at one of the mines the Goldbergs took over until they broke them during an extended strike, although Mr. Goldberg and his sons never used the word *strike*. They always called it a "work stoppage." What I was reminded of as I watched Mr. Goldberg that day in the boardroom was this: not everyone can do anger.

There are many strategies to get your way. You don't always need to say anything to make your point, to argue, to cajole, to convince. Sometimes all you need is power. When naked power is being exercised, it is not something you ever forget, and over the years, I saw it exercised around that boardroom table.

At the time, I rationalized it as being in the service of a good cause: that cause being Goldberg Limited. But sometimes absolute power in your own realm is not enough, such as when you're dealing with a politician you didn't bother to build a relationship with when he was in opposition, one who might actually gain approval with voters by being tough on you, or with a journalist who doesn't care about the things that most normal people care about, like the admiration of others and money and power and the prestige that comes from being on speaking terms with those who have more power than you. In times like this, you need words and your physical presence to make a point. Anger is also one of the ways you can augment your power, but not everybody can project it well. Mr. Goldberg was one of those men who could do anger. He could do it well because he believed wholeheartedly in his own cause and power. He had full confidence in himself. And he didn't care, not really, what people thought about him. But of Mr. Goldberg's sons, only one of them could do anger.

Sammy had always been emotional and quick to anger like his father, and he worked hard to live up to his father's image. But unlike Mr. Goldberg, Sammy was too congenial at heart. When he got angry and shouted at you, you never quite took it seriously. It was like being yelled at by an actor. The effect might have been loud and powerful, but we all knew it was just an act. In the course of business, Sammy got angry because he thought it was part of his job, part of his role as the oldest son of Mr. Goldberg. He often did it in his father's presence, as if he were trying to show his father how tough he was, how deserving he was of Mr. Goldberg's love and respect. But it took all our restraint not to roll our eyes.

Jake couldn't do anger because he was too quiet, always holding himself in reserve. He never raised his voice. He was always trying so hard not to be his father that he overcompensated when it came to trying to make his points. He was too introverted and conflicted to do anger, and luckily for all of us, he knew it and never tried. David, on the other hand, kept us guessing for years about his ability to do anger because he never got angry. At least not until he'd raised his voice at his father over his treatment of Jake after the lunch with Solomon. I had heard about that only from Jake, and I, myself, had never seen David become really angry, not even with his father, not even to stand up for his brothers or when Mr. Goldberg was putting a stop to David's drama career. Because he never allowed himself to show anger, we all assumed that when it finally came, it would be terrible.

Mr. Goldberg might have suspected before, but ever since Jake's lunch with Solomon, Mr. Goldberg's suspicions that his youngest son might indeed match him in the seriousness and effects of his anger had only been confirmed. This might have been why he restrained himself that day in the boardroom although his face was red and his big hands were shaking — I knew this not because I saw them but because he kept them under the table so I wouldn't see them. I'd seen that once before when we'd gone to meet the prime minister before Allan Keyes and that prime minister hadn't agreed to give Mr. Goldberg what he was asking for.

When Mr. Goldberg got angry, his eyes lowered, and he sometimes yelled and swore and grew red in the face. But during these fits of anger, he never threw anything that he truly valued and never broke anything that would cost real money to replace. He mostly threw books and inexpensive pens. Often, he would get up and storm around the room, spittle flying from his mouth. At times like that, most of us who worked with him knew not to say anything. We'd remain quiet and nod if we agreed with him, stay motionless if we didn't, and wait it out as he exhausted his anger. But when Mr. Goldberg was really angry, it was more frightening because he wouldn't say anything. A wall would descend over his face, over his eyes, over his jaw, and his eyelids would lower, looking even more like a reptile's. He would stare at you. If he was really angry, he would point to the door, and you knew that it was time to leave. The reason Mr. Goldberg's anger was so powerful was that at its heart it wasn't really anger. It was pure hate.

Years earlier, before Mr. Goldberg had ever been angry with me, a federal minister of industry was inexplicably ignoring our requests for a meeting. Mr. Goldberg was starting to get angry, and after one of our latest meeting requests had been denied, he quietly asked me, "Young Mr. McFall, do you know what's the worst thing you can do to somebody?"

I had some thoughts, but I knew Mr. Goldberg didn't want me to answer the question. He had his own ideas to share. "No, Mr. Goldberg."

"The worst thing you can do is to ignore them."

I WAS REMINDED of that when David entered the room and sat down at the far end of the table, opposite his father. David had arrived wearing jeans and a sweatshirt. Mr. Goldberg, as usual, was dressed in a dark suit, white shirt, and dark tie. All of us knew Mr. Goldberg was so angry that he wouldn't speak right away. But David, as he sometimes did, pretended not to notice. And he never bothered to explain why he was late that day.

As Mr. Goldberg watched David, his heavy lids came down low so that he looked like a lizard, and I thought of the mythical basilisk. Mr. Goldberg looked at his youngest son for a long time, as if he were trying to see through him to intimidate him. Most of us, if we had been as late as David had, would have been drawn to those eyes despite ourselves, and then looked away, horrified because they were filled with hate. But David looked in front of him at the table, like an oblivious teenager. This unrequited staring contest went on for five minutes. I know because I counted on the Rolex I had bought as a present for myself on my fifth anniversary with the company.

Mr. Goldberg realized he had to recover and retake control of the situation. With an extreme physical effort, he lifted the wall of hate that had descended over his eyes like a snake wriggling back into the skin that it had discarded.

"How nice of you to join us." The voice flat, no trace of sarcasm, which would have been a sign of weakness. Mr. Goldberg had never shown weakness in his life. David nodded. That out of the way, the discussion was about to begin.

2

"AS YOU ALL know, we are faced with an important decision. Over the years, we have taken a gold company of one mine and built it into a company of many mines. A gold company that is number two in the world in terms of production. We now have an opportunity before us, one that doesn't come around every day. We have the opportunity to buy another mine, which will make us the largest gold company in the world. The question before us, the question we need to answer for ourselves, is a simple one: to bid or not to bid?"

Mr. Goldberg spoke with his usual confident sense of self-evidence. He didn't appear to realize that his question sounded uncannily like another one spoken by a make-believe Danish prince about the nature of existence. He didn't seem to realize he was speaking on some level about another kind of material existence, about the corporate entity his father had bequeathed to him and that he had grown many times over. And he refused to mention that the other bidder we would be up against was Solomon. It was as if Solomon didn't exist in this conversation, as if he wasn't one of the essential factors we needed to consider in making our decision. But we all knew Mr. Goldberg was pretending. We all knew that, despite that fact that Mr. Goldberg refused to even say Solomon's name, he couldn't get Solomon out of his mind. The room went quiet after Mr. Goldberg finished speaking.

Mr. Goldberg took care to look at each of us in turn, not looking at any one of his sons longer than another. All three sons looked serious. Sammy was staring so hard at his father I thought the blood vessels in his eyes would burst. Jake was looking past his father at the picture of his grandfather as if he were hoping Abraham would rescue him, maybe even bounce him on his knee and tell him everything would be okay. And David was watching his father with an air of concern. Ira and I were both looking professionally at Mr. Goldberg like the lawyers we were.

As the oldest son, Sammy would speak first, so we all turned to him. Everyone except for Mr. Goldberg, who waited. Sammy hadn't been the same ever since his nervous breakdown. Outwardly, he had recovered, but his old veneer of confidence now gave way to a light sheen of sweat every time he had to speak in the presence of his father. His loud voice stuttered on occasion. Some first-born sons would have rebelled after being taken out of the running to succeed their father, but, if anything, Sammy had taken to agreeing with Mr. Goldberg more vehemently than before. It was as if he was hoping that if he were even more like Mr. Goldberg, then Mr. Goldberg would relent and see his potential. That was why Sammy now adopted at least the classic physical position of confidence. But since his nervous breakdown, Sammy could no longer hide his lack of confidence, and that weakness only made him less deserving of respect in Mr. Goldberg's eyes. As Sammy had recuperated and eased his way back into the business, Mr. Goldberg had responded to Sammy with only gentleness and kindness. But after Sammy had recovered as much as he was ever going to, Mr. Goldberg's treatment of his oldest son had reverted to form.

"I think," Sammy began, and despite his best efforts, he had chosen the wrong words to frame his remarks. Mr. Goldberg had little patience for men who used extra words, and he had only contempt for people who prefaced their views with "I think" or even "I believe." He wanted the people advising him to be certain. Starting off with "I think" had been a verbal habit of Jake's, not Sammy's, from the time he was a boy, and Mr. Goldberg viewed it as an unnecessary affectation.

This habit of starting a sentence with "I think" was new to Sammy, and it didn't really suit him in his middle age. I was not sure if this tentativeness was a side effect of the lithium his doctor had prescribed, and I pitied him for deciding to open this way. It was a sort of death wish in any conversation with his father. Sammy must have realized it because his initial physical confidence seemed to dissipate quickly, and from then on, he appeared even more tentative. He compounded his error by repeating the dreaded words when he said, "I think we have to go for it." Then he must have had a burst of inspiration because he added, "This is not the kind of opportunity that comes around every day, and so we have to go all in" ("we have to go all in" being one of the phrases that had become a favourite of Mr. Goldberg's in recent years). But then he reverted to his poor opening. "I think it's a no-brainer: we're the second biggest gold company in the world, and this acquisition would give us the chance to be number one. Number one," Sammy added for emphasis, although the repetition sounded weak. And then, for some reason, Sammy started to sound like Jake by slipping into jargon, like "global scale" and "supply chain efficiencies," and with this he was now compounding his opening errors because Mr. Goldberg hated corporate speak, just as he hated abbreviations.

Sammy finished off with what he hoped was his peroration, even though he didn't know the word. "We can't let Solomon beat us on this one." And then, knowing his father, he concluded with, "We can't afford to lose." He waited for his father's approval, but despite Mr. Goldberg's unusual gentleness with his first-born son in the months of his recovery, none was forthcoming today. In fact, as Sammy finished speaking to the room and looked over to his father, his father's eyes were already on Jake.

Mr. Goldberg looked at the thick folder in front of his middle son with impatience and contempt. If Sammy had started his presentation with the shallow confidence of someone who thought he was going to succeed because he knew that what he was about to say accorded with the opinion of the most powerful person in the room, Jake began his speech with the desperation of the salesman who knew he was not going to get to finish his pitch, let alone make the sale. I was hoping he wouldn't open the file folder because once he did, he would lose the slim chance he still had with his father. But when Sammy was done and Mr. Goldberg had dismissed him with a nod of his head instead of a "Thank you" and a "Hmm" instead of a "Nicely done," Mr. Goldberg looked over at Jake with a sour look on his face. "Well, go ahead, then," was all he said to his second son.

Jake swallowed and opened the folder. Mr. Goldberg was quicker than all of us. Before Jake had a chance to pass anything around, Mr. Goldberg said, "Jesus Christ, Jacob, that's not a PowerPoint, is it? Please tell me you haven't brought a PowerPoint. This is a discussion. We're not looking at PowerPoints." Mr.

Goldberg shook his head sulkily and waved his hand at Jake as if he were the least important person in the world.

Without his PowerPoint, Jake was as lost as an actor who doesn't know his lines. Yet although he was different from his father and his brothers, he was not a Goldberg for nothing; he soldiered on. But he nearly lost his father completely with his first sentence: "I've been speaking with some analysts and consultants who are familiar with the history of this mine as well as a former consultant to Solomon's company." Mr. Goldberg dramatically rolled his eyes. If there was anything he hated more than jargon, it was analysts and consultants. He thought analysts were parasites who enabled the short-term outlook of the market that drove companies to chase after quarterly results and who encouraged shareholder activism. Consultants were at the bottom of the heap.

And if consultants were at the low end of Mr. Goldberg's estimation, the only lower position was reserved for consultants to Solomon. Most CEOs would have jumped at the chance to speak to people who had worked for the other side, who, despite all the nondisclosure agreements, never seemed to be able to resist the temptation to share some valuable information about the competition. But not Mr. Goldberg. He found the whole practice of consultants walking into everyone's boardrooms and learning everyone's business and dropping what they knew behind them like golden breadcrumbs distasteful, and he didn't want to ever hear a word about Solomon. Jake had to have known this, and I began to wonder if he had mentioned Solomon's consultant deliberately, as if he somehow wanted to pre-emptively and utterly destroy the credibility of his own opinion in his father's eyes.

Mr. Goldberg could now barely bring himself to look at his middle son, so he stared into the middle distance, his face impassive.

Jake didn't glance down once at his slides, and it's hard to convey charts and graphs through mere words, but he did his best. "The global market for gold is still undervalued, and as the Chinese pull millions of their people into the middle class, demand for gold is only going to rise." None of us quite knew where Jake was going with this. None of us assumed he was going to come down on the side of recommending that we bid. We all knew that's what Mr. Goldberg wanted to do. We assumed Jake was setting himself up for a recommendation to not bid against Solomon by first acknowledging all the arguments for bidding against him. Jake went on for a few minutes in this vein as Mr. Goldberg lost interest; his attention started to wander, and he began to look around the room and fidget in his chair.

Before Jake had started speaking, he knew that he would be dismissed by Mr. Goldberg, because of the PowerPoint, because of his reliance on the opinions of "experts," and because he knew that Mr. Goldberg fundamentally mistrusted all his opinions. This had been the case for years, because ever since Jake had been a teenager, and even when they seemed to have reached a détente in Jake's forties, all of his opinions had run counter to everything Mr. Goldberg wanted to do. So Jake spoke quickly, as if he knew he didn't have a lot of time and his own father didn't want to listen to him.

All of us expected Jake to oppose bidding, in no small part because of the lunch he'd had with Solomon, so when he came down firmly on the side of bidding against Solomon, we were surprised. Even Mr. Goldberg was surprised, but it was clear from his reaction, his slightly widened eyes, that he didn't put a lot of faith in Jake's arguments, and I almost wondered if for the first time he doubted the wisdom of going ahead because of his middle son's support for it. That might actually have been Jake's intention, his version of reverse psychology or even a very private joke, but before we knew it, Jake was finished speaking, and it was David's turn.

So far it was three for bidding against Solomon. We all already knew that Mr. Goldberg wanted to bid because he was naturally competitive, because for the last number of years he had wanted to own the largest gold company in the world, and because he hated to lose to Solomon. And if he didn't want to bid, he wouldn't have brought us all together to discuss it. Who voted for going ahead or not didn't matter in itself because Mr. Goldberg still had the only vote that counted. But Mr. Goldberg would be interested in what David had to say, almost as much as he would be interested in Ira's view.

If Sammy was for everything his father wanted to do, and Jake was usually against his father except for today — and none of us could really figure out his reasons — David was not predictable. He didn't set out to please or displease his father. He gave him his best, objective advice. But David was complex, and unlike Sammy and Jake, he didn't rely only on words to convey his message. He never used PowerPoint, but the way he dressed, how slowly or quickly he spoke, whether he looked more at Mr. Goldberg or around the room, were all part of his overall message.

Every other person in the room would have started speaking right away, conscious of not being seen to waste Mr. Goldberg's time, starting to speak even if he hadn't had time to collect his thoughts, perhaps so that he wouldn't have time to collect his thoughts because we all knew Mr. Goldberg distrusted people who took time to collect their thoughts. He believed that anybody who took too long to formulate their thoughts and who spoke in well-constructed sentences had something to hide. At seventy-four, he was still famous for not preparing for any speeches that he gave, whether internally or outside the company. I had always known this about

Mr. Goldberg and had always, not even consciously at first, adjusted how I spoke to him. But David wasn't any one of us, and he took his time. Mr. Goldberg stared at him, and with every passing second his heavy eyelids fell a little lower. Mr. Goldberg had become much less indulgent of David ever since the shouting match after Jake's lunch with Solomon.

David and I had spoken several times before this meeting, so I knew that he knew what he was going to say. I'm not sure why he waited so long to respond. It could have been that he wanted Mr. Goldberg to think he had thought carefully about the question. In the end, I concluded David wanted his father to know that what he was about to say had not been easy for him. That he was showing his father deference, even though he was going to try his patience by not agreeing with him.

Despite the tension he was creating, David didn't look the least bit uncomfortable. He wasn't sweating; his forty-six-year-old forehead was free of lines. But he did look solicitous, which was almost always how he was with his father, even when his father's eyelids were descending or when he was yelling. It was that way when Mr. Goldberg put an end to David's career in acting.

"Dad, Aussie Gold is a good company, and this acquisition would fit with where you want to take the company, which is more global and with even larger economies of scale. It would make us number one." And here, like the actor he had once been, David paused for just the right amount of time before he said, "And I know there's nothing that would bring you more satisfaction than to outbid Solomon." Unlike Sammy and Jake, who had spoken to the room, as small as it was, David spoke only to his father.

David had the legendary manners of his *zayde* Abraham, which was to say that he was exceedingly polite. He would shake the hands of everyone in any room he walked into and take the time to learn their names. If someone attended a party he was hosting and that person didn't know many people in the room, David would make sure to introduce them to others, and he would find ways of staking out common ground — professional interests or hobbies or vacations — so that when he moved on, the newcomer had found someone to speak with. And it wasn't something he did because he felt he had to; he did it as a small, simple act of respect and kindness. And he did it every day.

David spoke in the same respectful tones to CEOs of other companies as he did to the employees breaking rock in search of gold at one of his family's mines. But at this moment, why pretend anybody's else's opinion mattered? He spoke to his father the way a kind, thoughtful son would speak to his father over breakfast about sports or about where to take a family vacation. The rest of us in the boardroom were observers, at least for now, even though David knew there was one other opinion that counted in the room, and that was Ira's. Mine counted too, but whatever David was about to say would be the filter through which Mr. Goldberg would view my contribution.

David didn't want to surprise Mr. Goldberg, and by the way he had started off, briefly listing the merits of the acquisition, acknowledging his father's strategic thinking, expressing empathy, Mr. Goldberg knew where David was going, and although you wouldn't notice if you had just met him, Mr. Goldberg's eyelids were already quite low. But even when he was late, David was Mr. Goldberg's favourite son, and so Mr. Goldberg didn't hurry him along. He would hear him out. David didn't alter his cadence or tone. "This acquisition would make sense at almost any other time, with almost any other competing bidder."

When David's "but" came, as we knew it inevitably had to, Mr. Goldberg almost flinched in his chair, but he blinked, and his eyelids were slow to rise, as if he were hoping that when he reopened his eyes, none of us would still be in front of him.

"But we're at the height of the cycle."

Although nobody ever knew when they were at the top or the bottom of the mysterious cycle or how long the particular pleasure or pain was going to last, David didn't qualify his statements with "I think." He knew it was obvious that when you express an opinion you are expressing a thought, and he knew Mr. Goldberg's feelings about the phrase. David was speaking based on his gut, which, after you cut through all the assertively rational models and data and projections about a future nobody can ever accurately predict, is all businesspeople really have to go on when they make big decisions.

"There's no point in having regrets or fighting past battles. In every decision we have made up to this point, with every new acquisition, we did what we thought was right. And gold has been climbing for a decade. But since the start of this year, we've seen some price dips, which would suggest we've reached the top of the cycle. Our gearing is already high; we're in danger of breaching covenants if we further increase our debt ratio and prices drop. As tempting as the opportunity might appear, we'd be paying a premium. We should walk away. We shouldn't buy."

I remember glancing around the room, wanting to see the reactions. Ira, despite all his reserve, couldn't help himself. He let a tight smile escape. Jake crossed and uncrossed his arms and glanced down. Sammy reacted like he'd been shot. His big, strong body moved in his chair, his eyes widened, and he looked at his father before looking back at his forty-six-year-old baby brother. He barely shook his head. But in his reaction, even though he had the same body and head as his father, Sammy revealed yet again that he wasn't the measure of him. Because Mr. Goldberg didn't react. He sat still, didn't move his arms or hands. He didn't blink; his eyelids lowered, he looked at David, and he said nothing.

Sammy stopped fidgeting and stared at David in a way that reminded me of the way Sammy had looked in that darkened auditorium more than thirty years before when David had come on stage as Juliet and Sammy's eyes had flickered between David in his wig and his father in his seat giving off that golden glow.

Mr. Goldberg continued to stare at David, and David didn't follow the advice he had just given to his father on bidding against Solomon. David didn't look away. He held his father's gaze. Mr. Goldberg's eyelids had dropped another couple millimetres. Mr. Goldberg didn't say anything in response to David but turned to me. After me it would be Ira. Before I had a chance to speak, Mr. Goldberg said to me in a flat voice, "Are you for or against?" Even though I was, as Ira had described so many years before, "David's man," and even though David and I were of the same generation and saw many things in the same ways, it wasn't nec- essarily a given that I would side with David. I had always tried to give my best professional advice to any Goldberg who asked, regardless of which side of a debate they were on. But in this case, David and I were in agreement.

I nodded and said, "Against."

"And do you have any arguments that are different from David's?" Mr. Goldberg was trying hard to appear unaffected by his youngest son's words, but he looked uncharacteristically tired, and I was reminded that, although he was wealthy and powerful and had recovered fully from his bout with lung cancer, he was still a man of seventy-four. I quickly ran through my arguments in my mind. Mr. Goldberg was not interested in hearing the contrary position presented again. I had prepared a few historical examples from other deals in case I needed them as evidence, but David had expressed the kernel of the argument. I couldn't measurably improve on it, so I would cede the field and let Ira speak. I shook my head. "No."

"Thank you. What about you, Ira?"

Like David, Ira knew the only person in the room who mattered was Mr. Goldberg. But unlike David, Ira made a point of speaking to the room. He wanted the unwritten record, the one that lasts far longer in people's minds, to show that he'd addressed everyone equally. Despite the fact he owed to Mr. Goldberg the last thirty-five years of his career and however many more years he wanted to keep actively making a lot of money, Ira was thinking ahead. He looked at each of us in turn, acknowledging our right to have an opinion. Before he started to speak, he did not look at Mr. Goldberg. He looked at Sammy. But, when he began to speak, he referred to David and his argument. Ira had made a career of managing the moods of Mr. Goldberg, and this time, on this day, regarding this decision that would make or break the company, he didn't disappoint. As someone who shared the same profession, I had to admire his skill, if still disagreeing with his intent and with what ended up being the result.

"Saul." Ira was the only one at the company who called Mr. Goldberg by his first name. He didn't do it often, especially when others were in the room, but he chose his moments carefully, and always with great effect. "David has neatly laid out the arguments against. I have to say they are logical and compelling. And it is difficult to counter them, let alone dismiss them."

Anyone who wasn't familiar with Ira's style would assume he was going to play the role of the brave, honest adviser and come down on David's side. But I'd known Ira long enough to know he was setting himself up to go in the opposite direction. He signalled his intention and his methods clearly with his next sentence. "Every analyst out there is saying we're at the top of the cycle. The bears are out in force. I agree that most companies would not be making this acquisition at this time. I don't even necessarily disagree with David's arguments in totality." Ira couldn't resist a lawyerly double negative and a few gratuitous syllables — the effect of billable hours dies hard even for in-house counsel — but already at this point Mr. Goldberg knew exactly where Ira was going. And he liked it.

"But, and I know you've heard me say it before, we are not an ordinary company. And you — you are not an ordinary businessman. If you and Abraham" — a typical Ira insertion, rhetorically pulling Mr. Goldberg closer to the only man he truly admired — "had always done what the analysts were advising you to do, what kind of company would we be? I don't know for sure, but I know it wouldn't be the same. You haven't made a career out of following the herd. You've followed your instincts. Every time."

And now Ira went in for the kill. He was giving advice, hedging his bets, speaking truth to power and agreeing with power all at the same time, and in the process ingratiating himself still further with Mr. Goldberg, if that was possible. "If it were me, I would probably be taking David's advice here. I'm a pretty cool customer, but I'm not sure I would have the balls for this acquisition, not at this time." Mr. Goldberg smiled primly. "But that's probably why I'm not sitting in your seat, Saul. You are. And you are for a reason. If you still feel, after listening to the counterarguments today, that this is the right decision, and you are still willing to take on this risk, then I support you. A hundred and fifty percent." In this final statement, Ira was exhibiting the pale professional courage of the corporate lawyer who prides himself on identifying a risk for the record but then going along with the CEO who is brave enough to actually take that risk.

We didn't have to wait for Mr. Goldberg's reaction. He smiled at Ira, and then he turned his smile on all of us. Through it all, Ira did not smile but looked as serious as befitted a man who had just given momentous advice. Mr. Goldberg's smile, despite his wealth and power, despite the obvious intelligence, if not wisdom, was the smile of a child. A child who was pleased with himself.

Sammy frowned, trying to figure out how what Ira had said was different than what he had said. Jake looked down at his stack of unused PowerPoints that he would now take back to his assistant, Judy, and ask her to shred. I looked at Ira, but he refused to make eye contact underneath his bushy eyebrows. He had eyes only for Mr. Goldberg. David alone looked at his father with concern, and I knew he was already starting to think about how he would serve and support Mr. Goldberg when this acquisition didn't go as planned. But there was a sign of something else in David's impossibly blue, symmetrical eyes. I must have fallen under Solomon's spell by this time; I didn't appreciate what I was seeing beneath David layer of concern. It was only later, in retrospect, that I realized David was trying, not quite successfully, to hide his hurt feelings. For the first time that any of us could remember, David's father had taken Ira's advice over his.

3

A WEEK LATER, as the markets were about to open in Western Australia, we were sitting down for the first seder of Passover at Mr. Goldberg's home in Upper Westmount in Montréal. The adults sat at the long dining table, and a separate table had been set up for the children, near the living room but still close. By this time, I had been to several seders at the Goldbergs' and I knew how important the presence of children was to this ritual and to all the Jewish rituals.

The whole family was there: Mr. Goldberg, Sammy and Jake, with their wives and children, David, Ira and his wife, Jane, who was in town, our children, and me. Mr. Goldberg presided at the head of the table, his golden kippah resting lightly on his golden-grey hair. It had all grown back after his chemo, but a little more grey had come with it. At one end of our table, and repeated on the children's table, was the ceremonial seder plate, with its symbolic foods set out in a circle. The chicken bone, the egg, the bitter herbs. The *haroset* — a mixture of apples and nuts and wine to represent the mortar used by the Hebrew slaves in Egypt to build the pyramids. The celery to be dipped in the salt water, symbol of the tears the Hebrew slaves had shed during their labours. The bitter horseradish. The still-covered matzoh — the unleavened bread that the Hebrews didn't have time to let rise when they received the distraught Pharaonic order to flee Egypt after the death of every first-born son, including the royal one — occupied pride of place on two large plates placed strategically along each table.

The first time I'd attended a seder at the Goldbergs' was just a few months after I'd first been invited down to Curaçao. When I saw my first seder plate and Mr. Goldberg explained the significance of each of the ritual foods, I found the Easter eggs that Mary so lovingly hid around our small house childish and inadequate in comparison. Over time I stopped thinking about it.

Mr. Goldberg put on his reading glasses and began to read aloud the opening paragraphs of the Haggadah, copies of which were placed before each of us atop our plates. We picked up our books to follow.

"Blessed are thou, Lord, our God, King of the Universe, who does create the fruit of the vine. Blessed are thou, Lord, our God, King of the Universe, who has chosen us above all peoples and has exalted us above all tongues, and hast hallowed us with thy commandments." Mr. Goldberg didn't hurry through the words as if they were part of a muttered prayer. He read slowly, enunciating the words. "And thou hast given us, Lord, our God, with love Seasons for gladness, Holidays and times for rejoicing, this day of the Festival of Matzoth, the time of our freedom, an assembly day of holiness, a memorial to the outgoing. For thou hast chosen us, and hast sanctified us, above all peoples, and thou hast caused us to inherit thy Sacred Seasons in gladness and rejoicing. Blessed art thou, Lord, who dost sanctify Israel and the Festivals." Under the table, Jane squeezed my knee. I squeezed hers back.

"Blessed art thou, Lord, our God, King of the Universe, who hast kept us alive, and has hast maintained us, and has enabled us to reach this time." Mr. Goldberg stopped reading and commanded us: "And now we dip." And he passed around the plate at our end of the table, and we each took a piece of celery and dipped it in the salty water while Mr. Goldberg recited the traditional blessing: "Blessed are thou, Lord, our God, King of the Universe, who dost create the fruit of the soil."

When he was finished speaking, Mr. Goldberg reached for the covered plate, lifted the golden linen cloth, took a piece of matzoh, and broke it. Then he disappeared with it into the kitchen. I had seen this many times before, so I knew that he was hiding for the children what was now not just a piece of matzoh but the *aphikoman*, which means "that which comes after."

Later, toward the end of the meal, the children would be sent to hunt for the aphikoman. Even the older children would join in, for there would be a prize for the winner. In some simple way, it was like my childhood Easter hunt. I don't imagine other Jewish households offered more than a few dollars, but the prize for the child who found the aphikoman at the Goldberg house was a small gold coin, printed with the company logo and worth anywhere from two hundred to four hundred dollars, depending on the price of gold on that day. Mr. Goldberg was usually back in a few minutes, but this time he didn't return. Ira went to look for him. The rest of us resumed our conversation. Fifteen minutes later, Mr. Goldberg and Ira came back to the dining room.

Mr. Goldberg put his reading glasses back on, lifted the plate of matzoh, and said, "This is the poor bread which our fathers ate in the land of Egypt. Let anyone who is hungry, come in and eat; let anyone who is needy, come in and make Passover. This year we are here; next year we shall be in the land of Israel.

This year we are slaves; next year we shall be freemen." The way Mr. Goldberg said "slaves" reminded me of the way he had said the word so many years earlier in Curaçao when had he told me about Tula and compared the ending of that story to the stories of the Jewish holidays.

The next part of the seder was my favourite part. The four questions. It had only taken me a couple of seders to realize the phrase was misleading. It was one question and four answers. First we drank our first cup of wine. Then Mr. Goldberg stood up and called for his grandson named for the Old Testament prophet whom we honoured on Passover with his own goblet of wine and a door especially opened so he could come into the house and drink and announce the Messiah. "Elijah, come to your *zayde*." Elijah was Jake's son and the youngest grandchild. He was ten and blond like the Goldberg family. He wore a blue linen sports jacket with little light-blue patches on the elbows. Like all the Goldbergs before him, his eyes had that strange symmetry, but in him, the third generation after Abraham, the effect had softened.

He ran to Mr. Goldberg and, without any shyness, even at ten, jumped onto his grandfather's lap. Mr. Goldberg placed his arms around his grandson and lifted the Haggadah for him to read. But Elijah pushed the book away and looked up at Mr. Goldberg. "I don't need the book, *Zayde*. I know the words." Mr. Goldberg nodded solemnly, as if he wasn't surprised. Everyone was silent. I looked over at Jake, who was staring at his son with paternal pride and a modest fascination, but also a tentativeness because his son was sitting on Mr. Goldberg's lap.

Elijah, without the least bit of nervousness, addressed the long table of adults and the almost equally long table of children. "Why is this night different from all other nights?" and like a born orator, Elijah let his rhetorical question sink in before proceeding to enlighten us. "On all other nights, we eat leavened bread and matzah; on this night we eat only matzoh." As he spoke, he gestured to the matzoh in front of us. "On all other nights we eat all kinds of herbs; on this night, we eat mainly bitters." A nod this time, to the herbs representing the bitter suffering the Jews endured when they were slaves in Egypt. "On all other nights, we do not dip even once; on this night we dip twice." And the youngest Goldberg made a dipping motion with his little hand. "On all other nights, we eat either sitting straight or reclining; on this night we all recline," and Elijah leaned back so hard against the chest of Mr. Goldberg that Mr. Goldberg was surprised. Everyone at the table laughed. This last answer had always struck me as strange because we never reclined.

Upon the successful completion of the four questions, Elijah clapped and his family clapped for him and Mr. Goldberg put his arms around him and rocked him slowly before gently placing him on the floor. Elijah hugged his grandfather and gave him a kiss on the cheek before running back to his table of children. Then we were launched on the story of liberation. The reluctant Moses, the obstinate Pharaoh, the tough desert God with his array of plagues, the final heartbreaking death of the first-born, and the angel of death passing over the houses of the Jews because they had done as instructed by their God and splattered the blood of a lamb on their front doors so that the angel of death would pass over their houses and strike down only the first-born sons of the Egyptians.

The subsequent softening of Pharaoh, the flight of the Jews with nothing, their bread that didn't have time to rise, Pharaoh's last-minute change of heart and his dispatching of soldiers to kill the Jews waiting at the Red Sea. The miraculous parting of the Red Sea just at the moment of greatest despair, the mad dash through, the Egyptians following and, when the last Hebrew had crossed, the mighty waters turning back on themselves, the drowning of Pharaoh's warriors and their horses, the forty years of wandering in the desert still ahead of them, but the Hebrews delivered by their Lord.

At the same time, half a continent away, just as the Australian Securities Exchange was opening in Sydney, lawyers handpicked by Ira and instructed by Mr. Goldberg were launching Goldberg Limited's hostile takeover bid for Aussie Gold, a major player with two high-producing, low-cost mines in Queensland and Canada. With Aussie Gold's production, we would become the largest gold producer in the world. Mr. Goldberg stepped away from the table two more times that evening, ostensibly to go to the bathroom, but each time he was away for longer, and each time Ira happened to join him.

Within hours, Iseli Gold — Solomon's company — joined the bidding. Iseli Gold had been generating and conserving cash for the last three years. Unlike Goldberg Limited, which had steadily been making acquisitions in recent years, Iseli's gearing — ratio of debt to capitalization — was low, and their war chest was deep. As usual, Mr. Goldberg had paid little attention to his competitors.

DAVID KNEW THAT we shouldn't be buying at the height of the cycle, but when the action was well underway, and when Solomon continued to sweeten his offer by such maddeningly small increments that Mr. Goldberg felt compelled to meet and exceed them, the rest of us began to feel more and more uneasy with every counterbid.

As the share premium for Aussie Gold reached twenty, then thirty, then forty percent above the market capitalization of the company, only David realized what Solomon was doing. Solomon had never intended to win the bidding war. But by this time — because in Mr. Goldberg's eyes David had shown him disrespect by raising his voice over his treatment of Jake and then compounded his transgression by giving unwanted advice about Aussie Gold — David had been banished from Mr. Goldberg's shrinking inner circle of advisers. Mr. Goldberg listened to no one except Ira. And Ira egged him on without seeming to, hedging his bets in his advice, telling Mr. Goldberg that obviously he was taking risks that he himself wouldn't have the stomach for, that of course caution was a common virtue, but that he trusted Mr. Goldberg's singular judgment.

IN THE DAYS of offers and counteroffers that followed, the option of withdrawing was still possible, and I asked David, "Did your father not read any of the analysts' reports?" After Mr. Goldberg had decided to go ahead, Jake had sent his father copies of the reports that he hadn't been interested in hearing about during the meeting.

David was not yet forty-seven at this point, but he smiled like an old man who has been living a secret life and knows that he is finally about to be exposed. With a mixture of relief and wistfulness, he said, "You've probably never noticed, but my father doesn't read."

"Doesn't read?" I remembered him reading for hours on the beach in Curaçao.

"The stock prices, yes, and the news, but he's never read a book, unless you count Carnegie's *How to Win Friends and Influence People* and the Bible, and I don't usually count the Bible because he doesn't so much read it as misread it."

I DIDN'T HAVE to ask David what he meant about Mr. Goldberg's reading of the Bible because I thought I knew. Solomon had told me, when he was telling me about Mr. Goldberg's praying for successful acquisitions at Shaar Hashomayim. I could hear Solomon's incredulous voice ringing in my ears: "At synagogue, he prays to God for the destruction of his enemies. He thinks all the biblical stories of sibling rivalry — Cain and Abel, Jacob and Esau, Joseph and his brothers — are positive lessons to be emulated, not to be avoided, because they toughen everybody up. 'Thou shalt remember the Sabbath day to keep it holy,' and what is more holy than going forward to smite your enemies through the divine instrument of a hostile takeover? 'Honour thy father and thy mother?' He concedes this one, but that didn't prevent him from cheating his father's and mother's other child out of his birthright." Solomon hadn't finished.

"'Thou shalt not kill,' unless it is in defence or for a good cause or metaphorical in the pursuit of business objectives. 'Thou shalt not commit adultery' because as Paul Newman said about his faithful marriage of forty years, worth several lifetimes in Hollywood, why go out for hamburger when you can have filet mignon at home?" Solomon had stopped for a moment to breathe and said, "Why are you looking at me like that? Hollywood's okay for others, just not for his son. 'Thou shalt not steal,' unless it is from thine enemies and it is legally sanctioned and Ira has approved. 'Thou shalt not bear false witness against thy neighbour' unless thy neighbour is a sworn enemy and deserves it. 'Thou shalt not covet thy neighbour's house' because thine own house is bigger and better, ditto for not coveting thy neighbour's wife because thine own wife is thinner and better looking."

"SEAN, ARE YOU all right?"

"Yes, sorry, what do mean your father doesn't read?"

"He's not alone. Many executives don't read books. They don't have the time or the patience or the energy after reading reports and being the centre of attention all day. Sometimes they make reading more business books one of their New Year's resolutions. But," and here David smiled for my benefit as if he were about to apologize for saying something to disillusion me, "my father doesn't even read reports. He doesn't trust them. I don't think he understands them. He claims he values the spoken word over the written one because it's more direct and honest, and he says he'd rather talk to 'real people' than read an analyst's report. But back in university, I realized that my father is practically financially illiterate. He dropped out of university and never bothered to pick up the basics of business that most people take for granted. He thinks it's all somehow beneath him."

"Financially illiterate?"

"Well, he can read the stock prices well enough, but I don't think he could explain to you the difference between an income statement and a balance sheet. Worse, I don't think he *cares*. He's run the company my *zayde* bequeathed to him on pure instinct. On improvised speeches and hearty handshakes. He buys companies not because he's looked carefully at the financials and considers them undervalued and knows exactly where he can drive down costs and improve efficiencies. He buys them because he *likes* them. He thinks success in business comes down to being the one with the most motivation."

"How can he run a company then? How has he been so successful?"

David laughed, but it was over quickly. "Abraham gave him a pretty good head start. You have to work really hard to drive a productive gold mine into the ground. But there's one other thing: when it comes to numbers, he relies on Ira for almost everything." Ira, long-time family servant and admirer of Napoleon, purveyor of historical military knowledge and anecdotes. And my mentor.

IN THE END, Solomon withdrew from the auction, and Goldberg had the winning bid. The price of gold dipped a little just before our acquisition of Aussie Gold closed in May 2012. Mr. Goldberg must have held his breath, because the price we paid in the end was an astounding premium of fifty percent per share. He never said anything to any of us. Gold began to climb again soon after we closed. At that point, Mr. Goldberg didn't have to stoop to saying "I told you so" to David because the way he looked at his youngest son and smiled like a child every time he saw him at the office or the house said enough. And so we became the largest gold company in the world, and Mr. Goldberg was happy and victorious and vindicated. All was very good until David disappeared.

4

IRA CALLED TO tell me the news at 6:00 a.m. on a Monday morning. "David has disappeared. Do you know where he is?"

"What do you mean, disappeared?"

"Vanished. No messages. Not returning calls. You have no idea?"

"No."

"Mr. Goldberg wants to see you at his home in half an hour."

"WHERE IS MY SON?"

"I don't know, Mr. Goldberg."

"You don't know, or you're not telling me?"

I didn't know for sure. "I don't know."

Mr. Goldberg shook his big head. "Is he in Hollywood? Once you get that bug, see what it's like in La-La Land, it never leaves you. It's like politics. It's a disease. He's been dreaming of going back his whole life."

"I don't know, Mr. Goldberg." David had never said anything to me about wanting to return to LA. I'd always assumed he had put Hollywood behind him. It was probably too late for him to become an actor or even a director. Perhaps he could still become a producer. I found myself embarrassed that I was jealous of Mr. Goldberg, jealous that he might know his son better than I did.

Mr. Goldberg watched me carefully. I think he reached the wrong conclusion, that I was lying to him, because he said, "You know I can fire you — for cause, so no severance package — for lying to me?"

"I suppose so."

"Not 'I suppose so.' I can."

"Okay."

"Is he in London?"

I remained silent as the famous Goldberg eyelids lowered. He waited, and I continued to say nothing. Finally, he shook his head in disgust. It was only then that I said, "I don't know for sure."

"If he reaches out to you, you are to contact me right away. Do you understand?"

I didn't understand, but I knew what had to be said. "I understand."

"If he reaches out to you, and you don't let me know, I will consider that lying. And insubordination. A firing offence."

I couldn't bring myself to speak. I just nodded.

"My son may not love me. But he will respect me." And Mr. Goldberg dismissed me with a wave of his arm, as if brushing away a fly.

LESS THAN AN hour later, I arrived at Goldberg Limited. Ira and I ended up on the same elevator. When we reached the top floor, he pulled me into his office and shut the door. He remained standing.

"You have forty-eight hours to find David and report back."

"And if I don't by then?"

"I'm to go after him."

"Why me first?"

"That's obvious. Because you're David's man."

"And what do I do once I find him?"

"You bring him home."

"And what if he doesn't want to come home?"

"He will, eventually."

"And if I refuse?"

"Mr. Goldberg says if you refuse, then you're not to bother coming back."

I had never lost my patience with Ira. Until then. "Do you never get tired of taking orders? Don't you ever want to run your own show?"

Ira laughed. But I must have hit a nerve, or else he was feeling boastful, because he turned serious again. "I love the Goldbergs. I love the company. I know I'll never be a member of the family, and that's okay. But that doesn't mean I don't have ambition." Still Ira remained standing. "Have you ever heard of Fabian Cunctator?" I shook my head. "It sounds a bit off-colour, but Cunctator is Latin for 'Delayer.' Fabian got his nickname fighting Hannibal."

Like Mr. Goldberg years earlier in Curaçao when he'd told me the story of Tula the slave, Ira gave me this history lesson in the present tense. He was standing only a foot away from me.

"It's the third century BCE. Rome is a small regional power in Italy, just beginning to feel its strength, but it's proud and has a sense of both its history and its destiny. Rome is taken aback when Hannibal, the general of Carthage, present-day Libya, crosses the Mediterranean at Gibraltar, moves quickly into Spain, and does what no Roman thinks possible. He crosses the Alps into Italy in the winter and begins wreaking havoc in the Roman heartland.

And not only does Hannibal bring his men over the mountains, he brings elephants, which few Romans have seen before, and he unleashes them on the battlefield. All of this would be bad enough, but it gets worse for Rome. The Romans have become good at war, but Hannibal is a tactical genius, and whenever the Romans engage Hannibal in battle, they lose to his army of North Africans.

"Finally, the Roman general Fabian comes up with a plan, not a tactical battle plan but a true strategy. He will refuse to meet the Carthaginians in a pitched battle but will pull back, retreat, lead Hannibal's army deeper into Italy, harry their flanks in an early prototype of guerrilla warfare, knowing that the city of Rome itself will be safe because Hannibal's mercenary army lacks the equipment and resolve for a long siege of a walled city. So rather than a typical Roman offensive strategy of taking the war to the enemy, Fabian invents the classic war of attrition. But the Roman Senate thinks it's cowardly, and they lose patience with him and strip Fabian of command.

"Enter another general, Varro, who bravely heads out like a good Roman soldier and, for his pains, leads his army into one of its most complete defeats at the Battle of Cannae. Hannibal tempts the Romans forward and then envelops them on all sides and cuts them to pieces. The Senate finally sees the wisdom of Fabian's strategy. Frustrated at being denied battle, Hannibal rapes and pillages. But time marches on, and his men become homesick and begin to desert. At the right moment, the Romans counterattack, and Scipio Africanus, a general who's good at pursuit, drives Hannibal back over the Alps, pursues him to Carthage, destroys the city, and sows salt in the fields so nothing will ever grow again. The ancients understood that patience is a virtue. The patient man wins in the end." Ira didn't look for my reaction. "Go look for David." He opened the door for me to leave.

I CALLED JANE that morning, 9:30 a.m. my time, 2:30 p.m. in London. I waited a couple hours before calling Jane because I didn't want to be Mr. Goldberg's messenger. I didn't want to tell David he had to come home.

"Is he there?"

Despite the hour, Jane sounded tired. "Yes. Of course, he's here."

"How is he?"

"Not good. He's not speaking."

"When did he get there?"

"Yesterday."

"Okay. I'll talk to Louisa about staying with Fiona and fly out tonight." After I packed, I called Ira to let him know that David was in London and that I was going after him. Ira seemed pleased with my quick progress. I asked him to inform Mr. Goldberg and said I'd be in touch.

WHEN I SAW David the next morning, he looked terrible. He hadn't been sleeping or eating. All he wanted was to play chess — the game he'd taught me in grade seven after he'd taught me how to play touch football. And so that's all we did for the first day. He kept his head bowed and didn't look at me as he moved his pieces or waited for me to respond. On the second day, he looked up from the chessboard and started to talk. It was while he was in the midst of beating me.

"My father taught me how to play chess."

I nodded.

"He taught all three of us. Like boxing, learning how to play chess was a rite of passage, as was the first time you beat him. It was something, to beat your father at chess for the first time.

Sammy did it when he was twelve. I think he felt guilty about it. Jake actually studied the game and did it when he was ten. He was proud. It was the first time he had beaten our father at anything."

"And you?"

David looked up. "I don't remember. Probably somewhere in between. But my father hated playing chess with me."

"How could he hate playing with you?"

"I didn't care."

"You didn't care if he hated playing with you?"

"No, I did care. He hated playing with me because I didn't care if I won or not. He found it infuriating. I think it took all the fun out of it for him. I enjoyed the game, and I enjoyed spending time with him. He travelled so much. But the fact that I never cared if I lost a game bothered him. He saw it as a lack of seriousness, almost a lack of personal respect. I think it made him wonder if I had the drive to win that he saw as essential in anybody who would eventually run the company. Sammy assumed that because he was the first-born and appeared to be most like our father, he would become CEO. We all knew Jake was too different, and I was always the baby, the third son who liked to act in plays. But my father treated me like he expected me to lead one day. Checkmate, by the way."

ON THE THIRD day, we only played chess while eating breakfast. It was the first time I'd noticed David eat something since I'd arrived. And then he wanted to go out. So for the rest of the week, we followed the same routine. We'd wake up, play chess, go for walks at Kew or Kensington Gardens. Lunch in Notting Hill or Soho. A museum in the afternoon. Take in a play in the evening, followed by drinks at a pub. Then come back, perhaps chat a bit, and fall asleep. With each passing day, David ate more, drank less, and looked more rested. During all this time, I took care never to initiate conversation.

Ira had given me forty-eight hours' grace, and then he started calling me every evening. His question was always was the same. "When is he coming home?" After the second call, I asked David how he wanted me to respond the next time Ira phoned.

"Tell him I'm working out some things. My father knows where I am. I'm not going any farther. You need to return to work, but I want you to come back in a few weeks. Tell Ira you'll give me some space and work on me when you're back."

Ira had to confer with Mr. Goldberg, but when we spoke the next day, Ira told me Mr. Goldberg had approved the plan. I returned to Montréal and went into the office as if everything was normal. Three weeks later, I flew back to London.

On my second trip, about a month after he had disappeared and after making the first move at the chessboard, David said, "I'm acting again, Sean."

"Acting?"

"Don't sound so surprised," David said. He was using his old constant, courtly, jesting tone. "Jane got me a small part in one of her plays."

"Don't believe anything he says, Sean," Jane said as she appeared in the kitchen and gave David a pat on the head. "I just got him an audition. He earned the part on his own."

"Even after all these years, Sean."

I shook my head and smiled and congratulated him. He had embarked on a new beginning.

UNCHARACTERISTICALLY, IT WAS Declan and not Mary who first asked me how David was doing. I was back in Montréal after my second trip to visit David in London. I had returned to tell Ira and Mr. Goldberg that David was doing well. I didn't mention anything about his return to acting. Nor did I give any timetable about David's potential return to the office. I just said he wasn't ready yet. Neither Mr. Goldberg nor Ira was happy with the situation, but no ultimatums were given. It was understood I would return to London in a few weeks.

I was sitting outside on the small backyard deck that Declan had built for my mother when I started university. Declan had just finished cutting his narrow plot of grass with his hand-powered mower and was relaxing with a Labatt 50.

"How's he doing, Sean? Your friend."

The question had come out of nowhere. My mother was preparing supper in a way that suggested she wanted to leave us alone, and my father and I had been sitting together in silence. My two older children, Dylan and Bridget, were away at university, Harvard and Yale, but the baby, Fiona, the rugby-playing teenager who must have got her athletic genes from Declan, was inside helping Mary in the kitchen with the apple pie. I could smell the lilac trees and the lily of the valley that my father had planted years ago. It felt like it was the first time in years that my father had asked me a question, and it took me by surprise.

In all our walks or chess games, David had said nothing to me about why he had left his father and the company. Sammy was crushed once and for all when it was clear he was never going to succeed Mr. Goldberg. Jake's destruction was slower and more drawn out, accomplished little by little on repeated occasions: each time he wanted to work outside the company and Mr. Goldberg said no, each time Jake acquiesced to his father's will. I had thought David, as the youngest and favourite son who wanted only to protect his father, would be spared his father's influence. And so he was, for the longest time.

With my father, even as an adult, I defaulted to short sentences, striving to get to the point as quickly as possible, feeling inadequate. "David has always tried to support his father. But his father didn't listen to him on an important business decision. His feelings were hurt. But now I think he's doing okay."

My father nodded and admired his garden handiwork. Even at seventy-one, even with a push mower, his grass was neatly cut. Every spring, he sharpened the blades himself. He had gained a bit of weight since he'd retired, but hadn't gone to fat.

"This Mr. Goldberg, he's quite a guy, isn't he?"

Declan had only met Mr. Goldberg once over the years, and it had been when Mr. Goldberg had apologized for exposing me to the robbery on Curaçao. I laughed, despite myself. I'd never heard Mr. Goldberg described as "a guy" before. "Yes, Dad, quite a guy."

Declan took a long swig of beer from the tall glass with the Olympic rings on it that he'd got as part of a Petro-Canada promotion and licked his lips slowly. "Power is a mysterious thing, Sean."

"Yes, Dad."

More silence. Then, "Do you think he'll go back to the company?"

"I don't know."

"It's hard to leave a company." My father had worked for the same subcontracting company for forty-seven years before retiring to his gardening and weekly beer drinking with the other sixty-something "boys." He surveyed his garden again. "But it's even harder to leave your family."

My father had never quite lost the spare, careful speech of the working class, and that was the end of our short conversation.

5

EVEN WHEN I was back in Montréal between trips to visit David in London, Ira called me every morning to ask me how things were going. I hadn't made any promises that I could convince David to come home. I just let Ira think that was what I was doing. All I ever said was, "I need to keep going to London," and Ira, for once reading incorrectly between the lines, would say, "Okay, I'll let Mr. Goldberg know."

On my third trip to London to see David, after he had been there six weeks, when we had just finished breakfast and were halfway through our first chess game of the morning, David said, "Remember when I said that I'd tell you about my family one day?"

We had been on the treadmill at the Westmount YMCA, jogging side by side just after Jake's disastrous lunch with Solomon. "Yeah?"

"Well, I'm ready now."

"Okay."

"Did you know we're descended from Cossacks?"

I didn't know what that had to do with Mr. Goldberg cheating Isaac out of his birthright. "I didn't."

"At least partly."

According to David, all the Goldbergs knew the story; it was passed down from generation to generation, usually after solemn anticipatory suppers, often accompanied by the whisky that none of the Goldbergs ever finished but which they thought the story demanded. It was passed down faithfully from father to son before the sons were out of their teens. The women who married into the Goldberg family usually found out when their first child was born. As for the Goldberg family men, once they started in on their story, they had no qualms about telling it. They passed it down as a point of pride and a warning. This is where we come from. This is what we are capable of.

David told me the story without emotion. He prefaced his comments with this: "Over the course of our history, we've been conquered or attacked and our men have been killed and our women have been raped. This is why, in the Jewish religion, the religion always goes through the mother. As long as the mother is Jewish, that's enough. You only ever know who the mother is." And then David told me about the origins of his family, back in Poland, in what used to be part of Russia.

THE COSSACKS DIDN'T come every year — if they had, the family of David's great-grandmother Aviva would never have survived — but the year Aviva turned fifteen, she was surprised by their arrival. Wild military men from southern Russia who rode their horses and fought for the czar, they came whenever they wanted, and if they were like an uncle they were like the uncle in your most terrible nightmares. When they came, they were drunk, and as a child Aviva remembered wondering if they were so violent because they were drunk or if they had to make themselves drunk to be violent. And they smelled, almost as strong as their horses.

Their smell was not what Aviva's family noticed first. It was the sound of their horses, galloping down the dirt road to their *shtetl*. Aviva's family heard the horses before they heard the men, shouting and swearing and laughing. The laughter was the worst. Because when your tormentor laughs, it means he holds you in contempt and he is confident you cannot win. The sound of galloping horses was the sign to Aviva's family of what was about to happen.

Aviva was a strong woman, but even after she had been living in Montréal for years, the sound and smell of horses was something she couldn't abide. To celebrate his first gold strike, Abraham wanted to take Aviva for a *calèche* ride around Mount Royal. When she found out what it was, that she would be pulled around by two horses, she nearly slapped her son's handsome face. But she controlled herself, saying she felt under the weather.

The Goldberg matriarch's *shtetl* in eastern Poland was so small it didn't have a name. There were only twelve families. Aviva's father ran a small grocery store out of their living room on the first floor of their house. Aviva went to what passed for a school in someone else's house. They had a few books. They went to synagogue. She had friends. That was their life.

When the Cossacks came that year, they didn't ride through town shooting their pistols into the air and through the windows as they usually did. At the last minute, as the Cossacks were breaking down the door to Aviva's home, her mother managed to hide her in the closet, behind some old clothes.

It took the Cossacks a few minutes to break down the front door, but then everything happened quickly. The Cossacks opened the closet as they stumbled around, but they were already

so drunk they didn't look very hard. They left the closet door
open, and Aviva saw everything. Afterward, she was amazed that
through it all, she never made a sound. When she thought she was
about to scream, she stuffed her father's winter coat in her mouth.

They raped Aviva's mother first. And they tied her father to a
chair and made him watch. While it was happening, the others
stood around drinking and joking and took their turns, like boys
waiting for a water fountain, pushing each other, slapping each
other on the back. When Aviva's father tried to close his eyes,
they slapped him and held his eyes open with their stinking, dirty
hands. Halfway through, Aviva's father went into shock and
started to whimper. The Cossacks hit him, and he stopped for a
bit but then started up again, and the Cossacks hit him harder.
The pattern repeated itself, but the Cossacks never hit him so hard
that he lost consciousness.

Aviva's mother didn't make a sound. She stayed silent and
immobile, and Aviva thought it was her mother's silence that
eventually drove away the joking and the laughter, made the
Cossacks sullen and angry so that rather than losing their desire
they abused her even more roughly. Unlike her father, Aviva's
mother didn't try to close her eyes. She didn't look beyond them
or at a place at the ceiling. She stared into the eyes of each man as
he lay on top of her, crushing her into the bed. She stared calmly
into their eyes. And at one point — Aviva didn't know how her
mother did it — she began to smirk. It was this final act of rebellion that drove the largest, dirtiest, loudest one mad. He began to
hit Aviva's mother as he raped her. But Aviva's mother continued
to stare and smirk. When he was done, he began to hit her harder.
When she didn't stop smirking, he took out a knife and cut her
throat. Her blood splattered. It was at this point Aviva's father
began to scream. It was a scream that Aviva had never heard

before. It was worse than the howl of an animal, as far removed from a human sound as Aviva had ever heard. It stunned the man who had killed her mother, and the other men. She thought they would slap her father harder, knock out his teeth. They stabbed him. Aviva emerged from her closet, wanting to hold her father and wanting to die herself. Her mother's death had happened suddenly, but her father was dying slowly. Aviva wanted to be with him. Afterward, she regretted showing herself. If she had stayed hidden, the men might have become bored and left. She felt ashamed of these thoughts.

When the men saw fifteen-year-old Aviva emerging in shock from her hiding place, their energy returned. Aviva knew that the Cossack who grabbed her and pushed her down had a beard and brown eyes and was big and heavy, but she had trouble remembering exactly what he looked like. What she remembered when she closed her eyes was his smell. He smelled like rotting meat, like he hadn't washed in weeks. But that wasn't all of it. He smelled like an unwashed man who had been drinking vodka and eating onions and never learned how to brush his teeth or sweeten his breath. As he grabbed her and pushed her down, his stink was overpowering. She had no real sense of what he was about to do her. She knew it was going to hurt.

He lifted up her dress and ripped at her underwear. Aviva's fear turned, and she no longer worried about dying. She worried his stink would make her sick and she would throw up in his face. As he pressed his sweaty, greasy face to hers, Aviva's stomach began to heave. She clenched her teeth tightly together, praying that she would not be sick. She didn't throw up. He didn't notice. He actually thought she was reacting to his thrusting, and he began to grin, and then her fear of being sick shifted to a fear of laughing. She wanted to laugh in his stupid, fat, ugly face. From what had just happened to her mother, Aviva knew that being laughed at was what men hated the most. They didn't mind being yelled at and kicked as long they were taken seriously enough to deserve the attention, the violence. But no man could tolerate being laughed at. She closed her eyes and imagined she was somewhere else. Eventually, what he was doing to her came to an end.

WHEN DAVID WAS finished, I didn't know what to say. It was a different story than the one I had expected. I could only acknowledge that it was terrible. And for the first time in David's life that I could remember, words failed him as well.

After that, we played chess together in silence until David beat me, and I thought that finally I had got to the bottom of things, that I understood the Goldbergs, all of them: Mr. Goldberg and Sammy and Jake, perhaps even Solomon, but most of all, David. But I didn't, at least not yet. It would take Solomon to help me really understand.

THE NEXT DAY, when we were walking by old trees in Kew Gardens, David said, "I'm not going back, you know."

I looked at him and said, "I know." I think I'd known it when I'd first heard he'd disappeared, even before I'd flown over to London. I think David had always known as well. And from the time Mr. Goldberg had told me to go look for his son, and Ira had told me on his behalf that I was not to return to the company if I didn't bring David back with me, I'd known that I was not going to convince David to return against his will. I was never even going to try.

MR. GOLDBERG TOOK the news stoically. And despite his threat, he didn't throw me out of the company.

David never mentioned it, but when he told me he wasn't going back, I assumed he would do something different with the rest of his life. He was too old at forty-seven and too much of a Goldberg to go work for someone else like Solomon. I thought maybe David would start a company of his own. Or devote himself to philanthropy. Or perhaps even revive his acting career. I thought that whatever he decided, I would again be there by his side, somehow, somewhere. I would get to leave Goldberg Limited behind along with all the doubts that I had accumulated over the years. Together, we would both start over. But that was in the future. In the meantime, I still had to earn a living.

AND SO BEGAN life at Goldberg Limited without David.

It was unlike anything that had come before. When he passed me in the hallway, Mr. Goldberg didn't look at me for longer than he had to. Ira became increasingly serious and especially so in my presence. Sammy spent more time in the office, and Jake stayed away more. In David's absence, there was a sense of suspension. David was banished. We worked hard to make the most of the latest acquisition. All went well in the beginning. It was during these short few months when everything looked like it was going to turn out all right for Goldberg Limited that I ran into Solomon in Moscow.

IT WAS AFTER Goldberg Limited was successful in its bidding for Aussie Gold that Solomon took me fully into his confidence. He had already come so far the year before, telling me how Mr.

Goldberg had cheated Isaac out of his share of the company, that this story must have been just the last, inevitable step, only a matter of time.

It started off innocuously enough. Solomon was all business. Mr. Goldberg had just paid a premium to acquire control of Aussie Gold and wasn't keen to invest in Russia. He had never liked communism, but he liked Putin even less. But he had sent me there to look at a small, highly productive gold mine and to have an exploratory discussion with its owners about a joint venture for expansion. It was clear Mr. Goldberg's heart wasn't in it, but he had heard Solomon was making forays into Russia and having some success building relationships with a few of the oligarchs. Even after besting him in the Aussie Gold acquisition, Mr. Goldberg didn't want Solomon to be ahead of us in anything.

I ended up staying at the Metropol, the golden art nouveau hotel across from the Bolshoi. Only after I had checked in and been up to my room did I remember it was Solomon's favourite Moscow hotel. I saw him later that night, drinking, if you can call nursing the same gin and tonic all evening "drinking" in Russia. He motioned me over with a wave of his hand and a measure of weariness. Without his usual ironic friendliness, he gave me the following free intelligence: "The Russians you'll meet tomorrow don't really want to do a JV. None of them do. Not even the Jewish ones. At least not in mining. Maybe ten years ago, or maybe twenty, when Putin was a newly resigned KGB colonel and the state was giving assets away, but even then, we would probably have been too late. Maybe outside of Russia, if they felt they needed a Canadian face, but not at home. Oil's another story, but the Russians have learned how to run mines. They don't need our help."

I never would have told Mr. Goldberg what Solomon had just

said, but if I had, he would have assumed Solomon was trying to throw us off the scent, that he himself was having excellent meetings and didn't want us going in the following day to make our pitch. But I knew Solomon well enough by then to believe that he wouldn't lie to me. I acknowledged his comment and sipped my scotch.

Solomon didn't mention his failed bid for Aussie Gold, but he continued in his serious vein until, all of a sudden, he turned personal. And for the first time since I had known him, his interest in the other side of his family seemed genuine and unironic. "How's Jake?"

"He's fine."

Solomon nodded, clearly not believing me. "And Sammy?"

Solomon would have known about his cousin's breakdown. It had happened before Solomon had had lunch with Jake. "He's better now. I'm not sure he's quite the same."

"No. I don't think he ever could be." Solomon looked around the bar at the other guests as if wondering what had brought them to Moscow. Then he turned his attention back to me. "We're in Russia, not Poland, although Poland was part of Russia from time to time. A poor excuse for a country, always getting conquered. But we're close to where it all began."

Moscow was a thousand miles from Poland, but I wasn't going to argue geography. And while I was probably imagining it, Solomon looked more Slavic in the dim light of the bar. "Where what began?"

"My family, Sean. At least the family I know. I'm going to tell you the story of my family."

"I think I already know the story, Solomon."

"Aviva and the Cossacks?"

"Yeah."

"David tell you?" I nodded. "Poor cousin David. That's not the real story. That's the made-up one. I'm going to tell you the real one." But first Solomon ordered another drink. Before he began, he said, "Our own stories are the hardest to tell, let alone to understand." Then he told me the real story of Aviva and Abraham's father and where the Goldbergs came from.

6

IN THE REAL story of Aviva, as compared to the one David had told me, there were no Cossacks. The Cossacks would ride into town occasionally and burn down houses and shoot at people to let off steam when they were tired of fighting and laying down their lives for the pleasure of the czar. But Aviva's family didn't live in a *shtetl*, they lived in a town, and they were reasonably well-off. They had a big house by the standards of the time. Aviva's mother was never raped by the Cossacks, and neither was Aviva, and her father wasn't killed. He called himself a merchant, but really, he was a travelling salesman. He'd go from town to town and sell. And apparently, he was very good at it.

"Do you know what he sold?" Solomon asked.

"No."

"Jewellery. And not just any jewellery, young Mr. McFall. Gold jewellery. Gold's been part of the family for a long time." Solomon shifted in his seat and looked around again. "And do you know to whom?" Solomon didn't wait for me to shake my head. "His biggest customers were not other Jews, although they did buy his stuff. It was the Cossacks. They loved him. He was almost like a mascot to some of them. He had red hair and a loud voice, and he liked to drink with them. They called him to his face 'an honorary Cossack' and their 'favourite Jew.' Who knows what they called him behind his back. But he didn't care. All he cared about was selling his gold jewellery. His customers are the only Cossacks in the real story." Solomon's second drink arrived, and he looked around the Metropol bar. Everyone else was drinking and talking loudly. Solomon spoke softly.

"My great-*bubbe* Aviva told my father the real story when he turned eighteen. He was a couple months away from finishing high school, and my uncle had just dropped out of McGill, in the middle of his final exams."

When they were boys, the young Mr. Goldberg and Isaac had visited their *bubbe* together, often with Abraham but sometimes on their own if Abraham was travelling. But in his teens, Mr. Goldberg had stopped visiting as often. The way Aviva always took his head in her hands and stared at him and looked into his eyes as if she were looking for some sort of sign was starting to make him uncomfortable. And his sense that Isaac was her favourite didn't help.

Up until then, even during the time he was a teenager, Aviva served Isaac milk and cookies whenever he came to visit with Mr. Goldberg or on his own. Sometimes she served ginger ale instead of milk. But on the day after Isaac turned eighteen and he came alone, it was a gin and tonic that Aviva poured for the two of them. She clinked glasses and said, "*L'Chaim*," and then, after she and Isaac had swallowed, she said, "I want to tell you the story of our family, of where we come from."

"Apparently, my father had the same reaction as you," Solomon said. "He said, 'I know that story, *Bubbe*.' She just laughed in his face, but not unkindly."

AVIVA TOLD ISAAC the story, in her deep voice, still resonant and musical at eighty-one, with more than a hint of an Eastern European accent, as if it were a story she had told many times before. Her thick white hair swept back and falling to her shoulders. Expensive, comfortable clothes. No makeup, even at eighty-one. Most astonishing of all, no old people's smell. She still walked two miles and swam thirty laps at the Westmount YMCA every day. When she wasn't walking, she drove the 1952 Jaguar convertible that Abraham had bought her for her seventy-fifth birthday.

"AVIVA'S FATHER, THE red-headed prosperous merchant who liked to sell gold jewellery to the Cossacks, also liked to drink. He liked to drink almost as much as he liked to sell gold jewellery. But there was one thing he liked even more than drinking and selling jewellery. And that, young Mr. McFall, was his daughter. Aviva. And so sometimes, when he came home from a selling trip, and he'd been staying up all night drinking with his Cossack friends after selling them gold jewellery for their wives and mistresses, he wouldn't go right to the matrimonial bed that he shared with his wife. He would stumble into his teenage daughter's bed and rape her. And Aviva, who didn't want her mother to know, would be careful not to make a sound."

I had never seen Solomon look so serious, so pale. His usual ironic humour and energy had drained from his face.

"It was when she turned fifteen and missed her period that Aviva decided she had to leave. But before she did, she went down to the basement. Her father had asked her to help him keep his books, and over time she had watched him open and shut the safe where he kept his stock. She knew the combination by heart. She opened that safe and took every single piece of gold jewellery that her father owned, and she ran away."

Solomon's voice faltered. He took a moment to collect himself. After this, the story became more innocuous. It assumed the form of an epilogue. It became a sort of transatlantic romance. Solomon took more time with this part of the story, shared more details. And gradually the colour returned to his face and his usual sense of humour returned.

AVIVA TRADED A pair of gold earrings for a ride to Gdańsk with a clothing merchant, a dark, silent man who miraculously wanted nothing else from her, or maybe he did, but after one look at Aviva's face he decided otherwise. Once at the coastal city, she booked passage on a ship bound for Montréal. She didn't know anything about Montréal, except that it was in Canada. She had originally wanted to go to New York because she had heard more about it, but she'd missed that ship, and the next one was going to Canada. She had to sell a gold chain to a man in an alleyway to make enough money to buy a third-class ticket.

Aviva had never seen the sea before. At first, she couldn't see it because the big ship blocked the view. It was painted black and red, and it reminded her of the whale in the story of Jonah. As she looked up at it and walked up the gangway, she had a strong sense that this whale was going to take her in its dark belly, carry her halfway across the world, and spit her up on shore amongst strangers. She had a moment of panic and hesitated. She didn't want to move forward, and yet she was afraid to move back. An elderly couple behind her were patient. They must have understood something of what was going through her mind because they let Aviva take her time, but the crowds behind them began to yell at her to hurry up. In the end, Aviva's fear of what she was running from was greater than her fear of what she was running to. She didn't look behind at the country she was leaving because despite what had happened to her, she knew if she did then she wouldn't have the strength to go.

Her cabin was in the deepest part of the ship, below the waterline. The light was both harsh and not bright. Whenever she could, she went out on deck. When the ship weighed anchor and pulled away from the dock, she was on the far side facing the sea, and when the ship left the coast behind and steamed through the Baltic Sea toward the English Channel, she looked out at the water stretching before her. She had never seen anything like it. If she had read any of the Romantic poets, she might have been able to give words to her feelings, she might have known to call what she was experiencing a sense of awe. But she hadn't, at least not yet, and so all she remembered feeling was a contradiction that she carried calmly in her mind, that told her she was tiny in this open space, that her little life and her problems and her feelings of guilt and anger were only a drop in the ocean, that she would be washed clean in the salt, but also and equally that she was an important part of something bigger, as much as every fish in the sea, no matter the largest whale or smallest minnow. For the first three days at sea, Aviva watched the ocean.

It had taken a week to travel from Warsaw to Gdańsk. Another two weeks to book passage on a ship. When she still didn't get her period, Aviva knew she had to find a husband on the voyage. It never occurred to her not to have the baby, even though it had been conceived in evil. It was still hers, and if she wasn't going to have a father anymore, she was going to have a son. She was proud that in the time leading up to his birth and while he was being born and for every day afterward for as long as she was alive, she had always thought of Abraham only as her son. Not also as her half-brother. When she left her father, he ceased to exist for her.

"SHE HAD TWO weeks at sea," Solomon said. "You can imagine the difficulties she faced — how to find a man who wanted to sleep with her right away so that when the baby came eight months later, he would think it was premature but his, but also a man who wanted to marry her and didn't think she was a woman of 'loose morals.' Aviva still didn't really know much about sex, and she knew less about love, but she must have known something because she was already pregnant by her father. They didn't call themselves incest victims then, let alone incest survivors. They didn't call themselves anything."

ON THE THIRD day on board, because she knew she had to, Aviva went to the rough eating room where the third-class passengers had the privilege of queuing up for poor-quality food and then washing their own dishes. She dressed in her best clothes — these too she had had the presence of mind to take with her when she left her home. She looked serious and demure, and if she had to say so herself, as she looked back from the vantage point of more than sixty years, aristocratic in a shabby way.

Eating her food, she looked at her fellow ship passengers. She discounted the men who were married. They might enjoy the excitement of a transatlantic fling, the great threat of discovery in the close quarters, but she knew they would never divorce their wives and marry her. And she didn't give a second glance to men who were travelling in a group of other men. These seemed to her to be fortune hunters, and Aviva already knew that when men were in a group, they brought out the worst in each other. Some of these smiled at her, and one went so far as to point at her and lean over and say something laughingly into his friend's ear. She pretended not to notice. By and large, these were the kind of men who would sleep with a woman just to boast about it afterward with their friends at the bar. She stayed clear of them and frowned in what she hoped was a haughty way whenever they looked in her direction.

"THE CHALLENGE WAS immense," Solomon said with admiration. "How to make the first move with a man without making it look like she was the aggressor? At that time, if a woman was too forward with a man, he would assume she was a prostitute, and most of the time he would be right. Despite her ulterior motives, she still thought, over half a century later, that her heart had been in the right place. She wasn't a gold digger. She didn't need money. She had just enough to take care of herself and start raising a son. She only wanted to find a husband so that her son would have a father. And, of course, she was dealing with a smaller gene pool from which to choose. Given what had happened to her, God might have forgiven her if she had decided to cast her net a little further, but she wanted a Jewish father for her son."

AS THE SHIP approached Newfoundland on its way to Halifax, Aviva was running out of time. With a few short days to go, she found her husband. He was gaunt. By the way he coughed, Aviva knew he was suffering from consumption, but that didn't dissuade her. She could tell he was smart because he was reading thick books and writing in a small, black notebook. He paid no attention to the voyage, to the sea, to the other passengers, or to the gently swaying motion of the large boat.

The first day Aviva saw him, he sat on the deck, reading and writing and smoking cigars, which, given his apparent condition, seemed a reckless defiance. When Aviva walked by him for the first time, he didn't notice her. He was too busy writing and smoking and coughing. The next time, an hour later, he noticed her but pretended not to. The next day, when Aviva walked by, he looked up at her with his beautiful, large, sad eyes and actually smiled. But then he looked down and began to write with more energy than Aviva had imagined he had in him. But on that day, because she had only one more before they docked, Aviva decided to be bold.

"Good morning," she said. "Is that seat taken?"

He could have been forgiven for thinking she was a woman of no great repute. But he smiled and said, "It is now."

She sat down beside him and looked out at the ocean. He looked at her, unsure whether to talk or write or read. And then he decided to sit beside her in silence. They looked at the water. Aviva imagined they were both content.

"HE DIED SIX months later," Solomon said. "But not before marrying Aviva three weeks after they got off the boat together, and not before giving her and her son his name." His name was Benjamin Goldberg. He didn't have a lot of money; he worked in a hat factory and wrote short stories on the side. But he left Aviva the little he had, and that, along with the remnants of the golden jewellery that she hadn't had to sell to pay for passage to Montréal and the two jobs she worked when she learned sufficient English, was enough to set Aviva up in a small apartment and allow her to raise Abraham. Unlike many children of immigrants, Abraham didn't have to drop out of high school to go to work. He was able to devote himself to his studies and do well enough to be admitted to mining engineering at McGill when there was a Jewish quota."

According to what Aviva told Isaac, she never said anything to Abraham about his true origins. She didn't want to burden him with the knowledge. But she didn't want to fully lie to him either, so she made up another story, about her mother's rape and murder. It was still terrible but less so in her mind, and Aviva thought it was believable and even true in a different sort of way. When Isaac asked why she was telling only him the truth, all she would say was that he was an adult now and it was so he would understand his family and be prepared for whatever happened.

AT LAST SOLOMON was finished. "And this, young Sean McFall, is where my family comes from. It is quite a saga, as you can see. And Goldberg is not even our real family name."

"Do you know what it is?"

"Only Aviva knew it. And she died before she told anyone." And then Solomon couldn't resist being ironically grand and ending on a light note, so he added, with a smile, "Our real name is lost in the mists of ancient family myth and mystery."

"Didn't Isaac ever try to track them down, your relatives?"

"Well, there was the Holocaust, and it's kind of hard to, without a name."

With this final story of the Goldbergs, I had reached the bottom. There was nowhere else to go, nothing left to know.

WE HAD STARTED bidding for Aussie Gold in April 2012, when gold was trading at a healthy U.S. $1,631 an ounce. When our offer to buy the company was accepted on May 16, gold had fallen to $1,537 an ounce. Mr. Goldberg assumed it was just a blip, and by the time our deal to purchase had closed three months later, he felt vindicated and destined as only a man who isn't made jittery by the markets can feel. By then, the price of gold had started to climb again, recovering to $1,691. And it continued to climb, reaching $1,771 in September. It was only in October that it really started to crash. And it continued to fall for the next months. By June 2013, it had fallen to $1,225.

Gold doesn't operate the way other commodities do. While gold was dropping, other assets like real estate and equities were rising and paper money was being printed and demand for gold was increasing, all of which should have caused the price of gold to rise. But as the financial markets had become more complex, and as our brightest financial minds were creating ever more exotic market instruments, gold was trading on paper — or in electrons — at over fifty times the multiple of actual gold, and this led to a loss of confidence. So just a few short months after we paid a fifty-percent premium per share for Aussie Gold, the value of the precious metal had dropped thirty percent.

7

A WEEK BEFORE the article appeared in late June 2013, a couple of increasingly frantic messages were left for Mr. Goldberg from my old childhood friend Michael Appleby. Michael was working on a story that he "was sure Mr. Goldberg would want to comment on." Mr. Goldberg didn't comment often, and it was always on his own terms, usually when he was seeking to promote an acquisition. But that week Mr. Goldberg was in Australia, keeping the mine managers motivated. He did not return Michael's calls. The day before the eight-thousand-word story appeared in the *Globe and Mail*, Mr. Goldberg received a courtesy email from Michael Appleby letting him know the story was going to be running the next day, in Saturday's print edition. Mr. Goldberg rarely checked email, but his secretary, Linda, printed the email off for him, and after he read it, he spoke to Ira, who started making calls that evening, but to no avail.

NONE OF US left work on time — usually around 7:00 p.m. — that day. After Mr. Goldberg received the email from Michael

Appleby, Ira asked Sammy, Jake, and me to stay in the office until the article appeared on the website. At 7:00 p.m. he gathered us all in Mr. Goldberg's office and ordered in pizza. Mr. Goldberg, who never fired up a computer if he could help it, checked for the article every hour that Friday night, knowing it was going to run in the print edition the following morning. He concealed his frustration and impatience each time he checked and it wasn't yet up on the *Globe and Mail* website.

When it finally appeared, just after 10:00 p.m., under the headline, "All that glitters is not gold: the astounding story at the heart of Goldberg Limited," Mr. Goldberg pulled his chair closer to his monitor, put on his reading glasses, and started to read. The rest of us read it on our own laptops, but I pulled my chair near to Mr. Goldberg so I could see the reflection of his face on his screen and read over his shoulder if I wanted to. I tried to read along with him, at the same speed.

Michael Appleby, after close consultation with his editors and with the approval of the *Globe and Mail*'s legal staff, prefaced his piece with a note to readers explaining why the story they were about to read was going to appear so one-sided.

Saul Goldberg is notoriously private, and even his nephew's decision to sit down with the *Globe and Mail* to tell his astonishing story did not cause him to revisit his policy of rarely speaking to the media, an approach he traditionally breaks with only when he wants to promote an acquisition. Several calls were made to Mr. Goldberg asking for comments for this story, and several messages were left for Ira Levin, the company's chief legal officer who doubles as Goldberg Limited's head of PR. Most of these messages, which provided a clear sense of the gist of this story, were left unreturned. Mr.

Goldberg declined to comment for this story, but Ira Levin did contact our publisher in his capacity as the company's chief legal officer to request that this paper not publish the story and even sought an injunction to halt the publication of the story, which was denied yesterday by the courts. Later that same day, a spokesperson for Goldberg Limited emailed the following statement to the *Globe and Mail*: "As a matter of principle, Mr. Goldberg doesn't respond to rumours, specu-lation, or reckless accusations, especially when they concern internal family matters."

Once the preamble was out of the way and the story proper began, Mr. Goldberg skimmed the extraneous details. The soft lead that made Solomon sound more like a touring rock star or actor shooting his latest film in Montréal would have barely reg-istered with him. I don't think Mr. Goldberg noticed that Michael had chosen the present tense to tell his story.

When Solomon Goldberg walks into the bar at the Ritz-Carlton in Montréal, he looks healthy, wealthy, and relaxed. Healthy because he plays racquetball three times a week in the summer and skis every weekend in the winter. Wealthy because he is one of the heirs to at least part of the Goldberg fortune, which on his side of the family is larger than it has been for two decades, thanks in no small part to his own efforts, and because of the success of Iseli Gold, the company he has built from scratch. And he's relaxed because he's finally decided to tell his story.

At forty-seven, the only member of the third generation of the Goldberg family to work outside the family com-pany that bears its name cuts a tall, trim figure. He wears his work-week uniform: a Tilford blue blazer over a white Harry Rosen shirt tucked into tailored, brushed-cotton khakis. But his business-casual outward appearance belies an inner intensity that only really comes through when he begins to talk about his family.

Mr. Goldberg wouldn't have bothered to wonder how my childhood friend Michael Appleby knew what brand of blazer Solomon wore or why Michael took pains to talk about Solomon's trim appearance or even how he recognized brushed cotton. None of the Goldbergs had ever been fat, and they took care to stay in shape in various ways. Judging from the way he scrolled down, Mr. Goldberg spent a little more time, but not much, on the glimpse into the family history, the scene-setting for the gist of the story. To Mr. Goldberg, it would have been very old news, and more than faintly distasteful to him, this public account of his family's private history. He would have found the childhood anecdotes that Michael Appleby chose to tell cloying and sentimental, and in poor taste.

> "My father, Isaac, and my uncle, Saul, were insepara-
> ble growing up. They did everything together: skating at
> Mount Royal, skiing in the Laurentians, tobogganing at
> Murray Hill, chasing girls."

At this point, Mr. Goldberg frowned, as if wondering what Isaac knew about chasing girls. Hadn't Isaac married the first girl he'd asked out on a date?

> "They practically grew up in the business. My *zayde*
> Abraham took them everywhere with him, to the mines, on

business trips to Europe and South America. It was always understood they would both work in the business together, and Abraham's expectation was that they would do it in harmony as brothers."

Yet even in this idealized early history, the tension started early.

"But despite their closeness, there was always a sibling rivalry. Even if it was terribly one-sided."

Michael Appleby was playing amateur psychologist, writing somewhat melodramatically.

And here a dark cloud descends over Solomon Goldberg's handsome features. He looks down at his half-finished salad. It is clear the family history is hard to talk about.

At this point in his reading, Mr. Goldberg uncharacteristically swore under his breath, an unadorned "Fuck" followed swiftly by, "If it's so hard for him, why is he doing it?" to nobody in particular.

"My uncle Saul was the oldest, and he never ceased to remind my father Isaac that he had entered this world first, as if he'd had something to do with it. He'd push his brother around on the hockey rink, he'd talk first at meetings, he'd talk longer when they were both asked to address the same audience. Saul assumed he would run Goldberg Limited one day and my father would find some other place for himself in the company."

After establishing that Saul was his uncle, at least by blood, Solomon was now only referring to him by his first name. He was refusing any obvious family connection, refusing to acknowledge the shared family name.

"Saul even tried to steal my father's girlfriend, the woman who ultimately became his wife and my mother."

Here Mr. Goldberg didn't swear. He sat up straighter in his chair. He was now paying attention because Solomon was establishing his case — that Mr. Goldberg was a thief — and rewriting history. Because it was Isaac who had stolen Eliana from him, and as Mr. Goldberg knew, a man who will easily rewrite the past is a man to be reckoned with.

Mr. Goldberg skimmed the rest — university years, more sibling rivalry, competing for Abraham's affections and endorsement, early years in the company — until he got to the pull quote, its large black font dominating the narrow screen. True to form, instead of bulging out, his eyes narrowed as his heavy lids descended. Solomon was not pulling his punches. Perhaps, being the good journalist that he was, Michael had goaded Solomon into using extreme language, but I doubted it. His well-spoken nephew knew exactly what he was doing. He had been nursing his hatred — quite effectively, it would seem — for almost forty years.

Mr. Goldberg didn't reprimand himself under his breath for admiring this resourceful nephew of his who was setting out on a very public quest to destroy him. Michael might have held the pen, but Solomon was dictating the story. Although Michael was a very minor actor in this drama, he would have gone automatically on Mr. Goldberg's blackest blacklist, as he had to. Perhaps Mr. Goldberg shouldn't have been be so surprised by this betrayal:

trust is a commodity, like any other. It can appreciate in value, it can decline, it can be traded for something considered more valuable, and it can be lost overnight. Solomon could be very persuasive. And in the end, Solomon gave Michael a better story than Mr. Goldberg ever could. But Michel Appleby was a parasite preying on an internal family matter. He would never be spoken to, or even of, by Mr. Goldberg again.

"But all of this childhood bullying paled in comparison to what my uncle did to my father when their father died. My uncle swindled my father, plain and simple, out of his rightful share of his Goldberg inheritance."

Solomon chose his words carefully. *Bullying* — what a modern word! And yet it sounded old-fashioned coming from Solomon. As for the word *swindled*, it legitimately sounded old-fashioned and somehow worse than *cheated*.

Mr. Goldberg was now reading carefully, every word in every line, sometimes twice. He hadn't studied law, but he had spent enough time around Ira and other lawyers to know how they thought. And he had spent enough time paying attention to events in courtrooms to know how judges responded to lawyers' arguments. The whole anatomy of the alleged fraud was being meticulously laid out by Michael Appleby, courtesy of Solomon, for the *Globe and Mail*'s readers. Geology reports saying one thing. Brotherly handshakes backed up by legal documents. Reports disproven weeks later by reality. Pained discovery. The Firehall mine running out of gold. The whole world would think Solomon was libelling him, and they would expect the atomic legal response they had come to know from Mr. Goldberg's army of litigation lawyers under Ira's command. Or perhaps the whole world would believe Solomon. Mr. Goldberg couldn't be sure what would be worse.

"At first, my father refused to reach the conclusion presented by all the evidence. His brain just wouldn't allow him to do so. But when he finally acknowledged it on an intellectual level, he still refused to believe it in his heart. My mother had to explain it to him. When he did finally believe it, he stopped wanting to live. I never thought it was possible that a man could actually die of a broken heart. But my father did."

Tears well up in Solomon's bright blue eyes as he speaks about his father's deep disappointment and death. This is the first time he is telling the story in public. Solomon doesn't sound angry. The words he is carefully choosing to tell his family story to the world have an incredulous tone to them, as if he can't believe his uncle's actions.

Michael was clumsily reminding his readers of his exclusive scoop, and here he inserted himself briefly into the story.

Laying your father's death at your uncle's doorstep is not an easy task. Why now, I ask him, after all these years?

Solomon has his extemporaneous answer ready. "I didn't want my father's memory to be forgotten or to be misinterpreted. I wanted to tell the story that he can no longer tell, that he was embarrassed to tell because he and my uncle were brothers. But my uncle is just my uncle."

Mr. Goldberg looked away from his computer and looked quickly at the large photo on his desk, the one of himself and Isaac standing on either side of Abraham, the two brothers in their late twenties. He, the young Mr. Goldberg, was smiling in the photo, and Isaac was looking serious. Then Mr. Goldberg returned his gaze to his bright screen. Solomon was throwing down the gauntlet on the pages of Canada's national newspaper. But Solomon didn't leave off yet with the sophomoric psychoanalyzing.

> "It didn't stop there. My uncle's megalomania and narcissism only increased as he grew older. He wanted to dominate everyone around. He was a tyrant at home. His youngest son, David, was somehow immune, but he terrorized his two older sons, Sammy and Jake, in different ways. There's no power, you know, like the power of a father within a family."

Still, the story didn't end there. There had to be more. It was not enough that Solomon was calling his uncle a fraud in front of all of Canada and the world through the medium of the infernal internet. In these modern times, Solomon's journey couldn't be that simple.

> "When my father died, and when I found out from my mother what had happened, I went through a very dark time."
>
> Solomon is reflective as he speaks. He has come to terms with his past. He almost sounds like he is talking about someone else.
>
> "When you're young, it's hard to make peace with the fact your uncle has cheated your father out of his birthright and that his treatment by his brother has killed your father. For the longest time, I didn't want to believe it. I am not embarrassed to admit that I was very angry. I tried to deal

with my anger by abusing drugs and alcohol. I thought of suicide. Essentially, I suffered a mental breakdown."

At this, Mr. Goldberg looked up from his screen. His eyes were wide open, but he couldn't bring himself to read further. I'm not sure what bothered him more: being accused of fraud in the pages of the national newspaper or reading his nephew admit to a breakdown. Sammy's breakdown was a private family affair, at least as much as possible. Whatever the Goldbergs were, they weren't weak. Why was his nephew doing this?

The rest of the story, as it had to be, was about redemption, about Solomon's recovery. His mother and girlfriend nursing him back to health and hope. The resumption of his studies at McGill. Joining the mining industry as a lowly mining engineer, not at another gold company but at a small bauxite mine in Zambia. His discovery that he was a natural leader and his quickly emerging rapport with the miners despite the great difference in their upbringing. His success there followed by several international postings, including running the bauxite company's Australian operations, the jewel in their crown, before striking out on his own at the age of thirty with his founding of Iseli Gold with one under-producing mine in Australia. His growing Iseli into a global powerhouse as the fourth largest gold mining company in the world, the accumulation of great personal wealth through his Iseli shareholdings, and his triumphant reclaiming of his place as global gold mining royalty.

Asked if Solomon's meteoric success outside of Goldberg Limited was fuelled by a desire to show that he could succeed outside the safe confines of the family firm, Solomon smiles.

"I don't think that motivation hurt. But regardless, I do feel proud of my success. I did it on my own, like my grandfather. I feel very good about the value I've created for shareholders with Iseli."

Solomon didn't mention the several billion dollars of value he had created for himself in Iseli Class A shares that continued to rise in value and accumulate each year. Would he ever return to the Goldberg family business? Michael had him pausing for a moment and, according to his photograph, looking thoughtful.

"It's a good question. I don't, as a rule, rule anything out. But it would have to be under the right circumstances. It would have to be the right kind of decision, for the right reasons, a decision my father would have approved of."

And then he stated the painfully obvious: "If he were still alive."

Mr. Goldberg had now reached the end of the story. When he looked away from the screen, he was slightly breathless and appeared conflicted. One part of himself must have hated Solomon for doing what he had done, telling the private stories of the Goldbergs to Canada's national newspaper so whoever still read newspapers would now have doubts about Mr. Goldberg and his private actions. But another part of himself, deeper, less articulate, must have had nothing less than admiration for his brother's son who had made something of himself and amassed such a level of power and confidence that he could so boldly take up arms against his uncle. This is a man who knows himself, who is his own man, who has made his own way in the world. He is a man that Mr. Goldberg would be proud to call his son. Even as Solomon was declaring war on his uncle, I am sure that Mr. Goldberg couldn't help thinking highly of him. His toughness. His cunning. It was this hard-to-admit admiration that prevented Mr. Goldberg from giving in completely to his anger. In its place, he turned to Ira. Yet even Mr. Goldberg knew that this time was more complicated than all the previous ones. Everyone would expect Mr. Goldberg to sue Solomon for libel. But Mr. Goldberg knew he couldn't because what Solomon had said was true.

IT WAS AT this exact moment, after the article came out, that Solomon chose to meet with the CEOs of the banks on whose boards he sat, two of which just so happened to be major lenders to Goldberg Limited. They had been lenders for years, and when Solomon had joined their boards, it had been too late for Mr. Goldberg to pay down his loans and take them elsewhere. But Mr. Goldberg had tried to reverse the decision of the banks when one board chair had called him the night before to let him know Solomon's appointment to the board would be announced the next day. Even the brightest people sometimes have trouble connecting all the dots when it comes to families and relationships and feelings.

But Mr. Goldberg experienced one of his rare defeats when the chairmen of each board refused to rescind the two separate appointments that had already been approved. It came down to a simple equation that any banker could understand: Mr. Goldberg was a cherished and highly valued client. But Solomon was considered to be one of the best financial minds of his generation. Clients like Mr. Goldberg, while richly appreciated, could always be found. Board directors like Solomon would only come around once in a bank CEO's career. The irony wasn't wasted on Mr.

Goldberg that if he hadn't cut Solomon so completely out of the business when he pushed out Isaac, Solomon could never have served as the director of a bank where a family member had such a major loan.

Solomon met with the CEOs, one at a time, in their large offices on the top floors of their office towers in downtown Toronto. It was, of course, unusual for board members to reach into the operating businesses of the banks, but Solomon was unusual to begin with, and he was able to have whatever conversations he wanted. And Solomon chose his timing well. Mr. Goldberg would have already been in breach of his covenants when, after our disastrous acquisition of Aussie Gold and crash of the price of gold, Goldberg Limited fell far below the ratio of earnings to debt as specified in the loans from both banks. The biblical word *covenant*, which has so much resonance for Jews, had always stood out for me in its financial context. It is fitting in a way that the banks should have taken a word that carries so much meaning and turned it into a word for a financial agreement. Solomon must have been convincing because both banks began to call the loans in for breach of covenant.

IT WAS TWO days after the article appeared and the banks were already calling in the loans when David phoned me.

"How is he?"

"I haven't seen him much. He's spending all his time with Ira."

Silence at the other end for the longest time. "I think I need to come back."

"What about your role in the play, your acting?"

"I'll finish it up, but I won't take on another one. I've given it up before. I can do it again."

It was my turn to say nothing.

"And Sean?"

"Yes?"

"You should know your concern is not unrequited."

For the briefest time, I thought I should fight for him, try to convince him otherwise, tell him that his future lay outside his family and their company, but I knew it would be fruitless. In the end, David hadn't been able to escape. He was coming back to fulfill his destiny to be by his father's side. And after more than thirty years of knowing the Goldbergs and more than twenty years of working for them, I still had to fulfill mine.

8

IF YOU DIDN'T know Ira — and most people didn't because this was the first time in his career with Goldberg Limited that he was stepping out of the shadows and appearing on TV — you could be forgiven for not noticing anything out of the ordinary. But if you had known and worked with Ira for twenty-three years and you watched the press conference carefully, you would have noted certain subtle signs.

He was wearing a new suit for the occasion. It was navy blue, and the dark colour was set off by a tie with little animals leaping across it — I knew he wore Hermès — that might have been only a shade of yellow but looked golden on TV. His hair was freshly cut and appeared even more distinguished than usual. And when he was speaking — which was most of the time because he was the only representative of Goldberg Limited present at the press conference — and the camera zoomed in on him, if you knew him well you could see that of his dark eyebrows, neatly trimmed for the occasion but still somehow bushy, the right one was twitching slightly. And if you really knew him, you could see that solid, dependable Ira was trying hard not to show how joyful he was at being appointed the first-ever non-family CEO of the Goldberg empire.

"It's an honour to be chosen by Mr. Goldberg at this time to lead the company through its present challenges. I have no doubt, with the quality of our people and our assets, and the tried-and-true Goldberg approach to running our business that has stood us in such good stead over the last one hundred years, that Goldberg Limited will emerge even stronger than before, ready to compete successfully for another hundred years."

I had to give Ira credit. For a man who had rarely been in front of the cameras, he was a natural: witty, concise, apparently transparent. The short press release that had been issued that morning had laid out all the facts: Goldberg Limited was entering bankruptcy protection to restructure itself. Underperforming assets would be sold, debt would be shed. The company was committed to emerging stronger than before. Perhaps most surprisingly, every single member of the family who had been directly involved in the business was relinquishing operational control to devote themselves singleheartedly to serving on the board where they had each been directors for years. Although Mr. Goldberg was quoted in the release, on behalf of himself and his sons, none of them was present that day at the press conference announcing the first non-member of the Goldberg family to run the firm and shepherd it through bankruptcy protection. It was Ira's show.

It was only when Ira had finished his prepared comments and the questions were about to begin that the cameras panned the audience and I noticed there was indeed one Goldberg in the room. It was Elijah, Jake's son and the youngest of the Goldbergs, sitting not on stage but in the audience, his parents nowhere to be seen. Elijah would have been about eleven years old, the same age I was when I met David. For the occasion, he had donned a suit and tie, and his hair was neatly combed. He looked like a businessman in miniature, a Goldberg businessman, with his blond hair and fourth-generation Goldberg eyes. The last time I had seen him — at the Passover dinner when Mr. Goldberg and Ira were stealing away from the table to bid on Aussie Gold — Elijah had asked the one question and given the four answers, but this time he had no speaking role. He was silent and appeared solemn and determined as only an eleven-year-old can, and the gently symmetrical shape of his eyes and his serious expression made him seem far older than his years. He watched the press conference as if he knew the first stage of his life was ending and the real story of his life was just beginning. He seemed to be absorbing everything that was happening to his family through his bright skin so that he would take it with him wherever he went. And then the camera moved off him and returned to Ira smoothly answering questions from the podium.

Like most of the Goldbergs, I wasn't there. I watched it all from home, Jane quietly by my side. She had flown home to be with me the week I handed in my resignation. I had delivered the letter and spoken to David the day before the press conference, in his office that Mr. Goldberg had kept waiting for him all through the time David was in London and said he wouldn't be back. Mr. Goldberg had known all along that his youngest son would be returning.

AS I HAD walked into his office and David rose to greet me, he saw my face and noticed the white envelope in my hand, and although his impossibly blue, symmetrical Goldberg eyes were duller than usual, he quickly mustered up a smile. I thought of the boy long ago who had chosen me early for his flag football team at LCC and taught me in a few short minutes how to play the game. "If it isn't young Mr. McFall."

"David."

As always, David made things easier for me. He spoke first. "After so many years, have we come to a parting of the ways?"

"Yes." David had found a way to make me smile, even now.

"Well, then." He held out his hand to shake mine.

I thought of his grandfather teaching him how to shake hands when he was a boy, and I wanted to say something about not wanting to see him, like his brothers before him, broken at the altar of his father, and that I understood he wasn't returning to his father for the same reasons as his brothers. Perhaps most of all, I felt I owed him the explanation that I no longer desired his father's approval or feared his wrath. But I wouldn't have been able to put such simple truths into words anyway, and he knew that, and when I began to try, he waved me off.

"You don't need to explain. Not to anyone. Least of all to me." And with that last sentence, he spared me having to say anything else.

"Remember I told you years ago that you had a choice about the company?"

"Yes."

"I still envy you." This time, when he smiled, it was his old smile and it was the old David. He gave me a hug, and it was as childhood friends that we parted.

WHEN THE PRESS conference was over and I had turned off the TV, Jane suggested we go out for a walk. We walked east toward the mountain.

While we were walking, my cellphone rang, and I saw that it

was Solomon. I didn't answer, and he left a message. On the walk back, I listened to it on speaker so Jane could hear it too. "Hello not-so-young-anymore Mr. McFall." Solomon's voice was cheery as usual. "I didn't see you anywhere near the press conference, but I have to assume that you've returned from your latest London sojourn. Given everything that is transpiring at what used to be the largest gold company in the world, the thought occurred to me that perhaps we should sit down and have a talk about the future." Jane raised her eyebrows, and I shrugged my shoulders and put the phone back in my pocket. I had finally decided to leave Goldberg Limited after David went back, but I wasn't sure I was quite ready to throw in my lot with Solomon.

We took summer and winter vacations every year in faraway places, but this was the first weekday I had been off work in Montréal in a long time. I read a novel for the remainder of the day — for years Jane had been trying to get me to read more fiction — and afterward we went out for dinner. It was early July, and as it was warm, we ate outside on a terrace. I had never been drunk in my life — Solomon would occasionally and mercilessly tease me about being a disgrace to my Irish heritage — but Jane had agreed to drive, and I drank that night. We came home, and I collapsed into bed with Jane beside me. It was then that she told me she was thinking of coming back to Montréal after her latest play.

I stroked her hair. "Don't you always come back after your play?"

"No, silly, I mean for good."

"Ah." I paused for the longest moment. "Jane?"

"Yes?"

"I've been meaning to ask you this for some time. It's about David."

"Yes?"

"If he hadn't been gay, would you have married him?"

Jane turned to me and pushed my hand away. She sat up. "Why would you ever wonder that?"

"I don't know. I just did."

"It's so ... hypothetical."

"I know. That's why I'm asking."

Jane laughed. "Lawyers and their hypothetical questions." She lay back down and put my hand back on her hair. "Sean, there are so many things in life to worry about, and that's not one of them. David always had a lot going for him. But I always loved you. Ever since the beginning."

AFTERWARD, WHEN NIGHT had fallen and Jane and I were falling asleep, a succession of images flew across my brain, starting from when I was a child. My father, Declan, taking me to the park to throw the ball around or play hockey. My mother, Mary, reading Dostoevsky, teaching me how to read, her fierce love and dreams for me carrying us both along into the future that neither of us could foresee. Going to LCC and meeting David Goldberg. Swimming in Curaçao. Encountering the moray eel. Being robbed at gunpoint. The blur of university and starting at the company. My first trip up to the mine. The hundreds of meetings, with Mr. Goldberg, Sammy, Jake, David, and Ira. Ira in his suits and with his bushy eyebrows, biding his time like Solomon. Solomon largely off stage until the end, making only cameo appearances to tell me stories in airport and hotel bars around the world until he at last succeeded in his ambition of bringing Mr. Goldberg to his knees. Up until then, my twenty-three years of loyal service to the Goldbergs and my friend David with his golden promise — despite the bright, immutable properties of the precious metal that his family dug out of the earth — slowly tarnishing over the years. Our three lovely children standing in the order of their birth, and Jane by my side through it all, there with me even when she was in London. Jane beside me now, hard asleep judging by her breathing, back beside me forever.

I knew I was going to visit Mary and Declan the next morning. I was going to eat my mother's apple pie, and I was going to sit in our little backyard and drink beer with my father. I was going to tell him something about David and his decision to return to his father, and I was going to tell him a little bit more about me and my decision, at least as much as I was able to articulate.

But, for now, I was letting sleep overtake me. I was forty-seven. I wasn't dying, only falling asleep. But in those final seconds before I lost consciousness, I had a vision of my death, in my bed with Jane by my side and our children and our grandchildren around me, looking on not with a detached respect for the aged but with genuine affection. I was dying at a proper old age, Mary and Declan having died years before, and Jane too was old, but still she looked to me like she always had when we were young.

ULTIMATELY, I DECIDED not to go over to Solomon. Even though by then I had lost the necessary faith in the Goldbergs I worked for, I felt it would be yet one more betrayal that I didn't want on my conscience. Instead, I joined another mining company, one that mined a respectable metal in Mr. Goldberg's half-serious words — iron ore — and I put my hard-earned knowledge and experience to work for them. Jane came back to Montréal, and I spent more time with her and the children as they set out on the trajectories of their own lives, and I watched Goldberg Limited from afar, with a detached interest.

Ira stewarded the company for a time as best he could until he ran out of ideas, money, and time, and his knowledge of Napoleonic strategy deserted him. He had to sell the company off in pieces. Ira even sold several to Solomon until eventually there was nothing left of Goldberg Limited. Solomon reigned supreme. The Springtime mine in northern Québec went last, and Ahanu's grandchildren put together an Indigenous consortium that increased their original ten-percent ownership stake in the mine to a majority one. The hundred-year-old company that Abraham had built and that Mr. Goldberg had grown and run with his three sons was finally no more. Soon after this, Mr. Goldberg died. I think he died of a broken heart, as his brother had.

David and I stayed friends, and we saw each other from time to time, although we never spoke about the company that used to bear his family name, and every time I saw him, I couldn't help feeling slightly guilty about the fact that I knew more about his family than he did. He did not return to acting, nor did he become a producer. He decided to live comfortably off the not insubstantial family fortune that he and his brothers had inherited, and he aged well.

David's older brothers reacted in their distinctive ways when Goldberg Limited ended. Jake no longer had a company to try to leave or a father to fail to defy, and at the age of fifty-seven, he went out and started his own geological consultancy. Sammy no longer had a father to fail to emulate; I had hoped this would free him, but it didn't. He had another nervous breakdown, from which he did not fully recover.

Only David continued much as before. His golden hair turned slowly but inexorably to silver and he put on weight around his middle, but his impossibly blue Goldberg eyes retained most of their original brightness and he managed to hold on to something of the boy who had chosen me for his flag football team on that first day of class at LCC. Gradually, with the passing of years, his sadness at not being able to save his father from himself and not being able to save his brothers from their father subsided, and as he entered his late fifties, he began to laugh more and the cheerful, ironic, indomitable optimism of his youth was nearly restored to him in full.

WHEN I'D VISITED my father in his little backyard and told him I had decided to leave Goldberg Limited, he didn't say anything at first. He nodded as if the news was not unexpected, as if he had known all along that things would turn out this way. He took a slow sip of his Labatt and looked out at his immaculate garden. When he finally spoke, his words took the form of a question. "Have you learned a lot from the Goldbergs, Sean? From your work with them?"

I had to think about it for a moment. I was three years short of fifty, and my father's slow economy with words was beginning to rub off on me. "Yes, Dad, I think I have. But I realize now that it's not necessarily what I set out to learn."

My father pondered that for a moment, took another sip. Then, without looking at me, he said, "No, I don't suppose it ever is."

Acknowledgements

MANY THANKS TO Marc Côté and the golden team at Cormorant — Sarah Cooper, Sarah Jensen, Angel Guerra, Marijke Friesen, Luckshika Rajaratnam, and Andrea Waters — for believing in this book and bringing it into the world in such a shining way.

I'm fortunate to have a publisher and an editor in Marc who knows so much about everything, from classic British sports cars and their suitability to Montréal weather (limited to summer months) to the eating arrangements of steerage passengers on early ocean liners (rudimentary at best) to the layout of Montréal's Ritz-Carleton restaurant before renovations (no booths) to where really wealthy people buy their suits in London (not Savile Row but Jermyn Street). His salutary interventions in these matters as well as in even more complex ones having to do with the inner lives of my characters made this a much better book and saved me from much embarrassment.

Thanks to my paternal grandfather Israel Goldberg for inspiring this book. No, my grandfather didn't have a gold mine or become a billionaire. He came to Canada from Romania in the early years of the twentieth century with nothing to his name and only the name and address of a cousin in Montréal. When, fresh off the boat, he knocked on his cousin's door, he was given a nickel and told to go buy himself a coffee. The door was closed in his face.

Resolving never to depend on the generosity of anyone ever again, Israel Goldberg devoted most of the waking hours of his life to making money. It was everything to him. He built a successful business selling religious jewelry to the nuns and priests who were plentiful in a Québec that was decades away from the Quiet Revolution. His private life was less successful. His relations with his wife and children were tempestuous at best. He had a bit of a mean streak. It was the story of him driving his three sons around Montréal and pointing out a man who owed him money that first sparked the writing of this book. From there, of course, I made everything else up, including all the Goldbergs, their gold mines, and their billions.

Thanks to my early readers. My father-in-law Peter Eadie. My cousin Judi Goldberg. My older brother Eric Goodwin. And my good friend Niel Golightly. I'm lucky to have such supportive relatives and friends who don't mind reading early versions of my work.

My endless thanks to my wife, Kara, and our three children — Ariel, Anneke, and Isaac — for their love and inspiration. Without each of you, nothing is possible.

We acknowledge the sacred land on which Cormorant Books operates. It has been a site of human activity for 15,000 years. This land is the territory of the Huron-Wendat and Petun First Nations, the Seneca, and most recently, the Mississaugas of the Credit River. The territory was the subject of the Dish With One Spoon Wampum Belt Covenant, an agreement between the Iroquois Confederacy and Confederacy of the Ojibway and allied nations to peaceably share and steward the resources around the Great Lakes. Today, the meeting place of Toronto is still home to many Indigenous people from across Turtle Island. We are grateful to have the opportunity to work in the community, on this territory.

We are also mindful of broken covenants and the need to strive to make right with all our relations.